"You don't think he'll change his mind?"

"He will not. He thinks me soiled." The word caught in Eve's throat. "He'll have me shunned if I don't marry. But I've never even been out with a boy."

Levi returned to his pacing. "You've got a problem here."

"*Ya*, I do." Eve gave a little laugh that reflected no humor. "And it's already been a week. My father is threatening to tell our bishop tomorrow and have me shunned immediately. He'll put me out then. I know he will."

"I can only think of one alternate solution here, Eve, and you may not like it, but—"

"Anything," she whispered, "because I'm afraid if I'm forced, I might choose to marry Jemuel rather than lose myself. Lose my life. And that's what would happen if I went into the *Englischer* world. I know it." She looked up to him. "What can I do?"

Levi held her gaze and shrugged. "You can marry me."

Emma Miller lives quietly in her old farmhouse in rural Delaware. Fortunate enough to have been born into a family of strong faith, she grew up on a dairy farm, surrounded by loving parents, siblings, grandparents, aunts, uncles and cousins. Emma was educated in local schools and once taught in an Amish schoolhouse. When she's not caring for her large family, reading and writing are her favorite pastimes.

Raised in Kentucky timber country, **Mindy Steele** has been writing since she could hold a crayon against the wall. Inspired by her rural surroundings, she writes Amish romance peppered with the right amount of charms for all the senses to make you laugh, cry, hold your breath and root for the happy-ever-after ending. Mother of four, Mindy enjoys coffee indulgences, weekend road trips and researching her next book.

EMMA MILLER

&

MINDY STEELE

An Amish Marriage

2 Uplifting Stories

Courting His Amish Wife and
His Amish Wife's Hidden Past

LOVE INSPIRED

INSPIRATIONAL ROMANCE

LOVE INSPIRED®

INSPIRATIONAL ROMANCE

ISBN-13: 978-1-335-44853-8

An Amish Marriage

Copyright © 2023 by Harlequin Enterprises ULC

Courting His Amish Wife
First published in 2021. This edition published in 2023.
Copyright © 2021 by Emma Miller

His Amish Wife's Hidden Past
First published in 2021. This edition published in 2023.
Copyright © 2021 by Mindy Steele

For questions and comments about the quality of this book, please contact us at CustomerService@Harlequin.com.

Harlequin Enterprises ULC
22 Adelaide St. West, 41st Floor
Toronto, Ontario M5H 4E3, Canada
www.LoveInspired.com

Printed in U.S.A.

CONTENTS

COURTING HIS AMISH WIFE

Emma Miller

And we know that all things work together for good to them that love God, to them who are the called according to his purpose.
—*Romans* 8:28

Prologue

Through the trees, Eve spotted her father's windmill and ran faster, ignoring the branches and underbrush that tore at her hair and scratched her arms and face. She took in great gulps of air, sobbing with relief as she sprinted the final distance. She had prayed to God over and over throughout the night. She had begged Him to see her home safely. Now the sun was breaking over the horizon, and she had made it the more than ten miles home in the dark.

Bursting from the edge of the woods, she hitched up her dirty and torn dress, the hem wet from the dew, and climbed over the fence. In her father's pasture, she hurried past the horses and sheep, her gaze fixed on the white farmhouse ahead. If she could just make it to the house, her father would be there. She would be safe at last, and he would know what to do.

Trying to calm her pounding heart, Eve inhaled deeply. At last, her breath was coming more evenly. She wiped at her eyes with the torn sleeve of her favorite dress. She was safe. She was home. Her father would protect her.

At the gate into the barnyard, she let herself through and slowed to a walk as she neared the back porch. Her father's beagle trotted toward her, barking in greeting. Through the windows, she could see into the kitchen where a light glowed from an oil lamp that hung over the table. Her father and sisters and brothers would be there waiting for her. As she climbed the steps to the porch, her wet sneakers squeaked. Hours ago, she had crossed a low spot in the woods and soaked her canvas shoes.

She had almost reached the door when it swung open.

"Dat," she cried, throwing herself at him, bursting into tears. "Oh, *Dat.*"

"Dochter." Her father grasped her by the shoulders, but instead of embracing her, he pushed her back. "Where have you been?" he demanded in Pennsylvania *Deitsch*. He looked her up and down, not in relief that she was safely home, but in anger. "Where is your prayer *kapp*?"

Eve raised her hand to her hair to find it uncovered. "Oh," she cried. "I must have… I must have lost it in the woods somewhere." She brushed back her brown hair that had come loose from the neat bun at the nape of her neck to fall in hanks around her face. She pulled a twig from her hair. *"Dat.* Something terrible happened. I—"

"Where have you been all night?" he boomed, becoming angrier with her by the second. "Who have you been with?" he shouted. "To sneak out of my house after I forbade you to go? I should beat you!"

When she looked up at him, Eve realized she had made a terrible mistake. It had taken her hours to find her way home. She had walked and run all night, choosing the long way home because she had been afraid to follow any main roads for fear Jemuel would find her. She had climbed fences, been scratched by briars and been chased by a feral dog. At one point, she had been lost and worried she had walked too far, or in the wrong direction. But she hadn't given up because she knew that if she could make it home safely, everything would be all right.

But looking at her father's stern face, at his long, thick gray beard and his angry eyes that stared at her from behind his wire-frame glasses, she realized she was wrong. She wasn't safe. And perhaps she would never be so again because she knew what her father was going to say before the words came out of his mouth.

He pointed an accusing finger. "You will marry that boy!" Amon Summy shouted, spittle flying from his mouth.

Eve lowered her head, tears streaming down her cheeks as she prayed fervently to God again to help her.

Chapter One

Levi snapped off a leaf of fresh mint from Alma Stolzfus's pot of herbs near her back door and popped it into his mouth. He was standing with a group of young women, all of marrying age, all looking for husbands. *A fox in the henhouse*—that's what his grandmother would have called him. Because he was single, too.

The difference was, he wasn't here to gobble up any of these girls. He wasn't even looking for a girl to offer a ride home this evening after the singing. He intended to ask Mari, Alma Stolzfus's niece, to let him take her home, though right now, he wasn't even sure she would say yes. They were a bit on-again, off-again. One week she was bold enough to ask him to drive her home from one of the Saturday night singings, and the next she barely spoke to him.

Levi had the idea that she was more interested in JJ Yoder than him. The problem was that JJ was the quiet, reflective type. He was too shy to ask a girl to ride home with him, which was the typical way young men and women got to spend time alone together in pursuit of the right spouse. JJ certainly wasn't asking any girl out for an ice-cream cone or inviting her to his family's home on a visiting Sunday. It was Levi's theory that Mari was going out with him occasionally only to make JJ jealous enough to ask her out himself, which was okay with Levi. He liked Mari, but more as a friend. That didn't mean he wouldn't have accepted a kiss if she offered, but that was about as unlikely as her aunt Alma giving him one.

"What about you, Levi?" Trudy Yoder, JJ's sister, cut her eyes at him. She was one of the prettiest girls standing there, and she knew it. "You going to the barn raising at Mary Aaron's grandfather's tomorrow?"

He suspected Trudy was openly flirting with him, the way she was swinging her hips ever so slightly, smiling and batting her feathery eyelashes.

His hunch was confirmed when her sister harrumphed and slipped her arm through Trudy's. "Come, *Schweschder*. We'd best see if Alma needs any help getting the lemonade and snacks on the table."

Trudy resisted her sister's tug on her arm. "So are you going?" she asked Levi.

"*Ya*, I'm going to the barn raising," he answered lazily. It had been a warm day, even for the end of May, and it was supposed to be sunny, warm and clear the following day, perfect conditions for a barn raising. The work crews would show up at dawn and work until sunset. It would be a long day, but Levi enjoyed barn raisings. He liked knowing he had helped a family, and the food served, often three full meals, was always exceptional.

"You are?" Trudy was grinning again. "And is there a kind of cookie you especially like, Levi? My *mam* and I are baking twelve dozen for the midday meal." The apples of her cheeks were as rosy as the dress she was wearing. Like the other girls, she had kicked off her shoes for the volleyball game they'd just played, boys against girls, and hadn't put them back on. She was cute and sweet, and he wondered if Mari didn't want to ride home with him if he ought to ask Trudy.

"We're making cookies, too. Peanut butter with peanut butter chips," Mary With-A-Y said. That was what they called her because she was also Mary Stolzfus, a cousin of Mari's, only she spelled her name differently. "I made some a few weeks back and took them to the Fishers' for visiting Sunday. I bet Levi ate a hundred of my cookies."

The Fishers, relations to the Fishers back home, were the folks Levi lived with. Though his home was in Hickory Grove in central Delaware, he was a buggy maker's apprentice to Jeb Fisher there in Lancaster County, Pennsylvania. Because Jeb and his wife had never been blessed with children, they opened their home to young men interested in learning to build buggies. Right now, Levi was sharing a room with Jehu Yutzy from Ohio.

"He ate a hundred of *your* cookies!" One of the other girls, whose name he didn't remember, laughed. "I bet Levi would eat *two hundred* of *my* chocolate-chocolate chip cookies. You like chocolate-chocolate chip, don't you, Levi?" She gazed up at him with big, green eyes.

Levi chewed thoughtfully on the mint leaf in his mouth, enjoying the sweet, cool flavor. "The truth is, I love all cookies," he said diplomatically. And that was a fact. He did love to eat. "You're all such good cooks around here, how could a man choose?"

The girls giggled in response and began to call out the kind of cookies they could make for Levi.

"Levi." Someone whispered in his ear from behind, and he turned, surprised because he hadn't seen her approach. It was Mari.

He smiled at her. "There you are. I was wondering where you had—"

"Sht," she shushed, speaking so softly that only he could hear her. "I need your help. It's important."

He looked into her eyes and immediately saw that something was wrong. Very wrong. He glanced at the circle of young women who looked like Englisher-dyed Easter eggs in their pastel-colored dresses of blue and pink and green. They hadn't seemed to notice Mari and were talking among themselves about the ingredients in their recipes.

He returned his gaze to Mari. "You need me now?"

"Right now."

By the tone of her voice, he guessed he wouldn't be getting a kiss. He studied her worried face, trying to figure out what was going on.

"So, are you coming or not?" Mari asked. She looked him up and down and then walked away.

Levi pushed his straw hat down farther on his head, nodded to the girls and followed Mari.

Eve sat on a bale of straw in the Stolzfuses' barn, her knees drawn up, arms wrapped around them. She stared at the toes of her water-stained, black canvas sneakers. "What am I going to do? What am I going to do?" she whispered. The phrase had become a chant over the last week. A prayer.

Where am I going to go? she wondered. *Where will I live? How will I make money to eat?*

A speckled black-and-white Dominique chicken

scratched in the wood shavings at Eve's feet and clucked contently. She watched the chicken, thinking how curious it was that life around her went on without acknowledging that her life, as she knew it, was over. Of course, no one but her father and her cousin Mari knew what had happened.

And Jemuel. *He* knew.

Eve took a deep, shuddering breath. It was warm inside the enormous dairy barn and smelled comfortingly of fresh hay, straw and well-cared-for animals. A black cat leaped up onto the bale of straw and rubbed against her. Eve stroked its back, and it purred, watching the chicken.

The chicken paid no attention to the cat and wandered off, still searching for a stray morsel of corn or grain on the swept concrete floor. The cat seemed to know that things wouldn't end well if it pounced on the chicken. Alma Stolzfus wouldn't have a cat on the property that harmed any animals but a rat or a mouse.

Eve glanced up at the closed barn doors. The larger of the two, meant to lead farm stock or equipment through, had a wide crack at the top that needed caulking. The late afternoon sun poured through the opening, and she watched the movement of dust motes. The way they were illuminated in the beams of sunlight, they seemed to twinkle, reminding her of the stars in the heavens.

Was her life truly over? Her *dat* had said it was if she didn't do as he ordered. But how could it be over? She was only twenty-two. She had too many dreams to have reached the end so soon. She had imagined having a handsome husband, her own home, a house full of children. She had imagined being happy.

Would she ever find happiness now? Or at least contentment?

Eve pressed her lips together, fighting tears that brimmed in her eyes. There had to be an answer to her dilemma. There *had* to be.

Mari had said she could help. Mari was a cousin she didn't often see because Eve's father had had a disagreement with Mari's father, *his* cousin, many years ago. And Eve and Mari didn't belong to the same church district, so the only time they saw each other was at young people's social events. There were plenty of chaperoned frolics for young men and women of marrying age in the county, but Eve didn't get to go often because of her responsibilities at home.

As the eldest of six children and because their mother had died years ago, it fell to Eve to do the cooking and cleaning and other household chores in her father's home. Her sister Annie, at nineteen, was a great help, but the burden of being in charge was still firmly balanced on Eve's shoulders. With meals to cook, the house to clean, laundry to do and clothes to be sewn for her growing brothers and sisters, she didn't get out often. That was at least partially how she'd ended up in this situation to begin with. She didn't get to spend much time with other young women or men, and she had never been on a date. Not only had she never been on a date, but a young man had never even expressed any interest in her before. That was why, when Jemuel had paid attention to her at her father's booth at the farmers market, she'd so quickly become enamored with him.

The sound of a door opening startled Eve, and she half rose from the bale of straw she was sitting on.

The standard-sized door beside the larger sliding one swung open.

"Eve, it's Mari," her cousin called as she entered the barn. "I brought someone with me. Someone who can maybe help."

"Ne," Eve said miserably, now having second thoughts about having come to the Stolzfus farm. Her father would be so angry with her if he found out she'd told someone what happened with Jemuel. The only reason he had let her come to the singing was because he had assumed she would be meeting Jemuel there to discuss their impending wedding nuptials. An assumption she hadn't corrected. She'd neither seen nor heard from Jemuel since she'd run from him, and she hoped she would never lay eyes on him again.

"I don't want anyone to know," Eve murmured. Then she saw him: Levi Miller. Though she didn't know him, she knew *of* him. Mostly because every woman in the county, ages 2 to 102, thought he was as handsome as a man could be. They had once been introduced at a girls-against-boys softball game, but it had been a year ago and she doubted he remembered her. She wasn't the kind of girl a boy remembered.

"I don't know if you've met Levi, but—"

"Ne," Eve interrupted Mari, mortified that Levi was whom she had brought. A boy? What was her cousin thinking? Did Mari really think she was going to talk to a boy about what Jemuel had done, what he had tried to do? She twisted her fingers in the skirt fabric of her threadbare green dress. "This isn't a good idea. My father would be so angry if he found out I had told anyone. Even you," she told Mari pointedly.

"Sounds to me like he's already pretty angry." Mari

turned to wave Levi, who stood in the doorway backlit by sunlight, inside. "Come in and close the door," she told him. "We don't want Trudy to know we're here. Otherwise she'll be giving her opinion."

Levi closed the door behind him. "I won't let anyone in. Not anyone you don't want here." He was speaking to Eve.

Eve waited for her eyes to adjust so she could see him and her cousin better. She imagined their eyes were adjusting, too, after coming into the barn from the bright afternoon sunshine. Which was a good thing because it gave her a moment to gather her wits. When Mari had said she might know someone who could help, Eve had assumed she meant her aunt Alma or maybe one of the other women there chaperoning the frolic. Eve would never have agreed to let Mari bring Levi Miller. What could Mari possibly be thinking to believe Eve would tell this young man anything about what had happened to her? Why would Mari think he would care?

As her eyes adjusted, there was no doubt in Eve's mind that Levi Miller was good-looking. He wasn't overly tall, but he had broad shoulders and nice hands that were clean, his nails trimmed. His hair was a medium brown, shiny and a little long, the way unmarried boys sometimes let theirs get when they were away from their mothers' watchful eyes. He had a strong chin, a long, straight nose and expressive blue-gray eyes, framed by heavy brows.

He was as handsome as she was plain.

Eve had always known she wasn't a pretty girl. But she didn't think she was ugly, either. She was just… plain. She was ordinary in looks with brown hair and brown eyes and a short, thick, round body. She was ordinary in the way a white dinner plate was ordinary. Nothing fancy, but well suited to the task. Eve's appearance was suitable to who she was: a woman of God, Amish, a big sister to three brothers and two sisters, and a daughter to Amon Summy. In that order.

"Please go." Eve lowered her gaze, unable to bear the two of them standing there looking at her.

"I don't mean to intrude," Levi said. He had a warm and steady tenor voice. "I came to see if I could help."

Eve clasped her hands together and glanced down to where the chicken had scratched in the sawdust. There were lines and shapes. As she studied them at her feet, she thought she saw a heart, and she stared at it.

A sign from God?

Eve had never been one for looking for signs from God, not like her father. He never liked to make big decisions without first praying and then waiting for a sign. When he had decided he wanted to take her out of school after she had completed the sixth grade, he had told her he would make his decision in a few days. The fact that she didn't want to quit school and stay home to work all day hadn't mattered. He had prayed and then waited for a sign. It had come in the form of a single black-eyed Susan in her mother's flower bed near the back door of their house. Her father said that was a sign from God that she was meant to be home alone during the day while the others were in school.

He had received the same sign when he decided that her sister Annie should leave school. However, their father had received no such sign from God concerning the boys in the family. Both older boys attended classes until they were sixteen, and Abiah would be in eighth grade in the fall. Eve and Annie had talked, wondering if their father would receive a sign that their sister Naomi, who had just completed the sixth grade, was to end her schooling.

"Please, Eve," Mari fretted. "I don't know how else to help you. Even though my *mam* said you might be able to stay with us for a little while, my *dat* said no. Your father and him being cousins, he said he didn't think it was right for him to get involved in a family matter. Especially since my father and yours are not on good terms."

"I can't promise you I can help, but if you don't tell me what's wrong, I know I can't," Levi said. He spoke gently to her as if she were an animal that might bolt at any moment.

"Come on." Mari sat down on the bale of straw and patted it. "Sit down and tell Levi what happened." She caught the hem of Eve's dress and tugged on it.

Eve dropped down. "You didn't tell him?"

"*Ne*, of course not. I gave you my word. I said I wouldn't tell anyone without your permission." Mari took Eve's hand in her own. "It's better if you explain to him, in your own words. It's your story to tell," she said soberly.

Eve hung her head in shame. "I can't," she whispered. How could she tell Levi Miller, the most eligible bachelor in Lancaster County, how stupid she had been? How naive?

"I wish you would." Levi walked away and came back with a milking stool. He set it an appropriate distance from the two young women and sat down, facing them. "I'm a pretty good listener. That's what my sisters say."

It took Eve a moment to find her voice. She couldn't

bring herself to look at him as she spoke. "You have sisters?"

"A bunch of them. My sister Mary is older than I am and married with children. She lives in New York, where we're originally from. But my sisters back in Delaware—stepsisters technically—we talk all the time. There's Lovey, who's married and lives down the road, Ginger, who just wed in the spring to our neighbor Eli, and Bay, Nettie and Tara are still at home." He spoke slowly, his voice growing on Eve.

But Eve still couldn't look at him. It took her what seemed like an eternity to speak, but he waited patiently. She was embarrassed to tell him what had happened, but she was running out of choices. She had prayed and prayed to God to save her. What if He had sent Levi with a solution?

Eve swallowed hard, digging deep within herself to find the nerve to speak. "I did a foolish thing," she blurted.

Levi threaded his fingers together, lowering his head thoughtfully before looking up at her again. "Haven't we all?"

"*Ne*, this was *really* foolish. I didn't think it through." Once she started to speak, she couldn't stop. It all tumbled out of her. "I met this boy named Jemuel. He's the same age as me. He seemed so nice. He came every Friday for weeks. Stopped by at my father's table at the farmers market. Jemuel and I talked, and we laughed. And one day, he brought me a turkey sandwich and an orange soda pop. He kept asking me if I wanted to go to a singing with him. I thought he was being nice, and not many boys—" Eve's voice caught in her throat.

"It's all right," Mari assured her, taking her hand again and squeezing it.

"No one ever asks to take me to a singing, or offers a ride home," Eve continued. "Not that I get to go to a lot of singings."

"Her mother passed twelve years ago, having her youngest sister. Eve cares for three brothers and two sisters, all younger. And her father. She runs the house, cooks, cleans—she does it all."

"I'm sorry to hear that. I lost my mother a few years ago. I understand how hard it is," Levi said. "Did your father not remarry?"

"He did," Eve murmured. "But she left."

They were all quiet for a moment until Mari urged, "Tell Levi what happened with Jemuel."

Eve exhaled. She was still shaky inside, but at least she didn't feel as if she was going to burst into tears at any moment anymore. "Jemuel kept inviting me out. I asked my father and asked. And every time he said no. He said he didn't know Jemuel or his family and that it wasn't—" She hesitated and then went on. "He said it wasn't safe for a young woman to ride in a buggy with a man she didn't know."

Eve was quiet long enough that Levi said, "Okay?" his tone pressing her to go on.

"I went anyway." The words came out sounding more defiant than Eve intended. "I disobeyed my father, and a week ago Friday night, I sneaked out of the house and met Jemuel at the end of our lane. We were supposed to go to a singing. I wore my favorite dress. Blue. I love a blue dress." She didn't know why she told him that detail. What did men care about what a woman wore? But she had loved that dress that was now ruined, torn in shreds, and waiting in her sewing room to become something else. The dress had reminded her of her mother because her mother's favorite color had been blue, and she had worn it all the time.

"You sneaked out of the house?" Levi pushed gently.

"*Ya.* It was after nine and dark when I left. Jemuel said the singing didn't start until later, so it would be fine going that late. I didn't use my head," she admitted. "I didn't think about the fact that singings don't start at ten o'clock at night. I was just happy that Jemuel wanted to be with me. That he liked me."

Eve took another deep breath. "So... I got into Jemuel's buggy with him. And at first, everything was fine. We were talking and laughing. He told me a funny story about chasing a calf through his sister's spinach patch. But the minute he took the beers out from under the seat, I should have been suspicious. I should have told him to turn around and take me home. Either that or I should have just gotten out of the buggy and walked home. Before it was too late." She whispered her last words.

Mari wrapped her arm around Eve's shoulders. "You're doing great. Keep going."

"I didn't drink the beer, but he did. He drank the beers and threw the cans out of the buggy. Right on the road. I didn't get suspicious, though, until I realized we were headed away from the direction where he said the singing was. But even then, I didn't make him turn around." She looked up to see Levi watching her, his face without judgment. It gave her the courage to go on.

"Instead of going to his aunt's, he drove down a long lane to an abandoned farmhouse. I told him I didn't want to go inside. That I wanted to go to the singing or home. Jemuel said we had to make a stop at the house to get something for his uncle, and then we'd go to the singing. He said the house belonged to them. He wanted me to go inside with him, and I didn't—"

Her words caught in her throat, but this time she feared she wouldn't be able to speak again.

"Take a breath," Mari encouraged, rubbing Eve's arm.

Eve inhaled deeply and went on. "I didn't want to go, but I went anyway." She spoke now in a voice barely above a whisper. She could hear the black-and-white chicken clucking in the far corner of the barn. "When we got inside, Jemuel, he...he tried to—" She felt her face grow hot and she couldn't speak.

"He tried to push himself on her," Mari finished for her.

"Push himself?" Levi didn't seem to understand what Mari was saying. Then, suddenly, the expression on his face changed. "He tried to take advantage of her," he said angrily. "Did he...harm you, Eve?"

Eve felt as if she were frozen. She couldn't speak. She couldn't move. She could barely hear. All she saw was Levi sitting there on the milk stool, handsome, smart Levi. And here she was, ugly and stupid.

"He didn't." Mari took over the explanation. "Eve hit him with a broken chair, and she ran. He chased her, but she was smart. She didn't take the road. Instead, she ran through the woods. It took her all night long, but she found her way home."

"I thought my father would go to Jemuel, to Jemuel's father, to his bishop and tell them what happened. I thought my father would defend me. I thought he would see Jemuel punished. He didn't." Tears welled in Eve's eyes. "He said it was all my fault."

"Wait." Levi came off the milk stool so quickly that he knocked it over. "Your father blamed you?" he asked, his hands on his hips as he stood before her.

Eve nodded, unable to verbally respond.

"Her father told her that she had shamed herself and the family, and the only way to make amends for her sin was to marry Jemuel," Mari finished for her.

"What sin did you commit?" Levi asked, his eyes narrowing. "Being too trusting is not a sin, Eve."

Eve pressed her lips together. "My only sin was not obeying my father, and for that, I confessed to our bishop, though I didn't tell him the details. And I apologized to my father."

"Let me make sure I have this right." Levi began to pace. "A man took you for a buggy ride, making you think he was taking you somewhere he had no intention of taking you. And then he tried to take *advantage* of you?" he asked in disbelief.

Eve hung her head.

"And if she doesn't marry Jemuel, *this week*, her father is putting her out of the house and having her shunned," Mari explained. "I tried to convince my parents to let her stay with us, but I couldn't."

"It's all right," Eve assured her cousin, smiling feebly at her. "I understand. My father can be a difficult man. I wouldn't bring those difficulties into your father's home. You don't deserve that. None of you do. But I cannot marry Jemuel," she went on, her voice so strained that she barely recognized it. "I will not. But I don't know where to go. What to do." She finally felt brave enough to meet Levi's gaze. "If I'm shunned,

I'll lose everything. I've already lost my family, but to lose my God…"

"You can't lose God," Levi insisted. "No one can lose God. He's with us always."

"I'll lose everything," Eve repeated. "And I cannot lose my faith. I cannot lose my church. I know that most people our age at least consider what it would be like to leave our homes, our Amish way of life, to be an Englisher, but I never have. I love our faith, our simple ways. I love God, and I will not abandon Him." Her last words were fierce.

Mari rose, crossing her arms over her chest. "You see the problem here," she told him. "If Eve doesn't marry immediately, she's out of her father's house, out of the Amish community."

Levi nodded, still pacing. "And you don't think that your father said these things impulsively? You don't think he'll change his mind?"

"He will not. He thinks me *soiled*." The word caught in Eve's throat. "He'll have me shunned if I don't marry. But I've never even been out with a boy. I don't know—"

The barn door opened. "Mari?"

Mari whipped around. It was one of her sisters.

"Aunt Alma is looking for you." Her sister squinted, her eyes not yet adjusted. "Who else is there with you?"

Mari rushed toward the door and grabbed her sister. "Mind your own knitting." She gave her a nudge out the door. "I'll be back as soon as I can," she called over her shoulder.

The door closed behind them, and the bright light was gone again.

"Mari's right," Levi said, returning to his pacing. "You've got a problem here."

"*Ya*, I do." Eve gave a little laugh that reflected no humor. "And it's already been a week. My father is threatening to tell our bishop tomorrow and have me shunned immediately. He'll put me out then. I know he will."

Levi stopped directly in front of Eve and looked down at her. "I can only think of one alternate solution here, Eve, and you may not like it, but—"

"Anything," she whispered, "because I'm afraid if I'm forced, I might choose to marry Jemuel rather than lose myself. Lose my life. And that's what would happen if I went into the Englisher world. I know it." She looked up to him. "What can I do?"

Levi held her gaze and shrugged. "You can marry me."

Chapter Two

Levi led his new wife through the train station lobby, a large duffel bag in each hand. He still couldn't believe he was a married man. He couldn't believe that he had impulsively asked Eve to marry him and she had said yes. Never in his wildest dreams could he have guessed he would have walked into that barn less than a week ago a single man and walked out betrothed. To a woman he didn't know.

It wasn't that he didn't want a wife. He had always seen himself someday, down the road, a happily married man like his father. But he'd seen no reason to be in a hurry to wed. His intention had been to finish his apprenticeship and return home to Hickory Grove and build buggies. He would establish a buggy shop, build and sell buggies, save money to build a home for a family and then—and only then—begin looking seriously for a wife.

And all of those carefully laid plans had vanished in a single moment.

That day in the barn when Eve told him what happened to her, his immediate impulse had been to help her. His heart had gone out to the girl, and Levi's father had always preached to him and his siblings to help those in need. When Eve told him she would sooner marry the man who had tried to attack her than allow her father to have her shunned, the idea that he could marry her had just popped up in Levi's head. In the moment, it had seemed the perfect solution. Eve would be able to escape her father and the awful man who had tried to take advantage of her, and not lose her church. Levi had known the moment he began talking to Eve that she was a good woman, a woman of faith, the kind he wanted to marry. What he had not considered was what it would mean to him to marry a woman he didn't know.

And now it was too late to reconsider. He and Eve were wed, and marriage was forever. But he'd done the right thing. He'd been telling himself that since he got up this morning and lowered himself to his knees, praying to God to show him the way to make his marriage a good one.

Levi glanced at Eve, and thoughts of himself slipped away. She looked tired and scared, and it was his responsibility as her husband to put her at ease.

"Let's find a place to sit," Levi said. "The train won't be here for another forty minutes, but I thought we best be early. Early is always better than late when it comes to catching trains and picking peaches." He chuckled nervously at his own joke.

Eve offered a smile but said nothing.

He understood how she was feeling. The last week had been overwhelming for him, as well.

This was the first time he and Eve had been alone since the day in the barn almost a week ago. When they

parted that day, he had taken a borrowed buggy and
gone directly to her father to ask for her hand in marriage. The stern-faced man had met him on the porch
and not asked him to come inside, not even when Levi
told him why he was there. Their conversation had been
brief. Her father had been expecting the man who had
tried to assault Eve. However, he had given his permission for Levi to marry his daughter anyway. Amon
Summy hadn't seemed to care all that much who Levi
was or why he wanted to marry Eve. Amon just wanted
his daughter married and out of his home. Mari's mother
had made the arrangements for her brother, the bishop
in their church district, to marry the couple, and a few
hours ago, Levi and Eve had wed in front of only a
handful of people.

Levi had always imagined his wedding would be like
the ones he had been attending since he was a child. He
thought he would marry the way his father had married
his stepmother and his brothers and sisters had married
their spouses. He had envisioned the solemn church
service and then a full day of celebration with good
food, the laughter of friends and family, and generous
gifts that would help him and his wife establish their
new home. He'd envisioned a traditional honeymoon of
traveling for a few weeks to visit relatives with his new
wife before returning home to set up housekeeping.

The only thing he'd been right about was the solemn
service. The sole member of Eve's immediate family
who had attended had been her father, who scowled
through the entire service. And while Mari and her
mother and sisters had tried to make it a happy affair,
not knowing the details of why they were marrying so
quickly, those attempts had fallen short. They'd not even

had a wedding dinner after the service. There had been no time because Levi and Eve had to get to the station to catch the train to Delaware.

"Why don't we sit here?" Levi suggested, pointing at a wooden bench in the cavernous waiting room. He glanced at Eve.

She was wearing the same green dress she had been wearing the day he met her and a dingy church Sunday apron over it. He suspected she didn't have another dress, something he would right as soon as they arrived in Hickory Grove. He was not a man of great means, but he had enough money to provide his wife's basic needs. She had brought only one small bag to Mari's that morning, a fact that he'd found slightly embarrassing because he had two large zip duffels and had made arrangements for the Fishers to bring the rest of his belongings to him the next time they came to Hickory Grove.

Levi set his bags down beside the bench and held out his hand to take the old leather case from her. There was an awkward exchange of him stepping toward her and reaching and her trying to set it down herself without touching him before he managed to take it from her. "Would you like something to drink?" he asked. "There are sodas and water in the shop. And snacks, if you're hungry."

Eve dropped down on the bench, setting her black cloak and wool bonnet on her lap. The garments were too hot to wear in the June heat and too bulky to go into a bag. "*Ne,* I'm not thirsty or hungry." She stared at the toes of her worn leather shoes poking out from beneath the hem of her dress.

Levi stood there for a minute, wanting to say something, but not knowing what. Eve looked so...so...

beaten down by all the events of the last two weeks of her life that he was worried about her. She was young, only twenty-two to his twenty-nine—too young to have already been through so much. After a moment of indecision, he sat down on the bench beside her and removed his straw hat. "Eve," he said quietly. When she didn't respond, he said, "Look at me. Please?"

She slowly lifted her chin until her gaze met his. She wasn't what most would call a pretty girl, not like Mari Stolzfus or Trudy Yoder. Still, she had smooth skin that was unblemished, big, dark brown eyes framed by thick lashes and glossy hair beneath the white prayer *kapp* pinned to her head. She was shorter and rounder than a lot of girls he knew, but she was strong and healthy. And she was a woman of immense faith. Her faith was what mattered more to him because he, too, was a person of faith. So what if she wouldn't be the prettiest new bride in Hickory Grove? She was *his* bride, and the thought made him smile tenderly.

"Everything is going to be all right, Eve." His words were as much to reassure himself as her, at that moment. "You're going to like Hickory Grove. Everyone is so friendly and kind and…and they're fun. You're going to fit in so well, so easily," he told her.

She pressed her lips together, lips that were the color of the roses in his stepmother's garden. "You should call your father. It's not right to show up without warning. Your stepmother won't appreciate it. She might not want me there."

He shook his head with a smile. "You don't know Rosemary. She would welcome anyone I brought into her home, anyone that any of my brothers and sisters brought home. You're going to like her, Eve. And she's going to love you."

Eve thought on that for a moment. "And she's your *stepmother*?"

He nodded. Her question reminded him of how little they knew of each other.

"Because the way you talk about her," Eve continued, "she doesn't sound like a stepmother. My father was married a few years after my mother died, and she—she wouldn't have welcomed anyone I brought home. She didn't even want me there." Her gaze fell to her lap. "She wasn't very nice to my brothers and sisters or to me."

"You said she left." Levi fiddled with the brim of his hat. "Was that why? Did she not get along with you and your siblings?"

The slightest smile tugged at the corner of her mouth. "I guess she didn't get along well with my father, either."

He smiled at her attempt at humor.

"I don't know where she went or how she managed to leave. There was no divorce. I guess she just went home to her family in Indiana. That's where my father is from."

"Well, I didn't know your stepmother, but I'll make a wild guess that she was nothing like our Rosemary. Rosemary's going to be thrilled to have another girl in the house. She was so sad when my stepsister Ginger left home this spring to be married. Of course, we won't live with my father and Rosemary forever. We'll build our own house. My brother Joshua and his wife just moved out of the big house to live in a small house my brother Ethan was building for himself and his wife. Only Ethan ended up moving to her parents' place down the road. So there's room for us in the big house for now. I'll talk to my father about where you and I will build our place on the farm. When we're ready."

"You need to call your father," she repeated.

Levi exhaled. She was right. The truth was, he'd been putting off this phone call for days. It was going to come as a shock to his father and he'd likely be at least a little hurt that the family hadn't been invited to the wedding. But Levi had been focusing on Eve all week and trying to make everything as easy for her as possible. Having his large family or even his parents attend the wedding would only have made matters more complicated. This had been the best way to do it, he was sure. And if he was wrong, it was done.

"You're right," Levi told her. "I'll call him now, and then I'll get us some snacks for the ride."

"Do they have pay phones here?" she asked, glancing around the big, echoing waiting area of the station. "They're hard to find anymore."

"There are a few here." He started to get up from the bench, then sat down again. "Eve." When she didn't look at him or reply, he spoke her name again. "You have nothing to be nervous about. My *vader* and Rosemary and my whole family are going to adore you."

"Until they know why you married me."

"*Ne*, they're not like that. But I already told you, I won't tell anyone. Not even my father. There's no need for anyone in Delaware to ever know."

She looked up at him, seeming so fragile that his first instinct was to put his arm around her and comfort her. He didn't, of course. It wouldn't have been proper in such a public place. Besides, they didn't know each other.

"It's not anyone's business. I married you because I wanted to." He gave her hand that was resting on the bench a quick squeeze. "Remember that. You and I stood before that bishop and before *Gott* this morning and made those vows of our free will. *Ya?*" he said softly.

Again, the hint of a smile. *"Ya,"* she repeated.

He rose again, taking his hat with him. "I'm going to go find a pay phone. I'll call my father and tell him that the driver I hired says we'll be in Hickory Grove around six. And then I'm going to buy a Coke and some spicy Doritos." He dropped his hat on his head. "You sure you don't want something?"

"Ne. Danke," she answered.

He backed away, dropping his hat onto his head. "I'll get you something anyway. Just in case." He smiled at her, showing more confidence than he was feeling. "Be right back."

Levi found the pay phones easily; he'd used them before. He'd been living in Lancaster County for almost two years and had traveled from Pennsylvania to Delaware several times. He pulled several quarters from his pocket, fed them into the phone, and then he lifted the receiver and punched in the phone number to his father's harness shop in Hickory Grove.

Levi took a deep breath as the phone rang.

"Miller's Harness Shop," came a young male voice. "How can I help you?"

Levi had expected one of Rosemary's girls to answer. They often worked in the shop, either at the cash register or in the back, doing the finer leatherwork. "Who is this?" he asked.

"Jesse Stutzman," the boy answered. "Who is this?"

It was his stepmother Rosemary's son by her first marriage. He had to be coming up on thirteen years old. Where had the time gone? When his father and Rosemary had married, Jesse had been only nine. "Jesse, it's Levi. I didn't recognize your voice. It's gotten deeper since I was last home."

"Everyone says that."

The boy sounded embarrassed, and Levi smiled to himself, remembering all too well what it was like to be thirteen. It was a trying age, no longer a child, but not yet a man.

"Is my *dat* around?"

"I just saw him walk into the back, hang on," Jesse said.

As Levi waited, he turned around. On the far side of the large, marble waiting room, he saw his wife sitting on the bench where he'd left her, still holding on to her bonnet and cloak.

"Levi?" his father said into the phone.

Levi turned his back to the waiting room. *"Dat."* The sound of his father's voice brought a tightness to his chest. It was easy, day to day, to not think about how much he missed his family, but hearing his father speak his name brought up a well of emotion. His father hadn't been keen on the idea of Levi apprenticing so far away. He preferred to have his adult children live nearby, but he had accepted the decision.

"Are you well?" his father asked in Pennsylvania *Deitsch*, the language they spoke at home.

Levi cleared his throat, responding in Pennsylvania *Deitsch*. "I'm fine."

"It's the middle of the day, *Sohn*. It's not that I don't like to hear from you, but aren't you working?" His father sounded calm; it was one of his personality traits Levi had always admired and attempted to emulate. However, his concern was still evident in his voice.

Suddenly nervous, Levi turned around again to check on Eve. She was still sitting where he'd left her, waiting for him patiently. Seeing her, the woman who was now his wife, gave him the courage he needed. "I wanted to let you know I'm on my way home. Today. Now."

"Is something wrong? Do you need me to send a driver?"

"No, nothing is wrong. I'm… We're taking the train. And I already have a driver picking us up at the Wilmington station. I'll be home by supper if there are no delays."

"You said *we*?"

Levi took a deep breath. "Eve and me. Eve is my wife, *Dat*. I'm married."

His father was quiet on the other end of the line for so long that Levi thought maybe they had been disconnected or that his father hadn't heard him. But there had been no click, no dead sound. And Levi knew his father had heard what he said because the older man had exhaled sharply.

When his father finally spoke, his voice was tight. "When did you marry?"

"This morning."

Again a pause. Then, "And you didn't think Rosemary and I would want to be there?" His tone took on a sharpness Levi rarely heard from his father. While Benjamin Miller had held high standards for his children, he had always been kind in doling out both compliments and criticism. Another trait Levi admired in his father.

"There was no time. The Fishers were there, though," he added, thinking perhaps that would somehow lessen the blow.

"Do we... Do we know the bride?"

Again, Levi looked at Eve, but this time he did not turn his back on her. He could tell his father was upset. There was no mistaking it in his tone, and Levi had the sudden desire to tell him everything that had happened to Eve and how it had turned his life upside down in only one week. But then he reminded himself of the promise he had made to Eve and a verse from some-where in the Old Testament came to him: *A man shall leave his father and mother and hold fast to his wife.*

Levi stroked his bare chin with his hand, his chin that would never be smooth again. As a newly married man, beginning today, he would grow a beard. "You don't know her."

There was silence on his father's end of the phone again. Then, at last, he said, "I will see you when you get home, Levi."

The phone clicked, and Levi felt the backs of his eyes sting. He blinked as he turned to the pay phone and hung up the receiver. His father had not said why he was so upset. He didn't have to. Marrying a woman sud-denly, a woman his father had never met, could mean only one thing in their community. It meant that Levi had taken from a woman that which was meant only for her husband.

Levi sniffed and took a deep breath. He reached into his pocket, took out a handkerchief his stepmother had made for him and wiped his mouth. A part of him was angry that his father had leaped to such a conclusion about him so quickly. Another part was sad that his father didn't know him better. Didn't know who he had become as a man.

It hadn't occurred to Levi that when he had offered to marry Eve, his father would think what he must now think. But what else could Levi have done? Marrying Eve was the right thing to do; he knew it in his mind and deep in his heart. He wished he could explain that to his father, along with why. But he couldn't because he had made a promise, and to that, he needed to resign himself.

Pushing aside thoughts of his father, of his dismay, Levi put on a smile and went to get some snacks to share with his wife.

Accepting the hand Levi offered, Eve stepped down from the minivan that had brought them from the Wilmington train station to the little town of Hickory Grove in Kent County. She had never been to Delaware, never been anywhere outside Lancaster County, Pennsylvania, and was feeling overwhelmed. But she also felt a spark of excitement, of hope for this new life before her. A new life with Levi Miller.

Her feet on solid ground, she withdrew her hand from Levi's, clutching her wool cloak and black bonnet to her chest. Against her will, she trembled a little as she gazed up at the rambling white clapboard farmhouse. It was two stories with multiple additions, rooflines running in several directions and two red chimneys to anchor the proportions. The farmland that surrounded the house was flat with no hills and valleys like home, but beautiful in its own way. There were barns, sheds and small outbuildings galore, painted red, all dwarfed by the enormous old dairy barn that Levi had explained as they came up the driveway housed Benjamin's harness shop and the new buggy shop where he would work. Beside it had been a greenhouse that Levi's brother and stepsister ran.

Eve's gaze settled on the big home again. The house and porches were neatly painted, and blooming shrubs and a colorful assortment of flowers grew around the foundation in wide, cultivated beds. While properly plain in color and design, the house looked nothing like the dull structure with its ever-peeling paint and hard-packed dirt lawn that she had grown up in.

Levi removed their bags from the back of the van, setting them in the driveway, and then paid the driver. As the van pulled away, voices and the sound of dogs barking from inside the house caught Eve's attention.

The door to the house flew open and a large, ruddy-colored dog with only three legs bounded across the porch toward them. A woman who looked to be some-where in her forties appeared in the doorway and held open the screen door. "Out with you," she called into the house. Another dog, almost identical to the first, also missing a rear leg, raced past the woman.

Eve watched in awe as the two dogs bounded down the porch stairs. Her father would never have allowed an animal with a disability on his property. Animals born with any disfigurement were put down at birth "for their own good," he had explained to her when she was a child. Her father had told her that a kitten with a blind eye or a pig with a clubfoot wouldn't be able to survive. Yet these full-grown dogs weren't just surviv-ing, they were thriving. Missing a limb didn't seem to hinder their speed or frivolity one bit.

The dogs ran up to Levi, obviously recognizing him

and happy to see him. "Silas and Ada," he introduced, stroking each on the head before motioning for them to sit. "My brother Jacob's dogs. Chesapeake Bay retrievers. They won't bite." He tilted his head one way and then the other. "They might lick you to death, but they won't bite."

Eve's gaze moved from the dogs to her new husband. While he appeared relaxed, the tone of his voice said otherwise. She could tell he was nervous about bringing her home with him, which made *her* nervous. What if Levi's parents wouldn't let them stay? Where would they go? Would *they* go anywhere, or would Levi send her far away to live with some distant relative? She'd heard of such things before.

"They're fine," Eve murmured. "I like dogs. Animals."

"Good, because we've got plenty of them—dogs, cats, goats, sheep, pigs, cows, horses. Oh, and last time I was home, my brother Jesse had a pet snake."

Her eyes got round.

The corner of his mouth turned up in a half smile. "Don't worry. Rosemary wouldn't let him keep it in the house." He waved her to follow him. "Come on, meet my family."

As Levi took the stairs, a man in his fifties who looked very much like Levi, though shorter and rounder, joined the woman on the porch. This had to be her in-laws.

"*Vader*, Rosemary," Levi called. "This is Eve, my wife. Eve, my father, Benjamin, and our Rosemary."

Rosemary met Eve's gaze, and for a moment, the older woman's pretty, round face was unreadable. *What if they don't want me here?* Eve thought again.

And then Rosemary broke into a bright smile. "*Ach*, you must be tired from your travels. Come in, come in, Eve. And let me take your cloak and bonnet. It's too warm on a day like this to be holding those things." She took them from Eve's arms. "Come in and meet my daughters. They're cleaning up. We expected you for supper but figured you must have gotten held up."

"*Ya.*" Eve nodded. "The train left Philadelphia late, so we arrived in Wilmington late, and then there was traffic. *Beach traffic*, Levi said?" She hadn't understood what he meant by beach traffic but hadn't asked because much of what he said she was unfamiliar with. Levi had been raised so differently than she had that she was beginning to wonder how hard it was going to be for her to transition to his way of life.

"*Ya, beach traffic.*" Rosemary rolled her eyes as she walked into the mudroom, obviously expecting Eve to follow. "The highways get very busy in the summer because of the beaches south of here." She was hanging up Eve's cloak and bonnet on a hook just inside the door. "So many Englisher tourists come from Pennsylvania and New Jersey to our beaches. But not to worry, we know the back roads to get where we need to go without tangling with cars."

Pausing in the doorway, Eve glanced over her shoulder at Levi. He was standing in front of his father; neither was speaking. She studied the older man for a moment. Benjamin was a sturdy, fiftyish man of medium height with rusty-brown hair streaked with gray. He had a weathered face with a high forehead and broad nose with a full beard that had a reddish cast, which had also begun to gray.

The last week had been such a whirlwind that Eve

and Levi had had little time to talk. However, on the
train ride, Levi had told her about his complicated family. He said that his mother and Rosemary's husband,
Benjamin's best friend, had died six years ago. Then
Benjamin and Rosemary had wed, and both families,
except for his oldest sister, Mary, who already had a
family, had moved from New York state to Delaware
to begin anew as a *blended* family. Levi had led her to
believe that his father, Benjamin, was a kind, understanding man. A happy man.

He didn't look happy now. In fact, he seemed so unhappy with his son that Eve was hesitant to leave Levi
alone on the porch with him.

Benjamin was speaking now. He hadn't raised his
voice, but it was obvious he was saying something Levi
didn't like.

Eve wasn't sure what to do. It was her fault Levi
had married without consulting his parents. Shouldn't
she be at her husband's side if Benjamin was dressing
him down?

Levi glanced her way. "I'll be in in a minute," he told
her. "Go in with Rosemary."

Eve nodded and followed her mother-in-law through
the mudroom into a big family kitchen that held not one,
but two tables pushed together in an L shape. It was a
kitchen nearly as big as the first floor of Eve's father's
house had been.

"They're here," Rosemary announced to two young
women standing at a large country-style sink doing
dishes. "Eve, that's Tara." She indicated the younger
of the two who Levi had told her was twenty. "And
Nettie." Nettie was a little older than Eve.

In green dresses of different shades, both girls were

pretty, Tara with very light red hair and Nettie with blond. Their eyes, like their mother's, were green.

Of course they were pretty, Eve thought. Everyone in this family was handsome or pretty. She was a plain wren among a flock of colorful finches, blue jays and cardinals.

"We're so glad you made it safely. I was worried something had happened, a train crash or something," Tara said, setting down a dish towel.

"Tara is a worrier," Nettie explained, rinsing off a dinner plate and setting it out for her sister to dry. "She worries so none of us have to."

"It happens," Tara threw in her sister's direction. She turned back to Eve. "You must be starved. I made your plates. It's fried chicken, pasta salad, broccoli slaw and pickled beets. I hope you like pickled beets, *Schweschder*. Is it all right if I call you sister?" She walked toward a refrigerator, not waiting for Eve to respond. "I know I have plenty of sisters, but can you have enough?"

"You're going to love her fried chicken," Nettie put in. "Tara's the best cook in the house, after *Mam*, of course. Tara's also the chattiest. Which gets her into trouble sometimes," she added in a fake whisper.

"I don't know why you say things like that," Tara flung over her shoulder at her sister as she set the plates on the table. "*Mam* said you shouldn't tease me so much. Didn't you, *Mam*?"

"Girls, girls," Rosemary admonished.

Eve glanced in the direction of the porch, where she'd left Levi. She didn't hear any shouting from the porch. She hoped Levi's father wasn't too upset with him.

Rosemary caught her looking at the door. "He'll be

in in a minute," the older woman soothed. "Sit. Relax." She smiled kindly. "You're home now."

"I can't tell you how nice it will be to have another girl in the house," Nettie said, bringing two place settings to the end of one of the tables. "Our sisters Lovey and Ginger married, and Bay is so busy with the greenhouse this time of year that I feel like all Tara and I do is cook and clean. One meal is barely over, and it's time to start preparing for the next. It will be nice to have someone else to spend time with besides Miss Worrywart."

Tara stuck her tongue out at her sister as she carried a foil-covered plate in each hand toward the table.

Nettie rolled her eyes. "Do you see what I have to deal with every day?" she asked Eve.

Eve smiled to herself. Tara reminded her of her sister Anne. She was a worrier, too, but also playful and fun. She used to stick her tongue out at Eve when their father wasn't looking.

Thinking of her sister brought a lump to her throat. She hadn't been gone even a whole day and she already missed Anne.

"Please, Eve. Sit down. Can I get you some water?" Tara asked.

The loud sound of footfalls and little boys laughing came from the hall and then filled the kitchen as twin toddlers burst into the room. They were followed by an older boy who Eve thought might be Jesse, Rosemary's son from her previous husband. The family was so big, and it was confusing as to who were Benjamin's children and who were Rosemary's. The twin boys, she knew, were Benjamin and Rosemary's. Levi had said that it had been a bit of a surprise to the family that Rosemary had given birth at her age, but the little boys had found their way into everyone's hearts and sealed the union of the two families.

Rosemary made another round of introductions, and then another sister walked into the kitchen—Bay, the one who had the greenhouse. Then Levi's brother Joshua arrived with his family, and the kitchen was so loud, with everyone talking at once, that Eve started to feel overwhelmed again. More handsome, beautiful people who seemed so content. How would she ever fit into this big, happy family?

What had she done in marrying Levi, a stranger?

When Levi walked inside with his father, Eve could tell he was upset. Levi sat down beside her to eat his supper, and everyone joined them at the table for dessert, diving into fresh strawberry pies Tara had made. Everyone was talking to Eve, asking questions, but no one, she realized, was speaking to Levi. He ate in silence, not looking up from his plate.

Was he angry with her? Eve began to wonder.

Thankfully, once she and Levi had eaten their supper and declined the pie, the family began to scatter. Nettie and Tara excused themselves to put the twins to bed, Joshua and his family went home, and the others went their separate ways to finish chores and prepare for the next day.

Eve insisted on washing Levi's dinner dishes and her own. When she took up a clean dish towel to begin drying, Rosemary told her to put it down.

"Let the dishes sit on the drainboard until tomorrow," Rosemary said. "Jesse took your bags up to your room. I know it's been a very long day for you. You turn in." She looked at Levi, who was just standing at the end of one of the tables. "I've prepared Joshua and Phoebe's old room for you."

"Thank you, Rosemary," Levi said, then looked to Eve. "Come on. It's this way."

Eve said good-night to Rosemary, the only one left in the kitchen, and climbed the stairs behind Levi. At the landing, they went down a long hall and then a second one. He opened the very last door on the right and stepped back to let her pass.

Only when Levi walked into the bedroom and closed the door behind him did Eve realize the full extent of her impulsive decision to marry a stranger. She stared at the only bed in the room, made up with a colorful log cabin patterned quilt.

She was married to Levi now.

And that meant she would share a bed with him.

Suddenly, she was afraid. And angry. Hot tears burned the backs of her eyelids. How could her father have forced her to make the choice between marrying a complete stranger and a would-be rapist?

And how had she been so foolish as to have put herself in such a position in the first place?

Chapter Three

Levi closed the bedroom door and leaned against it, his hands tucked behind him. He took a deep breath, suddenly so tired, he could barely think. He was trying hard not to second-guess his decision to marry Eve because what was done was done.

The exchange between him and his father had been worse than he had anticipated. He had suspected from the conversation on the phone back in Lancaster that his father was upset with him, but never in his life had the man he looked up to expressed such disappointment in him. Not even the time Levi had convinced his twin brothers, Jacob and Joshua, to jump out the second-story window of their barn back in New York. The twins had only been ten, he had been thirteen, and Jacob had ended up with a trip to the emergency department with a broken arm. Their father had expressed his disappointment in Levi's choices right before he assigned all of Jacob's chores to him for two months while his little brother's bone mended. But that had not been half as bad as what had happened on their porch that evening.

Levi closed his eyes, thinking back to the conversation. He'd been the one to speak up first.

"Thank you for letting me bring my wife home, *Dat*," he had said.

His father had slid his hands into his pockets and gazed out at their orchard before returning his attention to Levi. "You will always be welcome in my home, *Sohn*." His voice then cracked with emotion. "You know that. No matter what you have done."

Levi had had to bite down on his lower lip until he tasted blood to keep from shouting, "But I didn't do anything wrong, *Dadi*. I did the right thing!"

But, of course, he hadn't been able to say that because he was a man of his word. Instead, he had just stood there and listened to his father talk about the choices a man made in life and the consequences until Joshua, carrying his new baby, and his wife and young son had come walking across the yard. Then Levi's father had gone into the house.

"There's just one bed," Eve said, her voice bringing Levi back to the present.

He looked up. "What?"

"The bed." Eve's voice had taken on a tone of annoyance. She was talking quickly, her voice higher pitched than he had heard before. "There's only one bed. I can't… I won't—" She pointed, lowering her voice. "If you think I'm sleeping in that bed with you…" She crossed her arms over her chest, moisture in the corners of her eyes. "You've got another thing coming, Levi Miller!"

Levi was so surprised by the tone she had taken with him that he didn't understand what she was so upset about. And then he did. They were married. It was customary for a married couple to share a bed and procreate as God intended. She was worried he expected her to have relations with him.

He drew back, staring at her. As with his father, he was hurt, but angry, too. How could Eve think he was that kind of man? The kind of man Levi had just saved her from? He had sacrificed his father's opinion to protect her from Jemuel Yoder, and now she was accusing him of being cut from the same cloth?

"Eve, I don't expect us to sleep together," Levi snapped back. "Why would you think that?"

"That's why." She pointed at the bed again.

"But this is the room Rosemary gave us," he said defensively. "You think I should tell her it's not acceptable when she's welcomed us into her home with open arms? What will she think if I say we need separate rooms?"

Eve stared at him, a challenge in her dark brown eyes, which surprised him. In the week he'd known her, she had seemed so agreeable and thankful for his intervention. She had been so easy to please. And now she was making demands on him and causing him stress he didn't need piled on his shoulders on top of his father's disappointment in him.

Levi exhaled loudly, stepped around her, grabbed the quilt and a pillow off the bed and tossed them on the floor. Then he picked one of his bags from where Jesse had left it and strode to the door. "I'll go into the bathroom first. You put your nightclothes on while I'm gone. When I come back, you can take your turn in the bathroom. I'll sleep here on the floor." He pushed the pillow with the toe of his boot. "Will that work?"

Eve looked like she was about to burst into angry tears. Or throw something at him. Maybe both.

She gave a quick nod.

"Fine." He walked out the door, closing it behind him. The moment he was in the hall, he regretted the harshness in his voice. It didn't matter that she had spoken unkindly to him first. He knew better. His parents had raised him better. Eve was under stressful circumstances, too, and he should have kept that in mind. In fact, her situation was worse than his because she hadn't asked for any of this. *He* had offered to marry *her*. And now he was the head of their family and *he* was the one who had to take the lead in such matters. It was his duty to promote harmony in their married life.

As Levi walked down the hall, he made up his mind that he would apologize to Eve when he returned to their room. However, after preparing for bed, he returned to their bedroom to find her tucked into bed, sound asleep.

Settling onto a makeshift bed on the hard floor, Levi clasped his hands together and prayed to God to help him be a good husband to Eve. And then, exhausted, he fell asleep.

Eve woke to the heat of early morning sunlight on her face and the sound of someone moving around the bedroom. When she opened her eyes, she saw Levi, fully dressed in denim pants, a faded blue shirt and suspenders, his shaggy hair wet. He was unpacking his bags, placing items of clothing in the drawers. For a moment she watched him, then softly greeted him. *"Guder mariye."*

He turned to her, his face solemn. "I'm sorry if I woke you. Good morning."

She sat up, pressing her lips together. They'd not spoken since the night before after she'd been so terrible to him. After he walked out of their bedroom, Eve had quickly put on her nightgown, rehearsing her apology to him for when he returned. Once in bed, she said her prayers and then waited for him. But she must have fallen asleep before he returned. And now here they were, their second day of marriage.

She started to say she was sorry, but he spoke at the same time. Then both of them went silent.

"You first," she said.

He closed a drawer behind him and approached the bed. "I want to apologize for how I spoke to you last night, Eve. It's not an excuse, but I was tired and frustrated with my father and—" He looked out a big window that faced south, then back at her. "I took it out on you."

She gave a little sigh of relief, glad he wasn't angry with her. She felt so alone right now. She had no one but Levi, and she couldn't bear the thought of him being mad at her. "I wanted to tell you I was sorry, too." She clutched the bedsheet to her chest. "You didn't deserve what I said. How I said it. I was tired, too. And everything is so different here from home that I was feeling a bit…overwhelmed. Also not an excuse," she added.

He sat down on the edge of the bed beside her. "I should have brought up the subject of sleeping arrangements before we came upstairs." His blue-gray eyes were kind. "I had to accept whatever room Rosemary gave us because no one here knows that our marriage is anything different from any other marriage in my family. They don't realize we don't know each other very well."

She looked down, appreciating how delicately he was discussing the matter.

"Eve, I have no problem sleeping on the floor, but no one can know, otherwise they'll ask questions." He paused and then went on. "The same goes for how we speak to each other in front of everyone, how we are with each other. We're supposed to be newlyweds. Do you understand what I mean?"

She nodded. "You're saying we have to...act like we like each other." She lifted her chin, sneaking a peek at him when he didn't say anything. She noticed that he had not shaved except above his upper lip. Because he was married, he was now growing a beard. Which meant this was all real. She was married, and now she was Levi Miller's wife. She wasn't Eve Summy any longer, she was Eve Miller.

She met his gaze to see that he was smiling at her.

"Eve, it's not that I don't like you. What would make you say that?" he asked. "I'm just saying that we need to give the appearance of a newly married couple who, you know, planned to wed." He sat there for a moment and then pressed his hands to the tops of his legs and stood. "I'm going to go downstairs to the kitchen. You come down when you're ready."

"Ach," she said, copying the expression she'd heard her mother-in-law make the evening before. She threw off her sheet. "I should be in the kitchen, helping Rosemary and your sisters with breakfast."

He rested his hand on the doorknob and looked back at her. "I'm sure they'll appreciate your help but take your time. They know you had a long day yesterday. I'm going to go out to the barn and give my brothers some help with feeding, and I'll see you for breakfast." He offered a smile, and then he was gone.

The minute the door closed behind him, she jumped

out of bed and made it, using the pillow and the quilt that Levi had left on the floor. Then she put on the same green dress she'd worn the day before. It was her only dress now. She'd ruined the blue one two weeks ago running from Jemuel. The only other dress she had owned was the black one she wore to church, but her father had refused to let her pack it, saying it was his property. Thankfully, he had allowed her to keep the only prayer *kapp* she owned. After brushing and tying back her hair, she lovingly placed the starched white *kapp* over her hair and took great care to pin it down without mussing it. As with most Amish women, for Eve, the head covering was a symbol of her faith. It made her feel safe.

With the *kapp* set properly on her head, she took one last look at the small mirror over the chest of drawers where Levi had placed his things. Looking back at her, she saw the same brown-haired, brown-eyed wren of a girl whom she had seen in her father's home. But there was one difference, she reminded herself. She was no longer a girl; she was a married woman. She was Levi's wife. And she wanted to be the best wife she could be to him, the wife she knew she could be to such a good man. And that started today.

Despite Eve's intentions, once she was downstairs, her confidence wavered. She didn't know how it was possible, but the kitchen was even more hectic than it had been the night before. This morning not only were the family members who lived in the house there, but also his married siblings. The kitchen was full of men and women, all talking at once, talking over each other. With the women putting breakfast on the two kitchen tables, the men came in from outside, laughing and joking, giving each other heavy-handed nudges.

And there were children everywhere, more than just Rosemary and Benjamin's young ones. The children climbed over benches and ran in and out of the kitchen, squealing with laughter. One of Levi's little twin brothers Eve had met the night before chased a snow-white fluffy cat under the table and then back out. Tara, carrying a huge platter of freshly made pancakes, held the dish high as the other twin ducked under it.

"How can I help?" Eve asked Tara from the doorway.

"Oh, everything's ready. Sit down. And be sure to save a seat next to you for Levi." Tara giggled.

"Phillip," called one of the women Eve didn't know as she ducked her head under one of the tables. "Come out of there right now or I'm coming under." The young woman had to be one of the sisters. She had Tara's green eyes, and she was beautiful, with flaxen blond hair. She looked up. "Good morning, Eve. I'm Ginger." She smiled and pointed across the room. "The redhead is my husband, Eli. Eli!" she shouted. "Say hello to Levi's Eve."

In stocking feet, a red-haired man waved from the far side of the room. "Good morning, Eve. Welcome to Hickory Grove!"

"And somewhere around here is our daughter, Lizzy, and our sons Andrew and Simon," Ginger went on. "And under this table—" she ducked to look under again and then popped her head back up "—is our son Phillip, who will be washing dishes for a week if he doesn't come out from under his *grossmama*'s table." She threw her last few words in the direction of the boy's hiding place.

"*Ach*, could you put this sausage on the table?" Tara pushed a large round plate of sausage patties into each of Eve's hands. "The egg casserole is going to overcook if I don't get it out of the oven."

Eve had taken only two steps when Philip darted out from under the table right in front of her. Startled, she swayed to keep from stepping on him, and one of the plates began to tilt. "Oh no," she cried as the sizzling patties began to slide off the edge.

A blonde woman with brown eyes snatched up one of the plates off the table and caught three of the four patties midair. "Got 'em!" The fourth hit the table and shot out into the room.

Quick as a rabbit, a boy who looked to be a brother to little Phillip snatched the sausage off the floor. "Can I eat it, Abigail?" he asked, already bringing it toward his mouth.

Abigail cut her eyes at Ginger.

"*Ya*, why not?" Ginger answered with a shrug. "I'm sure he's eaten worse."

"Boys," the blonde agreed with amusement, then she returned her attention to Eve as she set the plate on the table. "I'm Abigail. My husband is the handsome one over there." She pointed toward one of Levi's brothers standing in the mudroom doorway. She put out her hands. "Here, let me take that."

Eve gladly passed the platter to Abigail and watched as she slid the sausages she'd caught from the plate back onto the platter before setting it down.

"Ethan, right?" Eve asked. On the train, Levi had gone through his family members' names and if they were married, along with their spouses' names, but there were so many of them. She feared she'd never learn them all. "The schoolteacher?"

"That's right. We live down the road with my parents. Our son, Jaimie, is around here somewhere. Up to mischief, I'm sure."

"Let's eat," Rosemary announced loudly above the din. Then she came up behind Eve and murmured, "Don't worry. You'll get used to the hubbub when everyone is here. They were all so eager to meet you that I couldn't tell them they weren't welcome to join us for breakfast."

She said it so kindly that Eve glanced up appreciatively. Rosemary was smiling at her and she smiled back.

"Go on, join your husband," Rosemary told her, indicating an empty seat on one of the benches beside where Levi sat. "We don't sit in any particular order around here. It's wherever you can find a place. Except for the head of the table." She pointed.

Eve looked over to see Benjamin taking a chair at the end of one of the tables.

"Makes him think he's in charge," Rosemary whispered in her ear.

Eve looked up and giggled, and Rosemary squeezed her hand, offering another kind smile. "We really are glad to have you here," she said quietly. "Now go on, before someone else takes your seat and you're stuck eating with the little ones." She looked up. "Not there, Jaimie," she ordered. "That's Eve's seat. Come over here with your *grossmammi*, where I can keep an eye on you."

After the entire family was seated and had silent grace, everyone began talking again, firing questions at

Eve. As they talked across the tables, holding multiple conversations at once, they passed around serving platters of fluffy egg-and-cheese casserole, sausage, bacon, toast, hash browns and dried apple muffins. As Eve ate, she tried to answer questions posed to her as best she could and keep up with as many conversations at once as she could manage. And she listened for names, trying to keep everyone straight, making notes to herself of questions she had for Levi later. She had so many.

How did Ginger and Eli have four children if they'd just married? Why did Marshall, Benjamin's eldest son, and Abigail live with her parents rather than on the family farm? And who was Benjamin calling Rosebud?

It wasn't until after breakfast that Eve realized how quiet Levi had been through the entire meal, and how little anyone had said to him. As he rose from the table, she got up, too. All of the men were pushing back from the table and making their way out the back to go about their day. As was customary, the women would clean up. Eve didn't mind at all, though. She had known Levi's family less than a day, but she already knew she wanted to be a part of it. Contributing to the day-to-day running of the household was a way she felt she could do that.

Eve scooped up several dirty plates and was walking toward the sink when she caught Rosemary watching Levi. The older woman glanced at Eve, then at Levi again. "Levi, did you forget something?" the older woman said.

"Sorry?" He turned to his stepmother.

"Aren't you forgetting something?" She gestured to Eve.

Eve pulled the dirty plates closer, feeling her cheeks

grow warm. She didn't like being the center of attention, especially in this big, lively family.

Levi stared blankly at Rosemary.

"Your wife," his stepmother said. "You didn't say goodbye to your new wife."

Embarrassment showed on Levi's face and Eve felt awful for being the cause. "*Ne*, it's…all right," Eve said. "He… He has work to do."

"Nonsense. Today is your first full day as a married couple," Rosemary lectured. "Habits you start now, you'll carry the rest of your days." She eyed Levi again as she took the pile of dishes from Eve. "Your father would never leave the house without telling me goodbye, Levi."

He looked down at the floor.

"Go on," Rosemary urged Eve. "Spend a moment with your husband. It will be hours before he's back for the midday meal, which we eat at one. This time of year, supper is at six thirty."

Not knowing what else to do, Eve met Levi halfway.

"I'm sorry," she mouthed, looking up at him. She twisted her fingers together in the folds of her apron.

"Not your fault," he told her, his tone measured. "I'm going to help Jacob with a problem with one of the plows, then meet with my *dat* so we can discuss plans to expand the size of what will become my buggy shop, and I'll see you for dinner." Their heads together, he spoke softly so no one else in the kitchen could hear them. "Will you be all right here with Rosemary and the girls?"

Eve studied Levi's stubbled face. This morning, Abigail had called her husband handsome, but Eve thought maybe the brother she had married was even better-looking. She smiled at him. "*Ya*, of course. I'll be fine. I'll help with the dishes and then I'm sure there's other work to be done."

Tara, who was walking by them with two dirty glasses in each hand, thrust her head between Levi's and Eve's. "Don't worry, Levi. I'll be here. I'm going to make strawberry jam. Do you like making jam, Eve?" She beamed. "I love making jam."

"I do," Eve answered.

"Thank you, Tara." Levi clapped his hand on his sister's shoulder and walked out of the house.

Eve immediately went back to clearing off the table, quickly finding the rhythm of Rosemary and her daughters who still lived at home. Lovey, who was obviously expecting, and her husband, Marshall, and son, Elijah, had said their goodbyes, as had Phoebe and Joshua and their two little ones. Abigail and her family had been the first to go. From what Eve had been able to gather, Abigail's mother was poorly and she needed to get home to her. Eve would ask Levi later about Abigail's mother's health.

Eve was gathering another stack of dirty dishes when Bay, Ginger's twin sister, called from the sink, "Want to wash, Eve?"

"*Ya*, I'll wash." Eve lowered the dishes into the dishwater. "I don't mind."

Bay looked to her mother, who was helping one of the twin boys get his socks on so he could go with his father to the barn. James—at least Eve thought it was James—lay on his back, his bare feet in the air. Rosemary was trying to slip on the sock, but the little boy was wiggling.

"*Mam*, Eve's going to wash dishes. May I go? I

have marigold seedlings to transplant before it gets too warm." Bay was already backing away from the sink to give Eve room. *"Mam?"*

Finally, wrestling the second sock on her son's foot, Rosemary glanced up. "Go, go," she shooed.

Bay rushed to the laundry room to make her way outside, whipping off her everyday apron. *"Danke!"*

"You're going to forget how to do household chores," Rosemary called after her daughter. "Then what will you do when you're married?"

"I don't know, maybe I won't marry at all." Bay poked her head back into the kitchen. "Or maybe my husband will do the housework and I'll support us running the greenhouse."

Rosemary frowned as she helped the little boy, who she realized was Josiah, not James, to his feet. "I wouldn't count on that, *Dochter.*"

The door closed loudly behind Bay, and Rosemary rolled her eyes. "That one." She gave her son a nudge. "Go on with you. Your *dat* is waiting for you on the porch."

The little boy took off, and Rosemary turned back to Eve. "If you're going to make strawberry jam today, Eve, you best change into a different dress."

Eve thrust her hands into the warm, soapy water and began to scrub a plate with a dish brush. "This is all I have," she said softly, embarrassed.

"Oh," Tara said, stopping in the middle of the floor. She had been flitting around in the kitchen like a little bee since Eve had come downstairs this morning, but now the bee was very still. Tara was thinking. "Well then, you could have a couple of my dresses." She shrugged cheerfully. "I have too many anyway."

Eve could feel Rosemary watching her, even though

her back was to the older woman. "I, uh…" Eve rinsed the plate in her hands. "I don't think it would fit," she managed.

"Well, why wouldn't it fit?" Tara set her hands on her hips. "Is it because you're too—"

"Too long," Rosemary interrupted. "Your dresses would be too long for Eve."

Eve didn't realize she had been holding her breath until she exhaled. And whispered a prayer of thanks to God for steering Rosemary to such a tactful explanation. Though it had to be obvious, she thought. Tara was much thinner and taller than Eve.

"Which means," Rosemary continued, bringing her hands together, "you and I, Eve, need to meet in my sewing room once this kitchen is *ret* up. I have a lot of extra fabric. I'm going to make you a dress."

"Oh, no. You don't need to do that," Eve said.

"*Ne*, I don't. But I want to so I don't want to hear another word about it," Rosemary said as she took a dish towel from a drawer and began to dry the clean dishes Eve was setting on the sideboard.

"But Eve and I are making strawberry jam," Tara protested.

"Not until you've picked the strawberries," Rosemary chastised.

And that was that.

Chapter Four

Levi lifted a couple of two-by-fours from the wagon onto his shoulder and carried them through an open bay door, sidestepping one of Jacob's dogs. "One way or the other, Ada," he muttered, walking out of the bright sunshine into the barn's shade.

When his family had moved to Hickory Grove from New York after his father married Rosemary, the two-story structure with a gambrel roof had been a dairy barn. His father had cleverly added interior walls to build a storefront for his harness shop, and several more rooms to create workspaces for the harness business that was their family's livelihood. Once they were settled in, and the shop had begun to thrive, the older man had built himself a small workshop for what had started out as a hobby but was becoming a passion. Benjamin Miller had always dreamed of building buggies, like his grandfather. The previous Christmas, Levi and his father had talked about adding space and bay doors to the buggy shop when Levi completed his apprenticeship and returned home. Now with Levi home to stay, the plans were being moved up, and construction on additional walls had begun.

Jacob followed behind Levi, carrying more lumber. Their father had put Jacob, a carpenter by trade, in charge of constructing the framework of the walls. Even though Levi had plenty of experience building interior walls, he was just his brother's assistant.

"Ada," Jacob called, steadying the boards on his shoulder to point into the barnyard with his free hand. "Get out from under our feet. Go chase a rabbit or something." The Chesapeake Bay retriever took off running, and he shook his head as he lowered the wood to the stack Levi had started. "Phew, going to be another warm one."

Setting down the wood he had carried inside, Levi removed a handkerchief from his pocket. He lifted his straw hat and wiped his brow, saying nothing. He had too much on his mind for small talk. Right now, he wanted to get the wagon of lumber unloaded and un-hitch the horse because the sooner these walls went up, the sooner he could get to the business of building his first buggy. With the proceeds, he would be able to open a bank account to begin saving for the house he would build on his father's property for him and Eve to live in.

"But better than rain, though, *ya*?" Jacob asked, re-moving his hat and fanning himself with it.

An orange barn cat rubbed against Levi's ankle, and he pushed it away gently with his boot, hoping it got the message. He didn't recognize the half-grown calico; it was probably one of his brother's rescues. Jacob loved animals and was always bringing strays home. He took a particular liking to the sick and injured. Back in Up-state New York, his younger brother had once rescued a litter of kittens from a tree's hollow after a neighbor's mother cat had been killed on the road. Jacob had insisted their mother let him keep the newborn kittens in the kitchen in a cardboard box where he had fed them cow's milk from a tiny bottle for weeks. Every single kitten had survived.

"You know what's for dinner?" Jacob leaned down to pet the cat Levi had shooed away. "Seems like breakfast was a long time ago. I'm starving."

"I don't know what we're having." Levi hooked his thumb in the direction of the bay door. "Let's get the rest of this wood unloaded. I'd like to see some progress on these walls today."

Levi started for the door, but Jacob stepped sideways, blocking his way.

"What's going on with you?" Jacob asked.

"What do you mean?" Levi didn't meet his gaze as he slid his handkerchief back into his pocket. "We need to get the rest of the wood so I can put the wagon away and unhitch the horse. Sassafras is old. No need to let her stand out in the sun." He set his hat on his head.

Jacob studied him for a moment, making Levi uncomfortable.

"*Ne*, it's more than that." Jacob studied him. "You don't seem like yourself. You seem…frustrated."

"That's because I *am* frustrated." Levi threw out his arms. "I came home to get this business off the ground. To build buggies. I have the skill, the knowledge, and *Dat*'s got me mending fences, hauling wood and—and framing walls." He swung one hand in the direction of the empty space.

The old mare they'd brought from New York lifted its head, gazing in Levi's direction when he raised his voice. Even their old horse was upset with him, Levi thought morosely.

"Come on. You've been home less than a week," Jacob argued, his tone calm. "And if we're going to make more space for you to build those buggies, we have to put up walls. *Dat*'s already moved up his plans by a good six months so you can start working."

Levi crossed his arms over his chest and said nothing. Tomorrow he'd have been back in Hickory Grove a week. He'd have been married a week, and still, his father was upset with him. And things weren't going much better with his wife.

Levi didn't see much of Eve during the day. She worked in the kitchen and in the garden with Rosemary and the girls, and Levi did what his father asked of him around the farm. They had meals together, of course, but then they were in a room full of people. Only at night were he and Eve alone and then, the moment Levi closed the bedroom door, both of them became irritable with each other. She seemed upset with him the minute she got within six feet of him, and he responded with equal, irrational crossness. He hadn't thought it would be easy to be a new husband under the circumstances, but this wasn't what he had expected at all. Not from Eve and, worse, not from himself.

"You need to have patience," Jacob urged gently. "You know how *Dat* is. He likes things to go as planned and when they don't..." He shrugged. "It takes him a little time to adjust."

"Are you talking about me wanting to start the business sooner, or my marriage?" Levi asked.

"Both."

Levi looked away. He respected Jacob's honesty

with him. He watched the orange cat trot across a two-by-four they'd added to the pile, comically trying to balance as the board tilted under its weight. "*Dat* is disappointed in me," he said quietly.

"He loves you, Levi. You just need to give him some time."

Levi nodded, appreciating the fact that his brother didn't go into the specific reason why his father was disappointed in him. "I know," he murmured. "But I want to get to work. I have to build a buggy so I can sell it, so I can have some money to start saving for a house for Eve and me. So we can get out of *Dat*'s house."

"Right. You're a married man now, aren't you?" Jacob smiled good-naturedly. "How are you finding that so far?"

Levi sighed. "Honestly?" He met his brother's gaze. Jacob had their father's brown eyes. "Not what I expected. It's…harder than I thought it would be. I'm not sure what Eve wants from me."

"Well…" He drew in a breath slowly. "I imagine Eve could use a helping of your patience, too. From what she had to say about her family life, Hickory Grove has to be quite a change." He chuckled. "This family has to be a whole lot different from what she's used to."

Levi responded testily. "How do *you* know what she came from?"

"Because I asked her," Jacob pushed back.

Levi set his jaw, surprised by the jealousy that flared in his chest. "When were you conversing with my wife? Where was I?"

"We were in the garden this morning. You'd gone to the lumberyard, and Tara asked me to help her and Eve with the pole beans' trellises. One of the wooden posts was leaning, and the wires had loosened up." He shrugged. "We talked while we worked. She seems very nice, your wife. I like her."

"I bet you do."

Jacob frowned. "What's that supposed to mean?"

Levi walked away from his brother and into the bright sunlight without another word.

Eve picked up a stack of white bowls from the kitchen table, then set them down again, flustered, not recalling what Tara had just told her. "Should I take the bowls outside now or wait?"

Tara closed the freezer door, wiping her hands on her apron. "You should leave them. We're going to go outside and sit for a while. Then we'll have the strawberry ice cream when the men get back from the barn. No telling how long they'll be. You know how men are." She brought the fingers of one hand to her thumb repeatedly. "Talk, talk, talk. *Mam* says women have nothing over men when it comes to gabbing on a visiting Sunday."

"I don't know. Maybe I should stay here." Eve gazed around the large, airy kitchen. "And get things ready."

"*Ne.* Everything is already set. Ice cream is in the freezer. Bowls and spoons are out." Tara grabbed Eve's hand. "I want you to get to know my new friend Chloe. She just moved here with her aunt and uncle from Indiana." She halted in the laundry room, turning to Eve, her eyes wide. "Did I tell you she was betrothed, but she broke it off? I don't know why. No one does, but I'm hoping once we're better friends, she'll tell me."

Eve hesitated before she spoke, considering whether it was best to keep her thoughts to herself. That had always been her father's advice. He used to tell her that no one wanted to know what she thought about anything. But it seemed to her that in Levi's family, opinions, as well as discussion, were welcome, even encouraged. And she so wanted to be a part of this family, to be one of them. She wanted to be a good wife and a good sister-in-law and daughter-in-law.

"Tara," Eve said gently, pulling her hand from hers. "It might be that Chloe doesn't want to share what happened between her and her betrothed."

Tara blinked her pretty green eyes. "Why?"

Eve shrugged, thinking of her own circumstances that brought her to Hickory Grove. "Maybe it's painful for her."

Tara seemed to consider that for a moment, and then her jaw dropped. "Oh. *Ya*, maybe you're right. I wouldn't want to upset her." She seemed a bit disappointed. "So you *don't* think I should ask her?"

Eve shook her head. "Definitely not. If she wants to tell you once you know each other better, she will."

"You're probably right." Tara gave Eve a quick hug. "Thank you."

Eve hugged her back. "For what?"

"For keeping me out of hot water with my *mam*. She's always saying my mouth gets me in trouble." She shrugged. "And for being my friend. For being my sister. *Mam* says that when you love someone, you have to tell them when they're about to make a mistake. Even if you might hurt their feelings. But don't worry. My feelings aren't hurt."

Eve bit down on her lower lip. Since her arrival, everyone in Levi's family had been kind to her, but Tara had gone out of her way to include Eve in her everyday life, offering friendship at every turn. This first week of marriage had been so hard for Eve that she didn't know what she would have done without Tara.

So far, marriage was not at all what she had imagined it would be. Of course, when she had thought about marrying when she was younger, it had been in only a dreamy sort of way. She'd assumed she would get to know her betrothed before their wedding day, courting for months, maybe even a full year. She thought she would know the man she married as well as she knew herself before they set up housekeeping together.

The truth was, she didn't know Levi at all. She knew that he was a good man, of course, a man of faith. She knew he was kind; else, he would never have offered to marry her. But she didn't know who he was as a person much beyond his devotion to his family—his father in particular—and his love for food. They'd barely talked in the week between his proposal and the wedding. Then once they arrived in Hickory Grove, they spent most hours of the day apart.

The only time they were alone was in the bedroom they shared, and that was quickly becoming a disaster. By the time they climbed the stairs to bed, they were both spent from a day of hard work. The forced closeness before they knew each other put them both on edge, and Eve found she could barely tolerate Levi once he closed their bedroom door. He was so handsome and such a catch that Eve felt unattractive and undeserving of him. And she took it out on him.

The night before, she had gotten up in the middle of the night to use the bathroom and accidentally tripped over his foot where he lay on the floor. When he cried out in pain, startled from his sleep, she'd been cross with him, telling him it was his fault. Levi's behavior hadn't been much better. Two nights before, she'd opened the window because she was hot. Then he'd closed it, saying he was cold on the floor. Still hot, she'd opened it again, only for Levi to get up and slam the window shut so hard that the glass had rattled and Rosemary had called from the end of the hallway, asking if everything was all right.

Eve knew this was not how a man and woman, bound by marriage, were supposed to treat each other, but she didn't know what to do about it. And she had no one to ask because no one in Hickory Grove, including Levi's family, knew them to be anything but a happily married couple.

"Want to go talk to Chloe until the men come back from the barn?" Tara asked, stealing Eve from her reverie.

Eve found a brave smile, thankful for the friendship Tara had offered so readily. "*Ya*, let's."

Hand in hand, they went out of the house and into the backyard. There, women sat in the shade of giant maple trees, small children played in the grass and babes slept in their mothers' arms.

Because it was visiting Sunday and there was no church for their district, Rosemary had taken the opportunity to invite friends over. According to Tara, her family either had friends and family over or went visiting every Sunday that they didn't attend services. While there were no church services on visiting day, it was still meant to be a day of rest. Any unnecessary work was frowned upon. The men fed and watered the animals, but no one hitched a plow or repaired a shutter. The women provided meals, but there was no scrubbing of floors or picking strawberries. Meals were simple: either foods like soups and casseroles were prepared the day before and reheated on the back of the woodstove, or they ate sandwiches or cold salads, also prepared before the Sabbath.

Benjamin, like Eve's father, had gathered his family in their parlor for morning and evening prayers, but there ended the similarity between Eve's old visiting Sunday and her new one. Benjamin did not force children to sit all day quietly. Instead, they were encouraged to run and play. And the adults were not required to spend the day seated on hard benches, in contemplative prayer. Also, no one in the Miller family wore their heavy, black Sunday clothing on visiting Sundays. Everyone simply wore comfortable, clean clothes. Instead of donning her black church dress, Eve had put on the brand-new peach-colored dress Rosemary had made for her.

The other difference Eve noticed that morning, her first Visiting Sunday with Levi's family, was how kind and gentle everyone was to each other in the house. It was as if on this day, they set aside the business of their lives to be sure they were living the lives God meant for them. There were no disagreements at the breakfast table, no chastising, only kind words exchanged and gentle laughter.

"Chloe!" Tara called, her arm linked through Eve's as they approached three picnic tables where the women were gathered.

As in Lancaster County, the married women naturally sat together, and the unmarried gathered separately. Without hearing a word said, Eve knew that the married women talked of children and housekeeping, while the younger women chattered about boys, singings and their dreams of the men they would marry.

Eve didn't feel like she belonged with either group so she was happy to go along with whatever Tara wanted.

"Chloe!" Tara called. "Here she is. Eve."

Several married women looked in their direction, and Eve felt herself blush. Rosemary had introduced her to them all earlier, before Eve found an excuse to escape to the kitchen, but as with Levi's family, it was all so overwhelming. Everyone knew who she was, knew her name and where she'd come from, but they were all mixed up in her head now. Chloe, however, she had not met because Eve had fled to the security of the kitchen before she and her family arrived.

Tara and Eve stopped short as a little girl in a pink dress and adorable white apron toddled in front of them on unsteady legs. Hot on her heels was Ginger's little girl, Lizzy, who was four.

"Come back, Ada!" Lizzy cried. Then she called over her shoulder to one of the mothers, "I'll get her!"

Tara's friend Chloe walked across the freshly cut grass to meet them. Chloe's hair, covered mostly by her prayer *kapp*, was so blond that it looked white. And when the young woman grew nearer, Eve saw that her eyebrows and lashes were the same hue.

"It's *goot* to meet you, Eve," Chloe said. "Nice to meet someone else new to Hickory Grove. We only moved here a few weeks ago."

"Tara! Tara, come here! I want to meet Levi's wife."

Eve turned at the same time as Chloe and Tara to see a woman in her forties waving them to where she sat in a lawn chair. Ada's mother, also a new arrival. "I want to meet Eve."

Tara leaned over and whispered in Eve's ear, "Sorry."

"For what?" Eve whispered back.

Tara only opened her eyes wider in a *you'll see soon enough* expression. Then, side by side, the three young women approached the older woman beckoning them.

"This is Eunice Gruber," Tara introduced. "They live down the road. I think you met her son John at church last week. Cute with the fuzzy eyebrows," she added in a whisper in Eve's ear.

Eve forced a smile and nodded to Eunice. "Glad to meet you."

Eunice was a slender woman with broad cheeks and a birthmark on her chin. "I was surprised to hear Levi had married so suddenly," the older woman said, coming to her feet.

That didn't take long, Eve thought.

"When the family came home from church—I missed it, because little Ada was running a fever—and my husband told me Levi had brought a bride home from Lancaster County, I said Barnabas, you don't know what you're talking about." She shooed away a fly buzzing around her head. "I said, I'd know if Levi had married." She opened her thin arms wide. "And now, come to find out, I was wrong."

Not sure what to say, Eve just stood there between Chloe and Tara.

As it turned out, she didn't have to say anything because Eunice kept talking. "I thought for certain Rosemary would have told me Levi was marrying, us being such good friends." She narrowed her gaze. "But then I started to wonder. What if Rosemary and Benjamin *didn't know* Levi was marrying? What if they had eloped?" She leaned closer. "Did you elope?"

Eve froze in panic, unsure how to respond.

Eunice took another step toward Eve. "Well, did you?

What town are you from in Lancaster County? Maybe I know your family."

Eve felt her heart thud in her chest. She didn't know what to say.

"*Ach!* Here come the men," Tara cried, looking in the direction of the barns. "And I don't even have the ice cream out." She grabbed Eve's arm. "Would you help me, Eve, else I know my *mam* will be cross with me." She began to pull Eve in the direction of the house, calling over her shoulder, "Talk to you later, Eunice!"

"Wait! I'm coming, too," Chloe declared, hurrying across the grass.

Eve heaved a sigh of relief and linked her arm through Tara's, thankful her new friend had rescued her from what was bound to have become a more uncomfortable situation than it already was.

"If you haven't already figured it out," Tara explained as the young women made a beeline for the house, "you've just met Hickory Grove's gossip. Eunice knows everything, and what she doesn't know, *she finds out.*"

Chloe giggled. "We had a Eunice back in Washington State. Her name was Trudy. She was always repeating other people's business."

Eve looked from Tara on one side of her to Chloe on the other.

"Did she tell the truth?" Tara asked. "Because Eunice isn't just nosy. She doesn't always get the facts right. When my *mam* had her surgery on her foot last year, she told Mary Fisher's mother that *Mam* was in the family way again. Then Eunice had gone on about how *Mam* was too old for babies, that James and Josiah were proof of that, and that she ought to be ashamed of herself."

"Ne!" Chloe exclaimed, her eyes growing round. "She did not!"

"Ya, and my twin brothers just learning to walk!" Tara led Eve and Chloe up the steps to the porch. "See, I told you you would like Chloe," she told Eve. "I know Chloe and I aren't married, but I still think we can be the best of friends, don't you?"

So relieved that Tara had saved her from Eunice's questioning, Eve almost threw her arms around Levi's sister. *"Ya*, I think we can be." She put her hands together the way she had already seen Rosemary do several times. "Now let's get that ice cream to our guests."

A short time later, the three young women were set up at one of the picnic tables. There, they scooped the last of the three gallons of homemade strawberry ice cream out of the plastic containers. Almost at the bottom of her tub, Eve looked up to see the last person in her line to get the homemade treat. She gulped.

It was Levi.

She'd been so busy with the task that she hadn't even seen him. "One scoop or two?" she asked, pushing the heavy spoon down into the tub.

"Three if you've got it. Tara makes the best strawberry ice cream I've ever had." He handed her a bowl.

"There's enough," she said softly, keeping her eyes down.

"And enough for you, too? If there isn't, we can split it."

Eve considered telling him she wasn't going to have ice cream. Back home, her father had often criticized her taste for sweets. But then, glancing around, she noticed that the young folks, married and unmarried, were settling down as couples to have their dessert. Even Ginger and her husband, who had four children by his previous marriage, were stealing a few minutes of time alone together.

This is what we need, Eve thought. *Levi and I need to spend time together to get to know each other.* And then, before she lost her nerve, she said, "*Ya*, Husband, there's enough for me, too. I thought we could have ours together. Under that tree," she dared, indicating an oak tree with her ice cream scoop.

Levi hesitated, chewing on the idea for a moment, then murmured, "*Ya*, I think that would be nice. Wife," he added.

Chapter Five

Eve's shy smile softened Levi's heart. And he was reminded that it didn't take much to make her happy—just a smile, a kind word, an extra moment of his time.

All week he'd been tense, annoyed with everything and everyone. And that had included his wife. But the way she looked at him now made him want to be a better man, a better husband. As he studied her rosy cheeks and pretty mouth, he thought of what Jacob had said the other day about being patient with Eve. His brother was right. Change had come quickly to her life as well as his, and she deserved patience from him.

As much as Levi hated to admit it, his little brother was probably right about their father, too. By returning home six months early, Levi had changed the timeline for expanding the buggy shop. With him home now, their father had been forced to build before he was ready, but also put out money he hadn't planned on spending yet. New construction was never cheap, and the up-front cost of purchasing the materials they needed to build a good, sturdy buggy wasn't inexpensive, either.

"There you go. The last drop," Eve said, pouring the last bit of melted ice cream into Levi's bowl.

Levi blinked, bringing himself back to the moment. "Here, let me take yours, too." He picked up both bowls.

"I'll get our spoons. And napkins." She grabbed the utensils and moved a rock they were using to hold down the napkins, so they didn't blow away. "Oh, dear. There's only one left." She held up the paper napkin.

He shrugged. "We'll share. Come on. Let's go sit down and dig into this before it all melts."

"Are you sure?" she fretted, following him. "I could go up to the house and get more napkins."

He stopped, reminding himself that her legs were much shorter than his, and he waited for her to catch up. "I'm not letting this ice cream melt. By the time you got back from the house, we'd be drinking it." He smiled at her, feeling like his old self. "We'll share the napkin, and if I'm too messy, I'll just use my shirt." He demonstrated by rolling his shoulder forward and wiping his mouth on his shirtsleeve.

She giggled and the sound made his heart sing. He hadn't known Eve very long, and he didn't know her well, but he liked making her happy. Something about the way she smiled at him brought a tightness to his chest. The good kind.

"Here?" he asked, gesturing with her smaller bowl of ice cream at the tree she'd picked out.

"Ya." She sat down in the soft green grass, and he handed her the bowl before sitting beside her.

His back against the tree trunk, Levi accepted the spoon she offered and dipped it into his bowl. The ice cream was smooth and cold and sweet on his tongue. "Mmm. Delicious. Tara has always made a good strawberry ice cream, but I think this is the best she's ever made." He cut his eyes at her. "Did you help her make this?"

Eve licked her spoon, nodded. "*Ya.* I showed her how to sugar the strawberries and let them sit before you mash them." She pointed her spoon at him. "But the real trick is to add a little bit of fresh lemon juice to the strawberries to brighten their flavor. Mind you, not to the milk," she warned. "It could curdle."

He laughed. "Good to know, but I hate to tell you, Eve, I'm not going to be making ice cream. If we have ice cream in our house, it's going to be ice cream you've made or something I bought at Byler's store."

She smiled and dug into her bowl. "Ice cream is so good on a warm day like this. Sweet, but not too sweet," she told him.

He watched her, enjoying the pleasure he saw on her face as she sampled the cold confection. "Oops, you've got a little—" He picked up the napkin she'd tucked between them and blotted her chin.

She looked up at him through her lashes, seeming embarrassed and pleased at the same time. "Got it?" she asked.

Levi was surprised to find how much he enjoyed such an intimate moment between them. A moment he didn't want to end.

"Levi?"

"Got it." He pulled his hand away and tucked the napkin into his pocket. "I like the dress, Eve. It's a good color on you."

She ran her hand down the skirt of her new hunter-green dress. "Rosemary made it for me. She was going to make me a blue one—blue's my favorite color for a dress—but she didn't have any blue fabric." Seeming to have second thoughts, she looked up at him. "Not that I'm not grateful that she made this for me. It's been a very long time since I had a new dress and I love it."

Levi leaned his head against the trunk of the tree. It felt good to just sit here with Eve, to relax and enjoy the Sunday afternoon. The air smelled of early summer: freshly cut grass, sunshine and honeysuckle. Around him, he could hear the muffled chatter of his family and their friends, and in the distance, the bleat of one of his brother's goats and the lowing of their cows. "Tell me why blue dresses are your favorite, Eve."

She glanced away, giving him a moment to study her. She had a round face with rosy cheeks and long, dark lashes that framed her brown eyes. She had gorgeous eyes; he didn't know how he hadn't noticed that before. The color of hot chocolate, they were big and round and expressive.

"My *mam* always wore blue. It makes me think of her. I had a blue dress before, but—" She shook her head. "It doesn't matter now," she mumbled.

He took another bite of ice cream that was bursting with bits of fresh strawberry. "When did your mother die?"

"Twelve years ago." She lowered her gaze to the ice cream on her lap, her voice soft. "Childbirth. The baby didn't make it, either."

His first impulse was to reach out and touch her to comfort her, but that didn't seem right. Married or not, they were still strangers. And what if she didn't want him to touch her? He spoke instead, hoping his words would be of some comfort. "I'm so sorry, Eve. I have an idea what that's like. I lost my *mam* six years ago.

Cancer. I wasn't young like you were. I was already in my twenties, but—" He shrugged.

Instead of looking away, Eve met his gaze. "It's hard to lose a mother. It doesn't matter how old you are." She smiled sadly as if recalling a good memory. "I still miss my *mam* every day."

"Me, too," he agreed, tapping his spoon on the rim of his bowl. "My *mam* was a good mother, a good woman and always full of fun. She used to play practical jokes on my father all the time. One time, she packed him a lunch and put a note inside his sandwich." He smiled at the memory, surprised by the emotion it evoked. He couldn't have been more than nine or ten when it happened. "My *dat* took a big bite right out of the paper before he realized it was there."

Her eyes grew even rounder. "Was he upset with her?"

Levi looked at her, drawing back. "My *dat*?" He chuckled. "He thought it was hilarious, even though his friends teased him about it for years."

She smiled and then asked, "Was it… Did it feel strange when your father married again?"

Scooping a last spoonful of ice cream, he considered his reply. "Yes and no," he said slowly. "I knew Rosemary and her husband, Ethan, before my *mam* died. *Dat* and Ethan were best friends, so he was always around. Rosemary, too, and the girls. Jesse. Rosemary helped care for my *mam* in the end."

Levi licked the back of his spoon, disappointed his ice cream was gone. It really was the best strawberry ice cream he'd ever had, and he was proud that his wife had made it. She was a good cook, that was already obvious, and that had been one of the traits he'd wanted in a wife.

People assumed that all Amish women were good

cooks, but that wasn't true. His sister Mary, who still lived in Upstate New York with her husband and children, was an awful cook. It was a family joke. Levi still remembered their mother teasing Mary on her wedding day, saying her husband, Jake, must have been madly in love with her to marry her, knowing she would never learn to make a decent *hasenpfeffer*.

"Was that hard?" Eve pressed, her brown eyes on him. "Having a new mother?"

"Well, I was old enough that she didn't become a mother to me. Not in the way my *mam* had been, at least. When it happened, it felt…right." He looked up to find her listening intently. She hadn't asked the question just to make conversation; she really wanted to know.

"My father was devastated after my mother died," he continued. "And it was the same for Rosemary." He shrugged. "It seemed natural that they should come together in their grieving, and when it became something more…" He exhaled. "It seemed God's will to me. To all of us." He hesitated when he saw a sadness come over her. "I know it wasn't the same for you when your father remarried. I'm sorry for that."

Her bowl empty, she took his and stacked them together in the grass. "My stepmother was nothing like Rosemary."

He chuckled. "No one is like our Rosemary. Before she and *Dat* wed, she came to each of my brothers and me, and to my sister, and told us she would never try to take the place of our mother. But she hoped, she said, that she could be something between a second mother and a friend to us. And she's been that. And more importantly, she's been a good wife to my father. She makes him happy."

When Levi glanced at his wife, he saw that she was smiling at him. "They have a happy marriage," he went on. "The kind of marriage I hope that one day you and I will have, Eve." This time, before he could think better of it, he covered her small hand with his.

She looked up at him. "I want that, too, Levi. For us to be a happy couple." She looked away and then back at him again. "But how can that be if we never see each other?"

Levi felt the prickly heat of defensiveness on the back of his neck. "We see each other."

"Not enough," she answered. "You work such long hours. I only see you for meals. I want to spend more time like this with you."

She smiled up at him, but he didn't smile back. Suddenly he was feeling the weight of his father's disappointment on his shoulders again. His father wasn't happy with him, and now his wife was telling him that she wasn't, either?

Levi pulled his hand away. "I work hard all day, Eve. To earn our keep here. And to make a life for us." He pointed in the direction of the barn. "Jacob and I broke our backs this week, putting those walls up to expand the buggy shop. I did that for us. For you."

"Levi, I didn't mean—"

He interrupted her without allowing her to continue. "Do you not understand that the buggies I build in that new workshop space will give us the means to have a house, to put food on our table? I assume that's what you want? A house of your own? Or do you want to live under my father's roof for the rest of our lives?"

She folded her hands in her lap, averting her gaze. "I wasn't criticizing you, Levi."

He stood up. Everyone else was finishing up their ice cream, too. The couples were parting, and the men were gathering to head back to the barn to see the airbags he was going to install in the buggy he would be building. As he turned back to his wife, he spotted Rosemary watching them.

"Stand up," he told Eve without looking at her.

"What?"

"Please stand up." He put out his hand to help her. "And smile."

She came to her feet and moved in front of him, forcing him to look at her. "Levi, please. I didn't mean to—"

"Smile," he repeated. "People are watching us. It wouldn't do to see us arguing. We're supposed to be the happy newlyweds."

"I wasn't arguing with you, Levi. I only—"

He held his exaggerated smile, frozen on his face. She went silent and forced a smile.

"*Danke*. Now, I'm going back down to the barn. I'll see you at supper." As Levi walked away, he could feel Eve's gaze on his back.

And once again, he felt her discontent with him.

Eve turned the wooden handle on the glass butter churn as hard as she could, watching specks of yellow appear in the thick, rich cream. It was a rainy afternoon, and the women of the household were all gathered in the kitchen. Rosemary was pressing the wrinkles out of a prayer *kapp* from a whole pile of clean *kapps*, while Tara was making sourdough bread. Nettie's sleeves were rolled up as she scoured the gas stovetop vigorously. And Ginger had come to visit, bringing her two youngest, and was busy shucking early peas she'd brought from her garden.

"I was talking to Chloe yesterday," Tara announced as she turned dough from a bowl onto the kitchen table across from where Eve sat, churning the butter. "She came with her aunt to the greenhouse to buy flowers, and Chloe said that her aunt said that we might be splitting up our church district." She became more distressed with each word. "Chloe asked me what I knew about it, and I told her not a thing. Is that true, *Mam*? Are we splitting up our church?"

"Tara, you and I have talked about gossiping," Rosemary admonished with a sigh. "Let no unwholesome talk come out of your mouth, but only what helps others."

Tara raised her floured hands. "But it's not gossip if it's true. Is it true? I don't want to split our church. We've been going to church with the same folks since we came to Hickory Grove."

"Calm yourself, dear." Rosemary picked up a can of spray starch and shook it. Something rattled inside.

Eve was fascinated by the canned starch. Back home, she had mixed powdered starch in warm water, dipped her and her sisters' *kapps* in it, let it dry and then pressed it. The way Rosemary was doing it wasn't nearly so messy and made much more sense, especially with a whole house full of women.

"Wait." Nettie turned from the stove, steel wool in her hand. She was wearing pink rubber gloves so she wouldn't burn her hands with the caustic cleaner she was using. "Are we changing churches? Does that mean we won't go with the Fishers anymore?"

"Nettie's sweet on Jeb Fisher," Tara explained to Eve.

"She's doing it again, *Mam*," Nettie said. "Make her stop."

Rosemary sighed. "Doing what, dear?"

"Teasing me about Jeb. I keep telling her we're just friends."

"Maybe." Tara giggled. "But she'd like them to be more. That's why she doesn't want our church to split up." She turned her attention to Eve again. "Because then she couldn't sit in the women's pews and stare across the aisle at Jeb every other Sunday."

Eve turned the crank of the churn harder as she followed the conversation. The butter was forming into chunks now. She loved the process, feeling the soft, squishy butter in her hands, adding just the right amount of salt and waiting to see if the blocks came out of the wooden mold in perfect shapes.

Nettie walked to the sink and tossed the pad of steel wool in. "Is there any truth to what she's saying, *Mam*?" She rinsed a clean washrag and walked back to the stove to wipe it off. "Why would our church split?"

Rosemary gave the *kapp* a good spray of starch. "For the same reason our church split back in New York. Too many people. With so many Amish moving to Hickory Grove, the church districts are getting too big. We have to be able to fit everyone under one roof for services, and with Chloe's family just arrived, we now have thirteen families. It's becoming unmanageable."

"But wouldn't the new families just start their own church?" Nettie asked.

Rosemary lifted the iron off the woodstove and when she skimmed it over the white *kapp*, it sizzled. "I don't know how it will be done, if it will be done, but my guess is that established families will have the opportunity to become a part of a new district, mixing the old with the new." She tilted her head one way and then the other. "Some families will go, some will stay."

"They did just that in Seven Hickories. I bumped into Hannah Hartman in Byler's store the other day, and she said that she and Albert and her daughter Susanna and her husband all joined the new church district." Ginger glanced Eve's way. "Hannah's second husband is Albert Hartman. He used to be Mennonite, and he's our vet. When they married, he became Amish, and the bishop lets him drive a truck for work."

An Amish man with a truck? Eve couldn't imagine.

"Well, I don't know if I get a say," Nettie went on, as she wiped the stove down. "But if I do, I want to stay. I like our district."

"Nothing has been decided, *Dochter*. It hasn't even been decided that we'll be forming a new district. We're just talking."

"See, then I wasn't gossiping," Tara declared happily. "I was passing on information that Nettie didn't know."

Eve unscrewed the lid on the glass churn and dumped the ball of butter into a clean cloth.

As she began to squeeze the liquid out of the yellow butter, the back door opened, and she heard the scrape of heavy boots. She recognized the rhythm of her husband's footsteps and a moment later Levi walked into the kitchen with Ginger and Eli's son Philip in his arms. The five-year-old was holding a clean rag to his nose, and it was clear he'd been crying.

"*Ach*, what happened?" Ginger set the pan of peas on the table and walked over.

As she made her way across the kitchen, Eve caught a glimpse of a slightly rounded belly beneath her apron and dress. She was obviously in the family way. Eve didn't know how she had missed it. No one had mentioned that Ginger and Eli were expecting, but that wasn't all that unusual. Of course women talked among themselves in quilting circles, but pregnancy wasn't something normally discussed in the presence of Amish men, even if the men were brothers or stepfathers.

Levi lowered the boy to the floor. "Just a little bloody nose. He was chasing one of the cats through the buggy shop, tripped and—" He shrugged. "It happens."

Ginger lifted her skirt and knelt in front of Phillip. "Let me see."

"I'm fine," Phillip said, his voice muffled by the cloth.

Ginger peeled away the rag and studied the red spots. "Tilt your head back."

The boy did as he was told.

"Looks like it's stopped bleeding," Ginger declared.

Phillip tried to pull away from his mother. "Can I go back out and play?"

The boy looked just like his father, Eli. Eve had learned from Tara, not Levi, that Eli's wife had passed a few years ago and that Ginger had been watching Eli's children for him while he worked. Their relationship had blossomed from friendship to love, and Ginger had married Eli, getting a ready-made family in the bargain, only a few months ago. Ginger was good with the children, and they adored her, so much so that Eve would never have guessed they'd been born to a different mother.

"Please, Ginger?" Phillip begged. "Can I go back to the barn with Levi?"

"I think you best stay inside in case it starts bleeding again." Ginger got to her feet and dropped the bloody rag into the trash can. "Go find Lizzy and Josiah and James. I think they're playing on the upstairs landing."

Phillip groaned, flopping his hands to his sides. "I don't want to play with babies."

"Your sister is hardly a baby." Ginger looked in Eve's direction. "At home, Lizzy may be the youngest, but she runs things. She's put herself in charge of her brothers, all three of them. And mostly they do as they're told." She looked to Levi. "Thank you for bringing him up to the house. I'm sorry if he was any trouble."

"No trouble at all. I just thought I best bring him in."

Levi turned to go, making no point to acknowledge Eve in the room. She tried not to be hurt. Men came and went all day, she told herself. If they stopped to say hello and goodbye every time, no one would ever get anything done.

"Oh, Levi," Ginger called after him. "Did Jesse give you the message about your dental appointment?"

He turned back, frowning. "I didn't get a message."

She rolled her eyes. "I stopped at the harness shop on the way up the lane this morning. Trudy was busy ringing up a customer, so I answered the phone. Your dentist's office called to say they had a cancellation Friday. They can fix your broken filling at two thirty."

"I saw Jesse. He didn't say anything."

Ginger rolled her eyes. "Boys. Anyway, I said you would take the appointment." She grimaced. "I hope that's all right."

"Friday? That's good, isn't it?" Rosemary remarked, returning the iron to the top of the woodstove, taking care to grasp it by the wooden handle so as not to burn herself. "I'm surprised you got in so quickly. You should go with him, Eve."

When Eve looked up, Rosemary was looking right at her. She glanced at Levi, not sure what to say. She would love to go to Dover with him, but he didn't seem so keen on the idea from the look on his face.

Levi shuffled his feet. "I… I don't know that Eve wants to ride all the way into Dover and back, just to sit in a waiting room."

"Nonsense, Levi. Your wife would enjoy getting out of the house and spending time with you." She turned to Eve. "Wouldn't you, *Dochter*?"

Eve loved that Rosemary had begun referring to her as her daughter. She had no one else to call her that, and it made her feel good. Like a part of Levi's family. "*Ya*, that would be nice," she managed. "I haven't been to town yet."

Levi opened his mouth, closed it and then opened it again. "Rosemary—"

"Then this will be a perfect chance," Rosemary said, talking over Levi. "And on the way home, you can stop at Spence's Bazaar and get me some thread from the fabric shop we like. I'll show you what color I need." She directed this toward Eve. "Levi would never find it on his own."

"We can do that for you." Eve made eye contact with Levi. He didn't look pleased, but he didn't look angry, either. Just…resigned.

"Anyone else have anything for Eve and me to do?" he asked, a hint of sarcasm in his voice. "*Ne?* Then I best get back to work."

Eve watched her husband put his straw hat back on his head and walk out the door. Then she returned to squeezing the freshly made butter dry, excited at the prospect of an afternoon out with her husband.

Chapter Six

Levi walked down the dentist's office hallway, his straw hat in his hand, looking for the exit sign. The place was a warren of hallways and doors. As he looked for a sign pointing him in the right direction, he massaged his jaw that felt like pins and needles the way his foot did when it went to sleep. His beard stubble still felt odd to him. As odd as the idea that he was a married man.

Seeing an exit sign at last, he walked to the door—only to realize it was an emergency exit. He backtracked. Eve was sitting patiently in the waiting room. He couldn't believe that Rosemary had invited Eve to go with him to his appointment. If he didn't like Rosemary so much, he might have told her so. It wasn't that he didn't want Eve to come with him, only that he wanted to make that choice for himself. He wanted to invite his wife on an outing himself.

Of course, he probably wouldn't have thought to bring Eve along if Rosemary hadn't suggested it in front of everyone the other day. That night in their bedroom, he had been cranky about the idea of Eve going, but she'd been so excited when he'd pulled the buggy up in front of the house that he felt guilty for not having thought to invite her himself. And Eve hadn't wanted to go just because she wanted to see Dover. She had come because she wanted to be with him. That was what she had told him on the buggy ride.

"Looking for the exit?" a woman in pink scrubs asked as she walked by him in the hall.

"Yes. I thought it was this way, but it wasn't."

"Don't sweat it," she said. "I've worked here for almost a year, and I still get confused sometimes." She laughed, pointing in the opposite direction. "Take a right down the next hallway, then the second door on your left. It's marked."

"Thank you," he told her with a nod.

"No problem!" she sang.

Levi followed her directions and was relieved to find Eve waiting in a chair. She rose when she saw him.

"Are you okay?" she asked him in Pennsylvania Deitsch. "You were in there a long time."

"Ya, oll recht." He switched to English because his father had taught him to speak the language that prevailed in a room. He said it made people uncomfortable when others around them were speaking a language they didn't know. So Levi spoke Deitsch among the Amish, and when with Englishers, he spoke English. "I'm still numb, but it didn't hurt." He glanced across the waiting room to a TV mounted on the wall. A commercial for bed mattresses blasted. He pointed at it. "Were you watching?"

"Ya. I was. That's not a problem, is it?"

He went to the door that opened into the parking lot and she followed. She was an interesting woman, especially considering the home she had come from. He had met Amon Summy only twice, but that was enough times to know that the man was a controlling bully. Having lived under his roof, Eve would have been meeker, more docile, he thought. She was pleasantly surprising him. She spoke her mind in such an innocent way, like when she had told him the Sunday before that they weren't spending enough time together. Levi had taken it as criticism then, but with a little distance from the moment, he realized she was only telling him how she was feeling. And as her husband, he knew he needed to learn to listen.

"What were you watching?" he asked curiously. They stood for a moment in the lobby, looking out the glass doors. It was raining.

"A cooking show. How to make a buckle. Any kind. You start with the same basic recipe and then change up the fruit."

"What's the difference between a fruit buckle and a cobbler?" he asked.

"That's easy." She looked up at him through her long, thick lashes. "A cobbler has fruit on the bottom and biscuit on top. With a buckle, it's cake and fruit mixed together, with a crunchy streusel on top."

She looked nice today in the new green dress Rosemary had made for her, a fresh white apron and a starched *kapp* over her dark hair. Her cheeks were rosy and her dark eyes sparkled. It was funny that the first time he had ever met Eve, before the day in the barn that had sealed both their fates, he hadn't thought she was particularly pretty. But beginning the day they had stood before the bishop and exchanged vows, he had started to see her differently. Now, there were times when he looked at her and felt she *was* pretty.

"I like buckles and cobblers." He held up one finger. "And crisps, too. I love an apple crisp made from a mix of apples."

She nodded enthusiastically. "Me, too. I put cinnamon and vanilla in the oatmeal crumble that goes on top of my apple crisp."

Levi rubbed his stomach. "Just talking about it makes me hungry." He glanced out the glass door. "Looks like the rain's let up a bit. We should go. You want me to bring the buggy around for you so you don't get wet?"

She laughed. "I won't melt if you don't."

He smiled and reached for the door.

"Levi?"

He let go and the glass door swung closed. *"Ya?"*

She folded her hands in front of her. "Do you not want me to watch TV when I'm in a waiting room?"

He knitted his brow. "What?"

"The TV. I'm asking you—" she looked down at her black sneakers that had a hole in the toe "—because if you don't want me to see TV, I... I'll sit with my back to it next time."

"You're asking me if you can watch a cooking show in a doctor's waiting room?"

She nibbled on her lower lip. "Well...you being the man of the house, you have the final say in—" She exhaled. "In everything. If you tell me not to watch TV, I won't." She paused again. "Though I have to say, I don't think there's any harm in it once in a while. I mean, to see a cooking show."

"Eve, I would hope that I would never *tell* you to do or not do anything. I may be the man of our house—

even if we don't have a house yet—but I hope that we'll be able to discuss matters. I want your opinion on things, and I hope you want mine."

She stared at him for a long moment, then said, "I knew you were a good man when I married you. Because you asked me to marry you when you heard what had happened, but—" She glanced away, then back at him. "But Levi, you're even a better man than I thought."

He just stood there for a moment, not sure what to say. He was touched that she felt that way and was willing to tell him. He tried to be a good man, but he knew he failed in small ways every single day. Her confidence in him made him want to try even harder. Except he wasn't sure how to go about that. A man was supposed to court a woman before they married. They should have spent weeks, even months, going to singings together, having supper with each other's families, taking buggy rides together on visiting Sundays. When he had impulsively offered to marry Eve, none of that had crossed his mind.

When he looked down, he found Eve watching him—waiting for him to say something.

Levi cleared his throat. "I think there's no harm in learning how to make a good buckle for your husband, even if it is from a TV in a waiting room," he told her, lightening the tone of the conversation. "Especially if it's a blueberry buckle. That's my favorite." He glanced out the glass door again. "Now, if we're going to get that thread for Rosemary, we better go before the sky opens up again."

Then he held the door open for his wife the way he had seen Englishers do.

* * *

Levi checked his pocket watch, a gift from his father when he started his first job at fifteen years old. It was three thirty. Jacob had gone into the hardware store to get a primer for the walls of the buggy shop, as well as another box of nails, leaving Levi to finish mudding the drywall. He should have been back by now. He should have been back forty-five minutes ago.

He dipped his blade into a tray of mud and dragged it over a seam in the drywall. If it had been up to him, he wouldn't have put up the shop's drywall—bare studs would have suited him fine—but their father had insisted the walls be finished. He said he took pride in his workspace, and Levi needed to do the same.

Levi scraped away the excess mud and moved on to the next tape-covered seam. It wasn't that he didn't take pride in the place where he worked; it was only that he was in a hurry to get started. Working alone, it would take him a full month to build a buggy. And now, with most of the supplies having arrived, he was eager to get to work.

His father walked in through the open bay door, carrying two boxes. "Another UPS delivery," he announced.

Levi glanced over his shoulder. Things between him and his father had been awkward since his return to Hickory Grove. His *dat* had not once brought up the circumstances of his hasty marriage, but he didn't have to. Levi knew what he was thinking. He could see the disappointment in his father's eyes every time he looked at him.

"Should be the mechanism for the airbags. Folks can adjust them according to how big a load they're carrying," Levi explained. It was considered new technology, and it might cause a stir in some of the church districts in the county, but he liked the idea of bringing progress to his community in a good way. He also had plans for better headlamps and taillights, which ran off a simple battery. The brighter LED lights would make a buggy easier to see in the dark and, therefore, safer.

Levi watched his father set down the boxes without responding. He'd missed talking with his father when he was away and had been looking forward to the conversations they would have again when he returned. He'd been home three weeks now, and his father was still ignoring him for the most part. His *dat* answered him when spoken to, but he didn't initiate any conversation, and Levi was beginning to feel as if he were the naughty child put in a corner as punishment. And he was becoming more frustrated by the day because this behavior was so unlike his father. When he'd first arrived, he had assumed his *dat* would get past his displeasure and their relationship would return to what it had been, but now he feared that would never happen. Several times in the last week, Levi had almost said something to his *dat*, then bit his tongue.

But suddenly he couldn't hold back any longer. *"Dat,"* he said, setting his putty knife down.

His father was restocking the boxes, his back to him.

"Dat," Levi repeated a little louder.

His father turned to him. *"Ya?"*

"Dat, I'm sorry that I've disappointed you, but…" He exhaled and glanced away, beginning to wish he had kept his mouth shut. But it was too late now. "I know that this is not how you wanted to see me married," he went on, choosing his words carefully. "But what's done

is done. I'm tired of being treated like a schoolboy who's misbehaved. I'm beginning to feel like you don't want me here. Want us," he added. "I'm starting to worry that maybe Eve and I should have stayed in Lancaster."

His father slid his hands into his denim pockets, looking down at the floor. He, too, was choosing his words carefully. "I've been wondering… Have you talked with the bishop?"

Levi's brow furrowed. "I saw him Sunday. We chatted during the meal."

"I mean…" His father cleared his throat. "Have you talked to him about you and Eve?"

Levi stared at his father for a moment, still not following. Then it hit him. What he was asking was if Levi had gone to the bishop and confessed his sin of relations before marriage. "I have not because there's no need," he answered stiffly.

The older man, the man Levi had looked up to his entire life, took his time in responding. He seemed to be turning Levi's words over in his head. At last he said, "You know that I love you."

Levi's eyes suddenly felt scratchy. "I do."

"I'm sorry if I've made you think I didn't want you here because that's not true." His father slowly lifted his gaze. "But I never expected this from you, out of all of your brothers. And to think that a son of mine would not confess to his sin…" He paused, then cleared his throat and went on. "As I told you the day you arrived, I still need some time, *Sohn*."

"How much time?" Levi asked, wishing desperately that he could tell his father that he hadn't sinned, so no confession was necessary.

Benjamin shook his head. "I can't answer that right

now. Rosemary is saying the same, and I can't give her an answer, either. Both of you—all of you—will just have to be patient with me."

"All of us? Who else has talked to you about this?" Levi asked.

"Tara." The barest smile appeared on his lips. "She accused me of being mean. She likes Eve. We all do. I'm not trying to be mean. I just need time to work through this."

His father went silent, and for a long moment, Levi just stood there. He hadn't thought seriously about going back to Lancaster, but he wondered if maybe that would be best for him the way he was feeling today.

He reached for the spackling compound blade again and scooped up some mud to continue his drywall work. "Where is Jacob with those nails?" he muttered.

Eve took the croquet mallet Jacob handed her and stared at the blue wooden ball resting in the grass in front of her. She looked up at him apprehensively. "I just hit it?"

"Just hit it through the wire thingies!" Tara called from twenty feet away. She had already taken her turn and had managed to hit her red ball all the way to the foot of a poplar tree that was outside the playing area. Jacob had instructed her to move it back inside and forfeit a turn.

Jacob looked to Eve. "Don't listen to her. They're called wickets. Just hit the ball with the mallet, so it will roll through these first two wickets." He pointed at the two wire arches directly in front of the wooden stake in the ground, which was the starting point.

Eve held her breath and then tapped the blue ball

ever so gently. It rolled halfway under the first wicket and stopped in a tuft of grass. She groaned. "I can't do this. I'm terrible at games."

"*Ya*, you can," Tara insisted, running toward them.

While she looked for more jelly jars in the cellar that morning, Tara had discovered the croquet set, practically new in a bag, left by the previous owners. After cleaning up from the midday meal, she had insisted Eve help her set up the game in the front yard. The fact that Eve had never played croquet, had never even seen the game, didn't matter to Tara. And in the end, Eve had agreed to help because she couldn't say no to Tara. Her new friend had been so kind and generous since her arrival. Tara made a point every day to include Eve not just in the work of the day, but in the family, as well as any fun that was to be had. And if there was one thing Tara knew, it was how to have fun. She reminded Eve so much of her sister Annie that it hurt sometimes.

Tara and Eve had been following the written instructions in the bag to set up the playing field when Jacob returned from town. He'd fetched some lime from the barn and marked the field with the white powder, then helped them place the remainder of the wickets at the correct distance.

"You have to hit it harder than that," Tara told Eve as she came to a sliding halt, bumping into her and Jacob.

Jacob caught his stepsister by the arm and ducked to keep from being hit by the wooden mallet in her hand. "Easy," he warned good-naturedly.

Eve turned sideways, caught her lower lip between her teeth and hit her ball. Except that this time she hit it too hard and at a bad angle. It flew through the grass, hit the brick edging of a flower bed filled with orange daylilies and popped into the bed. A disgruntled toad hopped out of the flower bed.

Tara burst into laughter, and Eve and Jacob laughed with her.

"Okay, that might be a little too hard," Jacob told her. He leaned down and placed his green ball at the starting point. "I'll go get your ball. You hit this one. Hit it harder than the first time, not as hard as the second."

"*Ne*, I'll get it!" Tara took off, swinging her mallet in her hand like a windmill.

"Okay, okay." Eve nodded again and again, telling herself she could do this. The game seemed like it would be so much fun, especially on a warm, breezy day like today. She hadn't played games outside since she was eleven or twelve, though she had loved them as a child. Her father saw no need for a girl that old to play anymore. He thought his daughters' places were inside the house, cooking and cleaning, or in the garden weeding. Anytime he saw one of his children idle, he found them another chore to do.

Eve pulled back the mallet, concentrating so hard on lining up behind the green ball that she swung back too far and hit her ankle. "Ouch!" she cried, laughing as she dropped the mallet.

"It's not supposed to be a dangerous game," Levi's brother told her, trying not to laugh as she jumped up and down in pain. He picked up her mallet. "You okay?"

"She's fine!" Tara hollered back as she dug Eve's ball out of the flower bed. "Try again," she told Eve. "It took me forever to learn how to play, and now I love it. We play it at the Fishers' all the time."

Eve looked up at Jacob. Like Tara, he'd gone out of his way to welcome her into their family. But while

Tara seemed oblivious, she had an idea that Jacob suspected something wasn't right between Eve and Levi. He'd just been polite enough, so far, not to bring it up. "I'm fine," she told him, reaching for the mallet. "I just don't know how to hold this thing." She turned sideways again, eyeing the green ball.

Jacob stepped behind her and reached out to turn the mallet slightly in her hands. "You have to hit the ball squarely. It's all about hitting it square on, every time," he explained. "That'll keep it out of Rosemary's flower beds and all of us out of trouble."

She laughed. "Like this?" She adjusted the mallet in her hand.

"Almost." He reached from behind her and turned it slightly.

She stared at the two wickets lined up just so, held her breath and swung. Just as the wood mallet hit the wooden ball with a satisfying sound and the ball shot straight through the two wickets, she heard Levi call her name.

"Eve!"

She spun around to see her husband striding toward her, his gait long and purposeful. He did not look pleased. "What are you doing?" When he reached her, he swung around to his brother. "More importantly, what are *you* doing? I'm inside working, waiting on you, and you're out here playing games *with my wife*?"

Tara ran toward them, carrying Eve's blue game ball. "Levi, what's gotten into you?"

Jacob took a step back. "Brother, calm down." He raised both hands, palms out. "I had to go to two stores to find the nails, so it took a while. When I got back, Tara and Eve were trying to—"

"Don't you have work to do inside, Eve?" Levi interrupted loudly.

Eve's first impulse was to lower her head, mumble something apologetic and hurry back to the house. In her father's home, that would have been her response. Otherwise, she might have gotten a berating or, worse, a slap across the face. It happened occasionally. But this man was not her father. He was her husband, and she would not cower. If this marriage was going to work, she needed to make Levi understand what was acceptable and what was not in the life they were building together—that she hoped they would build together. And shouting at her was not acceptable.

She crossed her arms over her chest, met Levi's gaze and said very softly, "You cannot speak to me like that, husband."

For a moment, he stared at her stony-faced, and then suddenly, his expression changed.

Chapter Seven

Levi saw a myriad of emotions on Eve's face. She was scared and angry, but there was also an admirable calm about her. He had caused the first two emotions, but the last was her own. This young woman whom he'd married on impulse was turning out to be so many things he hadn't expected. Initially, that day Mari had led him to the barn, he had offered to marry Eve for her sake. And on some level, he had to admit, at least to himself, that he assumed she would be forever grateful to him, maybe even beholden to him. But in the weeks since that afternoon, no matter what Levi told himself, everything had been about him. Secretly, he had been so proud of the *sacrifice* he had made in marrying this woman. Today it seemed as if it was her sacrifice.

And he was ashamed of himself.

Eve remained where she was, studying him. A lesser woman would have turned to tears and apologies, maybe even fled had her husband behaved as he just had. But not Eve. *Not my wife,* he thought, *because she's a better person than that, a better person than me right now.*

Levi lowered his head. "Eve, I am so sorry," he whispered, unable to meet her gaze.

"Come on," Jacob quietly said to Tara.

"What? Why?" Tara was watching the exchange between Levi and Eve with obvious interest.

Jacob took the croquet mallet and ball from his stepsister's hands, set them in the grass and led her away. Levi watched them go, whispering a silent thanks to his brother. Then he forced himself to meet his wife's gaze.

Eve was dressed in her new ankle-length green dress and a white apron and her feet were bare. She wore her prayer *kapp* over her glossy brown hair that was pinned up, though tendrils had managed to escape. She was watching him with her big, brown eyes.

"Eve, I'm sorry," he said, his voice barely a whisper. He cleared his throat and spoke a little louder. "I know this isn't an excuse, but I was frustrated and angry with my father, and with Jacob. Things aren't going as I had thought they would when I came home and—" He exhaled, ashamed and embarrassed to have behaved so badly. And with his wife, of all people. "I'm sorry," he repeated.

He thought about the words the bishop had spoken the day he and Eve had married.

Likewise, ye husbands, dwell with them according to knowledge, giving honor unto the wife.

He was not honoring his wife, nor was he honoring the sanctity of marriage, family, friendship or any of the things his parents had taught him.

"You're right," he told her, reaching to take her hands, hoping she wouldn't pull away from him. "I should not have spoken to you that way." He searched her eyes for forgiveness. "And I promise you I'll try very hard to never do it again."

She was quiet for so long that Levi was suddenly afraid he had ruined everything, but at last she spoke in a calm, firm voice.

"Thank you for apologizing, Levi. We all make mistakes. What matters is seeing them and trying to do better." She hesitated and then went on, still allowing him to hold her hands. "Jacob wasn't doing anything wrong except helping me learn how to play the game. He did nothing inappropriate. Jacob would *never* do that. I haven't known him long, but I know what he isn't. And I know that no son Benjamin Miller has raised would ever behave improperly with another man's wife."

"I know," Levi murmured.

"You need to apologize to him, too. And to Tara. We don't want her thinking this is the way married people talk to each other."

Levi nodded. "I'll find them now." Surprised by how good her small hands fit into his, how warm and comforting they were, he was reluctant to let go.

"I think that's a good idea. I'm going back inside to help start supper." She pulled her hands away. "And maybe we can talk about this later?" she asked.

Her gentle face made Levi want to pull her into his arms. But right now, he didn't feel as if he had the right. As her husband, he needed to earn her physical affection. He just had to figure out how.

"Go on, make amends," she told him as she turned to walk away. "They both adore you and look up to you."

"Thank you," Levi called after her.

She glanced over her shoulder and offered a sweet smile. And that smile was what gave Levi the courage to hunt down Jacob and Tara, make his apology and promise to try to be a better big brother.

Levi found Jacob in the buggy shop finishing up applying mud to the last seams on the drywall. Jacob was whistling to himself, obviously content with the task at hand. His younger brother was always so even-tempered, just like his twin, Joshua. Nothing ever seemed to rattle either one, and Levi envied them for that.

"Hey," Levi said.

Jacob glanced over his shoulder. If he was upset with Levi, he didn't look it. "Hey." He returned to his task, smoothing the spackling compound expertly over the taped seams.

"I see you got those last couple drywall nails in."

"*Ya*, the walls look good. We'll let this dry overnight and we can sand in the morning and put the primer I bought on tomorrow afternoon. We'll be done in no time, and then you can get to work building your first buggy."

"It sounds like Eli might be interested in placing an order. With their family growing, he said it's time they got a bigger buggy. I just have to sit down and come up with a price."

"With a family discount," Jacob suggested.

"Of course." Levi took a step toward his brother. "Jacob?"

"*Ya?*"

Levi took a breath, trying to find the right words to use in an apology to his brother. "Could you stop a second?"

Jacob drew the spackling blade over a nail dimple and then set the spackle and blade down on an aluminum bench they used to reach high on the walls. He turned to his brother.

"I want to tell you how sorry I am." He hooked his thumb in the direction of the house and the front lawn where Jacob and the girls had set up the croquet court. "I don't know what's wrong with me. You weren't doing anything wrong outside with Tara and Eve. You were being nice to my wife." Levi drew the back of his hand across his mouth. "Which is more than I can say for myself."

Jacob was quiet for a moment and then said, "Don't worry about it. I know you're under a lot of stress." He hesitated and then went on. "And I know something's going on between you and Eve."

"What do you mean *going on*?" Levi asked, tempering his tone.

Jacob shrugged. "I can't say for sure. It's not like I'm an expert at marriage or anything."

"No, I don't guess you would be, considering the fact that your chin is clean-shaven."

Jacob met Levi's gaze and went on. "For newlyweds, you two don't seem all that happy together. Eli and Ginger were married months ago and they're still holding hands and grinning at each other all the time."

"As I've said before…" Levi responded, reminding himself that he was the one who had started this conversation. And he had been the one apologizing for words spoken in haste. "…it isn't easy going from being single to having a wife and the responsibility it bears."

"And then coming home with your new wife, staying in the house with *Dat* and Rosemary and the rest of us. I'd guess that's not easy, either." Jacob smiled in understanding. "I just… I'm worried about you. I'm worried about you both. Eve seems like a woman easily content. I guess I'd like to see her that way."

Not sure how to respond, Levi ran his thumbs beneath his suspenders. "I guess these walls aren't going to finish themselves. What do you want me to do? Finish the mudding?"

"*Ne*, I've got this. Grab the nails and put a couple more in that stud near the door," Jacob instructed, pointing to an inside door that opened into a hall their father had created when he'd divided the old dairy barn.

Levi crossed the room to pick up the new box of nails Jacob had brought home from the hardware store. "*Danke*, Jacob," he said quietly.

Jacob picked up his spackling blade. "For what?"

"I don't know. For not being angry with me, I guess. Right now, I don't know that I could bear it."

Jacob squeezed Levi's arm as he passed. "You're going to be fine." He hesitated and then spoke again. "My advice, from a man who fully admits he knows nothing about marriage?"

Levi arched an eyebrow.

"Don't worry about *Dat*. He'll come around, and if he doesn't." He shrugged. "His problem. *Ne*, I think it's best you concentrate on Eve. Because you can change that relationship, and she deserves it. You both do."

Supper was a quieter affair than usual in the Miller household that night. There were no guests, and Bay and Tara had gone to their sister Lovey's place and stayed for the evening meal.

That afternoon, Tara had taught Eve how to make meatballs and a tomato sauce and they served it over noodles with Parmesan cheese sprinkled on top. They also made fresh garlic bread sticks and a salad from new greens in the garden. Eve not only hadn't known how to make the pasta dish, but she hadn't ever even eaten it. One bite, and she decided that spaghetti might be her favorite meal of all time. The week before, Rosemary had given her some index cards to write down recipes and she intended to add it to her growing stack.

When everyone had had their fill of the meal, there were sweet home-canned peaches covered in cream and sprinkled with cinnamon for dessert. After everyone was properly stuffed, Rosemary took her toddlers upstairs for a bath, and the men drifted out of the room one by one until there was no one left but Tara, Levi and Eve.

As Eve carried a stack of dirty dinner plates to the sink where Tara was already washing, she saw Levi begin to gather glasses from the table. She turned to him. "What are you doing?"

He carried the glasses to the counter, setting them down with the dirty dishes. "Helping."

Eve lifted her brows, confused. She had never once in her life seen her father pick up a dirty dish off the table. Her mother had done it until her death, and then he had left them for his daughters to pick up. "You're helping clean up the kitchen?"

He shrugged. "My *mam* always used to say 'many hands make light work.'"

"Is that from the Bible?" Tara asked, lowering the whole stack of dinner plates into the hot, sudsy water.

"*Ne*, I don't think so." He went back to the table and picked up the can of Parmesan cheese and a jar of home-made salad dressing and carried them to the refrigerator. "It's just something people say."

"Like a proverb," Tara said.

Levi pointed at her. He seemed as if he was in a good mood. "Exactly."

Eve frowned. "I don't understand. Isn't Proverbs a chapter in the Bible?"

"*Ya*, but a proverb can also be a general kind of thing. It can just mean a saying that has a lesson in it," Levi explained, seeming unperturbed by her question. Her father had never appreciated questions of any sort, but he particularly disliked questions that fell into the category of *fancy learning*. Levi's family, however, enjoyed sharing knowledge and even encouraged the children to be inquisitive.

Tara turned from the sink, water dripping from her hands. "It's like an adage."

Eve stared at Tara. "I don't know that word, either. Did you learn that in school?"

She shook her head. "*Ne*, but you know Ethan's a schoolmaster, right? He told me. He reads a lot."

"We like to tease him sometimes about knowing a whole lot of useless information," Levi said and Tara chuckled.

"My father only allowed us to finish the sixth grade," Eve said, collecting silverware from the table. "He saw no need for more schooling than that. At least for girls."

"We all went until we were sixteen in New York." Tara had returned to her dishwashing. "A lot of girls I knew stopped when they were fourteen. I wanted to do the same, but *Mam* wouldn't let me."

Eve carried the silverware to the sink, and Tara took a step back to drop it straight into the sudsy water. "I would love to have gone until I was sixteen. I like to read. At least I used to."

Levi began pushing chairs and benches under the table. "Ethan's got lots of schoolbooks. If you want, I can ask him if we can borrow some. You just have to tell me what kind."

"And that would be all right?" Eve asked her husband, surprised by how open he was to education—especially for women.

"Sure." Levi carried an empty serving bowl stained with red sauce. "Okay if I steal my wife for a little while once we get everything off the table?" he asked his sister.

"Sure. Go now." She glanced around the kitchen. "We're practically done straightening up, and only one of us can wash at a time."

Eve looked to Levi, not sure why he wanted to be alone with her. He hadn't once since they arrived made an effort to spend time with just her. Not that she could blame him. She had been the one who had suggested it the day they had ice cream, and look how that had turned out. Then there had been the incident with Jacob earlier in the day. Eve was beginning to worry that maybe she and Levi just weren't compatible. And then where did that leave them?

"Just us?" Eve asked.

He grinned wryly, reminding her of the man she had admired from afar before she changed both their lives forever with one bad decision. "If you're willing, after my behavior today."

Eve dried her hands on a dish towel. "*Ya*, I'll swing with you," she said, now excited and apprehensive at the same time. "But I… I should help Tara finish the dishes. Dry them and put them away."

He shrugged. "Then we'll do it together and then go outside."

Tara giggled. "Eve, go with him. I can finish here."

Levi headed for the door.

Eve looked at him, at Tara and then back at Levi again.

"Go!" Tara repeated, making a shooing motion. "You're newlyweds. *Mam* says newlyweds need time together without family around."

So Eve followed her husband through the house and out the front door, onto the front porch that she'd never seen anyone use since she'd arrived. Everyone came and went by the back porch, which was more accurately the side of the house. They sat in chairs there, too, sometimes while doing chores like snapping green beans.

"Nice evening," Levi said as he sat down on the swing that was big enough for two or three. "Come on, sit down with me." He patted the rattan seat.

Eve hesitated, suddenly nervous.

"Come on, Eve." He patted the place beside him again. "I won't bite, I promise. After the dressing-down you gave me today, I'm the one who ought to be afraid of you."

She pressed her lips together and sat down on the swing. He gave it a push and she lifted her legs, enjoying the little rush she felt in her chest as they glided forward. The warm evening breeze tickled the pieces of hair that had fallen from the knot at the nape of her neck.

She looked at Levi. "I didn't mean to dress you down."

"*Ya*, you did," he argued. "And I deserved it."

Though they weren't touching, they were close enough that she could feel the warmth of his body. She could smell the Ivory soap he'd used to wash up with before supper. And when she looked at him, he was smiling hesitantly. She liked his beard that was growing in; it made him even more handsome than he already was.

"So... I've been thinking on this matter. I took a walk after I apologized to Tara and Jacob, and I... prayed. I asked God to help me be the husband you deserve, Eve and..." He hesitated and then went on. "I was thinking about what you said about us needing to spend more time together. Because we don't know each other very well. Because we didn't court before we said our vows. And I agree with you. I just wasn't sure how to go about it."

Eve watched his face, trying to figure out where he was going with this conversation.

"But God answered my prayers," he declared.

"He did?"

"Ya." He gave the swing another push. "We didn't get to court, so I think we need to court now."

She knitted her brows. "What?"

He leaned back in the swing, sliding his arm across the back so that his fingertips brushed her shoulder. "I'd like to court you, Eve."

She looked at him suspiciously. He wasn't making sense. "But we're married."

"So better you court me than someone else, right?"

When Levi smiled at her the way he was smiling now, she felt a little light-headed and she smiled back shyly. "Okay." She drew out the word. "How are we going to court?"

He rolled his shoulders back. He was wearing a short-sleeved shirt the color of the blue dress she'd ruined escaping from Jemuel.

"We're going to go on dates." He gave a nod of confidence. "We're going to get to know each other. Dates we arrange, not Rosemary," he amended, referring to their trip to the dentist.

"Dates?" she asked, still not quite following.

"Like…" He held up his finger. "I ran into Sara Yoder yesterday at the grain store and she heard I'd married. She asked if you and I would be interested in chaperoning at a supper she's having next weekend. With it being summer, she says it's harder to get folks to help out."

"Sara Yoder." As Eve racked her brain, trying to remember who she was, she gazed out at the front yard. Someone had picked up the croquet mallets and balls and set them next to a tree, ready if anyone wanted to play. "Does she go to our church?" she asked.

"*Ne*, she lives over at Seven Poplars, which is a little north of here. She's the matchmaker."

"A matchmaker?" she asked. She had heard of matchmakers but had never met one. "In Kent County?"

"*Ya*, she came from out west a few years ago. She's a cousin to Hannah Hartman. Hannah is married—"

"To the Amish veterinarian," Eve interrupted excitedly. "I know who she is."

He laughed. "So Tara's gossiping is good for something."

"She wasn't gossiping," Eve said in her new sister's defense. "She's just trying to help me get to know people and how they're related. And actually, it was Ginger who told me first."

"Fair enough," Levi answered. He pushed the swing again and they drifted backward. "Anyway, Sara is expecting a pretty good-sized crowd of young folks and she likes having a little help keeping an eye on everyone. Mostly the guys, to make sure everyone behaves as the bishops would expect."

She nodded, touched that he would not only come up with such a plan but that he was willing to implement it. That he cared enough about the vow he had made to her to try to make things better between them. "I think I'd like to go to Sara Yoder's. With you. On a date."

"Good." He glanced at her. "It'll be fun. And we'll get a chance to be together, away from here. Time to talk."

"And… What other kinds of dates can we go on? Seeing as how we're married."

He shrugged. "We'll just have to be creative. Like… I thought we could take the old rowboat over to the pond and paddle around. Maybe throw a fishing line in."

"I've never been fishing," she said, her interest piqued.

He drew back. "Never been fishing?"

"*Ne*, my brothers went sometimes, down to a creek near our place, but our *dat* didn't think it was any place for a woman."

"I'm not going to get into how your father and I disagree in matters, but I don't see anything wrong with a female of any age fishing. Especially a wife fishing with her husband. So what do you say?"

"I'd like to do that, too. With you," she added, feeling a little shy, but excited at the same time.

"It's a date, then."

Levi picked at a tiny tear in his pants and Eve made a mental note to repair it next time the pants went through the wash.

"But the thing about this," Levi continued, "is that

we can't tell anyone that's what we're doing. That we're courting. We don't want them to be suspicious."

"Because they think we knew each other before we married," she said.

"*Ya*, I would assume they do, although truth be told—" he looked away "—I don't know what my father is thinking these days. He's barely talking to me."

"I know he's upset with you because he thinks you took liberties with me. Maybe you should tell him the truth?"

"*Ne*," he answered firmly. "We agreed no one need know."

"I'm sorry he jumped to that conclusion, Levi," she told him gently.

He looked at her again, a sad smile on his face. "We both are. But today, taking my walk and praying, I realized that I need to concentrate on what I can change and put everything else in God's hands. Because He always comes through for me."

Chapter Eight

Levi made good on his promise. The following week, after a light supper of sandwiches and salads, Eve and Levi set out through the orchard alone on another date. The thermometer on the back porch read ninety degrees when they left, but there was a nice breeze and the sun, now low in the sky, felt good on Eve's face. She hadn't had a chance all day to get outside except when she'd taken scraps to the chicken house. She and Nettie and Tara had spent hours straightening up a room of the cellar and washing and organizing canning jars in anticipation of putting up tomatoes that were beginning to ripen in the garden.

Swinging a basket on her arm, she glanced up at her husband. There hadn't been an overnight change in their relationship, but since their talk on the front porch swing, it was evident that Levi was going out of his way to get to know her better. With both of them so busy, it was hard to find time alone that wasn't in their bedroom, but he was making an effort. The day before, they had walked the long lane together to get the mail and back, talking the whole way. And a few days before that, Levi had taken her with him to the feed mill to pick up grain in a wagon, and they'd stopped for ice cream cones at Byler's store.

"I didn't know there was a pond on the property," Eve said, enjoying the feel of the warm grass under her bare feet as she walked beside Levi. "How did I not know there was a pond?"

He shifted two fishing poles on his shoulder. "I don't know. I guess it didn't come up. We've got a big piece of property. *Dat* and Rosemary ended up buying two farms side by side. There was no house on the smaller one, just an old house trailer and some chicken houses that were falling down. We bulldozed those over."

"How big is the property?" she asked, hoping she wasn't overstepping her bounds with such personal information about her in-laws. But if she was going to live here, if they were going to make their life together on his father's property, it was only right she know.

"About three hundred acres."

The number shocked Eve. Her father owned ten acres and sold meats at a farmers market to make ends meet. "That's a lot of land," she murmured.

He shrugged. "Not something we advertise."

Obviously, she thought. To talk about owning such a vast piece of property, with no mortgage, would be *hochmut*…arrogant. Prideful, in the wrong way.

"*Dat* and Rosemary both sold their farms in upstate New York to buy it," Levi continued. "They were set on having enough land to go around so that any of their children who wanted to make homes here could."

Eve turned that information over in her head thoughtfully. It seemed like a vast amount of land, especially here in Delaware, where most of the farms were smaller than the ones in the Lancaster area. "So…did Benjamin already give each of you a piece of land?"

"*Ne.* It's up to us to choose once we're married. And ready to build." He glanced at her. "I'm hoping that in a year's time, I'll have sold enough buggies to have the cash to break ground on our home." He offered a smile that almost seemed bashful, which made her smile.

She felt her cheeks grow warm at the thought of living alone with Levi. Right now, she was enjoying life in a big house full of family, a family who loved and respected each other. But with the subtle changes beginning to take place between her and Levi, she suspected that, with time, she would be ready for that next step in their married life. She didn't consciously think about children, but she had the same dream every Amish woman had. She wanted a house full of them, and though she and Levi had not discussed the matter directly, she sensed he wanted the same thing.

"I figure we have time to choose the best spot," Levi went on. "The property fronts on two roads, so we have the option to get a little farther away from the big house and have our own lane if that's what we want."

Eve nodded. "Plenty of time." She looked up at him. "How many buggies do you think you can build in a year? I'm just wondering," she added quickly. "It's not that I'm not content in the big house. I love being a part of a family where everyone works together, gets along together. It's only that I'm curious. I don't know anything about buggy making."

Levi tilted his head one way and then the other. "I figure the first buggy will take me the longest. I've constructed all of the parts lots of times, but only one buggy from start to finish, and that was a small, open two-seater. Jeb, who I worked for, was always building several buggies at a time. He taught Jehu and me how to do something on one buggy, and then we'd do it on the next on our own. My friend Jehu was the other apprentice. You ever meet him? Jehu Yutzy? From Ohio?"

She shook her head no, switching the basket from one hand to the other. It was beginning to get heavy. She'd packed them a little snack to share in the boat: sweet tea and mini lemon tarts she and Tara had baked.

"Nice guy. Anyway, we learned from Jeb Fisher, but also each other. Jehu's hoping to have his own shop someday, but he doesn't have a *dat* with the finances to help him get going like I do. He'll have to work for someone else and save his money until he can buy the equipment and supplies. Because *Dat* started buggy making as a hobby, he's collected the necessary tools."

"It's good of Benjamin to help you this way. To help us," she added.

"I know, I know." He sighed. "I remind myself of that every day and give thanks to God for his generosity. I just didn't expect him to react the way he has to me marrying."

Eve pressed her lips together. "I'm sorry. I know it's my fault."

Levi stopped, brushing his fingertips against her bare arm. It was so warm outside that she was wearing a short-sleeved dress, a second one Rosemary had made for her, this one in a peach color. Now she had two everyday dresses, so she always had a clean one when the other was in the wash.

"Eve, please don't blame yourself," Levi said. "Remember, I was the one who offered to marry you. You didn't ask me. And no one forced me. It was my choice, and I don't blame you. I would never blame you. This is between me and my *vader. Oll recht?*"

"Oll recht," she repeated, gazing into his gray eyes that were becoming more familiar with each passing day.

He smiled down at her and then cocked his head. "Come on. We better get going. This is the best time of day for fishing, you know."

They began walking again and fell into an easy conversation.

Half an hour later, Eve found herself seated on a wooden bench in a rowboat in the middle of a half-acre pond. Levi had explained to her that the state had helped folks dig them back in the 1960s for emergency water. They dotted the county, providing water so the volunteer fire companies could fight fires better in the rural areas. It was stocked with bass every few years and supported a whole host of animals like frogs and turtles and such. There was even evidence a beaver had tried to take up residence in the cattails on one edge, though Levi said it was long gone by the time they bought the farm.

Eve had already caught two bass. It had been fun to try her hand at fishing, but she'd felt so bad for the live grasshoppers they had used for bait that, after catching two fish, she'd had enough of the sport.

"Do you want to go back to the house?" Levi asked her as he slowly reeled in his line. He'd caught three fish. They had released all of them, as they often did, her husband explained.

She watched his red-and-white plastic bobber bob across the surface of the pond. She'd already reeled her line in, and her pole was lying in the bottom of the boat. She smiled at Levi, sitting in the bow, facing her. "*Ne*, not yet." She folded her hands on her lap, enjoying the slight rocking of the boat. "It's too nice out here. Unless you're ready to go back," she added, hoping he wasn't.

He shook his head. "Nope, I'm enjoying sitting in the middle of a pond on a warm summer evening with my wife."

He was smiling at her, and she couldn't resist smiling back. When he looked at her the way he was looking at her now, she felt warm all over. And…safe. That was the best way to describe it.

Her whole life, she had lived by the whims of her unpredictable father. He had always provided food and heat and some form of clothing, but she had tiptoed around him, never knowing when he would lose his temper. Usually, he just threw things or hit a wall with a fist, but occasionally his hand met with one of his children's faces. Or her mother's. Her mother always had an excuse for his behavior, making it somehow seem all right, but now, living with Levi's family, she knew that it wasn't.

No, actually she'd realized that the morning she had come home after Jemuel had tried to attack her. When her father had not protected her from that horrible man, she saw him for the terribly flawed man he was.

Not that Levi wasn't flawed. He was impatient sometimes. But she had never felt physically threatened by him. And now, as the days passed, she was beginning to feel more and more comfortable with her husband. Not only was she learning that she liked him but, in her heart of hearts, she knew he would always protect her. As he had the day he had offered to marry her.

Eve felt herself blush and glanced over the rowboat's side to watch a water strider glide across the surface, barely creating a ripple. "Don't look at me that way," she told Levi bashfully.

"What way?" He set his pole in the bottom of the boat and pushed up the brim of his straw hat in an exaggerated motion, as if to get a better look at her. "A man can't look at his pretty wife?"

She giggled, shaking her head as if he had said the silliest thing. No one had ever called her pretty before, not even her mother. She knew it wasn't true, but it still made her feel good inside. "Are you thirsty? Would you like iced tea?"

"I would."

She reached for the basket behind her. "I brought some fruit tarts, too."

"I was wondering what smelled so amazing in that basket."

Eve pulled out a pint jar of iced tea, the glass wet with condensation, and handed it to him.

Levi unscrewed the Ball jar lid and took a sip. "What a clever way to bring drinks. Doesn't spill a drop." He took a big gulp and exhaled loudly. "*Goot.* Just the way I like it. Not too much sugar, but still sweet, and lemony."

"We bought a whole bag of lemons at Walmart the other day." She lifted a square plastic dish from the basket, removed its lid and held the container out to him.

He leaned over, and his eyes got wide. "Lemon tarts!" He lifted one out of the container and held it up. "That might be the prettiest tart I've ever seen. It looks like something you'd buy in an Englisher bakery." He looked up at her. "What's the decoration on top?"

She took a tart for herself and leaned forward to set

the container beside Levi on the bench. "Lemon zest," she said, fighting a feeling of pride that tightened in her chest. She liked cooking for Levi. She liked making things for him that he enjoyed.

"Zest?" he asked. Then he took a big bite of the tart, and the crust was so perfect that it flaked but didn't crumble in his hand. "I don't know that word."

"It's the peel, but just the yellow part." She nibbled on the crust of her tart. "The white is bitter."

Levi finished his tart in three more bites and reached for another, closing his eyes in pleasure. "So good," he murmured. "I might have to have a third."

"You can have the rest." She dared to meet his gaze. "I made them for you, Husband."

"I like hearing you call me that."

Not knowing what to say, she glanced away, reaching for her iced tea.

"Wanna play a game?" Levi asked, taking another tart.

"A game?"

He shrugged one shoulder. He was wearing a blue shirt, and it made his eyes look even bluer. "Sort of a game," he said. "Let's take turns asking each other questions, then we both have to answer."

"Questions like what?"

He chewed thoughtfully. "Like…what's your favorite animal?"

"My favorite animal?" She laughed. "Do you mean to eat?"

He laughed with her. "*Ne*, like what animal did you always like as a child? It could be a barnyard animal, or something exotic."

"Like a tiger," she suggested, wide-eyed. Of course,

she had never seen a tiger, but she had seen pictures of them.

"Exactly." He wiped at some crumbs in the corner of his mouth with the back of his hand, and she pulled a cloth napkin from the basket and tossed it onto his lap. "I'll go first," he offered, using the napkin. "Easy. Mine is an alpaca."

"An alpaca?" She laughed, relieved she knew the animal. He was so much better educated than she was that she feared he'd name a creature she hadn't known even existed.

"*Ya*, alpacas. When I was learning to read, we had this book in school that had a letter and picture on every page, and the A page was my favorite because it had an alpaca on it. My teacher had to explain to me what it was. And then my *dat* took me to a farm to see some. Some Englisher he knew raised them for their wool."

Eve nodded, fascinated. She had never had anyone in her life who would have taken her to see an alpaca.

"I'd love to have an alpaca of my own someday. I know someone here in Kent County who has them," he told her excitedly. "An Amish guy. Have you ever seen one?"

She shook her head.

"Then I'm going to take you to see them," he declared.

"Who has alpacas?" She sipped her tea. The ice had all melted, but it was still nice and cool.

"Our veterinarian. Albert Hartman."

She pointed at Levi. "*Recht*. He became Amish to marry..." She couldn't remember the woman's name.

"Hannah," Levi said. "That's right. Let's plan to go see Albert's alpacas soon. For one of our dates, maybe. Would you like that?"

"I would," she told him.

"Okay, so what's yours?" he asked.

"Chipmunks. They're so small and cute, and I love how they race around," she told him. "I just love chipmunks. But not to eat, mind you."

He drew back, laughing. "I would hope not." They laughed together, and he said, "Okay, your turn. Ask me a question. Anything."

She thought for a moment, then asked, "Favorite cookie?"

He grimaced. "A hard one. Let's see...oatmeal cookies, made with chocolate chips, not raisins. Not that I don't like raisins in my cookies, but I love chocolate."

"I love chocolate in my oatmeal cookies, too!" she told him excitedly, thinking that would be easy to remember.

They bounced four or five more questions between them, and then Levi said, "Favorite color?" Before she could answer, he put up his hand. "Wait, wait. Let me guess." He squeezed his eyes shut for a moment, then opened them. "Blue?"

She smiled with a nod. "How did you know?"

Their laughter died away. "A guess. You said it was your mother's favorite color. And you told me you ruined your dress...that night."

Surprisingly, his mention of the night Jemuel had tried to attack her didn't upset her. Instead, she was touched that he remembered the dress and why it had been distressing to lose it.

"And your favorite color?" she asked, studying his handsome face.

He pressed his hands to his knees and leaned closer to her. "Blue."

"That's always been your favorite color, too?" she asked suspiciously.

His gaze never left hers as he shook his head slowly. "Not always. But it is now." He smiled and she felt a flutter in her chest. "Because it's yours, wife."

Eve was so excited to meet the matchmaker Sara Yoder on their next date that the buggy had barely rolled to a stop, and she was climbing down. This was her and Levi's first invitation as a married couple to serve as chaperones and she was thrilled to be asked. She'd never served as a chaperone, so she didn't know exactly what it entailed, but how hard could it be? she wondered. A chaperone's responsibility was to make sure single men and women behaved according to the *ordung*, rules established by the church.

It seemed to her that it would be especially simple to keep their eye on folks in a place like Seven Poplars, where Old Order Amish didn't practice *rumspringa*, and there were plenty of organized activities to keep them from exploring dangerous temptations like drugs, alcohol and premarital relations. Not that she was so naive as to think those failings didn't exist among the Amish in any community, but like Hickory Grove, Tara had told her that "everyone in Seven Poplars mostly behaved."

Levi got down from the buggy on the other side to tie up the bay to a hitching post as Eve looked around. Though they had arrived early, there were already several wagons and buggies parked. There was no activity around the house and no sounds in the barnyard, except for the lowing of a cow in the pasture in the distance and the bleat of goats she couldn't see.

Everyone was already at the hospitality barn, she supposed.

"Excited?" Levi asked, flashing her a smile.

"Ya." Eve beamed, looking down at the new canvas sneakers she'd bought at Spence's Bazaar for the event. Levi had generously given her fifty dollars to spend when she went with Tara and Nettie the day before. It had been more than enough to buy a nice pair of summer shoes, but when she'd tried to return the change, he'd told her to keep it. "Every woman needs a little pin money, don't they?" he'd asked her.

"I've never seen a hospitality barn," Eve told Levi. "That's what Tara said Sara called it."

Levi checked a strap on the horse's harness and then came around the hitching post to her. "I've never heard of it before, either. But if there's one thing I know about Sara Yoder, it's to expect the unexpected."

"What does that mean?" she asked, smiling because he was smiling.

"You'll see," he answered.

Eve walked beside her husband, and side by side, they followed a path that ran between the barn where Sara housed her animals and a long shed that looked to have been enclosed recently. A sign with writing burned into a large piece of wood hung over a door and read Bunkhouse.

"Tara said Sara was widowed." Eve hurried along eagerly. "She said Sara makes her living from matchmaking. Did she build this hospitality barn for her business?"

"Sort of. She had it *rebuilt*. When Sara first moved here from somewhere out west, she purchased it for practically nothing because it was about to be torn down at its original location to make room for a subdivision. With the help of friends and neighbors, a construction crew dismantled the barn and then rebuilt it here."

As they walked beyond the barnyard, the path opened into a grassy field blooming with black-eyed Susans. There, what had to be the hospitality barn came into view. Eve halted to admire it, planting her hands on her hips. It was a picture-perfect gambrel-roofed building with a metal roof, red siding and jaunty rooster weather vane perched high on a white cupola. Double white doors were thrown open, and the sound of voices drifted from inside to mingle with insect song and the peepers.

"Tara said single men and women stay here with Sara?" Eve asked.

They began walking again. "*Ya.* A few at a time, mostly those folks coming from far away. Girls sleep in the house, and while Sara did have boys sleeping in the barn for a while, she just had that shed renovated."

"The one that said 'bunkhouse'?"

He nodded. "And here we are." They walked through the open doors. "I imagine we'll eat inside and wander outside. I saw what looks to be the makings of a bonfire along the side of the barn." Levi looked at her. "Maybe we can roast some marshmallows and make s'mores." His gray eyes twinkled. "I love s'mores. You?"

She laughed. "I know what they are, but I've never had one."

"Never had one?" he gasped, bringing his hand to his chest. He was wearing the new short-sleeve shirt she had made him. It was grass green and she had to admit, he looked rather handsome in it. "Well, we'll right that wrong tonight for sure, wife."

Inside the hospitality barn, Eve gazed around at the interior, taking in the high ceiling, the massive wooden beams and the spotless whitewashed walls. Not only had the inside of the building been insulated, but the old wood floor had been sanded and refinished. Two enormous woodstoves stood in opposite corners, cold now, but she imagined they would make the barn cozy and warm in the winter. Tara had said that Sara used it year-round and was now holding weddings there, as well.

The space was a beehive of activity. Men and boys set up long tables and arranged chairs while women in Amish *kapps* and starched white aprons carried in large stainless steel containers and placed them on counters along one wall.

"Levi!" A short, sturdy, middle-aged woman waved them toward the food area.

"And that is Sara," Levi told Eve.

Sara Yoder was tidy in a blue dress, black stockings and shoes, and a white apron. Her dark textured hair was pinned up into a bun and covered with a starched white prayer *kapp*. And her skin was the color of caramel, still warm in the pan.

Eve had never seen a black Amish woman before.

Levi and Eve walked toward her.

"So this is your bride?" Sara announced with open arms, her dark eyes sparkling.

"Eve," Levi introduced. "And Sara," he told Eve.

"Congratulations on your marriage!" Sara sang, taking Eve's hand between hers. "You married a good man."

Eve felt her cheeks grow warm and she smiled. "That I have," she said, glancing at her husband.

"And I was thrilled when Levi sent word that you

could chaperone tonight. I'm bursting at the seams with men and women staying with me, and half the singles in the county are coming tonight. It seems as if love is in the air. I've made two matches this week," she added under her breath.

"Have you?" Eve couldn't imagine what it would be like to hire a matchmaker to find a husband. How could a stranger choose a spouse for a man or a woman? The idea was certainly unconventional. But then it wasn't any more unconventional than how she and Levi ended up married, was it?

Sara opened her arms wide again. "What do you think of my hospitality barn?"

Eve laughed. "You can hardly call it a barn. It's beautiful."

This building was nothing like the barns Eve had ever been inside; some had smelled of hay and animal feed, but others were not so pleasant. She shuddered involuntarily, remembering her father's dank and forbidding stable, all shadows, cobwebs and sagging doors and windows. The place had always smelled of rodents. Eve had spent many mornings and evenings there milking the cows in the semidarkness, and it wasn't a memory that she cared to linger over.

Levi pushed his straw hat back off his head a bit. "I know you have plenty to do, Sara, so we won't keep you. How can we help?"

"Well, once everyone gets here, I just need you, Levi, to keep an eye on the young men. If you see a group of them wandering off, you can pretty much assume they're up to no good. Obviously, no drinking of alcohol is allowed, and the same goes for cigarette smoking. I won't have it. And no fighting," she added. "A couple of weeks ago, I had two get into a fight over who was going to carry a cup of lemonade to a new girl who'd just arrived from Michigan."

"And what can I do?" Eve asked, clasping her hands together.

"Keep an eye on my girls. I can't be everywhere at once. Young women can be naive. They don't understand how easily they can put themselves at risk with a boy they don't know. I thoroughly vet anyone coming to stay with me, but any single in the county is welcome to my events and I can't speak for the character of everyone's cousin's friend."

Eve lowered her gaze. She knew Sara had no knowledge of the details of her marriage to Levi, but the matchmaker's warning about the innocence of young women struck home. If she'd had a woman like Sara in her life, would she have known better than to have gotten into a buggy with Jemuel?

"I think we can handle the chaperoning. What can we do now?" Levi asked.

Sara glanced around. Everyone there seemed to have a task and was getting to it. "Let's see… Would you mind going outside to check to see if we have enough wood for the bonfire? I asked Lem, a nice, shy boy just arrived from Kentucky. He said he would see to it, but he appears to have found something more important to do." She indicated with her chin and Eve followed Sara's line of sight.

A nice-looking young man with a head of white-blond hair and a big grin was taking an armful of paper plates from a short, round woman who looked like she could have been Eve's twin. Seeing the good-looking boy fawning over the plain, chubby girl made her heart sing. Her mother had always said that there was someone for everyone in God's world. Eve guessed she had been right.

"I can take care of that," Levi told Sara.

"What can I do?" Eve piped up.

"No doubt, there's still work to be had in the kitchen. We're having burritos tonight, so there's a lot of prep work."

"There's a *kitchen* in your barn?" Eve asked.

"Right through that doorway." She pointed. "Every hospitality barn needs a kitchen, don't you think? You can go help if you like. I know there are still tomatoes and cilantro from my garden to be chopped up for the salsa."

Levi turned to Eve. "You okay in here while I see to the firewood?"

She smiled up at him. "Of course."

She watched him go and then turned back to Sara. "So, what exactly is a hospitality barn?" More Amish were coming into the building now, and two teenage girls in black prayer *kapps* were spreading the tables with white tablecloths. "I've never heard of such a thing."

"That's because I made it up myself. I wanted someplace larger than my home where I could get young people together," Sara explained. "For my matchmaking, so that men and women of courting age could meet. Also, our church community needed a safe place to hold youth meetings, singings and frolics. This barn was an answer to our prayers, and it practically fell into my lap. It's more than a hundred years old and is in wonderful shape."

"But the expense of moving the structure." Eve looked around, still in awe.

"A bargain at any price. A lot of Amish communities have problems with their teenagers and young adults being lured into bad habits by the free ways of the English. Even Amish kids need somewhere away from adults to let down their hair, so to speak."

Eve nodded in agreement.

"On Wednesday evenings, Seven Poplars' youth group, the Gleaners, meets here. They do game nights, birthday parties and work frolics here, as well. It's good that Amish children learn the value of work and responsibility, but boys have a lot of energy. If we can positively channel that energy, the entire community benefits."

"Sure seems nice." Eve smoothed her skirt. "Nothing like this where I grew up. Singings and frolics were always at people's homes, the same as when my *mam* grew up."

"Tradition is good." Sara nodded thoughtfully. "It's served our faith well for hundreds of years, but as I see it, we don't live in a vacuum. We have to be open to change when it can be done without endangering our way of life."

"Sara!" A young woman carrying one of the big stainless tubs called from across the room. "Did you want the fixings on this table or that one?" With both hands occupied, she had to use her foot to point.

"I'd better take care of this before we have eight pounds of shredded cheese on the floor," Sara said as she walked away, squeezing Eve's arm.

Eve glanced around the airy barn one more time and then found her way back to the kitchen that was as well equipped as any in an Amish house. There were two large gas cookstoves, two cavernous sinks, a large refrigerator and counters along two walls, as well as an enormous prep island. A slender red-haired woman she didn't know was standing at a big gas stove, stirring sizzling ground beef in several cast-iron frying pans. "Ah, reinforcements have arrived," the woman announced when she spotted Eve. "Want to stir this beef? My hand is about to drop off."

Eve hurried to the stove, introducing herself as she accepted the spoon, and she and her new friend, Lena, were soon chatting as they worked. The next hour was a whirlwind of activity as Eve joined the other women to make and get the fixings out on the buffet table. There were trays of flour tortillas, ground beef, shredded chicken, lettuce, tomato, cheese, pinto beans and rice. They also set out jars of homemade salsa and tubs of sour cream. By the time all the food was on the table and a silent grace had been said, Eve was nearly starving.

She was just adding a serving spoon to a stainless steel tub of pinto beans when she heard Levi behind her. "There you are. I've been looking for you."

She stepped away from the buffet table where folks were lining up, wiping her hands on her apron. "Sara is very organized, but there was still a lot to be done."

"It looks delicious." Levi glanced over her shoulder, checking out the food. "Want to get in line?"

Eve nodded enthusiastically. "I've never had a burrito before."

"Never had a burrito?" He feigned shock.

She shook her head. "You eat so many Englisher foods here in Delaware," she said, thinking of the spaghetti and meatballs and pork medallion stir-fry Tara had taught her to make.

"Is that a bad thing?" he asked.

"*Ne.* I like trying new foods."

"Then come on." He took her hand. "Let's see what you think of beef and bean burritos."

A short time later, Eve held a paper plate with her very first burrito on it, as well as a pile of corn chips covered in gooey yellow cheese. Levi stood beside her, gazing over the crowd, looking for a place for them to sit.

"Wow, there must be fifty or sixty people here," he remarked. "I don't see two seats together." He hesitated. "Wait. How about over there, near the front door?"

She looked in that direction, but there were no dining tables set up. "Where?"

"That little table against the wall." He indicated a card-sized table with a couple of pillar candles and empty glass vases.

She pursed her lips. "No chairs." Her gaze drifted to the long tables packed with young men and women. Everyone seemed to be talking at once, voices and laughter ringing out in the barn. "Do you think, as chaperones, we should be sitting with Sara's guests?"

He looked down at her. "I don't think a matchmaker will object to newlyweds having supper alone together."

She smiled, feeling shy, but pleased. "And we are on a date."

"We are." He tilted his head in the direction of the little table. "Let's put our food down and get bottles of pop." They walked together, plates in their hands. "Root beer, cola or orange?"

"Definitely root beer," she told him.

"Me, too!" He smiled down at her, and his voice grew husky. "Know something?"

"What?" she asked, looking up.

"I like you, Eve."

She nibbled on her lower lip, looking up at him. "You do?"

He nodded, and she felt a warmth wash over her as she thought to herself, *I sure could get used to dating my husband.*

Chapter Nine

Eve veered off the dusty lane, taking the path that led to the side of the vast dairy barn where Levi now spent his days building his first buggy. When they'd arrived in Hickory Grove, he'd been so eager to get started. Looking back, she knew now that his frustration concerning not working—and therefore not earning money—had added to his bad behavior. That and his father's reaction to the unannounced marriage. Now that he was working, he seemed so much better. Levi's relationship with his father still wasn't what it had been before the marriage, but it seemed to her that it was better.

Enjoying her time outdoors, she swung the basket she carried on the crook of her arm, watching dragonflies float lazily in front of her. Someone had mowed the orchard that morning, and even from a distance, Eve could smell the sweet scent of cut grass. It was a perfect summer day.

Her thoughts drifted to the evening before when she and Levi had sat on the edge of her bed and chatted. She smiled at the memory. They hadn't spoken about anything of importance, just their day, but Levi had commented to her how much he looked forward to coming to bed each night because he knew she would be there. He had complimented her on what a good listener she was, and his words had made her heart sing.

After praying together, they had sat side by side for a long moment, looking into each other's eyes. Levi had been silent for so long that she had gotten the impression he'd wanted to say something more, do something, but then he had risen suddenly, and they had said their good-nights. Long after Eve had heard her husband's rhythmic breathing, she had lain awake thinking about how warm and safe she had felt sitting beside Levi. How now, whenever she saw him, she felt a light-headedness that nearly made her giddy.

Was this love? she wondered. Was that what she was feeling? She didn't know because she'd never been in love.

She had, of course, loved, but that was different. She had loved her mother; she loved her brothers and sisters. She knew what that kind of love felt like, but this, this feeling in her chest, it was different. It excited her and scared her at the same time.

It was times like this that she missed her mother the most. Because if her mother had still been alive, she could have asked her about the love between a man and a woman, what it felt like—but her *mam* wasn't here so she had no one to ask. Tara had become a dear friend, but she was still unmarried and had never even had a boyfriend, so Eve couldn't talk to her about these feelings bubbling up inside her. Besides, for all Eve knew, Tara thought they had fallen in love and that was why they had married.

And Eve couldn't talk to Levi about it. She would be

too embarrassed, especially because she didn't know how he felt about her. He had told her several times over the last couple of weeks that he liked her, and she was pleased by that. And she certainly liked him. Liking the man you married seemed like an important part of a good marriage, she thought.

But she wasn't naive enough to think that all Amish marriages were love matches. She knew that from watching other married couples. Men and women wed because it was expected of them by their community, because they wanted children and it was God's way. Sometimes matches were arranged by parents; sometimes two friends or even two strangers just agreed to marry because it was logical. Maybe a widowed man needed a mother for his children, or a woman needed a home of her own.

While knowing all that, secretly, Eve had dreamed of falling in love with a man and marrying him. Her marriage to Levi hadn't happened that way, but what if God gave them the gift of falling in love *after* they married?

Was that too much to hope for? To pray for? she wondered.

Reaching the buggy shop, Eve held tightly to her basket and peered in through the large, open bay door. She heard the loud, grumbling sound of a gas-powered generator. "Levi?" she called, unable to see anything because the bright sunlight was behind her. She stepped inside. *"Hallo?"*

As her eyes adjusted to the light, she saw her husband leaning over a sawhorse, sanding something. Afraid she might startle him if she approached, she raised her voice. "Levi!"

He looked up, then when he saw it was her, he broke

into a grin. He flipped a switch on the electric sander attached to the generator and then turned it off.

"Eve! I didn't think I'd see you until supper," he said, looking at her through a pair of clear safety glasses.

"Nice glasses," she teased as he approached her.

He chuckled and removed them. "My old boss was a stickler for safety. Jehu and I used to complain to each other all the time, but now that I'm my own boss, I see the value in it. I've even got *Dat* wearing them." He set the glasses on a workbench that was covered with parts for a buggy, she guessed, though she couldn't identify any of them. "Tara let you out of the kitchen?" he teased.

"Only for a few minutes." She nibbled on her lower lip, enjoying the back-and-forth with him. "We picked more tomatoes this morning, so we have more to can."

He nodded. "I see. You bring me something?" He pointed to the basket.

"Ya." She swung it on her arm, smiling up at him.

"I hope it's not a jar of canned tomatoes." He held up his hand that had little bits of sawdust on it, palm out. "Don't get me wrong. I love tomatoes fresh on a salad, or in a soup or spaghetti sauce, but I'm not much for eating them out of the jar."

She laughed, loving that he could be playful. "I brought you some limeade."

"Limeade?" His face lit up. "We usually only get lemonade around here."

She set the basket down on a workbench and dug into it. "Limes were on sale at Byler's store. We bought a big bag of them." She held up a pint canning jar with a screw-top lid.

Levi accepted it, unscrewed the lid and took a big drink. "Mmm, that's good," he muttered.

She smiled at him. "And I brought cookies, too."

"Cookies!" He took another drink. "What kind?"

"Our favorite." She pulled a plastic container from the basket.

"Oatmeal?" he guessed.

"Oatmeal with chocolate chunks. I cut up chocolate bars." She pulled off the lid and offered the container to him.

He took one, reached for another and drew back his hand. "Okay if I have another?"

She laughed. "They're all for you."

"*Ne*, I can't eat all of these cookies," he told her, setting down the jar of limeade after he took a second cookie.

He stepped closer to her, and she smelled the fresh sawdust on him and the underlying scent of his skin that she'd come to associate with her husband. When he met her gaze, she felt the same dizziness she often experienced now whenever he was around.

"One for you, one for me," he told her, offering one of her cookies.

She accepted it and they both bit into them at the same time.

"Best cookie ever," he told her, closing his eyes in pleasure.

"I sprinkle a pinch of salt on the top of each one, just as they come out of the oven," Eve explained.

"Never heard of that. Maybe that's why they're better than Tara's." He opened his eyes. "But please don't tell her that."

"Of course not." She was smiling so big that she could barely chew her cookie. "I would never want to hurt Tara's feelings. She's been so sweet to me since I got here. Like a sister."

"She's a sweet kid," he agreed, taking another cookie from the container.

"Not exactly a kid anymore," Eve told him, looking down at something rubbing against her bare ankle. It was a fluffy white cat.

"Snowball," Levi told her, pushing the rest of the cookie into his mouth. "A rescue. Ethan brought her home when she was just a little thing. Jacob took over her care. He loves strays."

Eve leaned over and petted the cat. "I like cats."

"Me, too." He hooked his thumb in the direction of the workbench covered in buggy parts. "Want to see what I'm doing?" he asked. Then he shook his head, grimacing. "Probably not, right?"

"I would love to see what you're doing." He moved toward the workbench and she followed him. "I keep wanting to come down to the barn to see what you do, but I don't want to bother you."

"Never think you're a bother, Eve. I wish you'd come down to the shop more often. Especially if you bring me cookies." He hesitated. "You want to see what I'm working on right now?"

She nodded excitedly.

"Okay." He started to lead her over to where he'd been working, then turned. "Wait. I almost forgot. We had a big delivery this morning and I have something for you."

"For me?" she whispered. "What?"

"A gift," he said, walking over to a large stack of cardboard boxes in various shapes and sizes. He moved several small boxes, picking up one and then the other to read the return addresses. "Ah ha!" he declared. "Here it is." He turned around and offered it to her.

"What is it?" she asked, staring at the box she'd accepted from him.

He tucked his hands behind his back. "Guess you'll have to open and see."

Eve hesitated, trying to extend the moment. She'd only ever received a couple of gifts in her whole life, and they had been from her mother when she was a child.

"Open it," he encouraged.

She set it on a pile of boxes and opened it. Inside was a brown paper bag and inside of that, something soft. She looked up to see him smiling, then gently slid the gift from the bag.

It was yards of a blue cotton blend fabric, and she knew exactly what it was for. And she was touched by his kindness in a deep place in her heart that she hadn't even known existed until now. *"Danke,"* she managed when she found her voice.

"It's for a dress. For you," he told her. "Blue, because it's your favorite color."

She looked up at him, clutching the fabric to her chest, her eyes glistening. "You remembered."

"After I ordered it, I asked Rosemary to make you the dress, but she suggested I give you fabric first. She said it would mean more to you that way. And she thought you might like to make it yourself. Because it came from me," he explained.

"She was right." Eve gently slid the fabric back into the bag and placed it in her basket. "Such a kind thing to do. But I don't want you to think I need things bought for me."

"I think nothing of the sort. I'm just glad you like

it." He tipped his head in the direction of his work area. "Still want to see what I'm doing?"

"Of course," she told him, setting down the basket to follow him.

Grinning, Levi began explaining to her what he was working on: the chassis of the buggy. He explained to her how the chassis was the frame beneath the buggy the wheels were attached to and then showed her the long, wooden reaches he was sanding that would connect the front and rear axles on the chassis.

He chattered on about head blocks, spring bars and shaft couplings, and as he talked, Eve's thoughts kept drifting. As Levi spoke, she admired how handsome he was and how, when he smiled, his whole face lit up and she couldn't help but smile back at him. She still couldn't believe he had given her a gift, and such a perfect gift. Now she would have a blue dress that would remind her every day of her mother. And of the kindness of the man she had married. When they had first arrived in Hickory Grove, Eve had worried she had made a mistake in marrying Levi, but she knew now that it hadn't been.

Levi kept talking and she tried to pay attention.

When he led her to a workbench to show her the parts of the drum brakes he was putting together, his hand brushed hers as he passed her parts to show her how they went together. The brakes of a buggy, he explained, kept the buggy from running into the horse when you pulled back on the reins.

Eve swallowed hard. His hand was warm and rough in the places where he had calluses, and she wondered what it would be like to hold it. To walk together, holding hands. She had rarely seen Amish men and women holding hands, but Rosemary and Benjamin did. Every other Sunday, when they walked to church, they went separately from their big, blended family. They walked close together, holding hands, talking and laughing. Eve wondered if it was too much to hope for, to someday hold hands with Levi on their way to church.

Levi stopped midsentence and stared at her.

Eve wondered if he was waiting for her to answer a question. She'd been so lost in her own foolish dreaming that she hadn't been listening.

"This is boring," he declared, throwing up his hand. "I'm boring you."

"Ne." She shook her vehemently. "You're not. I want to know what you do. I like hearing about it, even if…if I don't understand everything. My day is so boring— cooking, cleaning, hanging clothes on the line. Not that I mind," she added quickly. "I like being useful. But what you do—" She gazed around his shop that was stacked with cardboard boxes full of parts he had ordered and benches covered in parts in various stages of assembly. "This is so much more exciting," she declared enthusiastically.

When Eve met his gaze, she realized he was staring at her. "What?" she asked, wiping her mouth, afraid she had cookie crumbs on it.

He shook his head, taking a step closer to her. He was smiling. "Nothing, I just… It's all I can do to talk when you're standing so close because I…" He reddened. "I keep thinking that I'd like to kiss you, Eve."

She blushed and looked down at her bare feet that had gotten dusty on the walk over. Suddenly her heart was pounding. "I… I've never kissed a man," she heard herself say.

Levi took another step and stood in front of her. "I don't want to be forward." His voice had become husky.

Realizing he was as nervous as she was, Eve relaxed and giggled. "We're married, Levi. You have a right to kiss me."

He lifted his gaze. Held hers. "Would you like to kiss me, Wife?"

Not trusting herself to speak, she nodded. Then she closed her eyes and waited.

Eve didn't know what she expected, but when he wrapped his arms around her and brushed his lips ever so gently across hers, she felt enveloped in a warmth she had never felt before. In his embrace, she felt safe and content and…and cared for, if not loved.

Levi kissed her and she opened her eyes to see him studying her. "How was that?" he asked.

She raised her hand to touch her lips. "Warm and tingly," she told him with a shy smile. "How was it for you?"

Still holding her in his arms, he chuckled. "*Goot*. You smell like vanilla."

She stepped back. "Probably spilled some on myself," she told him, laughing as she ran her hand over her apron.

He was still studying her. "I don't think so."

"*Ach*, I should get back to the house," she said, feeling awkward. And excited. She would never have believed it could happen, that a handsome, smart, capable man like Levi could fall in love with a plain wren like her, but suddenly, she saw that possibility. And all she could think was *God is good*. "Tara will wonder what happened to me."

"*Ya*, you'd best go. We wouldn't want her coming

down here looking for you and finding us kissing." He raised an eyebrow, his tone teasing.

"*Ya...* I mean, *ne!*" She shook her head, vehemently. "We wouldn't want that."

They stood looking at each other for a long moment and then Levi said softly, "Wife, you best get going, else I'm liable to kiss you again."

She covered her mouth with her hand to stifle another giggle and turned and hurried out of the barn, grabbing her basket with the fabric as she went.

"Eve!" Levi called after her. "You forgot the cookies."

"They're all for you!" she called over her shoulder. Then she hurried back up the lane to the house, feeling as if she might burst with joy.

On a Sunday morning, Eve walked beside Levi along the road, headed toward his brother Ethan's home. They were both in their Sunday best, her in her black dress, crossed cape and bonnet, him in black pants, a white shirt and black vest, his wide-brimmed black felt hat on his head. His beard was coming in nicely, making him all the more handsome. Some husbands let their beards grow without trimming them, leaving them to look unkempt, but not Levi. For a man who worked with his hands, he was fastidious about cleanliness. No matter what he did on the farm, whether it was muck horse stalls or work in the buggy shop, when he came to the supper table, his hands and nails were meticulously scrubbed, and his face was freshly washed.

Pride swelled in her chest. With every passing day, she was surer of her impulsive decision to marry Levi. They were still getting to know each other, but as July slipped into August, she became more assured of her choice. As she began to feel more confident in their growing relationship, she was finding the desire in her heart to forgive Jemuel for what he had done. She prayed for him every day now because it was the right thing to do. But also because, had he not done what he had, maybe she would never have ended up where she was now, safe and happy.

"I hope you baked plenty of brownies." Levi touched his hand to her shoulder as they moved farther off the road to allow a motorcycle to fly by.

"I made three pans. They're in the wagon with Bay, and the girls took them to Marshall and Abigail's this morning." They had left early, with the children, to help their sister-in-law with last-minute preparations to host church. Eve had been invited to go with them, but she had stayed behind to clean up the breakfast dishes. Her offer hadn't been entirely selfless. She had remained so that she could walk with Levi to church. While bad weather or distance required families to take buggies to Sunday services, Benjamin preferred his family walk when possible. Which was just fine with Eve because it gave her time alone with Levi. Rather than walking with the family, they had fallen into the habit of making the trek alone together, as Benjamin and Rosemary often did.

"We made three pans of scalloped potatoes, too," she went on. "And four dozen buttermilk biscuits."

"Buttermilk biscuits!" Levi exclaimed as they moved closer to the road so they didn't have to walk in the tall weeds. "I love buttermilk biscuits. They're my favorite."

Eve looked at him quizzically. "Yesterday you said cheddar was your favorite."

"Can't I have two favorites?"

She rolled her eyes. The amount of food her husband could eat in a day astounded her. And yet he never gained a pound. She looked at a buttermilk biscuit and could feel it going to her hips. "Why are you worried about how much food we brought? There's always more than enough to go around when we break for the midday meal on Sundays."

"It's going to be a long day," he told her, walking slowly so she could keep up. "I heard *Dat* discussing it with Ethan last night. He didn't say anything to me about it," he added quietly.

Eve took his hand and squeezed it, knowing it pained him that his relationship with his father remained strained. She was still shy about their physical affection for each other, but she found it easier out of sight of anyone else. And she wanted to comfort him.

"We'll be talking today about splitting up our district after the first service. After we eat, the afternoon service will be shortened, and the plan will be announced, then discussed."

Eve's eyes widened. Hickory Grove had been abuzz with the topic for weeks. Everywhere she went, to Byler's store, to Ginger's quilting circle, to Spence's Bazaar, the women were talking about it and what it would mean to each family, the positives and the negatives. "So we're definitely splitting the district?"

"*Ya.* The elders have decided it's time. Past time. We've gotten so big that we can only meet in the larger homes. A church isn't meant to get so big that we can't meet in any member's home. We each have to take our turn and share the responsibility."

"So we'll have a new bishop?" she asked, thinking how much she liked Bishop Simon.

"*Ne*, Bishop Simon offered to take the new district, but we'll be choosing men to become preachers and deacons from the new congregation." He took her hand, threading his fingers through hers. "The older district will choose a new bishop from our preachers."

"I see," Eve said.

"I talked to Ethan after *Dat* left for home. Ethan said *Dat* was the first from the oldest, most established families to offer to join the new district. The division is sort of based on where we live, but it's important that families who have been here a while join the new district, too. Ethan thought he and Abigail would be going with us, as well as Joshua and Phoebe and Ginger and Eli, but Lovey and Marshall will be staying with our old district. Just because of where they live."

"Will Rosemary be upset, not getting to see her daughter and grandchildren on Sundays?"

"Both districts will be on the same schedule, so even though we meet in different places for services, visiting Sundays will be the same."

She nodded thoughtfully. "And how will the preachers and deacons be chosen for the new church?" Her whole life, she had belonged to the same district she had been born into, so she didn't know how it was done.

"The new congregation's baptized men and women will nominate whoever they feel is being called as a leader. Any man who receives three votes or more is placed in a pool. The two new preachers will be chosen from the pool."

"That means it could be anyone?" she asked, enjoying the feel of her husband's hand in hers.

"Any man who's been baptized, is married and is in good standing in the church, *ya*."

"But how do you know you've chosen the right men?" she asked.

He looked down at her. "God chooses through us. God always chooses well."

"And you truly believe that?" she asked, appreciating what a man of faith her husband was.

He thought over her question for a moment and looked at her. "I do."

The sound of hoofbeats reverberated on the pavement, and they both looked over their shoulders to see an open wagon headed in the same direction they were going. As the wagon moved closer, Eve realized it was Eli and Ginger. Eli was easy to spot from a distance because of his bright red hair. Ginger, her first pregnancy now obvious to everyone, waved, and Eve waved back. Then she realized she was still holding Levi's hand and she tried to pull away.

"Ne," Levi told her, holding on. "A man has a right to his wife's hand."

"But it's the Sabbath," she whispered as his sister and her family grew closer.

"The Sabbath is a gift from God, and so is a wife," he told her.

Eli slowed the wagon and called out to them with a grin. "I'd offer you a ride to Ethan and Abigail's, but my wife says I'm to let the newlyweds be."

Levi smiled as they rolled by. "A wise woman, your wife."

Eli glanced at Ginger and called back to them good-naturedly, "Don't I know it."

As they drove away, Eve studied their four little ones

in the back of the wagon, all clean and neatly dressed for church, and she couldn't help wondering if someday she and Levi would be driving to church with their own children. Was it too much to hope for?

She felt the warmth of Levi's hand and prayed it wasn't.

Chapter Ten

Excited to be going on another date with her husband, Eve walked out of the house on a Saturday morning, smoothing the fresh apron she wore over her new blue dress. The fabric Levi had ordered by mail, both sturdy and easy to wash and hang on the line, was perfect for an everyday dress. And it was so beautiful. She had a feeling Rosemary had picked out the fabric because Levi knew nothing about women's clothing, but it didn't matter because it had been his idea that she should have another blue dress.

Eve was so excited for the morning's adventure. Levi was taking her over to Seven Poplars to see Albert Hartman's alpacas. There, she'd also get to meet Rosemary's friend Hannah, whom she'd heard so much about. And after visiting with the Hartmans, they were going to stop at Gideon Esch's shop on the way home to pick up fresh sausage and scrapple.

As Eve followed the oyster shell lane toward the harness shop where she would meet Levi, Jacob's dogs rushed past her. The Chesapeake Bay retrievers crisscrossed in front of her, nipping at each other playfully.

She smiled at their antics as they cut behind her and raced toward the house again.

It was going to be another hot August day, with barely a breeze, but the heat wasn't going to bother Eve. She'd cross a desert in a buggy just to sit beside Levi and hear him talk about disc versus drum brakes and the newfangled shocks he wanted to add to his buggy design. She didn't even know what shocks were, but she didn't care. She just liked to hear the sound of Levi's voice.

As she grew closer to the harness shop, her gaze settled on Levi and his father standing in the parking area. There were two buggies and an old blue pickup in the lot, and a white car was coming up the lane. Saturdays were so busy at the shop that Tara was going to be working the cash register every Saturday morning for the foreseeable future.

Eve slowed her pace to study the two men who were obviously father and son. Levi's head was bowed slightly, and Benjamin was staring out in the direction of the hay feed that ran along the side of the oyster shell lane. She didn't have to be there to know that it was another tense conversation between father and son.

She sighed, her heart going out to her husband. She wished there was something she could do to help bridge the gap between the two of them, but Levi had been adamant that it wasn't her concern. He had told her on multiple occasions that his trouble with his father was not her fault, and he had made it plain that he wanted her to stay out of it.

She watched Levi shake his head in disagreement and wondered what they were discussing. She debated whether she should go to her husband or wait there in the driveway for him. She saw no sign of the buggy they were taking, which meant Levi hadn't made it to the barn yet.

"Eve! Eve!" a voice called from behind.

Eve turned around to see Rosemary hurrying down the lane after her. In her hand was a piece of white paper. Behind her, her and Benjamin's toddlers trailed, both barefoot, and one was carrying a stick. When she'd first arrived, she'd been embarrassed to admit that she couldn't tell the difference between the little boys. However, after James fell off a fence and had to have stitches, it had been easy for her to identify him because of the tiny red scar on his forehead. They were adorable little boys, full of vim and vinegar, as her mother used to say.

"Glad I caught you before you left," Rosemary said, flapping the paper in her hand. She was out of breath by the time she reached Eve. "I completely forgot that Eli asked me yesterday when we'd be picking up an order of scrapple again from Gideon's shop. Would you mind picking up a couple of things for Ginger? Her ankles are swelling up in this heat and the midwife insists she stay off her feet at least a few hours a day." She shook her head as she caught her breath. "Eli's about to come undone. He fusses over her as if he were a mother hen."

Eve smiled, wondering, if God were to bless her and Levi with children someday, if he would be the same. She could imagine how frustrated Ginger probably was with Eli fretting over her, but how good it had to feel to have a husband who cared so much.

"We can do that." Eve accepted the white envelope with the list on the back. Rosemary liked using junk mail to keep her lists. She said envelopes fit nicely in her apron pocket and it was a good way to save on paper.

"Levi said he's going to put a cooler in the buggy with some ice."

"Good idea." Rosemary wiped her forehead with the back of her hand. "Going to be another hot one." Her gaze strayed to her little ones, who had wandered off into the grass. They were trying to get one of the dogs to fetch, but so far, it appeared that the dogs were watching the twins play the game.

Eve smiled as she watched James throw the stick and then Josiah run to get it and take it back to his brother. She returned her gaze to Rosemary. "I'm meeting Levi at the harness shop, but—" She exhaled, not sure what to say, so she just looked in that direction.

Rosemary's gaze followed Eve's and settled on the two men in the parking lot. *"Ach,"* she muttered. "Those two, at it again. They're too much alike, I say. They butt heads like two billy goats."

Eve looked at Rosemary. "But it hasn't always been that way, has it? Not before I arrived." The moment the words were out of her mouth, she wished she could take them back. Levi didn't want her talking to his stepmother about him and his father. And her husband certainly didn't want Eve bringing up the suspicious circumstances of their marriage with anyone. Not even in an offhand way.

Rosemary's gaze shifted to Eve and she settled her hands on her hips. In her late forties, she certainly didn't look like she had given birth to eight children in twenty-five years. She was still slender and had barely a gray hair beneath her starched white *kapp.*

"Relationships between a father and son are complicated," Rosemary said. "Especially when the son becomes a man and the father isn't quite ready for that. And sons forget that their fathers aren't always right or fair."

Eve pressed her lips together, running her finger along the edge of the envelope in her hand. It was all she could do not to blurt out how guilty she felt because even though Levi denied it, she knew the trouble between him and his father was all her fault.

Rosemary reached out and stroked Eve's arm. "Both of them are so stubborn. The father thinks he has the right to certain details and the son doesn't. And neither wants to give in."

Eve knew very well Levi's stepmother was referring to their marriage. "And what do you think?" she said softly, not looking at Rosemary.

The older woman sighed. "I think the details Benjamin is seeking no longer matter." She hesitated and then went on. "While I agree that Benjamin had good reason to be concerned when you and Levi arrived in June, it's plain to see you two are finding your stride in your marriage. And I think in time, my husband will see that and let go of whatever anger or disappointment he's still holding on to."

Eve looked up, fighting tears that she could feel working their way out. She didn't know what to say. Her heart was so filled by Rosemary's kindness that she couldn't find the words to thank her.

"Marriage isn't easy, not for anyone," Rosemary went on. "Benjamin and I hit a couple bumps on the path in our early days before moving here." She smiled, seeming lost in memory. "And I can tell you that Levi's father, my first husband, and I went head-to-head in the beginning. We were so young and headstrong and selfish sometimes, I think. But, with time, we found our way. Together. As God intended."

Rosemary glanced over to where her boys were playing. They were now using the stick to dig a hole. She returned her attention to Eve. "I guess what I'm trying to say, in a roundabout way, is that I'm not worried about you and Levi anymore. I was at first. I could tell the two of you weren't in harmony. But I see the changes, and my heart is glad for you both. And Benjamin will get there, too. Levi just needs to be patient."

Eve smiled. "I wish you'd tell him that."

Rosemary chuckled. "I tell them both, sometimes at the same time, but—" she shrugged "—men. With matters of the heart, they can move at a snail's pace."

Eve met Rosemary's gaze. *"Danke."*

Rosemary drew back, her green eyes crinkling at the corners. "For what?"

"For your kindness." Eve lowered her head and then raised it again to look her in the eye. "For welcoming me here, even if it wasn't in the circumstances you had expected. I'm so happy here, and part of that is because of you, Rosemary."

The older woman smiled. *"Ach,* I'm glad you're happy." She gestured with her chin in the direction of the harness shop. "Now, what say you and I break up this discussion between our husbands before they raise their voices and scare off all our customers."

Eve laughed at Rosemary's practicality and walked beside her, the list tucked safely in her pocket, along with hope that her relationship with Levi's stepmother would only grow stronger over time.

The following church Sunday, Levi stood a few feet from a group of older men who had gathered beside the Fishers' fence, his hands deep in his pockets, head bowed so that the brim of his wool hat shielded his face.

He couldn't hear what was being said, but he didn't need to. He had heard his name spoken, and by the body language he was observing, he knew what they were saying.

After services and the midday meal, those adults who would become a part of the new church district had gathered to accept nominations for the two preacher positions and one deacon. Members of the congregation had been instructed two weeks before to spend time in prayer to seek God's will in their new church's founding. The duties of the preachers would be to give sermons at services. The new deacon would serve as Bishop Simon's assistant of sorts. He would collect donations, when required, in their community, speak to those in need of moral righting or counseling, and make marriage announcements, among other duties. Deacons and preachers were unpaid, and many hours and sacrifices were required from both the candidate and his family. They were no positions any man wanted, but when called by his people, by God, it was a sacrifice required by their faith.

Earlier, folks had stood and called out names. Any man whose name was given up three times or more would be included in the list of possible candidates. At the next church service in two weeks, two slips of paper would be placed in two hymnals, and those books would be placed in a stack with hymnals that did not have a slip of paper in them. Each man whose name has been offered up as a possible preacher would choose a hymnal. The two men who chose the hymnals with the slips of paper in them would be the men God had chosen to be the new preachers. The same process would take place to select a new deacon.

Levi's gaze shifted to his father, who stood in the circle of men. His heart ached that his father still believed he had sinned and not confessed. All men and women sinned; that was a given. But to not to confess—that was what stuck in his father's craw. He knew that because during their evening prayers, led by his father, the subject was often addressed.

Levi had probably been more surprised than anyone else the first time his name was announced as a possible preacher candidate. Having his name repeated twice more had shocked him. So he would be one of the men to choose a hymnal during the next service. And possibly become one of their preachers.

The first time his name was spoken, he'd heard a shuffle of feet, a few whispers. By the third time, there were audible sounds. No one spoke, but throats were cleared, and there was coughing and shifting on the pews.

It was obvious to Levi that there were those who did not believe his name should be in the pool. Because Levi had married without his parents' knowledge, everyone had jumped to the conclusion that he had sinned. Because they believed that Levi was not a man right with God and should not, therefore, be considered.

Levi stood there a few minutes longer, listening to the rumble of the men's voices. A raindrop fell on his hand and he looked up into the sky. The air was humid and rainclouds were gathering.

He wondered if he ought to find Eve and set off for home. If they didn't go soon, they'd get wet on the two-mile walk, but it was either walk or get into a buggy with his father, and right now, he didn't know if he could do that.

Just as Levi was about to turn away, he heard his

father's strong baritone voice. "I value everyone's thoughts on this matter, but I have to ask you this…" He paused, looking from one man to the next, taking his time, drawing their undivided attention. "Do we trust in the process?"

"What?" someone asked.

"Do we believe in this process of selection for our church?" Levi's father asked.

Men responded one after another.

"Ya."

"We do."

"It's how it's done. How it's always been done," came the voices.

"Then why, my friends," he asked, "would we remove a man's name that has been offered up not once, but three times by our congregation?" Again, Levi's father paused. He waited for a ripple of muted utterances to pass and then went on. "If we trust this process, if we accept that it is God who will be choosing these men by setting their hand on the right hymnal, why would we think we should remove a name from the candidates?"

No one said anything. Men stared at their shoes.

"If Levi Miller is not meant to be a preacher, God will not choose him," his father said in a calm, steady voice.

Sadness washed over Levi. His father had not defended him, only the process. His father didn't think him fit to be a preacher.

Levi walked away.

He crossed the barnyard as the sky grew darker and walked up to the house. Spotting his brother Jesse, he called out to him. "Have you seen Eve?"

Jesse was sitting on the porch rail with two boys about the same age. "*Ya*, in the kitchen, I think."

"Could you go inside and tell her I'm ready to go?"

Thirteen-year-old Jesse, who had grown tall and lanky over the summer, jumped down from the rail. "But Levi. It's going to rain. That's why—"

"Please do as I ask," Levi interrupted.

Without another word, Jesse went into the house.

Levi walked out to Marshall's driveway and waited. A few minutes later, Eve hurried down the porch steps, her bonnet in her hand.

"What's wrong?" she asked as she joined him.

"It's going to rain. If we don't go now, we'll get wet." Levi started down the driveway toward the road.

Eve put her bonnet on her head and began to tie it under her chin. "That's why we brought two buggies, so—"

"I'm going home. Come with me," he intoned, lengthening his stride. "Or stay and return with my family. Your choice."

She hurried to catch up with him, hurt obvious in her voice. "*You* are my family, Levi. Of course I'll come home with you."

They walked in silence to the road and turned toward home before she spoke again. "What's wrong?" she asked.

He kept walking. He wanted to tell her, but he was afraid he would cry if he spoke of it right now. He knew his father was disappointed in him, but he couldn't believe he hadn't spoken up for his own son's character.

"Levi, please," Eve murmured, slipping her arm through his. "Please talk to me."

He shook his head. "Not now," he muttered.

And then the rain began in earnest and he wondered if it had been a mistake ever coming home to Hickory Grove.

* * *

On her hands and knees, Eve spread the thick green leaves of the closest sprawling plant and spied a cucumber just the right size and color for picking. She snapped it off the vine and added it to the peck basket in the row between her and Tara.

"You're quiet today," Tara said. "What's troubling you?"

Eve took a moment to respond. A part of her thought she shouldn't say anything about Levi. He was her husband and it wasn't right to talk about him behind his back. But a part of her thought it was time she did something. Else she feared their marriage might not ever be what she had begun to think was possible.

Eve had tried to be patient with Levi. For two full days, she had kept quiet and waited for him to tell her why he had become so upset after church on Sunday. She had waited for him to tell her why he had barely spoken to her, to anyone since leaving Lovey and Marshall's. She suspected it had something to do with his name being one of the five who had been proposed for preacher, but she had no way of knowing because he wouldn't tell her.

That morning, now the third day, she had stood in the doorway of their bedroom, blocking his escape, and asked him outright what had him so upset. She didn't tell him that his black mood made her fear they were losing everything they had accomplished in their marriage in the last two months. Since church on Sunday, he had gone back to avoiding her, barely speaking, and bordered on rudeness with her and his family. He had turned so far inward that she wasn't only worried about the health of their marriage, but about him.

Levi had refused to meet her gaze. He told her he would talk about it when he was ready and he wasn't ready. And then he had ducked under her arm and walked out of their bedroom.

Eve had been so frustrated, so angry with him, that she had wanted to throw something at him. Not something hard that would hurt him—maybe a pillow or a balled-up sock, something to knock some sense into him.

"Did I do something wrong?" Tara asked, getting Eve's attention again.

Eve sat up, settling her dusty hands in her lap. She was quiet for a moment and then made a decision. "It's Levi," she said softly. "He's not been himself since church Sunday and I'm not sure why."

Tara looked surprised. "He didn't tell you?"

"Tell me what?"

Tara, who'd been picking cucumbers a few feet ahead of Eve, crawled the distance between them and sat up. Her knees pressed against Eve's. "There was a big hullabaloo after services," she said in a half whisper.

Eve frowned, feeling her forehead crease. "About what?"

"Choosing the preachers!" She leaned closer. "Some people don't think Levi is an acceptable candidate."

"Why?" Eve asked, slapping at a mosquito. Since the rain Sunday, they had been bad. Because of the pests, she and Tara had waited until late morning when the sun was higher, but not so high as to be roasting, to come out to pick cucumbers to make pickles.

Tara bit down on her lower lip.

Eve rose to her knees and grabbed Tara's hand. "Please, Tara. You have to tell me because Levi won't…

or can't. And I can't help him if I don't know what's wrong."

Tara pursed her lips. "*Mam* says I need to do a better job of minding my own knitting."

Eve released her. "This is not gossip. I'm Levi's wife, and I need to help him. And I need your help to do that." She frowned. "Why don't they think Levi should be considered for the job of preacher?"

Tara folded her hands in her lap and looked down at them. Her cheeks reddened. "Because no one knew you were getting married," she whispered under her breath. "And... And some say he should have made a confession to Bishop Simon."

Tara's words practically knocked the wind out of Eve, and she sat back hard on her heels.

"I'm sorry," Tara said softly. "That's what Martha Gruber said she heard her mother telling their neighbor."

Wiping her damp brow, Eve looked away. The huge garden was beautiful, with its neat rows of bright green plants and the soft, turned-up soil that created paths between them. She watched a butterfly flutter above a flower in a small patch of mixed wildflowers. Rosemary had interspersed beds of herbs as well as flowers in the vegetable garden.

Eve took a breath and turned back to Tara. "It's okay," she assured her. "It's going to be all right." She straightened her spine. "Levi and I are going to figure this out." She glanced across the garden to stare at the big dairy barn in the distance. Then she looked back at Tara. "Could you finish up picking the cucumbers? I have something I have to do."

"*Ya*, of course, *Schweschder*." Tara offered a shy smile. "I would do anything for you."

Touched that Tara would call her sister, Eve threw her arms around the younger girl and hugged her tightly. Determined to get to the bottom of this matter with her husband, she rose, dusted bits of dirt and leaves off her apron and strode barefoot down the row.

She was scared, but she would go to Levi. Because she wanted their marriage to be a good one. And even though he didn't love her, she was still hopeful that someday he would.

Chapter Eleven

At first, Eve was disappointed when she didn't find Levi in his shop. Then she was annoyed when Bay, who was busy watering mums in her greenhouse, told Eve that he had left in a wagon an hour previously to repair a buggy axle a good distance away. When Eve had asked her how long she thought he'd been gone, she'd shrugged and said something about as grumpy as he'd been, she was hoping he'd be gone a week or so.

With nothing to do but wait, Eve went about her day. She returned to the garden to help Tara finish harvesting cucumbers and then spent hours washing them, slicing them, and making bread and butter pickles to can. Again and again, she went to the kitchen window, hoping to see the wagon parked near the shop. As the hours on the wall clock ticked by, she went from being annoyed with her husband to becoming worried. He'd never said a word to her about being gone all day, and she began to fear that he'd been in an accident on the road. It wasn't unheard of. Horse and buggies and wagons were hit on the road all the time, and Amish folks died in those kinds of accidents.

When Levi finally walked into the house, Eve was putting supper on the table. Her chest heaving with relief, she had greeted him with a smile, but he only nodded and excused himself to wash up.

Levi was quiet through the entire meal of cold ham slices, chow-chow, mustard potato salad and sweet and sour beets. He didn't even comment on the cheddar biscuits he had to know she'd made fresh just for him. Several times as the evening dragged, Eve tried to make eye contact with him, hoping they could step outside together to talk, but he avoided her gaze.

After evening prayers, Eve climbed the stairs alone, prepared for bed and waited for her husband in their bedroom. He was so long in coming that she feared he wasn't, but she was still awake when he opened the door.

Levi walked into their bedroom and seemed startled to find her sitting on the edge of the bed. She'd washed up and was wearing a white summer nightgown Rosemary had given her. Eve's prayer *kapp* was lying neatly on top of the chest of drawers, stuffed with white paper to keep its shape. She wore her hair loose down her back, which fell to her waist.

He looked so surprised that, for a moment, she feared he might turn around and walk out.

"Close the door," she said softly, but in a tone that told him she meant business.

He hovered in the doorway. "Eve—"

"Close the door," she repeated evenly, making a point to keep her voice down. "Unless you want everyone in this house to hear what I have to say."

He got a stricken look on his face and closed the door.

Eve pressed her lips together. She'd been rehearsing

what she wanted to say to him, but now her knees were shaking beneath her gown. She sent a little prayer heavenward, asking for God's help in finding the words she needed to get through to her husband. Her whole life, she'd tried to be quiet, meek and mild. She had tried to be the woman her father wanted her to be. He had warned her repeatedly that it was not a woman's place to speak against a man. She imagined he had given her mother the same lecture.

But what if her mother had spoken up when her father had tried to silence her? Would her father have become a different man? If Eve's mother had established a different sort of marriage in their early days as husband and wife, would her father have not grown to be so harsh and rigid?

On Sunday, the deacon had read a verse from the Bible that came to Eve's mind. The only words she could recall right now were: *Be courageous, be strong.* Had those words been meant for her? For this moment?

When she heard the sound of the door click closed, she stood up. "Why didn't you tell me?" she asked.

He pressed a thumb and forefinger to his temples and blinked. He looked tired. "Tell you what?"

"That people spoke up against you after church. That there are those who—" Her words got caught in her throat and she had to take a moment before she could go on. "There are those who think you aren't fit to be a preacher."

His hand fell to his side and his gaze to his bare feet. He'd already cleaned up for bed. "I didn't want to be a preacher anyway."

She took a step toward him. "That's not the point, Levi. It's not up to you. It's up to *Gott*," she said, somehow finding the strength she needed to keep from backing down. To say what needed to be said.

He set his jaw, still not meeting her gaze.

"You should have told me," she repeated. "I'm your wife, and to make this marriage work, we have to be able to tell each other things. Even if we're embarrassed. Even if they hurt."

"I'm sorry," he murmured, shaking his head. "It was only that I didn't want to...upset you."

"Not a good reason." She crossed her arms over her chest. "Those people who spoke against you, it's because of me, isn't it? It's because we married so quickly and everyone made the assumption that we—" She felt her cheeks grow warm with embarrassment, but she pressed on because this was not the time to be shy and girlish. "They thought we acted as man and wife when we were not." She hesitated and then asked, "Is that why you're so upset? Because they don't think you are morally fit to speak God's word?"

He sighed and pressed his hand to his forehead. "*Ne*, I don't care about what others think. God knows what I have or have not done. But—" His voice cracked. "I... I overheard the men talking about it after services. My father was among them and he spoke up."

"For you?"

"*Ne*, wife. Not for me. For the tradition. For the way we choose our preachers and deacons. He said that they should trust in the process because God would not choose me because of my sin."

Eve's breath caught and it took her a moment to find her voice. "Oh, Levi," she murmured. She glanced at the window that reflected the light from the oil lamp beside the bed. She looked back at him. "This is all because of me. Because I disobeyed my father and got myself into trouble."

He lifted his hand in a tired gesture. "See, that's why I didn't tell you. Because you'd say it was your fault."

"Because it is!" she responded in frustration. "I made a terrible mistake with terrible costs, and you offered to marry me to protect me. You saved me, Levi."

He lowered his gaze to the floor again.

She sighed. "You have to tell him," she said, her voice calm again. "You have to tell your father and Rosemary what happened to me. Why you married me. And you have to tell our bishop, too. He'll know what to do about the gossip."

"*Ne, ne*, Eve." Levi shook his head again and again. "I told you I would never speak to anyone of how we came to be husband and wife. I will not speak a word of this to our bishop. As to my father, if he doesn't know me better than this, then—" He exhaled sharply. "*Ne,*" he repeated again. "I will not do it." Then he reached around her and grabbed the pillow, blanket and sheet he'd been using for his pallet on the floor from the end of the bed.

Before Eve could protest, he was out the door, closing it behind him.

Eve brought her hands to her face, near to bursting into tears. Instead, she took a couple of deep breaths and lowered herself to her knees. Clasping her hands together, she rested her elbows on the bed, squeezed her eyes shut and prayed fervently to God. Because if she didn't do something, she feared the marriage she thought could be possible would never come to be.

"Dear *Gott*, what do I do?" she whispered. "How do I make this right for my husband? How do I save my marriage?"

And God's response came to her as loud and clear in her head as if He had been in the room.

Levi did not return to their bedroom, but Eve slept surprisingly well that night. In the morning, she rose before anyone else in the family, just as the sun was washing the day in all of its glory. Wearing her favorite blue dress, her hair tucked neatly in a bun under her *kapp*, she went down to the kitchen and put two large percolators of coffee on the gas stove. When it was ready, she poured a cup black, the way Levi liked it, and went in search of him.

Eve located her husband in a tiny bedroom on the second floor that was used for storage. When she pushed open the door, she found him asleep in his clothes, curled up on some old sleeping bags on the floor.

"Levi?" she whispered. When he didn't respond, she leaned over and touched his shoulder gently. "Levi, wake up. It's morning."

He rolled over onto his back and opened his eyes. He looked at her, then the single window where sunlight poured in, then at her again.

"Best you get up before anyone else finds you here," she said. Then she set his cup of coffee beside him on the floor and walked out of the room before he had a chance to respond.

By the time Tara arrived downstairs, Eve had three baking sheets of bacon in the oven and was mixing up ingredients for blueberry muffins. Lovey had sent an entire bucket of blueberries over the day before, and while most would be frozen for use later, there was nothing better than fresh blueberries in a muffin.

"You're up early," Tara said, going to the dish cabinet to begin setting the table. "Are you all right?"

Standing at the kitchen counter, Eve took a deep breath. *Was* she all right?

She was.

Because her prayer had been answered. Because she knew what she had to do. And she knew it was the right thing.

"*Ya*, I'm *goot*." Eve smiled at Tara and shrugged. "I woke early, so I thought I'd get a start on breakfast."

"Sorry I slept in," Tara said. Then she whispered, "I was up late reading a book Chloe gave me. It's a *romance*." She grinned.

Eve cut her eyes at Tara but said nothing. Whether Tara's parents would approve of her reading choice wasn't her concern. At least it wasn't today. As her mother had always said, she had bigger fish to fry.

Eve returned to the task at hand, adding baking powder to the dry ingredients. Once the flour, salt and leavening were properly mixed, she would fold in the wet ingredients. She would mix it just until the flour and such were wet, paying no attention to a few lumps. Then she would add the blueberries, continuing to gently stir so as not to make the muffins tough. Once they were in greased tins, they would have fresh blueberry muffins in half an hour.

Levi managed to arrive at the breakfast table just in time for the silent prayer of thanks. He sat beside Eve the entire meal, not looking at her or anyone else. If anybody noticed, they didn't speak up.

The family laughed and teased as they ate, often talking over one another. Eve tried to keep up with every conversation, but as usual, it was near impossible. Bay went on about a new type of poinsettia plant that was growing well in the greenhouse. Benjamin complained about the cost of shipping for items he had to order for the harness shop, and Jesse told a long story about a goat that seemed to go nowhere and arrived at no conclusion. James and Josiah managed to each spill their milk not once, but twice over the course of the meal. It was a typical breakfast.

Levi spoke to Eve a couple of times during the meal, and not unkindly. She could tell he was upset with himself about their disagreement the night before, but he didn't say anything more than to ask her to pass the butter or another blueberry muffin. When everyone scattered after breakfast, Levi lingered in the mudroom, fussing with his hat. It seemed as if he wanted to speak with Eve privately, but she gave him no mind. She knew she had to take matters into her own hands, and that was what she intended to do.

When everyone had set off on their day's business, including Levi, who would be working in his shop today, Eve helped Tara clean up. Tara chattered as they went about their familiar tasks, talking about plans to go with her friend Chloe to pick sunflowers in a neighbor's field that afternoon.

When the kitchen was at last *ret* up, Eve hung the damp dish towels on the handles of the stove and asked Tara, "Do you know where your *mam* is?"

Tara was moving food around in the open refrigerator, taking stock to be sure everything was on the grocery list for shopping the following day. "In her sewing room, I think. James tore the knees out of another pair of pants." She rolled her eyes.

Eve chuckled and walked out of the kitchen. She followed a long hallway to the open door of Rosemary's sewing room. She heard the steady sound of a treadle sewing machine coming from inside, and she took a deep breath. If she was going to do this, now was the time. She took a deep breath, said a silent prayer and knocked on the doorframe. "Rosemary?"

The sound of the sewing machine paused. "*Ya!* Come in."

Eve walked into the room to see Rosemary seated at her Singer sewing machine. The sound began again as Levi's stepmother used both feet to pump the treadle and eased the seam of a small pair of navy trousers through the needle.

"Almost done. Just two more seams," Rosemary said above the *click, click* sound measured out by the rhythm of her feet.

"No hurry," Eve answered, gazing around. Rosemary had invited her to use the sewing machine anytime and, on several occasions, she'd spent a comfortable afternoon here. Besides the blue dress she had made, she'd also sewn herself a second nightgown and a pale green work shirt for Levi. She was presently working on a black wool coat for her husband to wear to church when it grew colder. The one currently hanging on a hook in their bedroom was threadbare at the cuffs and missing a hook and eye, and he had admitted sheepishly that he had been wearing it since before his family moved to Hickory Grove.

Nearly square, the sewing room was painted a pale blue with two large windows with a blue, white and yellow rag rug in the middle of the floor. There were two rocking chairs placed side by side where sisters, or mother and daughter, or mother-in-law and daughter-in-law, could sit and knit. One wall boasted an oversize walnut cabinet that looked like it had come from an old millinery shop. Eve recognized the style from one she had seen displayed in a Lancaster fabric store once. Open drawers in Rosemary's cabinet revealed various sizes of thread, needles, scissors and paper patterns. A small knotty pine table with turned legs stood between the windows, and in its center was a big terracotta planter filled with flowers.

Tara had told Eve that her mother changed the flowers with the seasons. While there were multicolored zinnias blooming in it now, this fall, there would be white or gold chrysanthemums. In December, Rosemary would replace the mums with poinsettias, and after Epiphany, it would be filled with herbs like rosemary and tarragon to be used in winter soups and stews. When Tara had told Eve this, she had giggled. Her mother's naming of her daughters had been unusual for an Amish woman, she had admitted. And then she had gone on to explain. Tara was named after the herb tarragon. Her sister Nettie's name was actually Nettle, Bay's was Bay Laurel and her oldest sister, Lovey, was Lovage.

"Ach," Rosemary cried as she ceased pumping the treadle. "One seam left to go, and the thread breaks in the needle." She raised her hands as if in surrender. "Always happens, doesn't it?" She turned on the bench where she sat to look at Eve and fell silent for a moment. "What's troubling you, Eve? I can see it on your face."

Eve clasped her hands and looked down at her clean, bare feet. Suddenly, she was unsure of herself. Was this a mistake to come to Rosemary? Was it wrong to go against her husband's wishes? The husband was the head of the family. Some believed that as his wife, she was required to obey him.

"Let me guess. This has something to do with that dejected look on Levi's face that we saw at the breakfast table." Rosemary got to her feet. "And my stubborn husband."

Eve slowly lifted her gaze, steeling herself so that she wouldn't cry. *"Ya."*

"Then tell me, but first, I think you need a hug. Then you should sit down and unburden yourself." Rosemary smiled kindly. "I can't tell you how pleased I am that you feel you can come to me, Eve."

Eve's voice trembled a little when she spoke. "Levi wouldn't like it if he knew I was here. He… He thinks this is between him and Benjamin."

"Ya." Rosemary planted her hands on her hips. "But we've left it up to those two for the hind part of two months, haven't we? And have they settled it? They have not. So it's time we women had a hand it." She opened her arms. "Come on. Let me give you a hug, *Dochter*. You look as if you need it."

Eve hesitated, then stepped closer and allowed Rosemary to hug her. "This is all my fault," she told Rosemary, fighting against tears again. Her mother-in-law's arms felt good around her and she hugged her back. "Levi is such a good man and I've ruined his life."

Rosemary clasped Eve's shoulders and leaned back to look into her eyes. *"Ne,* you have made his life. And life has its hills and valleys. Now come and sit with me and tell me what's weighing on your heart. Because I have to tell you, I've about had enough of this quarrel with these men of ours. They're bringing disharmony to our home and heartburn to Benjamin's stomach."

Rosemary smiled with amusement and Eve couldn't help but smile back.

So she and Rosemary sat side by side and Eve told her story. She started with the charming Jemuel Yoder at the market and barely took a breath until she finished with her and Levi's wedding day. Throughout the story, Rosemary listened patiently, asking questions occasionally and patting Eve's knee when her voice trembled.

When she was done, Eve took a deep breath and slid farther into the rocking chair. She was so short that only her toes touched the floor when she sat all the way back.

"Oh, my poor dear," Rosemary said when Eve fell silent. "I'm so sad about everything you've been through." She reached out and squeezed Eve's hand. "And thankful that God brought you to us. You're truly a blessing to this family."

Eve took a shuddering breath. "I don't think Levi feels that way right now."

"And why do you say that?" Rosemary asked pointedly. "Has Levi said that to you?"

Eve thought before she answered. "He has not. He... He promised to protect my secret. He said he would never tell anyone about Jemuel. About my father."

Rosemary smiled kindly. "That's our Levi. A kind, admirable man. A good man."

"He is a good man," Eve said, twisting a bit of her apron between her fingers. "I don't deserve him."

"Nonsense," Rosemary responded. "Do you love him?" Her question was pointed. "Or at least do you think you can love him in time? I'm not talking about the girlish, giggling kind of love. I'm talking about the deep love that binds us all of our days."

"He doesn't love me."

Rosemary gave a little laugh. "I suspect he does. Whether he knows it or not, that's why this has been so hard for him. That's why he can't ask you to let him tell his father why you married." She took Eve's hand. "And you didn't answer my question. *Do you love Levi?*"

The warmth of Rosemary's hand gave Eve the strength to respond with honesty. "I do love him. And that's why I have to make this right." She went on faster. "I can't stand having his father think he committed a sin he didn't commit. Nor his community. And I can't have our bishop and our congregation believing that, either," she added firmly.

Both women were silent for a moment. Then Eve said, "I want to talk to Bishop Simon. I want to tell him everything. Will you take me?"

Rosemary squeezed Eve's hand and got up from her rocking chair. She paced one way across the sewing room and then the other. "Are you certain about this?" she asked. "You have the right—you and Levi have the right—to keep this to yourselves."

Eve set her jaw. "I'm certain."

"And are you certain this isn't because you want Levi to be a preacher? Some women, especially young women, think it makes them more important in the community. To have a husband who serves as preacher or deacon."

Eve drew back in horror. "Why would I want my husband to spend long hours away from me, planning his sermons, making visits with the bishop and deacon, always having the responsibility of the church on his shoulders? I don't know if Levi is supposed to be a preacher." She got to her feet. "That's up to God. But I want Bishop Simon to know that Levi Miller is a Godly man. And I want Benjamin to know the truth about his son."

Rosemary came to a rest in front of Eve. "And you've really thought this through?" she asked, looking into Eve's eyes.

"*Ya.* I've thought for weeks that it was the right thing to do, and then when Levi's name came up at church, I knew…" She glanced away and then back to Rosemary. "I prayed on it and God answered me," she said, half-afraid Rosemary wouldn't believe her. Who was she, a plain little wren of a woman, to hear God's voice?

Rosemary took a deep breath. "Well, I suppose a trip to Bishop Simon's place is in order," she declared, walking to the sewing room door.

Eve felt a moment of panic. "What? Now?"

"*Ya,* now. No time like the present, and if we go now, we can still be back in time to get dinner on the table."

And so they did. Eve was surprised how easy Bishop Simon was to talk to. Over a glass of lemonade on his front porch, in Rosemary's presence, she spilled out the whole story, and with it her tears of regret as well as hope.

The bishop thanked Eve for coming to him and told her again and again what a fine wife she was and what a good life God had in store for her and Levi. Then he instructed her to say nothing to Levi or Benjamin. To leave the matter to him. He told Eve and Rosemary that he needed to pray on the matter and that he would be by their farm in the next couple of days.

So Eve waited, busying herself with canning tomatoes and beets and making pickles with Tara, and trying not to dream of a life with Levi and a houseful of little ones.

Chapter Twelve

Levi was giving a piece of trim work for the dashboard a final sanding when, from the window in his shop, he spotted the bishop's buggy pulling in. His first thought, childishly, was to slip into the warren of halls and rooms his father had constructed in the old barn and hide until Bishop Simon gave up looking for him and went home.

But even if he avoided Simon today, Levi couldn't hide from him forever. And he couldn't hide from the decision he had made when he offered to marry Eve and promised to never tell anyone why. So if the bishop asked Levi his side of the story, Levi would tell him nothing. He would not sacrifice his vow to his wife, not even to defend his own morality. And that would be that. The bishop would say Levi left him no choice but to remove his name from the list of preacher candidates. And that would be that.

Levi didn't really want to be a preacher anyway. It was a lot of work that took a man away from family and work, often causing financial consequences. And being a preacher, responsible for speaking God's word to His people, was a heavy burden on a man's soul.

Levi didn't feel he had a calling to stand up in front of a congregation and preach God's word. He had been as surprised as anyone when his name had come up, not once but three times.

Of course, had this whole mess unraveled differently and he was a candidate, and he did choose the hymnal with the slip of paper, he would not have turned down the position. It would have been his duty to his congregation and to God. Because when God called a man to be a preacher, the man responded with faith that his Lord would give him the words to speak.

But all of that was a moot point now, Levi thought with a tired sigh. With time, the whole thing would blow over and few would even remember who could have been a preacher but wasn't chosen. But Levi would remember. He would recall that members of his tight-knit community had deemed him unfit for the role. And his father could be counted among them.

With resignation, Levi flipped over the board he was sanding and ran his finger along the edge, feeling for any burrs. At least the construction of his very first buggy was going well. That was something, wasn't it?

"Levi," Bishop Simon called as he walked into the buggy shop. He was wearing black pants, a white shirt, black vest and his wide-brimmed black hat—this was an official call.

Levi glanced up and acknowledged the older man with a nod.

The bishop was a short, round man with perpetually rosy cheeks and frameless eyeglasses that he wore on the tip of his bulbous nose. When Levi had first met Bishop Simon, he had wondered how the glasses didn't slip off his nose and fall on the ground.

Levi liked the older man. He was kind and jovial, a good man who took the responsibility of looking after his flock seriously.

His hands deep in his pockets, Bishop Simon studied the new buggy frame Levi had resting up off the floor on wood chocks. "Going to be a fine-looking carriage," he mused. "I've been told you're a gifted craftsman, Levi. And the telling was accurate." He took a step closer to the shell and peered down over the top of his glasses. "Annie and I have been talking about getting a new buggy. I'm still driving the one my father drove before me. Body has been patched more times than I can tell you, front axle keeps bending, and the windshield is leaking again."

"I can have a look at the windshield. I might be able to pop it out and then put it back in with a new seal and caulk it. Axles can be replaced. If you just want to fix it," Levi told him. "If it's a new buggy you're looking for, I'm taking orders. This one is for my brother-in-law Eli. He and Ginger are in need of a bigger buggy."

Bishop Simon nodded approvingly. "I'll discuss it with Annie. I'm thinking a new one might be in order." He slid his hands from his pockets as he turned to look at Levi. "Do you have time to talk to me for a few minutes, Levi?"

Feeling his shoulders slump, Levi set down his sanding block. *"Ya,"* he said dejectedly. "I've time." He wondered how he would tell Eve his name had been withdrawn because their congregation and their bishop thought him unfit. It wasn't a thing a man wanted to have to admit to his wife. And in his case, it would lead to another discussion with her insisting he had to tell the bishop why he had married her.

Bishop Simon faced Levi. "I'm going to come right out and say this."

Levi heard a strange buzzing in his head, and he glanced away, trying to emotionally steady himself.

"I know everything," Bishop Simon said.

Levi blinked, looking back at the older man in confusion. "Everything about what?"

"About Eve. About why you married her. Why there was no formal betrothal before the wedding."

It took a moment for Levi to process the bishop's words. Surely he had misheard. But the way Simon was considering him, it didn't seem that he had. Because Simon didn't look disappointed, he looked...*pleased*.

"I'm sorry?" Levi narrowed his gaze. "*How* do you know?"

"Eve told me. Yesterday."

Levi's eyes widened in shock. "She came to you?"

"She did. She and Rosemary. Your wife came because of what some people in our congregation have been saying," the bishop explained. "It was important to Eve that I know that you marrying her, without following our usual traditions, was for honorable reasons."

Levi stared at the bishop, still not quite believing what he was hearing. "Eve told you?" he repeated.

Bishop Simon nodded, the slightest smile turning up one corner of his mouth. "She told me the whole story, start to finish. I was sorely sorry to hear how her father treated her." The white cat, Snowball, curled around his leg and he leaned over to stroke her soft coat. "She made a mistake in not listening to her father when he warned her about such men, even among our own. But young folks make mistakes." His smile broadened. "As do old folks. Which brings me to the apology I owe you."

Levi had no idea what to say. What reason could a bishop have to apologize to him?

Simon cleared his throat, looking up at Levi through the smudged lenses of his glasses. "I have to admit that I kept expecting you to show up at my house to talk over whatever brought you and Eve to this place in your lives. I anticipated a confession and forgiveness for your and Eve's sins. Only as time passed, and you didn't come to me, did I begin to suspect there was more to the story than at first glance."

"I can't believe she told you," Levi murmured, a strange sensation in his chest. He pressed his hand to his beating heart. *For him.* Eve had done this for *him.* She had confessed her own missteps to the bishop for Levi's sake.

"She didn't have to tell you," Levi heard himself say. "I would never have asked her to do that for me."

"*Ne*, she did not have to tell me. She explained that. She said that you had promised her no one would ever have to know. And I believe that you would never have told, Levi. Which is why she came to me on her own. It was important to her that I know the truth about you. To know you did not act inappropriately. She wanted me to know that you should be eligible for the position of preacher."

"But I told her I didn't want to be a preacher anyway."

"I don't think Eve thought it mattered what you want. She believes it should be left to God. And I agree." Bishop Simon stroked his beard. "That said, Eve told me, should you be chosen, you would make a fine preacher. She talked to me about what a man of faith you are. How your quiet faith has made hers stronger."

"Quiet faith?" Levi asked. He was completely overwhelmed by the sacrifice Eve had made for him. And her confidence in him. He was so astounded, in fact, that he was struggling to follow the conversation.

"Eve says you live your faith every day in deed as much as word and that you set a good example for her. She said you were there for her, a stranger, when her own family wasn't willing to stand up for her."

Levi smiled, not because his wife had praised him to the bishop, but because she thought those things of him. "She's a good woman. Better than I deserve."

"I think you deserve each other. Talking to Eve, and knowing you as I do, I believe this was God's plan. Bringing you together." He tilted his head. "An unusual way to bring a man and woman together in matrimony, I'd admit. But as Paul said in his letter to the Romans, 'And we know that all things work together for good to them that love God, to them who are called according to his purpose.'"

Levi, actually feeling a little light-headed, sat down on a stool his father used when tackling a time-consuming task. His head was spinning. Suddenly, all he could think of was that he needed to talk to Eve.

Simon stroked his long, gray beard. "I have to say, Levi, I was uneasy when others expressed concern over your eligibility to be a preacher. Not so much because I was worried about you, but because unrest of this sort is not good for our community. I didn't know why you had married so swiftly, but as I said, I suspected you had good reason. I told your father that when he came to me."

Levi looked up. "*Dat* came to you about me?"

"*Ya*, more than once. I counseled that he be patient,

and we prayed together. We discussed the idea that he needed to believe in you and have faith in God. I told him all would be revealed in time. If it was God's will." He raised his hands and let them fall. "And all has been revealed. So I will not be withdrawing your name. Should you, when the time comes, choose the hymnal with a slip of paper in it, you will be one of my preachers. And your wife is right, I think. A fine preacher you'll make."

Feeling a little steadier, Levi got up from his father's stool. "I don't know. Maybe I should just let you withdraw my name, Bishop. I don't want anyone in the congregation to know about Eve's past. It's not their business. I don't mind that you know what happened to Eve because she told you, but I don't want others to know and possibly judge her. I see no need."

The bishop chewed on that thought for a moment. "I agree, Levi. It's not necessary that the other parishioners know the circumstances. I've prayed heavily on this matter and come to the conclusion that it's not my place to interfere in God's ways. I will not be withdrawing your name. Your name was offered up, so you must be one of the men to choose a hymnal."

Levi ran his hand over his short beard, still not used to feeling it. "But what will you say to anyone who questions my suitability? Some folks are going to want an explanation. Details." Eunice Gruber immediately came to mind, but he didn't say it.

"They won't be getting details from me. I'll tell the congregation I know why you and Eve married and that I have deemed you a suitable candidate. That will be the end of the discussion."

A knock on the inner door that led deeper into the

barn sounded and both men turned around to face it. *"Ya?"* Levi called, wondering who was knocking on the shop door from the inside. Any potential customers would be approaching from the outside entrance.

The door swung open and his father filled the doorway. *"Oll recht* if I come in now?" he asked.

"Now?" Levi asked, looking to Bishop Simon.

"I told your father what happened to Eve," the bishop admitted.

"Don't be angry with him," Levi's father said, crossing the shop to join them. "I went to Simon yesterday, not knowing Eve and Rosemary had been there. I was pretty upset about what happened. Even if you weren't my son, I would have been upset by what some members of our congregation were saying," he told Levi.

Levi felt a weight fall from his shoulders. "So you know, *Dat.*"

His father held his gaze and, in the older man's eyes, Levi saw sorrow and happiness and an overwhelming sense of pride.

"I know," Levi's *dat* murmured.

"I'm going to leave you two," Bishop Simon said, backing away. "I'll speak with you both before we meet for services again."

Levi waited for the bishop to go before speaking. It actually gave him a moment to collect his thoughts and think on what he wanted to say because now that his father knew the truth, Levi's anger had fallen away. And he was glad of the release of that heavy burden. He was still trying to form the words in his head when his father beat him to it.

"I cannot tell you how sorry I am that I thought you had done something you had not, *Sohn.* I'm sorry I allowed doubt to overshadow what I knew of you, what I knew here." He laid his hand on his chest over his heart.

Emotion rose in Levi's throat. "It's *oll recht, Dat.*"

"Ne," he argued, emotion thick in his throat. "It's *not*. When you called from the train station to say you had wed, I should have trusted you. When you arrived and I met Eve, I should have known there was more to your marriage than you were telling me." He bowed his head. "I should have just asked you."

Levi shook his head. "I wouldn't have told you. I had promised Eve."

His father smiled and sighed. "Ah, Eve. Our Eve. When Bishop Simon told me about her visit, I was as proud of her as I am of you, Levi." His voice caught in his throat and his eyes grew moist. "You married her for different reasons than we usually marry, but they were the right reasons."

Levi hesitated then, wondering if he should ask the question that was on the tip of his tongue. Or would it be better to let it go, because what did it matter now? It was over.

The words fell from Levi's mouth anyway. "If you suspected there was a reason why we married, why did you not support me Sunday when people were saying I shouldn't be considered? Why did you say God wouldn't choose me?"

"What?" His father stared at him, his bushy eyebrows knitting. "I never said God would not choose you. When did you think I said that?"

"I was standing nearby, *Dat*. You were all at John Fisher's fence."

His father hesitated for a moment, thinking. "I know what conversation you speak of, but I did not say God wouldn't choose you. I never said that because I've lived long enough not to assume I know God's ways. What I *said* that day was that we had to trust the process. I said that if God didn't want you to be a preacher, you wouldn't be chosen." He raised his hand and let it fall. "The reason I didn't just come out and say you should be one of the candidates was because some of those men might have assumed I was taking up for you because you were my son. Because I wanted you to a preacher so I could walk around telling people you were." He paused. "I never said you wouldn't be chosen because that wouldn't have been for me to say, *Sohn*. Only *Gott* could make that decision."

Levi exhaled, thinking back to that day. He had been so upset. Had his emotions clouded his senses? Had he heard wrong? He racked his brain and realized that now that his father had spoken those words, he couldn't *actually* remember his father saying differently. He pressed his hand to his forehead, pushing his hat back. Now he felt foolish. He had gotten himself so worked up about something that had never been said.

"You have a good woman there, you know," his father said. "She loves you so much. She would do anything for you."

Levi's head snapped up when he heard his father use the word love.

Eve loved him?

Where had his father gotten that idea? He was mistaken.

Wasn't he? She had certainly not said she loved him. But that didn't mean it wasn't true, did it?

"I can't believe I was so reckless in my thinking and my behavior." Levi's father was still talking. "I was shocked when you called to tell me you were married. And my first thought wasn't to believe you had taken liberties with Eve, but that there was a Godlier explanation. But then by the time you arrived, I'd had time to get myself worked up. I… I think that secretly I was angry that you didn't include me in your decision to marry. I was upset that you made the decision on your own. And I… I didn't get to decide for you. Or at least help you decide." He shook his head. "That makes no sense, does it? I raised you to be a good man, to make good decisions on your own, and then I was mad that you did?"

Levi smiled, realizing that an amazing calm was settling over him. His father knew now why he had married Eve, and he'd not had to break his promise to his wife. He exhaled and took a deep, cleansing breath. His mind shifted to thoughts of Eve, even as his father continued to talk. Levi wondered where she was. Up at the house, he hoped. Because he needed to talk to her. And he needed to talk to her now.

"Rosemary warned me I was getting myself worked up without knowing the full story," his father went on, beginning to pace. "But I didn't listen to her. I—"

"Dat," Levi interrupted, stepping in front of his father. "I'm so thankful for your words, but I have to go. I have to find Eve. I have to thank her for going to Bishop Simon."

Levi's father smiled. *"Ya,* you should go. We can talk more later, *Sohn."*

Before Levi could turn away, his father wrapped his arms around Levi's shoulders and hugged him tightly. Then, without another word, he released him, and Levi went in search of his wife.

* * *

Levi looked for Eve in the kitchen, but no one was there and an illogical sense of panic flared in his chest. Where was his wife? Had she reached the limit of her patience with him and left him?

But where would she go? And after breakfast, she'd told him she'd see him for dinner. She'd made no plans to leave him or go anywhere. So she had to be there somewhere.

Levi found Tara feeding the chickens and she sent him to the garden. The short walk from the clothes-line in the side yard to the garden in the back seemed to stretch for miles. Then, at last, he spotted Eve in a row of summer squash, filling her apron with the ripe yellow vegetables.

Levi thanked God under his breath and called out, "Eve!"

She glanced up, and seeing him, smiled hesitantly. As he approached, she looked uneasy, which he completely understood. Things had been going so well between them the last few weeks. They had been getting to know each other, and the better he knew his wife, the more he found he liked her. And she liked him. At least he *thought* she did. But then the business with choosing preachers had happened and Levi had become brooding the way he had been when they arrived, separating himself emotionally from her. Instead of cleaving to his wife as God wanted married couples to do, in the face of hardship, he had abandoned her.

And her response to his emotional abandonment had been to go to their bishop and confess to him the mistakes she had made. To protect Levi's reputation, she had sacrificed herself and possibly her own reputation. Why would she do that after the way he had treated her?

Levi's father's words pushed their way into his head: *She loves you so much.*

Did she love him? And if she did, would she forgive him for all the mistakes he had made since they wed?

Levi hurried down the path between a row of summer squash and zucchini. "I've been looking for you everywhere."

"You have?" She dropped the squash, one by one, from her dusty, oversize apron into a basket. "Why? Is everything all right?"

He walked up to her, taking her hands in his. "I hope so, Eve." He looked into her brown eyes that seemed, at this moment, to be the most beautiful eyes he had ever seen. He studied her round face, taking in the length of her eyelashes, the pink in her cheeks and the bowed shape of her mouth. He had the sudden urge to kiss her on her beautiful mouth.

But he didn't because, at this moment, he didn't feel he had the right to kiss her.

"Bishop Simon came to talk to me, and he told me what you did." He squeezed both of her hands in his. "I can't believe you told him everything. For me," he added, the words catching in his throat.

She nodded, her smile still hesitant. "I did."

"But why?" he asked.

Her brows knitted. "Because it was the right thing to do, Levi."

"But we agreed no one needed to know."

"I know we did, but, thinking back, I realized that decision was made in haste. It was a selfish choice. It didn't occur to me that you family, your community would question your motive for marrying me." She shook her head. "We should have told Benjamin and Rosemary as soon as we got here. And then, when your name came up as a candidate for preacher and folks questioned it, I knew I had to do something."

He drew his head back. "How did you know about that?"

"Tara."

He frowned.

"Don't be angry with her. She loves you and wants the best for you. She only told me because you didn't." Eve paused and then said firmly, "You should have told me about the men at church and what they said, Levi. You're my husband. You're supposed to tell me those kinds of things."

"I know, I know. You're right." He glanced up, squinting in the bright sunlight that was beating down on them. "You want to sit down for a minute? There's something else I want to tell you."

"Of course."

Levi led Eve by her hand out of the vegetable garden and into Rosemary's fenced-in herb garden. Along one side of the white picket fence was a small, oblong pond with cattails, miniature lily pads and a decorative rock border. A wrought-iron bench sat beside the pond under the shade of several pink flowering crepe myrtle trees. The pond had been there when they bought the farm from Englishers, Rosemary had told her. It was the little pond and the fenced-in herb garden that had sold her on the property as much as the amount of land and rambling white farmhouse.

"Let's sit over here," Levi told her.

Eve was so relieved that Levi wasn't angry with her about going to Bishop Simon that, for the first time since she'd spoken with Simon she actually felt as if she could breathe again. In celebration, she inhaled deeply.

At the bench, Levi waited for her to sit first and then he sat down beside her, and not on the other end, but right beside her. He took her hand again and she shifted, pleased and uncomfortable at the same time. Even if Levi had been angry about her going to the bishop, she knew it had been the right thing to do. But knowing her husband wasn't angry made her heart sing. But she was also concerned. What did he want to talk to her about?

Eve waited for what seemed like a long time, waiting for Levi to speak. She could tell by the look on his face that he wanted to say something, he just wasn't ready. To ease the tension, she asked him, "What did Bishop Simon say about your name coming up for one of the new preachers?"

"He said that I would be one of the men to choose from the stack of hymnals the next time the congregation meets."

She looked up at him, thrilled by the feel of Levi's hand in hers and his undivided attention. "And what about what the men were saying about you?"

"Bishop Simon said he would tell anyone who brought the issue up that he had discussed with us why we married as we did and that he deemed me eligible to accept the job of preacher, should I be chosen. He said no one else ever need know."

Her palm feeling sweaty, she pulled her hand from his. "I think we need to tell Benjamin. If Rosemary hasn't already told him."

"The bishop told him." His voice broke with emotion, emotion Eve felt in her chest along with him. "And *Dat* came into the shop and talked to me after Simon."

"And everything is okay between you now?"

Levi smiled, his relief obvious. "It is."

"Oh, Levi," she sighed. "I'm happy for you. I know how your father's disappointment was weighing on your heart."

"*Dat* said he was sorry for being angry and disappointed with me. He also said he thinks I would make a good preacher." He shrugged. "If it's God's will."

"Of course you would be a good preacher!" she exclaimed. "I told Bishop Simon that."

"He told me," Levi said, sounding almost bashful.

"I think the faith you could show a congregation, faith in scripture and in God's word, could do so much good here in Hickory Grove."

"I'm young for a preacher, though," he said.

"*Ya*, but I'm not sure that matters. And I bet your father thinks the same," she told him, happy beyond words for him. No matter what he said, she knew how upset he had been about the riff between him and his father. And that had upset her because she had been responsible for Benjamin's assumptions, if not directly, then indirectly.

"Oh, Levi. I'm so happy for you." Without thinking, she threw her arms around him, then, realizing what she had done, started to pull away.

But Levi held on to her and hugged her tightly. "I've been such a fool, Eve," he whispered in her ear. "I'm so sorry for my behavior toward you. God gave me a gift in you. He gave me a beautiful wife and I was so caught up in myself that it took me too long to see that." He leaned back so that he was looking into her eyes. "But

I see it now. And…and I need to tell you that standing in my shop, listening to Bishop Simon and then to my father, I realized…"

He swallowed hard and glanced away.

"You realized what, Levi?" she whispered. "Tell me. You can tell me anything."

"I realized…" He met her gaze again and this time it didn't stray. "I realized that I've fallen in love with you, Eve. I don't know how." He shook his head. "Or when, but it's happened. I love you."

Eve didn't realize she had been holding her breath until it escaped in a great sigh. "You do?" Tears welled in her eyes.

"I do, and I don't care that you don't love me." He kept gazing into her eyes, talking faster than before as if he needed to get it all out at once. "I know that can only come in time, but—"

"Oh, Levi—"

"But I hope that someday you can love me," he went on, not seeming to have heard her. "I hope you can love me someday, if only half as much as I love you right now. I know it's a lot to ask but—"

"Levi," she interrupted and then she laughed when he finally fell silent. "I love you, too," she told him, her heart pounding in her chest.

He placed both of his hands on her cheeks and gazed into her eyes. "You do?"

She nodded, no longer even trying to fight her tears of joy. "I think I've loved you since that day in the barn when you saved me from Jemuel and my father."

They were both silent for a long time, lost in the moment, and then Levi got up off the bench. "Well, if you love me, and I love you, there's only one thing I can do." He reached for her hand.

"What's that, husband?" she asked, accepting his hand and coming to her feet. Behind her, she could hear the trickling water of the little waterfall in Rosemary's pond. The sun was warm on her face and there was a breeze carrying with it the scent of freshly cut grass and roses.

Levi faced her, taking her hand between his. "Eve, will you marry me?"

She blinked and then threw back her head in laughter, but also in joy. "Marry you?" she asked. "Levi, we're already married."

"We *are*?" he asked, sounding as if it were news to him.

Her laughter turned into giggles. "*Ya*, that's why I call you husband, and you call me wife."

"Is that so?" He moved even closer, wrapping his arms around her until they were so close that their noses were nearly touching.

"*Ya*," she giggled. "It's so."

"Huh." He looked away as if contemplating the truth of her words, then fixed his gaze on her again. "Then if we're already married, wife, I have another question for you."

The feel of Levi's arms around her, the scent of him so close, made her giddy. Her heart was singing, *He loves me! My Levi loves me!*

Her husband looked into her eyes again. "You want to hear my question?"

She nodded. "I do."

"May I kiss you?"

Eve's breath caught in her throat. "*Ya*, I would like that," she whispered.

For a long instant, Levi gazed into her eyes and then, slowly, he lowered his mouth to hers. She closed her eyes, recalling the first sweet kiss they had shared. But then, the kiss turned from one of innocence to a kiss meant to be between a man and his wife who were in love. And when Levi at last drew back, she gazed into his gray eyes.

"Wow," she whispered, knowing she was blushing.

"*Ya*, wow," he agreed.

She took in a ragged breath. "I should get back to the house with the squash before Tara comes looking for me."

"And before I kiss you again, wife," he said huskily. "And again, and again."

She looked up at him through her lashes. "Maybe tonight?" she dared to suggest in a whisper.

"*Ya*, that I can promise," he answered, his voice still husky.

And then Levi took Eve's hand and together they walked toward the garden, knowing they were on the right path, at last, to a life of happiness and love.

Epilogue

One Year Later

Enjoying the feel of the warm grass beneath her bare feet, Eve pulled a wet towel from a laundry basket and tossed it over the clothesline. Next, she grabbed two clothespins from a blue gingham bag hanging in front of her. As she attached the towel to the line with the wooden pins and reached for another towel, she glanced at Rosemary, who was hanging little boys' denim britches and blue and green shirts.

"*Ach*, I'm sorry for all of this complaining," the woman who had become a second mother to Eve said. "At my age, it's hard to do things differently sometimes. You know that Benjamin and I have given our blessing for this marriage. It's not that I think it's wrong, only that it's not the path I saw a daughter of mine taking."

Eve smiled at her across the clotheslines as she scooped up a handful of washcloths and hung each one from a corner. The sun was shining and, while it was already in the eighties, there was a nice breeze coming out of the orchard, carrying the scent of apples from the trees. "You're not complaining, *Mam*, just telling me your concerns. Sometimes we need to say things out loud to settle them in our minds."

"Ya," Rosemary said with a sigh. "And to settle them in our hearts, as well." She looked up, past Eve, and lifted her chin. "Hmm, I think you have a visitor."

"A visitor?" Eve knitted her brows. "Now? Chloe said she wasn't coming for Tara and me until after dinner." The three women had a trip to Fifer's Orchard planned to get a couple baskets of the last of the sweet corn for the season. Their own sweet corn hadn't been as plentiful as it should have been because of a fungus early in the season, and they wanted to can at least another dozen quart jars for winter.

Rosemary's mouth twitched into a smile. "It's not Chloe."

Eve glanced over her shoulder and was surprised to see Levi walking toward her, grinning. He was wearing the blue shirt she had recently made him, a shade of blue that matched her favorite dress. He was smiling so broadly that she couldn't help but smile back and giggle with happiness. Seeing him between breakfast and supper had become a welcome surprise. He had been so busy all summer with new buggy orders that sometimes he packed a cold lunch, so he didn't have to stop working to trek up to the house for dinner. "What are you doing here? I thought you and Benjamin had business in Dover and then you were going to work on your sermon for Sunday."

As it turned out, it had been God's choice for Levi to be elected preacher of the new church district, and a fine one he was becoming. Her husband was still finding his way, speaking the words of God to the congregation, but every time he stood before them, her heart swelled with pride.

"The sermon can wait. And, *ya*, we did go to Dover." His grin seemed to get even bigger. "We had an appointment with a lawyer."

"A lawyer?" Eve drew back her head, glancing at Rosemary. She could tell, at once, that Rosemary knew what their men had been up to. But her mother-in-law wasn't going to be the one to tell her.

Eve returned her gaze to her handsome husband. "Why did you have to see a lawyer?" She felt comfortable asking because in the last year, she and Levi had worked hard to always be honest with each other and to tell each other everything.

"It's a surprise," he told her. "Rosemary, okay if I borrow my wife for a little while?"

"Of course. Go." She waved Eve away with her free hand. "This is the last of my basket." She clipped a wooden pin, attaching a little boy's peach-colored shirt to the clothesline. "I'll finish up the towels and see you later."

"Are you sure?" Eve asked, even as Levi was taking her hand to lead her away.

"Go," Rosemary assured her. "Enjoy a few minutes alone with your husband."

Eve looked up at Levi, still hesitating.

"If Rosemary says go, you go," he warned her.

Eve nodded and looked back to Rosemary. "I won't be long. I'll pick the rest of the grape tomatoes and bring them in when I get back. Tara wants to have cucumber tomato salad for supper."

"Take your time," Rosemary insisted with another wave as she picked up Eve's laundry basket.

Taking Eve by the hand, Levi led her across the backyard.

"Where are we going?" Eve asked, tickled to have him to herself in the middle of the day.

"I told you. It's a surprise." He squeezed her hand. "How's Rosemary today?"

"Oh, she's fine. You know how she is. She just wants everything to be perfect for Bay's wedding. She wants it to be the same." She shrugged. "And it's not going to be like Lovey's and Ginger's. It can't be."

Levi sighed. "I understand." He smiled down at her. "You're good to be so patient with her." He cut his eyes at her. "And I'm sure that Bay will be forever grateful for your assistance in easing the tension."

She smiled up at him, her heart so full. In the last year, her whole world had changed so much. Not only had she gained a husband to love and be loved by, but she had gained an extended family that had welcomed her with open arms and a glad heart. "I'm thankful I can help."

Levi leaned down and kissed her cheek.

"Levi!" she murmured, pressing her fingertips to the place where he'd kissed her as she looked around to be sure no one had seen them. "Really. You're so naughty. Kissing me in broad daylight where anyone can see."

He shrugged. "There's no one around, but if there was, what would they say? 'Oh my, how terrible that Levi loves his wife so much that he kisses her in broad daylight?'"

Eve giggled. "Tell me where we're going."

"The pond."

"The pond?" She made a face. "I don't have time to go fishing and I know you certainly don't."

He clasped her hand in his warm one. "We're not going fishing." Releasing her hand, he looked down at her, pretending to be irritated. "What makes you think I have time to fish in the middle of the day, Wife?" He waved both arms, speaking in a fake gruff voice. "I have work to do. Important work. *Man's* work."

She laughed, catching his hand and pulling it down. "Tell me why we're going to the pond," she begged.

"If I told you," he said, taking her hand in his again, "it won't be a surprise, will it?"

So, hand in hand, they took the path through the orchard and down the old dirt road that led to the pond. As they walked, they talked, though not about anything vastly important. Eve told him about the mouse she found in the pantry and the cheese and potato casserole recipe she was tweaking. Levi told her about a new order for a buggy and his concern that he was going to have to start a waiting list because he was worried about overcommitting himself and ultimately disappointing his customers.

They passed through a field of milkweed and wild black-eyed Susans, and the pond came into view. Eve stopped and glanced around. Nothing looked any different from how it had the previous week when they'd gone fishing on a Saturday afternoon. "Okay, we're here," she said, resting her hands on her hips. "Where's my surprise?"

"Just a little farther," Levi told her and together they walked past the pond and up a little bluff where weeds, saplings and grass grew.

"Here it is!" Levi declared, facing the pond, opening his arms wide.

She turned in a full circle looking for something, anything that looked different. But it all looked the same and she was beginning to think he was pulling her leg. "This is my surprise? A bunch of weeds?"

"*Ya*, well, no." His hand shot out and he grabbed her hand. "Careful, you don't want to walk into the wall."

Smiling, she looked at him suspiciously. "What wall?"

He moved to stand beside her and together they gazed at the pond in the distance. "This is the front wall of our house," he whispered in her ear.

Eve's jaw dropped and she looked up at her husband. "Our house," she breathed. "Here?" She looked out at the pond again. Dragonflies flew lazy circles around the cattails on one end, and there was a cacophony of frog and insect song.

He was smiling down on her. "Right here," he said softly. "If this is where you want to live. *Dat* and I went to the lawyer's today so he could give us this land. You and I now own fifteen acres, and they include the pond." He caught a wisp of hair at her temple and tucked it behind her ear. "If you don't like this view, we can find another spot." He pointed west. "We have woods over there, if you prefer that."

"Oh, Levi," she murmured, tearing up as she studied the pond, *their* pond. "This is perfect."

"I thought you would like it. Which was why I wanted to surprise you," he told her.

She nibbled on her bottom lip. "But I don't have a surprise for you."

He shook his head. "I don't need a surprise. All I need is you, Eve."

"Wait," she said suddenly. "On second thought, I do have a surprise for you. You might have to wait for it, though."

It was his turn to grin suspiciously. "And what am I waiting for?"

She took his hand and pressed it to her rounded belly. At five months pregnant, she was, at last, showing, which made her so happy. It was finally becoming real: her marriage, the love she and Levi shared, and now their baby.

Levi gently caressed her belly. "*Ya*, I know I'll have to wait on this, but this isn't exactly a surprise." His grin was wry. "I've known about our little one for months."

"But that's not your surprise," she told him, beginning to slowly move his hand to different places on her belly. "Try here." She pushed his hand a little harder and was rewarded with a response.

The movement so startled Levi that he pulled his hand away, staring at her swollen belly, covered by her favorite blue dress and an oversize white apron. "Is that…" He looked up at her and then at his hand on her abdomen, then back to his wife. "That's our baby?"

She teared up again. Everything these days made her cry. "*Ya*, our little *bobbel*, husband."

The baby gave another kick, and Levi inhaled sharply and looked down at Eve, his face full of wonder. "Our *bobbel*, Eve. We're going to have a baby."

She laughed, covering his hand with hers again. "*Ya*, I know, Levi." She lifted one foot, showing him a bare ankle. "And hot days like today, I've the swelling to prove it."

Smiling down at her, Levi slid his hand from her belly to wrap his arms around her and hug her tightly. "*Danke*, Eve."

She laughed and snuggled against his broad chest. "For what?"

"For marrying me. For forgiving me for all the mistakes I made the first months we were married. For loving me. For carrying our son or daughter."

She slid her arms around his neck, gazing up into his blue-gray eyes. "You're welcome."

"I love you, wife," he whispered in her ear.

Eve opened her eyes to gaze over his shoulder at the pond that would soon grace their front yard. "And I love you, husband."

And then she kissed him on the mouth in broad daylight and silently thanked God in heaven for Levi and his family and the love He blessed her with every day.

* * * * *

HIS AMISH WIFE'S
HIDDEN PAST

Mindy Steele

To Julie and Connie

Thank you.

In the fear of the LORD is strong confidence:
and his children shall have a place of refuge.
—*Proverbs* 14:26

Chapter One

Daniel Raber stood on his mill office porch, watching his two hired mill hands amble toward their buggies. Another long day was over and Daniel was glad to see it go. Even he was feeling the effects of rushing to finish another lumber order in his tired bones.

September had started out humid and full of misery, but today, as ashen clouds moved gradually overhead, he felt the change of the seasons ignite. A slight chill of a rare northern wind blew over the Kentucky dirt. He looped both thumbs into his suspenders, closed his eyes, and inhaled the cool whiff mingled with sawdust and dusty earth. Life was shifting again. Imbalance was absolute.

Opening his eyes, he shoved the inkling aside. He had long broken away from trusting his gut, accepting *Gott*'s will in his daily life, but even in trusting *Gott*, one couldn't ignore awareness.

Slapping his dusty straw hat against his britches leg, he headed for the house. It was a mere stroll away over one slight rise in an earth dressed in pastured grasses where his horses and a few lowly cattle grazed. He had a lot to be thankful for. A successful milling business, a comfy home and all the things one needed for a peaceful, content life. So why today was he feeling off-kilter? He had long been cured of his bouts of melancholy, and learned to never look back, just forward.

Late-afternoon skies threatened rain above, but Daniel doubted they would make good on it. He finished milking, managed to wrangle four pesky goats back into their fences and put together a nice meal for one before the first stars winked. He was used to solitude within the quiet two-story home, but there were days when he missed companionship, the sense of family. He had his community, and it was enough, mostly, but occasionally when the rains lingered too long or the nights were simply cold and dreary, that loneliness snagged hold and left him wanting.

He was thirty-six, too old to be a bachelor, too young to start courting again. However, a family seemed to be niggling his thoughts of late. No one had caught his attention, not even Margaret Sayer, who made a habit of visiting every Tuesday with a new dish for him to sample. It was selfish, he thought, daring to ask *Gott* for more after He directed Daniel home and blessed him with so much already.

He turned off the gas burner and removed the pan of boiled potatoes from the stove. He sprinkled a dash of salt and set them by his plate before fetching the leftover chicken from the oven. It was a good thing he had tried his hand at cooking growing up when *Mudder* encouraged it. *A man who can cook will never go hungry,* *Mudder* had said. He poured himself a glass of water and took his seat at the head of the table.

The dim room grew dimmer, eerily so. Maybe that

storm was going to hit Miller's Creek after all. Daniel
lowered his head to pray for the void in his life to be
filled, ignoring the first pings on the porch roof. His
animals were safe and secure in the barn, his business,
the same, and the house had proven years ago when
a tornado blew near that it could withstand a mighty
storm sure enough. So why did he feel unsettled? He
only got that gut-jerk feeling when something bad was
about to happen. So he prayed for strength.

Halfway into his supper, a hard knock came at the
door. He pushed back his chair and went to answer. The
wind outside howled, the rain gaining momentum, making a racket against the tin roofs of the porch, barn and
outbuildings. He opened the door and found himself
looking down at his uncle, the bishop.

"Joshua." Daniel quickly stepped back at the sight
of the drenched willowy man and let him hurry inside.
"What brings you out in this?" Another shadow followed. Under his dripping, more-sleek version of rain
gear, Daniel noted the suit. The stranger wasn't Amish,
but the dark foyer gave little help on his identity.

"Evening, Daniel," the bishop greeted in his oddly
deep voice for such a small frame. His long beard glis-
tened against the light from the lamps burning in the
next room, revealing a healthy dose of silver woven into
dark coarse hairs. "This is Bryan Bates. He is a gov-
ernment agent." Daniel's forehead lifted in surprise.
"He asked that he may speak with you," Joshua added,
removing his black felt hat and shedding his raincoat,
comfortably hanging them on an empty wooden wall
peg nearby. Though *ferhoodled*, Daniel ushered both
men into the kitchen where the gas lanterns burned
brightest.

"Let me put on the kettle," Daniel said. He hated that his instincts were so keen. Both his *onkel* and the agent took a seat. *"Was ist letz?"* Daniel asked his *onkel*, but only received a sorrowful expression in reply. Joshua wasn't a man of limited words, ever. Daniel turned to the pudgy agent with shoes shinier than the blackest onyx littering the creek beds out back.

"Well, I'm actually a US marshal," Bates replied as he took in the room, a simple home free of adornments with more dust than Daniel could tackle daily given his business and farm duties. "It seems we have disrupted your supper." Before Daniel could offer either man a plate—he always made more than he needed—Joshua spoke again.

"The marshal," his uncle corrected, "has news to share with you." He stood and joined Daniel at the stove. Another sign something bad was coming. "I think you should sit down. I'll tend to making *kaffi*." Daniel found nothing in that solemn expression.

"Are you here as my bishop, or my *onkel*?" Daniel had no immediate family aside from Joshua, his business followed all the English-made mandates and not one horse had ever escaped the field. And if one of those pesky goats Caleb Byler tricked him into taking on had gotten out and caused an accident on the main road, well, the county deputy would be the one sitting in his kitchen right now, not a US marshal.

"Please, Mr. Raber, have a seat." It was an order, the way he said it, but Daniel detected a hint of pity in it. "You have been a hard man to find." The marshal pinned him with a probing gaze. Daniel sat in the nearest chair, always one to obey authority, unlike his *bruder* who'd had a habit of headbutting it.

"This is nice country you got out here. Not many neighbors. Quiet," Bates assessed as Joshua poured three cups of *kaffi* and brought them to the table. His northern accent only added to the mystery of his presence. "Have you lived here long?" Bates asked, taking a sip of the stout brew without so much as pruning his features. His *onkel* was known for his kind outreach to others, his penchant for hard candy, and his powerful *kaffi*.

"It was my family's homestead, and *jah*, going on eleven years now. You should say what you came to say. I'm not one who likes dragging a thing out if it can be helped." Daniel crossed both arms across his chest, ignoring the look of amusement smeared on the marshal's face.

"Then I will get straight to it. I'm from Indiana, where we have been investigating a homicide," Marshal Bates said. "The killer shot a detective after he and another man broke into his home. Tell me, Mr. Raber, do you know a Micah Reynolds?"

"*Nee*, I do not, nor have I ever lived in Indiana." Daniel remained calm though his confusion was building.

"Micah was a close friend of mine, a detective for about eight years. He was working on a case involving stolen firearms and other undesirable things. We suspect he got too close and Marotta, a very bad and wealthy man, wanted to see that Micah didn't get any closer." The marshal lowered his head and stared into his cup.

"I'm sorry about your friend, but I still don't know why you're telling me any of this or why you brought my bishop out in this weather to do it," Daniel said.

"Micah Reynolds wasn't my friend's birth name. It took some digging but I found out his real name was

Michael Raber." The news slammed like a hammer into Daniel's chest. The sudden shock to his system felt like a streak of lightning had made its way in and found him, on purpose.

His brother was dead?

"Michael? Are you sure?"

"Yes, Mr. Raber. I'm sorry, but yes. Michael Raber was murdered on Tuesday in his home by a man named Nicholas Corsetti." Thunder crashed outside matching Daniel's rumbling emotions.

Daniel got to his feet and went to the sink. "He's dead. My *bruder* is dead," he muttered, staring out into the storm that found him living peacefully here in his birthplace. He gripped the sink to keep his hands from shaking. Part of him always expected Michael to succumb to his bad habits or shady friends, but the news still made a dent in Daniel's heart.

"*Kumm*, Daniel. There is more to discuss and many decisions to be made this night," Joshua urged. Daniel didn't want to hear more.

He hated tears. Not for their weakness, but for what they represented. He let a couple freefall without caring either way. His brother was dead. Now he truly was alone in the world.

As the marshal continued, Daniel leaned forward and tried to absorb everything he was saying, but he was going to be sick. His brother had a family, three children, and one had witnessed the unimaginable. Daniel worked through his own emotional battle and grasped the severity of what the marshal was saying. Michael's family was in danger. "We can't let anything happen to them," he muttered.

"Glad we can agree." Both men locked gazes. Daniel understood the family, *his* family, needed a place to hide until a killer could be found. One didn't need to be a smart man to predict what came next. Straightening, Daniel braced himself for it.

"They want to hide them here," Joshua put in.

"No one would think to look in Amish country for them," the marshal said sweeping an arm over the room. "It's perfect."

"And yet, you found me." It was a stupid idea, and one that might get Michael's family killed. Amish didn't believe in confrontation. Surely the marshal wasn't thinking clearly.

"I found you because of an old photo your brother carried." The marshal pulled a photograph from his coat pocket and slid it across the table. Daniel gingerly lifted it and stared into the past, the family they once were smiling back at him. The outside world had taken them all and now that outside world was here, knocking on his door.

"Do they know Michael was Amish? That he had a *bruder*?" Daniel ran his thumb over the images of his family and tried wrapping his head around the situation.

"No, and they don't need to until after this is all over. I insist on that part. She has been hit with a lot in a short time. I don't want to overwhelm her with more." Daniel understood that well enough. For as heavy as his heart was feeling right now, Michael's wife was surely burdened with more.

"I will help any way I can for my *bruder*'s family, but I'm not sure how to hide a woman and three *kinner* here. Amish do things differently. Men and women don't simply live under the same roof unless they're…" Joshua touched his shoulder and squeezed. Daniel got to his feet again. "I can't marry my *bruder*'s wife, an *Englischer*."

"So you have another interest then," his *onkel* challenged.

"You know I do not," Daniel shot back. "And this is not the time for you to be addressing my single status, *Onkel*." Daniel narrowed his look. Joshua ran his boney finger over his *kaffi* cup and grinned. *So he is using this horrible ordeal to marry me off.* Daniel groaned to himself.

"You have a responsibility. She is a widow with three *kinner* and needs a husband, a protector and a provider. Many in our community marry for far less."

"They need someone who knows the outside world enough to help them fit in to this one." The marshal continued to persuade him. Daniel let out a slow breath as the reality sank in. A loveless marriage to a woman of his brother's choosing and three kids. "I'll give you two a minute to talk this through. I need to radio in and have the family brought on over." The marshal moved toward the door and pulled his phone from his jacket pocket.

"Here! Tonight?" Daniel called after him.

"I know this is a lot, so take that minute I mentioned to absorb everything I have told you, because that's what Magnolia is doing right now as she is being briefed about what she must do for her children's safety. I understand the commitment here, the sacrifice. But you aren't the only one making them. They need you." How could Daniel refuse now?

Appetite gone, Daniel began clearing the table. There were no instructions on how to handle a matter such as this, and if there had been, he would have never thought to read them.

He poured Joshua's bitter brew down the sink and started a fresh pot to percolate on the back burner. This night was certainly going to require it.

Thiry-year-old Magnolia Reynolds swiped the rain from her face and stepped into the dimly lit house behind the US marshal. Three days ago she was complaining about real estate contracts and how her husband breaking another promise to their children meant she would spend a night camping in the backyard while September gnats ate away at her flesh. Now, as a storm barreled overhead, she found herself widowed and running for her life.

She pulled Roslyn closer against her side as Sadie, her youngest, clung to her neck like a life raft. With all the emotions swirling inside her, she couldn't imagine what waves of confusion her daughters were feeling, but fear was certainly high on the list.

And now she was expected to put their lives in the hands of strangers. It was ironic, seeing as she had married a man who had built his fortune on lies and broken promises. A man who left her alone to face the consequences of his actions.

No matter the mixture of anger and fear, her heart was shattered. Micah was gone, her children traumatized, and Roslyn—at only six years of age—was a possible target for a madman. She accepted witness protection, trusting the marshal's concerns held value, but how was their best option for hiding marrying a stranger and pretending to be something she was not? Being tossed about most of her life had prepared her for many things, but this time, Magnolia feared she might not adapt, or blend in, so easily.

Marshal Bates, a longtime family friend, led the way inside the large house and she and her children cautiously followed, flanked by the two agents assigned to them. Agent Lawson was brawny and quiet, just as one might picture secret agents to be. Agent Moore, a female version of protection, was petite and far less serious. She made certain Magnolia understood what was expected of her to keep her daughters safe. Agent Moore urged her forward, just as she had done from the moment Magnolia's life had spun out of control.

"I want to go home. It's not fair," her eldest, Jasmine, protested as they moved into a large open kitchen. *It wasn't fair*, but what choice did they have?

Her gaze lifted immediately to the stranger as he turned from the stove and locked eyes with her. He was tall, with a dark stare and surprisingly was not as she pictured at all. Agent Moore had explained the common Amish dress, the stern nature, conformity, and devout faith they presented. He looked nothing of the sort. He had no beard or scowl and didn't look much older than her. If not for the suspenders and hair much too long to be considered appropriate, he looked like any man on the street back home in Indiana.

His gaze made a quick study of them and she clutched her children protectively closer, careful not to tug on Roslyn's long, dark braid as she did. She might not have many choices right now, but she wasn't about to hand out her trust too swiftly.

Her youngest two daughters were still dressed in matching pink pajamas. Roslyn had her favorite purple shoes, but no socks. If only she'd had more time to pack before the marshals swept them away from their lives only to drop them into a world completely foreign to her.

Jasmine gave her that signature sulk. They shared the same blonde hair and blue eyes, but Jasmine had also inherited her father's long legs and short temper. Magnolia passed her a begging glance to try harder and accept what was taking place. She had explained they would now live here, pretend to be other people, until life was safe again. Her daughters understood mostly what was necessary for their survival right now.

Turning her attention back to the stranger again, she wondered what was going through his thoughts, and what kind of man who looked like this one wasn't already married but agreeing to put his life at risk for strangers. She tried not to appear too fragile, but the last few days had taken a lot out of her.

In jeans and a plain rose-colored button-up shirt she looked far from a perfectly Plain woman. Her flip-flops revealed red painted toenails that matched her fingertips. She didn't look showy or arrogant, absent from her normal attire, but under his scrutiny, she knew she didn't look like a potential Amish bride either. It was her lot in life, seldom fitting in anywhere. She would deal with this as she did everything life tossed at her. By the skin of her teeth.

In his narrowed gaze, her chin lifted slightly, defining her willingness to do what she had to, marry a stranger, no matter how she wished not to. When he offered a curt nod, Magnolia accepted it as a silent agreement that he too would do what he had to do. Exhaustion was clearly navigating her steps at this point. But for the first time in three days, her shoulders relaxed a little.

"Mags, this is Daniel Raber. Daniel, this is Magnolia Reynolds and her daughters, Jasmine, Roslyn and Sadie." She swallowed the lump in her dry throat as

Marshal Bates introduced them. Indecision and panic swept through her but she feared speaking out now might be a mistake. The only way to steel her emotions was to focus on their troubles, not her unhinged world.

"Welcome to my home. It is very nice to meet each of you," the stranger welcomed in a low, but friendly, voice.

Sadie lifted her head at the sound of him and studied Daniel closely. Her unruly blonde curls bounced with the tilt of her head. Upon her youngest's request, Magnolia put Sadie down to stand on her own two feet. Her arms were immediately grateful for the rest. The room fell silent as first impressions ran between strangers.

Sadie's big brown eyes took Daniel in, seeing what to make of a man dressed in Amish garb. Then she took three cautious steps forward and held out her hand. Magnolia started to reach out to stop her, but fatigue was making her unsteady. Her youngest had never met a stranger. To Magnolia's surprise Daniel bent eye level to Sadie, and smiled.

"Nice to meet you too. I'm five. Mommy says we have to live here now." Magnolia steeled a breath when Daniel looked to her again. Permission perhaps. When she gave it, his lips tugged to one corner and she knew. Sadie had a way about her to melt most hearts. When Daniel accepted her hand, it felt as if the deal had been made. If he had second thoughts about helping them, he didn't any longer. "I like your house, but…?" Sadie leaned closer and whispered loudly. "I don't like the dark."

"I can add more lamps to help with that." Daniel winked, making her giggle. "But don't be afraid of the dark, little one." He tapped her little button nose.

"At least he likes kids," Agent Moore whispered beside her. For that, Magnolia was thankful.

"But it's the dark." Sadie cocked her head adorably and said in a comical cuteness that had the whole room smiling, "All kinds of things are in the dark."

"*Jah*, but if you can't see anything, what is there to be afraid of?"

She touched her finger to her chin as she was prone to do when contemplating. If Magnolia wasn't mistaken, the tall dark stranger was melting under her daughter's innocent charms. A fleeting thought pronounced itself right then. What kind of man who melted in little girls' smiles would protect them? "Just because I can't see the bad things hiding, don't mean they aren't there."

"*Jah*, true." Daniel matched her finger-to-the-chin gesture. "But just because you can't see *gut* things watching over us, does not mean they aren't there either." Sadie clearly didn't understand, but as always, she smiled anyway. It took so little effort to warrant a smile from that one. "We will just add more light for now, until you can trust me that there is nothing in the dark here to fear."

"You talk funny," she added. "I like it." Chuckles flowed around them.

"I like the way you talk too." Daniel patted her head and stood. His eyes locked with Magnolia's. Though she would remain guarded, respectfully so, she felt that living here for a time might not be so terrible after all.

Marshal Bates chimed in. "We have new identities for each of you like we talked about earlier. You both should help the girls try to remember them so they don't slip. I would suggest as few outings as possible and keep a low profile, even here." Daniel shot a glance at an older man standing to the shadows. Magnolia hadn't even considered his quiet presence until now. He must be the bishop that Agent Moore spoke of, the one who would marry them, until this nightmare ended.

"Being Amish does not mean one can hide away in solitude." The bishop stepped forward. "Plain life is much the opposite. Our communities thrive on connecting, gathering with family and neighbors regularly. It is the heart of our existence."

"As long as you all understand the limitations," the marshal added in. "The less they are seen, the better." Bates offered the manila folder to Magnolia. Still pondering over what community gatherings included, she ignored him. There was still time to back out and change her mind, wasn't there?

She felt a surge of lightheadedness. She had been living on coffee and prayers up to this point and now exhaustion was taking its full toll on her.

In her hesitation, Daniel stepped forward, accepting the envelope that contained their temporary identities.

"I hope I get a pretty name like Princess Sophia," Sadie said giddily.

"I don't need a new name. You can't just go changing my name," Jasmine protested, and added a foot stomp, punctuating it. With a fresh headache tempting and Jasmine putting up a fuss, Magnolia couldn't think clearly. It was times like these she simply had to accept surrender, let God take control. She was certainly in no frame of mind to take the wheel.

"We will do what is necessary. This isn't about what we want anymore, but what must be done for your safety," Magnolia reminded her eldest as Agent

Moore's hand steadied her elbow. Sometimes life simply wasn't fair.

Daniel opened the envelope and pulled out its contents. "That's your marriage license to keep things official," Bates chimed in. Without changing his blank expression, Daniel tucked the long sheet behind the following pages before looking to her again.

"You are now Hannah." She was glad the agent was keeping her upright as Roslyn shifted from clutching her right leg to gripping her left. He turned to Jasmine's pouting face. She opened her mouth to protest, but quickly drew it shut again. "You are now Catherine Faith." As their former lives began to be stripped away, thunder outside cracked.

Daniel took a few steps closer. This close up he seemed taller and larger than at a distance. He also smelled faintly of sawdust and a summer rain. It was a surprisingly pleasant combination.

"Shall I continue or do you need a moment?" His sincerity shocked her.

She didn't need a moment, she needed to curl into the nearest corner and cry. "Please, continue." He lowered on one knee, bringing him eye level with Roslyn, still clinging to her leg.

"Rosemary. Now that is a beautiful name." Roslyn didn't dare smile or comment, but her fingers loosened slightly from the denim. For the last three days her daughter hadn't spoken a word and Magnolia feared no matter what others said, it would be a long time before she would again. One didn't see death so close and simply forget it. Daniel's brows gathered, detecting the difference in her middle daughter aside from the other two. How much had the marshal shared with him? Bryan insisted Daniel didn't need to know about Micah's dark dealings, only that she and her children needed shelter and safety, and she for one wasn't about to tell him about the man she had married or what he had done to land them here. But it was clear he knew Roslyn had been the one who had seen her father murdered.

"My turn. Sadie Reynolds is hard to spell." Daniel pulled his attentions from Roslyn to her little curly-haired wonder centering the room.

"I agree." When he pulled the next sheet of paper with attached social security card forward, Magnolia noted the pause, the sudden flicker of recognition. He glanced at the bishop lingering in the shadows, clearly distraught and then quickly reined it back in. "How about Martha Jane?" Perhaps he knew another by the common name.

"Martha is pretty and starts with *M*. Mommy taught me all my letters. Jane is *J*. So, M.J." Her brown eyes twinkled. "I like it!" Apparently Daniel did too by the way his dark eyes lit up.

Feeling her legs grow more unsteady, Magnolia quickly put in, "Thank you for agreeing to let us stay here, but it's been a long day. If you could show us which room is ours, I would like to get the girls cleaned up and settled down for bed before we finish what is necessary down here."

Daniel swallowed hard, obviously not in any hurry to finish the duty expected of them. She couldn't blame him but she needed this day over before she collapsed.

"I have rooms for each of them, but I wasn't prepared for..." *Visitors* was too careless a word. "I haven't readied them."

"That won't be necessary, Mr. Raber. We will stay together in one bedroom." She clutched Rosemary closer to her hip. His jaw tightened before he turned to lead the way. Did he already hate this arrangement as much as she did? *Keep on keeping on*, words once gifted her that always helped her remember to keep putting one foot in front of the other no matter the path ahead.

So that's what she did.

Chapter Two

Somewhere in the morning hours, Magnolia had succumbed to exhaustion and slipped off to sleep. Now, she knew she needed to get up, face whatever obstacles another day poured onto her, but she had never felt so tired, so greedy to pull the covers up over her head and waste daylight hours. She reached out an arm and found the sheets cool to the touch. It was only then she realized she wasn't surrounded by little warm bodies. Bolting upright, she found herself disoriented. She wasn't dreaming. These last three days were very real.

Bright morning light filtered through a sheer curtain, revealing a very large and very empty room. A queen-size bed, a small wooden side table and miles of pecan-colored hardwood flooring. Adrenaline seized her and she jumped to her feet and ran out the bedroom door. In the long dim hallway, she tried to collect her bearings, felt her heart begin to gallop. Giggling rose up the stairs, penetrating the rooms in a surprisingly joyous sound. She took a shuddering breath, threw a hand over her racing heart. Giggles were good, very good. After what they had endured the last three days, giggles were a blessing. Emotionally overstrained, she nearly burst into tears at the sounds of laughter. "Thank you, Lord, for landing us someplace safe," she whispered.

Then reality hit her and safe seemed something one shouldn't throw quick trust at. Everything from last night came in a flood. The storm that announced their coming, the Amish house the US Marshals promised would be a safe haven for her daughters and that hurried wedding to a dark stranger to secure that measure of safety. Now her head was spinning again. Hannah gripped the banister with one hand, fisted her stomach with her other and began taking deep breaths.

There was no turning back and changing her mind now. The wheels were in motion and she couldn't stop them even if she wanted to. She had agreed to live with a stranger in his house. It was for them, she reminded herself as her stomach rolled with angst. She needed to be strong, adaptable, and yet the thought of crying for days seemed right too.

"You three enjoy your eggs and pancakes while I run this upstairs," the man, Daniel, spoke below. Could she trust this man? Putting their lives in another's hands was going to take some work. But what other choice did she have? This place, that man, was her safest choice.

Footfalls crossed old wooden floors. The tall figure with midnight black hair climbed the steps, a tray of food in his hands. He looked nothing like a man who served, or cooked. He was all brawn and simple, except for that first impression when he seemed to understand her plight, smiled kindly at her daughters. But how could he understand any of this?

"Gut morgen," he greeted before looking up, knowing she was there. Magnolia blinked as he drew closer

and taller in the vanishing distance. Then again, neither of them looked at each other once during the whole stupid charade she was too numb to recall in detail.

"You should eat something," he said, coming to a stop at the top of the landing. His eyes settled on her, sympathy in sorrowful hazel eyes. She couldn't muster a reply, her mind still adrift. She owed him plenty considering he was allowing them to stay here, but what could she say right now? In her silence, he brushed past her and aimed for the shared bedroom.

The scent of warm bacon, something she had sworn off after birthing Roslyn, caused her stomach to gurgle. Daniel pushed back a thin white curtain, letting more of the outside light in.

"Thank you for feeding my children. I never sleep this late." He turned to face her, and she felt her legs grow unsteady. In full light without the play of shadows and a brain too rattled to function, his sturdy frame and handsome looks held her at full attention now. Those few curious glances from last night hadn't given her such a clear view. His tanned face said he was a man who worked outdoors, though she scarcely recalled Bryan mentioning something about him working with wood. He was at least six foot and built like a lumberjack, long legs under dark, broad fall pants, and with shoulders that suggested he could carry some weight without complaint. His light blue shirt had no buttons, no collar. Magnolia hadn't seen a man in suspenders since her second foster home, and Daniel looked nothing like sweet old Henry Clayborn. Hazel eyes, a mossy green with rich earthy tones blended in perfectly. His jaw clenched, noting her dissecting of him. He tilted his head slightly, revealing a slight mark, a scar along his neck. The small trail of raised flesh long healed but present.

"You needed the rest." He lifted a curious brow, eyeing her copiously in return. She still wore the clothes she had arrived in last night and knew her hair required a proper washing or at least a brush. Without the use of her iron, the blond strands tended to wave and stray in various directions. It took ample amounts of product to tame the frizziness. She was most certainly a sight.

"The bathroom is just down the hall, second door to the left. Take the lamp, there's no window in there for light. Everything else should meet your satisfaction." *Indoor plumbing, thank the Lord*, she mentally praised. Agent Moore said she would have to adjust to using an outhouse. Thankfully, the agent had been wrong about that. "Up here, there is no gas lighting. Lamps must be used." She nodded.

"Thank you again for letting us stay here. I hope it won't be long."

"Not a problem." His rich voice softened.

"I think it would be best to establish which rooms are strictly off-limits, while we're here. I don't want to disturb your space." She shrugged, nervous being alone with a man she didn't know. "More than us being here already has, I mean." His forehead lifted mindfully, taking a good bit of dark hair with it. She hated the sound of her trembling voice.

"It is your home now too. Nothing needs to be off-limits, even to children." M.J.'s laughter rose up again. "It's good laughter fills these rooms again, even for a time." Her mouth opened, but nothing came out. "You should eat and rest a little longer before Edith Schwartz arrives." He made a motion to leave.

"Edith Schwartz?" She stared at the full plate on the bedside stand. Even the glass of milk looked tempting and she wasn't a fan of dairy.

"Joshua's wife. The bishop you met last night."

"Married us," she finished in a tone that even shocked her. It wasn't Daniel's fault she was here praising indoor plumbing and asking about boundaries instead of back home with a fully intact family, but someone needed to know she wasn't happy about this witness-protection arrangement and now that she was rested and fully alert, Daniel was the only one standing here. In her right mind, she would have never agreed to marry a stranger. It had all happened so fast, and in her delicate shocked state, she had numbly followed whatever Bryan felt was best for her children. Now, it all seemed too ridiculous for words.

"I'm sorry, I know that must have been difficult for you, but the marshal felt it was the best place to keep you all hidden. Our faith doesn't allow for a man and woman to live under one roof, unwed. But your children will be safe, fed—" he glanced at her food tray "—and given a place to heal, for however long you need." He didn't address her snarky tone, which surprised her. Whatever she thought, felt, he was being kind.

"I'm sorry too." And Magnolia was. This fake marriage wasn't only something she had to accept. He did too. Marriage was a sacred thing. She thought of Micah, how he'd wanted to leave and break that union. She had begged him not to let their children be raised in a broken home. He had acquiesced to her, but nothing was the same afterward. He lived his own life, she lived for her children, and for six years, passing a kind word had become her normal. Some men had so much, and yet wanted something different and Magnolia just wasn't new or different enough.

She considered the man before her again, this time for something more than his chosen apparel and the way he fit into it. This stranger was helping her without any reward, any reasoning. No one did something for nothing. Her eyes suddenly widened at the thought. Did he think he would be gaining a true wife with this arrangement? "What does this faith of yours expect from me?" Magnolia asked.

He again lifted that strong dark brow, measuring her meaning. It was a good look on him, if only aimed at another. "The truth?"

"The unedited version would be appreciated," she said in a professional tone.

"We have a set a rules, our *Ordnung*, which we each strive to follow. Our faith is the very center of our lives. The way we dress, how we do things, and even how we deal with others, are important." He shoved both hands into his pockets and lowered his gaze. "Edith will help with much of this. What being separate from the world truly means." He let out a sigh and looked to her again. "Mrs. Reynolds, I don't expect anything from you, if that is what you mean. You are only my wife, my *fraa* as we say it, in public. Here, you may speak plainly, live without expectations. We will work together to take care of your children, help them fit in here. Keep them safe until this man is caught."

She held his gaze a bit longer. He made it sound simple. This was all far from simple. Hannah wanted to believe him to be a man of his word, but then again, she was the worst judge of character on the planet. Micah had proven trustworthy, romantic, until Catherine came

along, then he'd made work his priority. By the time
M.J. was born, he put his work and his secrets first.
And no matter how much she gave to him, the further
he slipped away from her. She had kept her vows, remained the dutiful wife. And now, he was gone. She
wasn't sure what she was supposed to feel about that
aside from guilt. *If she had only been a better wife. If
he had only been a better man.* The thoughts battled
in her head.

"Thank you." She lowered her head, not wanting to
linger on the subject long.

"Edith will be here shortly, as I mentioned. She will
help you and the children…navigate. You will need to
dress Amish first." He turned away but she didn't miss
the spark of amusement before he did. "I am a fair hand
in the kitchen and can handle a few meals, but I own
a lumber mill." He turned to the window and pointed.
"Just over that hill. I have two men who work with
me. When you are more settled, I will introduce you.
It would be good to have plenty of eyes looking out
for each of you." Hannah didn't want any more eyes
on them. The fear that even here, in the middle of nowhere, the wrong set of eyes might find them sent a
chill up her spine.

"Our nearest neighbors are less than a mile that
way." He pointed in the other direction. "The Troyers.
They have a large orchard, and Millie is a very kind
woman, a widow with daughters herself. If you are here
long…" He paused, clearly hoping that wasn't the case.
"If you're here long, Millie would be a good friend to
talk to, but only the bishop and Edith can know the true
reasons for your being here."

"Of course," she hastily said. "We won't be talking

to anyone if we can help it. I don't need any friends, just my girls kept safe until all of this is over."

"Again, I'm sorry for your loss. I will do what I can to make it more bearable being here," Daniel said. He headed for the door again.

"Oh, and I can cook," she quickly shot out. "Isn't that part of an Amish wife's duties? I'm not sure what Amish eat but…"

"The kitchen is yours then," he said, slightly amused. "I need to run to the mill and get a few things in order, but we will have the rest of the weekend to get each of you settled, find a routine. Routines are good, I think." He paused. "Don't let the *kinner*, the children," he added for her benefit, "go to the barn."

"Why? Is it dangerous?" She looked out the window for the barn. It was brick red and massive, near three stories high. In the storm last night, she hadn't a clue it even existed. Still, how had she missed such a structure?

He laughed, jerking her back to his attention. "*Nee.* I just have four pesky goats I really don't need M.J. falling in love with before I get them rehomed. I never saw a child so eager for my pancakes. I reckon animals might send her overboard." He chuckled again and strolled out the door. So Amish men had humor, could muster up pancakes, and didn't walk around frowning and carrying pitchforks.

She grinned. Glancing out the window, she nibbled on a slice of bacon. The barn was even bigger than the house and Daniel was right. M.J., as her little Sadie was now called, didn't need to see any goats. If he owned a cat, she could only imagine what would happen. It was sweet M.J. had already gotten to the man in charge of their care. In fact, the way he'd addressed Rosemary last night had taken her by surprise. Of course, he knew most of their situation, but he also took the time to be patient, speak slowly and bend to her level so as not to frighten her. Almost as if he wanted her to know she was safe. If he had regrets for helping them, it didn't show. But the question still lingered there. How did the US Marshals find an Amish man willing to take them in? After pulling her hair into a ponytail and picking up the tray, Hannah went downstairs to join her daughters.

"Morning, girls." Hannah sat the tray down where three little girls ate busily. Despite the churning in her belly, she ran on automatic. Mothers didn't have the freedom to wear their emotions freely. She needed her children to feel safe and establish normalcy as quick as possible.

"Morning, Momma," M.J. greeted cheerily. The scent of fresh coffee permeated the kitchen. She glanced around, searching the many cabinets and drawers for a coffee mug. Daniel opened the next cabinet, reached in and revealed a dark brown cup. Hannah offered a sideways smile of gratitude.

Daniel wasn't sure what he'd expected when he promised to care for Michael's wife and children, but now that he had a few hours' sleep and a better handle on everything, the petite blonde who sold real-estate in Indiana looked far from what he would have predicted.

Hannah entering his kitchen last night, draped in children, he hadn't been overly shocked to find she was pretty even with all she was enduring. Michael had always been more taken with outward appearances. Her fragile state of vulnerability matched a look of one tragically consumed with exhaustion. Dark circles under blue, watery eyes revealed fatigue and fear, making him want to offer assurances he couldn't. He was but one man, human, and full of flaws and forced to recognize his own disheveled state. Now on a new dawn, she was beautiful. They had both somewhat rested and had a duty to do. He still wasn't sure how any of this was to work, but a glance toward her plate, he noted she had eaten most of the food he had prepared. It was a start.

Living alone for so long he wasn't used to having others about. It would take some getting used to, but he would take his time getting to know them individually and making them feel at home.

"It's not Starbucks, but it will do," Daniel muttered haphazardly as she took her first sip of his muddy morning brew.

"You know what a Starbucks is?" Hannah questioned too hastily, her eyes widened in surprise. He gave her a half-hearted grin. She would be shocked if she knew just how much he knew of the world. He could tell her, but talking about that time in his life stirred up too many painful memories.

"I don't like this. You always make our breakfast," Catherine interrupted, pushing food around her plate as if it might be poisonous.

Daniel gave the eldest another long look. She had inherited her mother's coloring, but that cold stare she was gifting him was familiar, taking him back in time.

From what he learned last night, Catherine was nine. Coincidentally, the same age he was when his life changed too. He mentally stashed away that bit of information, hoping as the days passed he could use that to reach common ground between them.

At nine, his father had lost his faith and found living Amish too constricting, too suffocating. Dan Raber packed up his family, abandoned his faith, and moved them to a world that was flashy, fast, and tempting. In the end, that world had swallowed up everything Daniel loved. He seldom gave in to thoughts of yesterday, but seeing Catherine exhibit the same angry emotions he once felt, only reminded him that much more of the family lost to him too.

"I'm sorry about that, baby. It won't happen again." Hannah sat the cup down and went to her daughter. "I just overslept, but don't worry, I will be making all your meals from now on." Watching Hannah try smoothing out Catherine's rebellion, Daniel thought of his *mudder*. She never wanted to leave her upbringing, her family or the steady faith she had clung to until the end. Mothers were strong like that. At least Catherine had had Michael. He had obviously turned his life around becoming a man upholding the law, nothing like their own father. Forgiveness was essential, but part of him knew he may never be able to forgive his *daed* for taking them away from their Amish home. But he was here now, and so was Michael's family. Here, faith, family and community were the backbone of life. Here brothers didn't run away and stores weren't robbed. Lives weren't taken for a mere 209 dollars. Here, little girls didn't lose fathers to men like Corsetti.

"He doesn't even know what we like. We could have been allergic to something." Catherine slammed down her fork jerking Daniel back to the present. "What if he killed us?" Daniel remained unaffected in the outburst, though when Rosemary burst into tears, he wanted to go to her.

"That's being a bit dramatic, is it not?" Hannah said

in a more firmer tone as she scooped Rosemary into her arms. "Mr. Raber worked hard to provide this meal for you and you will say thank you," Hannah ordered. Catherine mumbled a thank-you before sliding her plate away.

"Mommy, Mr. Raber said I can help milk a cow if you say it's okay," M.J. said with a mouth full of pancake, syrup dripping off her fork in a thick stream.

"Don't talk with your mouth full, Sadie."

"It's M.J. 'member?" her daughter scolded. "We got to learn our new names, Mommy. My new name is pretty, and I like it." Daniel stifled a laugh. The child had some charms, turning grown men into mush with smiles and an "I like it" stamp of approval for new things. Daniel knew from the moment they shook hands, he was done for. How was it even possible for a man to feel such love for children he just met?

And how fitting M.J. had been given the very name of her own grandmother. Martha was a common Amish name but what were the chances she had been given this one? Someday Daniel hoped to tell them each about the woman who'd left her mark on them, because it was as plain as the nose on his face; *Mudder* marked them all.

"Of course it is, pumpkin. I will try harder to remember your new names." Hannah eased Rosemary back into her seat now that she had calmed, and turned back to him. Daniel quickly withdrew his current infatuation with her five-year-old when she bore a perplexed look his way. "And I thought they weren't to go to the barn."

He offered her her forgotten cup of *kaffi*.

"I don't mind showing her the barn and an old milk cow before heading to the mill. This evening, I think it best to show you all around the property." He sipped at his cup, looking over the rim at her children. Rosemary glanced up, catching his attention. She was the spitting image of the grandmother she would never meet. The knowledge pricked his heart. Her fingers toyed nervously with the dark braid hanging over her shoulder. He'd give her a wider berth. Allow her all the time she needed to get settled. The marshal had told him she'd seen Michael's murder and had since not spoken a word. He knew so little about how such traumas affected the young, so little about children in general, but he knew time and prayer had ways of healing most of what plagued a soul and he would be sure to give her both.

"That's not necessary. Thank you for the offer but the children and I can stay right here until…" The sound of buggy wheels on gravel outside brought Hannah to alert. In her sudden jolt, she nearly dropped her coffee cup.

"It's just Edith Schwartz." Daniel reached out, touched her elbow with his palm to steady her. Her panicked look sent an unreasonable chill over his bones. "The bishop's wife. Remember?"

"I'm sorry, it's just…" Her voice trembled and she glanced over to her children. Daniel couldn't ignore the matching looks spreading on their small faces.

"You are safe here. All of you." He looked toward the table to include each of them. *Assurances. They needed assurances.* "No harm will come to you here," he said without an edge of doubt.

"But, Daniel," Hannah whispered as Catherine resumed complaining over her eggs and M.J. boasted about getting to milk a cow beside them. It seemed those two had complete faith in his words, but Hannah was not so convinced. "I don't mean to offend, not when you have been kind enough to take us in, but you're Amish. If danger does come, how can I..."

"Defend your family alone?" he quickly put in. "You'll never have to know." Had she already forgotten his promise to her, the oath they swore by? "Hannah." Her name came on a promise that he hoped she understood. She wasn't alone to face what threatened. "No one is coming through that door that I don't invite in." With that stern promise, Daniel sat his cup aside and brushed past to let the bishop's wife in. He hadn't expected to feel this protective need or how Hannah's eyes pleading up to him would make him feel. Daniel exhaled a breath and reached for the door handle. He hoped if the need ever did present itself, he could make good on his promise.

Chapter Three

Edith Schwartz walked in the door, and was ready to get to work. Dressed in a rich blue dress and white apron front, she quickly lifted her black bonnet revealing a white smaller one underneath. Hannah wasn't sure what the purpose of two head coverings were. In less time than it took to pour a second cup of coffee, the healthy-framed woman walked into the kitchen, sized up Hannah and her daughters, and said, "Now let's get to making you each look more… Plain." With a toothy smile, she urged them all up the stairs. Edith knew all about their circumstances, Daniel had said, and she had offered quick condolences, but she wasn't the type to dwell, and quickly introduced them all to the Plain life.

Hannah heard the door downstairs shut. Daniel had finally left to see about his mill nearby. She appreciated all he was doing but having him breathing over them would become a nuisance. She'd had plenty of that with the US Marshals.

In the shared bedroom, full light exposing the layers of dust on the windowsills and bedside stand, they gathered. M.J. was already trying to sneak a peek into one of the bags Edith carried with her and distributed on the bed. "Patience, *liebling*." Edith patted M.J.'s curly head, affection glinting in her soft brown eyes.

"Many will be disappointed to know you have married our Daniel," Edith said as she emptied the first bag. She held up a length of material the color of the sky right before dark clouds rolled in, a rich blue hue. "A man with so much to offer is much sought after among the unwed *maedels* of our community," Edith said with a pleasant candor. Hannah couldn't help but feel Edith didn't approve of one of their own marrying an outsider.

"He has been very kind to help us," Hannah replied, though she wondered what Edith's thoughts truly were considering her marriage of convenience. Accepting the dress, she kept the question to herself and slipped into the neighboring room to change. She listened to Edith speak to her children in a grandmotherly tone through the walls. Just like her, her children had never known their grandparents. Edith's accent was much richer than the man she had married.

Hannah slipped out of her two-day-old jeans and shirt, neatly folding them as if just pulled from the dryer. Slipping into the dress Edith had brought, Hannah realized there were no buttons to secure the upper half of the dress closed. She gathered her dirty clothes into one arm and held her dress front with the other, then looked up and went rigid. It seemed the neighboring room was by all accounts Daniel's room.

Unlike the room she and the children shared last night, this one was smaller. Masculine, yet simplified. A tall dark stained wooden dresser and shorter matching one sat along one wall, beautiful doilies, handmade and slightly yellowed with age, draped over their tops.

The large bed was made up, striking her as fascinating, considering Edith had only just arrived and Daniel lived alone. Micah had never made a bed once in their ten years of marriage.

The bed was draped in the most beautiful quilt she had seen in years. Blues and whites and a few shades of green arranged into a simple block pattern with a dizzy blend of mint and baby blue trim. Even a few feet away, Hannah could see the hand stitching. Mrs. Clayborn, the only foster mother Hannah had ever considered to resemble a mother, had loved to quilt and even taught Hannah a thing or two about tight stitches and proper binding. She didn't dare step closer, though she was eager for a closer look. On tiptoe, she stretched her neck to better view everything. On the bedside stand, there was a small black clock, wind-up style with bells on top. A small dish of change to the right and a long flashlight lay between the two. A man's room indeed, she thought, studying the naked windows in full morning light, breathing in the heavy scents of man and wood. It was a foreign mix, but surprisingly memorable.

The sound of M.J. in the next room, going on and on about her anxious need to have her first barn adventure, jerked Hannah's attention back. She hurried back into the room. Edith was helping M.J. into a soft blue dress slightly tattered at the hemline, while Catherine stood nearby, wearing a darker blue shade, arms crossed in an obvious temper. Her eldest had never known the feel of second-hand clothes before and it showed.

"And Mr. Raber says we don't give cows names because we eat them." Hannah wondered if Daniel perhaps had another dresser, somewhere, and then noted she needed to see her girls had a few extras, underwear, toothbrushes and so forth, as well. She had barely had time to pack what they needed. If they were going to spend the next few weeks here, there were essentials needed. Bates had given her plenty of cash with conditions she would let him know when she needed more.

"This is true. Now look at you. You look like a real Amish *kind*," Edith praised. "That means child." Edith winked. Hannah looked over the final results of her children's new identities. Who would have thought they could get more beautiful than they already were? She nodded her approval to each set of eyes looking to her for praise.

"Well, don't you look nice too," Edith said to Hannah.

"I didn't see any buttons." Hannah shrugged, revealing she was literally holding her dress together.

"Buttons aren't permitted here. They are considered showy and brazen. *Hochmut.* We are permitted to use hooks and eyes on dress backs and such, but I brought pins for that, dear." Hannah's eyes went wide. *Pins.* "Don't look so worried. Amish women have been wearing pins for centuries." Edith smiled amusingly. "This dress belonged to a new *mudder* with a *boppli* herself. It is a practical fashion for such, but I will see you have one like mine soon. I already cut out the pattern, along with a simple chore dress."

Edith helped Hannah pin her front so she wouldn't draw blood every time she moved. The children's dresses were simply pullover fashion. For that, Hannah was thankful.

"But, Ms. Edith." M.J. tugged at Edith's apron front. "If she is a milk cow, we won't eat her, will we?" M.J. was not one to let a thing go until it was fully understood.

"*Nee*, we need their milk." M.J.'s smile returned with

that fact. "You must convince Daniel to let you meet her and name her properly," Edith said, tapping her nose. "Now sit on the bed and let's see about taming those sunshine curls of yours."

"I was going to name her anyway." M.J. bounced onto the bed, happy for all the extra attention Edith was showing her. "You think my hair looks like sunshine?" Hannah and Edith passed smiles. Martha Jane was beyond her years and stubborn to a point, but like most females, loved being fussed over.

"This looks stupid." Catherine stomped out, the door of the bathroom down the hall slamming shut soon after. Hannah walked over and picked up the prayer covering she'd tossed in her rant. This caused Rosemary to start crying. Torn, Hannah pulled Rosemary into an embrace. Catherine always took her time dealing with change.

"It's okay, baby. How about you sit on the other side of the bed, and Mommy will fix your hair." Rosemary nodded, and Hannah thumbed away her little tears. Rosemary's long locks, the color of Micah's, felt like satin against her fingers. She worked it into a braid, listened for Catherine down the hall with one ear and Edith's instructions with the other. Hannah formed a dainty braided bun held by three bobby pins before finally speaking.

"I'm sorry. It has been a lot to take in for her," Hannah apologized for her eldest daughter. Catherine had a mind of her own and it took an act of nature to bend it from its own thinking. Time was her only friend now, Hannah knew. And just as Rosemary had been affected by witnessing her father's death, Catherine had been the one to keep M.J. hidden upstairs and safe until help arrived. For that, Hannah was thankful Catherine had kept her head and protected her sister. Each child was different, had their own way about them. It was best not to push her eldest, but simply remain present until she came to you. Still, Hannah ached to hold her, bring her to her chest and show her all would be well soon enough.

"She is hurting. It is to be expected. Little girls are not meant to shoulder such things. There is much healing needed here." Edith glanced around the room. "You will all find that soon enough," Edith said with a firm certainty that had Hannah almost believing her. "We can wait for wearing the *kapps*. I should have considered how different this would be for you and brought kerchiefs instead. *Jah*, that would be best. Except when going out, you see." She pointed a finger. "Then the prayer *kapp* is necessary." M.J. hopped down and so did Rosemary. "Now your turn." Edith held out an arm in invitation and Hannah sat down obediently. No one had ever done her hair before, at least not since she was thirteen.

"Can we play in that empty room?" M.J. pointed and Hannah nodded her approval. The room was dusty, but bare, and close enough Hannah could hear them.

"Explain the dress, the head covering to me, the reasoning of it. I know being set apart is important."

"An Amish woman dresses plain to promote modesty. It is the same with covering our heads. To stand apart from the rest of the world, and yet not attract attention." Edith grinned at the irony of her own words. "A prayer *kapp* is not only meant to cover our uncut hair. We are to not wear our hair down, except with our husbands." Hannah sucked in a breath. No way would

Daniel be seeing her hair down for however long she was to be here.

"It is also to remind us."

"Remind us?"

"To pray, always. To pray about everything and to step in Christ. Everything we do, our discipline, rules of our *Ordnung*, is to strive to live as simple and pure a Christian life as we can. To submit to His will. Now we make mistakes, like all, and must repent for them, but we are not so different. Tell me, Hannah, are you a woman of faith?"

"I must admit it has been hard. Micah, my husband, never encouraged it, but I was baptized when I was younger and took the girls each Sunday to a small church a few blocks from our home. I know much of the Bible but not well enough to recite verses on demand," Hannah said.

"Your husband did not attend church services with you?" Edith asked while reaching for the brush beside her.

Hannah laughed. "No. Micah was not interested."

Edith began working out the knots and kinks of three-day-old untended hair. "The Lord kept you close to Him, and now you are here, with us."

"He had nothing to do with that," Hannah said to her. God didn't take fathers from children. Killers did.

"Oh, but He brought you here for a reason, *jah*? You could have gone anywhere. It is a big world and yet you are here. *Gott* always has a plan." Edith smiled coolly and slipped the stiff *kapp* over Hannah's head. "Now you look as you should. The heart will simply follow," Edith remarked, gathering up bags off the bed. Hannah wasn't quite sure what she meant but didn't want to offend by asking. There was much to learn about these people, their ways. Edith was being so kind and help-ful. Hannah was grateful God had heard her prayer, bringing her and the children someplace that felt safe and kind.

"Let us start this day with a list of things you will need, and then tidy the *haus*. Daniel is not much for dusting, I see." Edith laughed, heading downstairs.

"I'm not sure a fake marriage and false names is what God wants," Hannah said, following faithfully behind. "But I do trust that the Lord knows best," Hannah told Edith as she followed her down the stairs.

Edith slipped into the kitchen, bustling about, put-ting things in order. "*Gott* always knows best. You will see." She smiled cunningly.

Hannah stiffened. "Daniel seems like a nice man, and I hope this doesn't tarnish his reputation or chance to find the real thing. I do have every intention of hav-ing our marriage annulled as soon as I can." Hannah hoped Edith believed her.

Edith pulled open a drawer and retrieved a pen and paper.

"What *Gott* brings together cannot be separated. If and when you leave, to Daniel, to the eyes of our com-munity, and *Gott*, you will always be his *fraa*. Can you give me the *kinner*'s shoe sizes?" Hannah was in shock at her bombshell statement.

"No divorce?" Hannah buried her face into her palms as the reality of what Daniel had sacrificed hit her. She thought they would simply get an annulment and all of this would be a thing of the past once the authorities found the man who killed Micah, and her daughter was safe.

Edith reached across the table and took her hand. "Daniel is a *gut* man who will treat you all with respect and kindness. Your *dochdern* need a *daed*'s love and gentle hand." Edith patted her hand and smiled. "If this helps you, our Daniel has never courted anyone before." Edith chuckled. "I tried my hand at matchmaking, and failed. He agreed to this for your *kinner*'s sake, *jah*. He has offered his home, his name, to you and to them. That is something to respect and be thankful for." Hannah was thankful, but had no desire to stay here forever, as Edith was suggesting.

"He will provide for you and keep you safe for as long as necessary and you will learn how to care for his needs, as well. I will teach you this, *jah*?"

Daniel had promised them safety, but acknowledged they would eventually leave. He'd promised she was his wife only in public. Why hadn't he mentioned their marriage could not be annulled? "Edith, what kind of man would give up his life for strangers?"

"The best kind," Edith replied with a tender smile and another pat on Hannah's hand. "But he didn't give it up, as you mean. Daniel simply added to what was already here. This house needs what you have brought."

Hannah still couldn't believe it. What kind of woman became a widow one day and three days later a bride? Shame washed over her, despite knowing it was all necessary.

She went to the stove and poured herself a third cup of coffee. She offered Edith one, which she graciously refused. Hannah sat back down and took a sip of coffee. Her heart was broken for the man she had loved, her stomach was nauseous at the betrayal he had delivered. Now she was responsible for ruining another man's future. How did one handle such emotions without the need to scream?

Chapter Four

For the rest of the day, Edith instructed Hannah how to use the washer ran by a gas-powered motor that was so loud Edith's instructions came in shouts. Hannah learned how to ring out clothes and hang them on the clothesline Daniel had outside the back door between T-shaped posts. Who would have guessed clothes had to be hung a certain way; but according to Edith, they did.

Out here, she caught a glimpse of the small garden of flowers where marigolds brightened the crisp, late, foggy morning. A single rose bush stood out at the corner of the house, yellow canary blooms thick as ants on a picnic basket of sweets. Strange to see such beauty this time of year. Hannah couldn't remember the last time she stopped and simply smelled the roses.

They dusted and mopped, ate peanut butter and jelly sandwiches, and on occasion laughed at something Edith said. Each girl helped, eager to please the woman dressed plain and ordinary, but clearly Edith was extraordinary.

Daniel's house was large, two full stories of dark, dusty rooms and sparse furniture. Old bookshelves in the sitting room revealed a man who liked to read more than just scripture. She'd spotted three Bibles in her ventures so far, and one old book that she couldn't tell what language it was but held the same worn-out appeal. She noted *The Count of Monte Cristo* and *A River Runs Through It*. Hannah had read those, but only because a teacher suggested them once. Her reading preferences leaned more toward romantic fiction where every ending was a happy one.

The upper-level rooms consisted of five bedrooms. She didn't figure her children would leave her shared bed for months, possibly years, and that was fine by her. There was one full bath and hallways that carried sounds far too easily. She liked the simplicity of it all. Primitive, yet functional. She didn't mind having no ties to the outside world. Not only was it safer, but it was quieter. It felt strange not to have her cell phone, but she understood why the authorities had insisted she toss it away.

The house was also empty of life. Well, she could add a large heaping spoonful while she was here, as Edith mentioned. Throughout the next hour, she forged on, wiped away years of dust and neglect, and emptiness. No matter how she felt, Daniel had indeed sacrificed for them and put his own future in peril. She would do her best, with what time she had, to show her appreciation.

She filled a fresh bucket of water at the sink and thought about him, the stranger she was chained to for the foreseeable future. Daniel's eyes had glinted slightly when he mentioned laughter was missed here. Hannah wondered how much laughter once filled it. He knew so much about her, but she knew nothing about him. Edith said he never married, nor held an eye for another.

Not a widower. She moved to the stairway, her small bucket of warm water and wood oil soap mixture at her side, and began washing the railing and delicately curved spindles.

He wasn't that old, no wrinkles or touches of silver. Daniel was rather nice-looking too. She moved down to the next step, dipped her rag in the bucket and repeated the same motions. Daniel was a business owner, had a mill somewhere over the hill where four horses grazed. So why, she asked herself, didn't he have a wife and children to fill his big empty house? Wasn't that one of the most important things to the Amish aside from God? Family?

She shook her head. It was none of her business, she reminded herself. Daniel had indeed sacrificed his own future to protect her and her children. She would never wrap her head around that one, but she would repay him best she could. She would learn to clean and polish and cook like an Amish *fraa*, put on the proper appearances when in certain company and hope their suffering would end soon.

By evening, Hannah had a meal cooking in the oven and a kettle of coffee percolating on the back burner. This was as close as she could get to normal, for the sake of her children who needed normal badly. She had watched Edith climb into a small buggy and leave, promising to return again tomorrow and the next day, until Hannah was at ease with her new life. She had silently thanked God that He had sent someone to show her the ropes. She had a list of supplies on the table, a few recipes Edith knew by heart and three little girls who now had a glimpse of what having a grandparent felt like. To see actual smiles on their faces was enough to push her forward, accept this deception of pretending to be an Amish family.

She looked down at her feet. The bulky plain black shoes Edith brought surprisingly fit perfectly. They beat three-inch heels any day of the week. She wasn't going to miss her Realtor job or the apparel it demanded. That oddly made her smile. Then again, Hannah always did appreciate the little things.

With the girls content playing with a deck of cards found tucked in a drawer with batteries, screwdrivers and other handy items, Hannah stepped out onto the long front porch. The swing in the far corner seemed a nice place to enjoy a fresh cup of coffee.

Fresh sheets blew on the line, their clean scent carrying around the house, into the air. Two large oaks stood gallantly in the yard and shuddered in the late-September wind. She glanced down at one hand, the dried skin from cleaning and washing all day. No stranger to hard work, there was something satisfying in it that she couldn't explain.

Seeing no threats immediately lurking, she allowed herself to relax a bit more against the swing. A rooster crowed, though it was neither sunrise nor sunset, startling her. She figured she would be a bit jumpy for days to come, and chuckled at herself. No one would dare suspect them hiding so far off the beaten path as this.

The late September air was cooler than the last few days had been, and she closed her eyes, inhaled a deep breath and slowly let it out. The world had never been so peaceful, so still. "Thank you, Lord," she whispered.

"Mom!" Catherine shouted from the other side of the screen door. Hannah jerked back to attention and hurried inside. "Where's the TV? I looked everywhere and can't find it." Before Hannah could answer her nine-year-old, Rosemary started crying. She did that at least twice a day. Raised voices, tight spaces, it all seemed to be the new normal Hannah would have to help her adjust to. Hannah hurried into the kitchen, sat down her coffee and quickly scooped the six-year-old into her arms. Catherine fussing, Rosemary crying, and M.J. watching it all with big sad brown eyes, Hannah simply reminded herself to breathe. This was their new normal. They would adapt, just as she would. At least, this time Hannah hoped she could.

"It's okay, baby. I've got you. We're safe, Roslyn. No one is here and we are safe. Just breathe." It took little effort to calm her in her arms, and within a minute, Rosemary was resting against her mother's chest as they rocked back and forth in the chair at the kitchen table.

"Mommy, goats! Aren't they pretty?" Hannah turned to the kitchen door leading out of the side of the house where her five-year-old was currently hugging a strawberry red goat munching on what looked like yellow roses.

Rosemary suddenly perked up at the sight of their newest visitors. "Come on, girls," Hannah instructed on a frustrated breath. "Let's get this creature back to the barn before it decides to eat all the laundry I just washed."

Daniel veered down the long driveway with the newly purchased rope. All children like to swing, he thought, though he had few memories of such things himself. He looked forward to seeing the girls smile, and tasting whatever Hannah had cooked up in the kitchen.

Nearing the barn, Daniel pulled back on the reins, bringing Colt, his best buggy horse, to a halt. His brother's wife in a dark blue dress, a size too big from the looks of it, stood near the corner of the house, both hands planted firmly on her hips. To his right, Catherine, in matching Amish dress, ran around the back of the house and soon appeared out the other side chasing a goat, the nanny's Nubian ears flapping like a basset hound giving chase.

Daniel growled. How had those critters gotten out of his newest pen? On the porch steps sat M.J., smiling as wide as the Kentucky sky while his brown-and-white-spotted nanny munched on his yellow roses. If Daniel weren't mistaken, M.J. was feeding the blooms to the pestering critter, not confiscating them. The old bush had been planted by his *mudder* when he was just a boy. He quickly jumped out of the buggy, tethered Colt to the fencing and went to put an end to all the ruckus. It was time to seriously try harder ridding himself of those goats. They were getting overly fat on grain and great at masterful escapes. They ate too much, cried too often and the rose bush was the last straw. *Jah*, they had to go.

Laughter filled the air, crossing the yard and reaching the barnyard. Daniel's gait slowed as the sound scraped over him. Hannah's laugh was not something he'd expected from a grieving widow on the run, and he didn't know what to make of it. No matter his scrutiny of his brother's wife, the soft pleasant sound brought him a sense of nostalgia and something else—something unfamiliar.

Hannah stopped running, blew a strand of hair from her face and let out an exasperated breath. To his surprise, Catherine was laughing too, chasing the black nanny goat who Daniel considered the ringleader of the unruly lot. Hannah watched her daughter, a soft loving look on her face. It registered within him, and brushed against his heart. *Mudder* used to do that when watching him and Michael run about. A mother's love was an undeniable sight. The woman had gone to great sacrifices for her children. He watched a breath longer, undecided what to make of her. One thing he did know, her beauty couldn't be easily ignored. Daniel was a man open to beauty. A sunrise over the hill often made him take a few extras moments to thank *Gott* for His careful hand. When new life was born, as it was on a farm, it warmed him in a way few things in life could. Finally sensing his presence, she turned to him, shaking her head before running toward him. Daniel quickly collected himself. He had no right to be noticing such things about her. This was Michael's wife.

"*Pest* was too kind a word," she said breathless. "They ate two sheets. Ate them." Her voice pitched. "And that rose bush behind the house is done for. Rosemary is watching over two we managed to get into the barn. M.J. thinks that one is her newest pet. But that one—" Hannah pointed an angry finger toward the black nanny "—needs a lesson in manners. She might not have horns, but can butt just fine without them." Hannah absentmindedly rubbed at her hip as she looked over her shoulder to see that the old nanny wasn't rearing up for another attack.

Daniel suppressed a laugh. No, she looked nothing like an *Englisch* businesswoman born in the city. In her pretty blue dress and apron, her crooked *kapp*, she looked like an angry Amish woman ready to strangle a goat. Helping them fit in wasn't going to be such a difficult task after all, which surprised him, and little in this world surprised Daniel anymore.

"I'll go get some feed. Usually works well enough." He stepped away before she could see he was smiling.

"I'll have supper on the table in a minute. Please send Roslyn—I mean Rosemary—inside," Hannah said on a hurried breath. He nodded and headed for the barn, a play of humor teasing his lips into a grin.

"Oh, and, Daniel," Hannah called out and he turned back to her. "Thanks for not laughing, out loud." She walked away, her two daughters faithfully following. He tried not to think about the way her hair had escaped her *kapp*, or the way she stubbornly marched when in a tiff. He didn't need to notice how easily she moved about as if she hadn't a care in the world. He needed to ignore how appealing such things were. Michael's wife, like his children, was his to protect, and that was that.

Daniel announced himself before entering the barn so as not to frighten Rosemary. She was the easiest to startle and required a patient hand. He hadn't expected to find her nuzzling Colt. She jumped back as if caught doing something unlawful. Daniel moved casually toward her, offered a genuine smile.

"His name is Colt. And he likes when you pat his nose like this." Daniel demonstrated, taking Colt's bridle. Rosemary reached up and did the same as he worked to unhitch him properly. "I'll pick up some carrots and you can feed him. He is very fond of carrots." She hesitated for a moment and then suddenly ran out of the barn and into the house. It seemed Rosemary held a fondness for animals, and no fear of them. Another thing he hadn't expected.

"One day at a time, Lord. One day at a time," Daniel

whispered. Things didn't seem so grim now. God had made him strong, compassionate. He knew the pain of heartache. Michael's daughters needed him and if Daniel were being honest, he needed them too.

When he stepped into the house, Daniel was instantly hit with the smell of crisp lemon floors and fresh air. The aroma of warm chicken took that over quickly. A man could get accustomed to coming home to such smells. So Hannah could cook, as she'd said she could, and clean too, apparently. He would make sure to thank Edith properly for her help. He felt almost ashamed at how dusty the house had become, but a working man had little time for such tasks, and living with a saw-mill nearby only made what little effort he gave in vain. Dust was inevitable.

"Mr. Raber, Mommy made chicken and dumplings. I got to help. Edith says I'm neutral."

"Natural. She said you're a natural," Catherine corrected her sister.

"And look." M.J. twirled wistfully, ignoring her sister's words, one blond curl hanging out of the confines of two perfectly aligned braids. "I'm a real Amish girl."

"And pretty as a sunbeam, I might add." He tossed Rosemary a smile and almost believed she would shyly return it but Catherine had brushed by her with a stack of plates and a frown. Unlike the mother, whom she shared those fair looks with, Catherine was determined to resist his friendship, and anything else that didn't represent their old life. She just needed more breathing space, he considered. Michael had been like that, tempered when confined. Perhaps seeing more of the farm would help soften her.

"I hope you like dumplings. Edith made fresh bread

and we found canned peaches in your pantry. So I made a simple cobbler. I didn't have an Amish recipe," Hannah stuttered nervously as she carried a large pot to the table. "I'm sorry. I hope mine is suitable for your taste." She didn't seem as guarded as she had when he'd left for work. Daniel couldn't ignore how often she used the words *I'm sorry* either.

As he went to the sink to wash up, Daniel replied, "Food is food, and it all looks and smells delicious. *Danki*, Hannah." When she ducked her head and began retrieving forks and spoons from his disorganized drawers, Daniel noted a hint of pride glint over her features. She was eager to please, even if he had a feeling she didn't want to. A natural born thing, he observed. Did she always blush when thanked or complimented? He aimed to find out. "The dress looks nice," he muttered beside her. "You will have no trouble fitting in to our community."

"Just part of the role," she shot back. A hint of warmth had pressed on her soft cheeks. *Jah*, he would have to thank Edith for much. Everyone seemed more relaxed, except for him. His brother's family was now, at least for now, his. Michael would be furious to know they were here, eating at the very table they once had, wearing the clothes he once wore himself.

Catherine reached for a slice of the fresh bread. Daniel spoke up. "Catherine, we have prayer before we eat." The quicker they learned what was considered normal, expected, the faster they would take to it and avoid unnecessary attention.

"We did that at breakfast already," she shot back, not hiding her sharp tone.

"*Jah*, we did. There is no amount too great when it

comes to prayer. The Lord has provided us with food to nourish our bodies. Some aren't so blessed. We have seen another day, and you are all here, safe and together. We have much to be thankful for."

"And Daisy. Don't forget we are thankful for Daisy," M.J. quickly added.

"Daisy?" Daniel queried, turning to Hannah.

"I had to take them into the barn to know where to put your pest." Hannah smiled knowingly.

"Milk cow," M.J. interrupted. "You said we can't name cows because we eat them. But Edith says we don't eat milk cows, which makes me happy. So I asked milk cow what she wanted me to name her and she said Daisy."

Hannah shot him a grin that said, *That's my M.J., try and tell her no.* Well, Daniel couldn't. Naming animals wasn't smart on a working farm, but what harm was it to name one if it made at least one child smile today.

"Well, if she said it was okay, then I can't go against it. I like Daisy. Now let's bow our heads and say a silent prayer." He leaned toward M.J. "That means we don't say our prayers out loud, but we should thank *Gott* for what we have been given." M.J. nodded hard, indicating she would follow instructions. Everything about the little one had his heart fluttering in his chest, filling empty voids that had long echoed with grief.

After the best meal Daniel had eaten in months, he stood from the table. "That was *appeditlich*, delicious, *danki*. After the girls help you clean up in here, I want to give them a tour of the farm."

"That isn't necessary," Hannah said and began stacking plates on top of one another. "We won't be here long enough to need a tour, and cleaning up is my duty, not the children's."

"We can't know how long you will be here. And children need something to do. It teaches them skills, and douses boredom," Daniel countered. Last thing he needed was four bored females wreaking further havoc on his life.

"I understand that is how things are done in your world, but not in ours," Hannah responded in a clipped tone. "And we don't know what's out there. It's best we stay inside, close to the house."

Daniel noted her rigid posture, her arrogant tone. Five seconds ago, she was smiling. He would never understand women. He didn't want to argue with her in front of the girls and he did understand her concerns, but it was important they each knew their surroundings. He had an old well and some of the fences were solar electric. Then there was the matter of the creek. Did any of them know how to swim?

"We live in the same world. Best to know your surroundings," he said before turning toward three sets of young eyes gawking at him. "Ladies, help your *mudder* clear the table and wash the dishes, then get on your shoes and meet me on the porch. We *will* be taking a little adventure." Now that he'd sparked interest in three little hearts, Daniel walked out the door. From what he could see so far, Hannah had a hard time saying no where her children were concerned. He wasn't the type to take advantage of a situation, but this time, he would. Outside, Daniel leaned against the railing and listened to the bustling indoors.

"Mommy, I want to see the farm and horseys and go on a 'venture." Daniel chuckled knowing he hit lit that spark and there was no way Hannah would refuse those big brown eyes.

"He called us ladies," M.J. went on, making Daniel smile.

"Dad would never make us do dishes," Catherine added. Daniel sighed heavily. It wasn't going to be easy, helping Catherine fit in, but he had made a promise to protect them, help them adjust and find healing, and he was a man who kept his promises.

Chapter Five

As the children finished drying dishes, Hannah stepped out onto the porch. Daniel was leaning against a porch post, taking in the horizon, its brilliant orange and red flames illuminating the sky. She took in a breath, never one who liked admitting she was wrong, and stepped forward. They had lived life a certain way—Micah's way—for so long, she hadn't considered it before now. Catherine didn't even know the basics of life, like washing dishes. What harm could be done seeing the farm? A walk would do them all good in truth.

"I understand about the girls needing things to do, but you must understand that my husband insisted that his daughters would never be treated like…"

"Like responsible and capable young women," Daniel tossed out quickly. He must have heard Catherine's outburst. She met his slow lifted glare, "You are not the only ones having to adjust, Hannah, but if we are to make this look real, they have to do what other Amish children do. Chores would be good for them and will keep their minds off worrying."

"You're right," she said. "Busy is always best. It will simply take a bit of getting used to, perhaps."

"And hiding inside, never seeing sunlight, is no good for anyone." He was right again, and she hated it.

She didn't argue. "Things happened so fast, and when the marshals said this was our best option, I accepted that. I'm fine playing dress-up to fit a role, for their safety, but they didn't ask for any of this."

"I understand. Neither did you." His eyes held her captive for one shuddering minute before traveling down and pausing at the ring on her hand. The simple band, a forever promise melted into gold. Hannah stared at it with mixed emotions; anger, grief, a large dose of regret with a side helping of guilt. If she had been a better wife, maybe... She shook off the thought. Life had kicked her plenty enough to know control was never in her hands. *Adjust and adapt*, she reminded herself. And for now that meant keeping the peace and accepting new ways.

"I married a man who lied and stole and put us all in danger. I don't know that we need a tour of a farm we may not stay at for long. There's danger out there," she said, putting the ringed hand behind her back. She would need to remove her wedding band, for the sake of this lie, but it had been a part of her for so long. How did one just toss out the one thing meant to stay with you for a lifetime?

"So he was not a good man?" Daniel's jaw tightened. He was Amish, surely hearing about the things Micah had done troubled him. Hadn't Bryan given him all the facts surrounding the threat out there?

"It would seem he wasn't. That's why we should stay inside, away from dangers."

"The marshal gave me a number to call each afternoon to check in. They believe that man, Corsetti, is heading north." He paused, nodding to where north was. His dark hair held more curls than she'd noticed before, a ridged line where his straw hat sat. "I don't know how to convince you this is the last place anyone would look for you. You will have to trust me, Hannah. You are safe here."

She looked around, seeing only roads, fields and forest, and just one house in view.

"The *kinner* need to know where they are so they can explore, do little chores, feel part of something. They need to know about old wells to avoid, neighbors they can turn to. They need to be children." He looked to her again. How could she argue with someone who was right, about all of it? She wanted them to live in peace with a sense of normalcy too. She was smart enough to know she wouldn't find it, maybe ever again, but this might be as close as she would get for now delivering it to them.

"So do you have family up north?" He studied her with those fascinating hazel eyes. Probably to see her *kapp* was straight and her hair hadn't found its way out of the three bobby pins holding it in place. Could they really pull off presenting themselves as a family to others?

"A foster grandmother," Hannah replied. "She isn't really my family. I never truly knew her. The Thompsons never adopted me, really, just let me stay until I was of age to leave. The authorities already warned me they might head there first, but I haven't talked to her for over twelve years." She went to the railing, looked out at the long gravel drive, fencing aligning the sides. It was rural and earthy, serene.

"You were a foster child?" She detected a hint of surprise in his low tone. Micah always spoke louder than necessary, his words fast and hurried. Yes, everything here was slower. Maybe, after all of this was over, she could find a quiet little space in the world like this to raise the girls in. Some place small with few neighbors, but not fully detached.

"Three times over at least," she replied, leaning against the post opposite him and picking at her nail, removing more of the polish instead of looking at him, wondering what he must think. Then wondering why she cared what he thought at all. Surely, he knew nothing of the real world. The Amish had big families, and, as she was learning, big hearts. No way could Daniel understand her world when his was so quiet and peaceful, and safe.

"How did... Sorry. It's none of my business." He looked out again. Hannah studied his features, the slight hint of an afternoon shadow on his face.

"It's not one you could understand, given who you are," she replied awkwardly. Daniel turned to her again.

"You would be surprised, given who I am." He arched a brow, revealing a man who might be a bit of a mystery himself. "Do you think because I am Amish, I'm exempt from knowing how the world can be?" His arms crossed over his chest, signaling she hadn't a clue about his world.

"No... Yes. I don't know," Hannah scrambled. "I was told you lived among the English for a while, but not how long." But wasn't that something all teenagers did? What was it called…*rumspringa*? At least that's what Agent Moore had said.

"Long enough to know their ways, their reckless regard for others and that I didn't belong there." A thousand scenarios flashed through her mind. That's when she saw it, the pain those eyes carried between the flecks of gold. Right now, Daniel Raber didn't look like a stoic savior to her current woes but a man who had lived and loved and lost. There was more to this man than met the eye, that was for certain. One thing Hannah learned early on, was you didn't get something for nothing. If she wanted to know more about him, that meant she had to give something of herself up.

"I was given up by my mother when I was born and adopted by the Delaneys." His eyes remained on her, unflinching. "They couldn't have children, but when I turned four, Mrs. Delaney got pregnant after years of failed attempts. So I was no longer needed." She couldn't remember them, but she did remember the feeling of being pushed on to the next temporary home and the next. And all her years of trying to fit in, and be loved.

"Children are a gift from *Gott*. I will never understand some of this world."

"It's a waste of time trying. Anyway." She shook off the old memory. "I was passed around a bit, I don't remember how many times, but when I was seven Henry and Anna Clayborn became my foster parents." Hannah smiled, thinking of the couple who taught her how to bake cookies, catch fish and took her to church three times each week. "They were older, had lost their daughter, but I never felt like a replacement. Not to them." Their love for her was undeniable. "They were wonderful people." She toyed with her *kapp* strings as the breeze picked up, letting them tickle her neck.

"I'm glad you had them," Daniel said, studying her intensely. She never liked people who stared, making her uneasy, but with Daniel she didn't feel uneasy. Hannah felt…listened to.

"It was the happiest time of my life." Until she had become a mother. Nothing outmeasured the miracle of bringing life into the world.

"Are they still part of your life, your daughters' lives?"

"No. They are both gone now. Anna got sick when I was thirteen, with cancer." She glanced at her feet, ran her shoe over the planks nervously. "Social services removed me from their care and handed me over to the Thompsons. I never got to say goodbye to her. The one woman who loved me most in this world, and they didn't let me say goodbye." She didn't mean to cry, but losing Anna and Henry had been the hardest loss she ever endured.

"I'm sorry." Daniel offered her a handkerchief. Plain white, all but one little flower in the lower corner. Who even carried those anymore? Apparently, men like Daniel.

"Me too." She took a breath. "The Thompsons, home number three, were what we foster kids called kid collectors." Hannah shrugged. "They house as many children as the state allows, collecting larger checks, which is seldom spent on their wards. As soon as I came of age, I left and went back to find Henry."

"And?"

"He had passed too."

"You have lost much," Daniel said with sincerity but not surprise. She guessed right about that part. Daniel Raber understood loss well.

She hadn't a clue what possessed her to share so much with him. Perhaps it had been too long since she'd had someone who listened to her. Someone who wanted to hear her. It was sweet and, surprisingly, too easy. If she wasn't careful, Hannah might just start to consider Daniel a friend.

Daniel hadn't predicted Hannah had endured so much in her short life. He only hoped his brother had treated her better than those who'd come before him, but was realizing that might not be the case. No wonder her eyes lit up every time he offered a proper thank-you when she made a meal, washed clothes or swept his house. As far as her tidbits of information, he would speak to Marshal Bates about those. No one mentioned his brother had stolen from these men. The threat they were all hoping to avoid might be more dangerous than previously thought.

They both grew silent. The moment drifted into an unexpected intimacy, sharing emotional wounds, as each stood leaning on their own post with a few steps separating them. No more than four feet, but continents apart.

Daniel contemplated the best methods of closing the distance. The marshal insisted he withhold his connection to Michael for now. Hannah didn't need to know Michael had left his family at seventeen and never once called his grieving mother. When their parents died, Michael hadn't even attended their funerals.

She had shared something of herself with him in hopes he too would offer up something of himself in return. Daniel simply wasn't ready to open up as freely as Hannah had, but he pondered over the similarities they did share. He did know what it was like to move around, learn to adapt to new surroundings, and how it felt to not fit in.

After his parents' passing, Daniel had a few friends, a good job at Bentley's Construction, and he had tried to carve out a life for himself. But the city never stuck. He was always the odd man out, the orphan without roots. That's how he felt those years back, but it seemed Hannah had truly been the one without roots, the real orphan.

His mundane life took a pivotal turn the day he opened *mudder*'s Bible and found pages and pages of her heartfelt words, scribbled and tucked away. She'd described a life he had craved for, one he barely remembered, with rules and restrictions, and he wanted it. Without hesitation, Daniel traded the worldly for the simple. Here, in Miller's Creek, is where he belonged. So at twenty-five he packed up his scarce belongings, whispered a dozen prayers, and knocked on Joshua Schwartz's door. His *onkel* had just become bishop and not only remembered him, but welcomed him to the flock. Daniel gave up what he knew, gave in to what really mattered, and joined the Amish community of his roots. It was one brave act that led him here. Hannah had had to act brave most of her life, he was learning.

When the girls scurried out to them, he was glad for the distraction. Listening to Hannah talk about her upbringing made his childhood look like a flick of dust in her heavy dustpan. His father may have made life hard, his life uncertain, but his parents loved him and he knew they did. Daniel never felt unloved.

"Who is ready to meet David and Goliath?" Daniel announced. M.J. immediately threw up a hand, her big brown eyes full of wanderlust to see two big work horses. It couldn't be ignored how Rosemary timidly took in a breath and nearly smiled. He hadn't expected the bridge he hoped to build between them to be constructed so quickly. When it came to Catherine, he knew a lot more hammering would be in order. He just needed to find the right tools.

After a quick tour through the barn, introducing all the animals and explaining electric fencing, Daniel took them to the location of the old well. It was long dried up and forgotten but clearly a hazard to children. He would make arrangements to have it filled soon so as to avoid any accidents. Considering they were so close already, he turned northeast. Not toward home, exactly, but to the creek where willows and birch grew thick. He'd kept the path clear, mostly. There weren't many hours in the day to complete every duty. He walked ahead, smashing down any threats of briars or weeds that might slow their stroll and scratch small ankles. Cool air and the waft of water filled his lungs. How long had it been since he just took a walk? Whip-poor-wills called between frog songs and the first crickets of the season chirping.

"You have so many horses. Which is your favorite?" M.J. asked, stumbling along behind him, a shadow he found pleasing. He glanced over the parade, white *kapps* trailing one after the other as eyes marveled at the simplicities of the country.

"They are all important. David and Goliath are my stronger horses. They pull wagons and hay mowers and sometimes logs for my mill. Maybelle was my buggy horse for a long time, and now that she is getting older,

I like to let her rest as much as possible. That's why I use Colt so often."

M.J. toddled up closer. Daniel slowed his gait near the tree line. "Rosemary likes Colt, but she won't tell you that. I like them all, even Daisy. *Mudder* says your barn is bigger than our house."

"Dirtier than it too, I imagine." Daniel shot Hannah an apprective smile. She had in just one day restored the home of his childhood with scents that invoked pleasant memories.

"Can you milk a horse?" M.J. inquired.

Daniel whipped around abruptly. "*Nee.* We only milk cows." The things kids asked.

"Are there small cows you can milk? Like my size?" Daniel chuckled at her eagerness to try something new.

"*Nee.* I guess you can milk a goat, but that would mean they have to become moms first." Daniel regretted the remark as soon as it escaped his lips. M.J. lit up like a new spark on a dark night and opened her mouth but before she could spill out another question he wasn't prepared to answer, Catherine spoke up from behind them.

"What's that sound?"

"Don't tell me you don't know." Daniel grinned and slowly stepped out of the way. Like scared sheep, Hannah's daughters moved into the clearing. The moment their eyes discovered the source of the sounds, they went wide with excitement. The creek was gently flowing, trickling over rocks and pebbles in a cadence. A few cicadas welcomed them, droning their call. On the opposite side were deep enough depths for a summer swim, but Daniel kept to the shallow shore leading them to an open rock bed area. He should be mucking stalls, storing feed. Anything but this, but he had to admit that he too was enjoying a meandering walk through the woods and along the creek beds.

"Say." He turned to M.J. "Have you ever skipped a rock?" Anyone who didn't know what a creek was, he thought not. Days were warm but the nights were growing chillier. He wished he could strip them of their shoes, lift a few stones and catch crawdads, but he could see they were already spellbound. Simply pleased by this new wonder. Who would have thought such a simple stream of water could build more bridges?

a day's worth of chores done before breakfast and it wouldn't hurt to take a look around, ensuring the safety of the farm. His life had been predictable these past few years, and now four females had changed that. Watching the children's faces light up, their curious natures flicker to life yesterday, Daniel felt a part of something he hadn't predicted. What it felt like to be a father. Their safety, as well as their happiness, meant a lot to him. It wasn't duty or obligation any longer. Was that wrong? He thought about that as he slipped quietly into his boots and out the back door.

Over the quiet weekend, Daniel had moved two dressers into the shared bedroom for Hannah to stow a few items in. She glanced down at her hand, turned the gold band counter clockwise twice, and slipped it off her finger. Jewelry, wedding bands included, wasn't permitted within the Amish. She tucked the ring under a few garments and shut the drawer. In a fast moving week, Edith had managed to gift them two dresses each, undergarments and shoes. Time flew by briskly in the shadow of chores and establishing new habits. Hannah liked routine. Routines promoted stability. As long as she was here, she might as well embrace it. *Until the next shake-up.* Because if there was one thing Hannah knew, life never let you get comfortable for long.

As she descended the stairs, Hannah thought about the meal she'd served tonight at dinner. Micah had had his preferences, what meals he wanted her to serve on a regular basis, but now, with Edith's generous contributions and a pantry filled with possibilites, Hannah was experimenting with new flavors. With so many fresh ingredients, peppers, onions, canned tomatoes,

Hannah had added chicken, a healthy portion of spicy mustard she once read about in a magazine recipe and a light splash of vinegar. The stew was gold. If there was a food Daniel didn't like, Hannah hadn't found it yet. It took so little to earn appreciation here. Daniel always thanked her for every effort she made, even when she burnt toast without the convenience of a real toaster. She smiled, recalling a failed Sunday breakfast. Normally she would have been devastated to fail at something so small, but Daniel rushed into the room, flew open the windows, and instead of stirring up a fuss, he laughed. Hannah was learning that not all laughs were cruel. And oh, how she missed laughter.

She slipped into the kitchen, poured a small cup of coffee before rinsing out the kettle and headed over to the sitting room where her girls awaited Daniel's nightly reading of the Bible. It too had become habit, his idea of normal. Surprisingly, Hannah liked this routine just as much as his nightly patrols of the farm he hadn't a clue she was aware of. He sold her on their safety here by remaining vigilant, convincingly so, and Hannah watched out her window each night for his silhouette moving into the barn, outbuildings and parcel before the lock on the front door clicked to his satisfaction. It was comforting, his hedge of protection, and having an extra set of eyes watching out for her children. She never thought trust would come so easy with a stranger, especially where her children were concerned, but Daniel carried the very essence of trust, the perfect partner to help her endure the coming days.

Hannah slid between Rosemary and Catherine on the long couch. She sat her cup down as M.J. curled into her lap. The sitting room was vast, open and airy with hints of masculinity added. So much open space Catherine could do cartwheels, she mused.

Daniel read from the last verses of the Book of Ruth. Hannah remembered the story well. Ruth had suffered many hardships, but she had Naomi. Hannah had no one. Ruth had Boaz, though Hannah was skeptical. Boaz had looked out for Ruth, but hadn't he been rewarded with much land for marrying her? Hannah would never understand men, or love for that matter. Then again, she was no Ruth.

The slow timbre of Daniel's voice was easy to listen to. She had never known a man who read aloud other than the pastor at their small church. She caressed M.J.'s hair, let her mind recount the events leading her to this night, this place. From the moment the police appeared at her Realtor job to the rush into witness protection, a lot had conspired. In hindsight, Hannah was beginning to piece together why Micah had insisted on her returning to work and why he kept all their financial problems from her.

Daniel closed the Bible, jerking Hannah back to the present. "Let me help you carry them up to bed," he offered, setting the Bible aside and getting to his feet. She hadn't realized the time had raced by and now her daughters lay fast asleep.

"I know you speak to Marshal Bates, but would you mind if I use your phone to talk to him myself?" Hannah got to her feet and repositioned M.J. in her arms.

Daniel gingerly lifted Rosemary from the couch and offered her a look. "*Jah*, that shouldn't be a problem. I have a business phone at the mill. I'm surprised you waited this long to ask." So was she, but she had been so busy with Edith, learning her ways, she somehow had forgotten that she needed to check in with Bryan herself, not just trust Daniel to deliver her the most precise updates. She had a feeling he kept things to himself. Past experience had taught her many things, and men leaving their partners in the dark was one.

"I don't like being a burden, but I would like to talk to him. I've known Bryan a long time. He and Micah were close friends."

"You're not a burden, Hannah. You may ask anything." She wondered if he really meant that. Daniel seemed guarded when it came to himself.

They carried the children up, Daniel making a second trip to fetch Catherine, and together they tucked the girls under the covers of one of the quilts she had found in a chest in one of the other rooms.

"I think I bored them to sleep," he jested, a boyish smile on his face as he looked over her three little girls blissfully sleeping.

"I think it's the highlight of their day actually, aside from going to the creek again," she added. "I must say I have never skipped rocks before."

"Well, maybe we should do it again one evening." Something in the way he suggested it caught her off guard. Was skipping rocks regularly part of his life?

"You weren't very good at it, you know." He grinned. Did he even know just how handsome those grins were? "We could stroll over the orchard fields next door. It's quite a sight in spring when it's in full bloom. They're harvesting now, which is wonderful to see too."

"They would like that," she responded. Daniel opened his mouth to say something else, but closed it again. "So about the use of the phone." She moved toward the door and he followed. "Can I do that soon?"

"*Jah*, tomorrow around noon?" She hated the way the dim lamplight made his eyes look so…intense.

"Noon?" she questioned.

"You can bring lunch for all of us. You should know Eli is allergic to peanut butter, but we Amish men will eat just about anything, as you well know." She fought the urge to shake her head at his cunning.

"Lunch?" Hannah crossed both arms but couldn't hide her amusement in his subtle request, or how much she really enjoyed his laid-back humor. If Hannah weren't mistaken, Daniel Raber was a bit of a charmer too. She would do well to keep things strictly friendly.

"You can use the phone and M.J. can entertain the men with stories about rock skipping and milk cows." Daniel moved through the doorway and turned back to her.

"I don't think that's a good idea, Daniel. The Marshals said the fewer people we meet the better."

"I think it's a fine idea. So bring us lunch tomorrow, use the phone and let me show off those pretty girls." He moved down the hall before she could even object. He said it as if he wanted to parade her children around, as his own. Part of her took offense. They were not his children, but Hannah couldn't help thinking, what would be the benefits of a father figure like Daniel for her girls? She shook the thought off quickly. None of this was real. Daniel was her husband in name only. A pretend father. She was leaving as soon as it was safe. He knew that. He agreed to it. No way could a man like that really want a woman like her. They weren't his, and neither was she.

Chapter Seven

"**H**ow's it feel being a married man?" Eli Plank elbowed Daniel as they finished stacking a lumber order for Lynch Construction.

"It's different," Daniel said honestly, ignoring Eli's wiggling brows. It was like being a fish out of water. What had possessed him to invite Hannah for long walks and lunches? Those soft smiles and two ovals of heavenly blue caused a man to succumb to a momentary weakness. He raked a hand through his hair. Eli poked him again and bellowed out a laugh. "I bet it is." Daniel handed both his employees a sports drink, and chugged his down like a man wandering the desert. He didn't want to talk about his complicated married life, wished he hadn't informed his hired hands about his newly acquired family, but he wasn't showing up for *Gmay*, the biweekly church service, with a family. Tongues would be wagging but Daniel knew, between Edith and Eli, the community would all know by now he was a married man.

Being responsible for Michael's family was a gift. At least that's what Joshua called it. Daniel didn't regret taking on the extra responsibility, but to them he was a stranger. A mere safe haven until the authorities took them away again. But Daniel was becoming attached. Each girl needed something different and he was edging closer to discovering what that was. He would never have children of his own, this being as close as he would ever get. When this was all over, he would tell them who he was, how they were connected. Hopefully, Hannah would allow him to see the children from time to time. They were becoming friends he liked to think. Surely, she wouldn't find a problem with that. Then again, it was Michael who had gotten her into this whole mess after all. Guilt took a stab at him. Would she sever their family ties once she discovered who he was?

"She a good cook? Nothing worse than marrying a woman and finding out she can't boil water." Eli's question interrupted him from his thoughts.

"That's poor Simon Beachy's problem," Vernon Schwartz added in. "He thought he was getting a jewel when he married my sister, Tracie. Found out soon enough she can't cook a lick. *Mudder* tried plenty. It never stuck." Vernon shook his light brown head in bewilderment. His straw hat shed a thick layer of sawdust into the breeze. Standing left of the mill usually earned him a good dusting of sawdust. "She can sew and grow just about anything, but can't fry an egg or bake a cake to save the farm."

"Well, Hannah cooks fine. Though she makes some dishes I have never heard of. She made pork with some barbeque sauce and ranch dressing mixture that was awfully *gut*. The woman liked her spices too." Daniel rubbed his belly. "I've no complaints in that department."

"And don't complain either. That doesn't work.

Women don't have good ears like we do," Eli said. "Is she *schee*?" Hannah was more than pretty, Daniel wanted to say. "You *have* been keeping her hidden away for more than a week." Eli lifted a brow. "Makes one wonder."

"That isn't an issue," Daniel replied with a red-faced laugh. Hannah was beautiful, inside and out. "And is it not what's on the inside that counts?" Daniel poked back.

"That's what *they* say." Eli winked. "But it's awfully nice if you can stand to look at her." Vernon and Daniel laughed. They would both see for themselves just what Daniel had gotten himself into in another hour or so. Edith felt that slow introductions into the community were best, and with church Sunday in just a couple days, Daniel hoped Edith was right. Hannah was still tense, always looking over her shoulder, waiting. Rosemary seemed more relaxed outdoors, but every creak of a floorboard drew her back. Strange, how indoors she seemed skittish, while outside she let down her guard.

"I will never understand why Sara ever agreed to marry the likes of you," Daniel teased. Sara Plank was too kind a woman to be married to his bolstering foreman.

Eli gave Vernon a wink. "What about the *kinner*? They growing on ya yet?" *Crawled into his heart*, Daniel thought.

"They've been through a lot, losing a *daed*, moving, getting a new one." But it was getting better he believed wholeheartedly.

"Makes sense," Vernon said and went back to stacking lumber.

"Hard thing, death. Especially on *kinner*. They might need more time to adjust," Eli said without any sarcasm.

"Not that little one," Daniel added. "I'm not sure how to get through to the oldest two and Hannah is a bit protective. They have been a foursome for a spell. I don't understand all her ways of thinking." Like why the girls didn't need to do chores. Daniel suspected it had little to do with Michael and more to do with Hannah's need that her children not be subject to hard work. He tried seeing her side of it. Had her time as a foster child been all about work? Had she never been given a proper childhood of her own? He had his suspicions.

"Don't bother trying to understand women. Just be glad *Gott* created them," Eli advised.

Daniel chuckled. "You're probably right about that."

"Always am." Eli beamed arrogantly.

"I think your house full of women is about to get a welcoming they won't forget," Vernon added.

"Huh?" Daniel turned in the direction Vernon was nodding.

Eli burst into laughter. "Is it Tuesday already?"

It was clear to see lunch was now canceled thanks to his weekly visitor.

Hannah added freshly sliced cheese to each chicken sandwich currently spread out on the counter. She'd made chocolate chip cookies, baked beans, and managed to put together a small salad that included tomatoes, cucumbers and onions, with a homemade vinegar dressing. Her recent bread-baking attempt was a complete failure, but thankfully Edith had seen to it they had plenty to spare from their cooking practices. She would try again tomorrow, hating that she hadn't gotten the hang of something seemingly so simple with only four ingredients. Water, flour, yeast and salt, and she managed to ruin it.

Catherine tucked plates and forks into the large basket Daniel had laid out for her this morning as a reminder. The man wanted his lunch delivered. It was the least she could do, considering he was housing and providing for four extra mouths to feed.

"The mill will probably be dirty," Catherine quipped, always trying to find the downside to everything. Hannah ignored her. In fact, she looked forward to seeing where Daniel worked, how he spent his day. Just the walk over the hill alone would brighten her spirits. For as restless as her daughters were becoming staying near her side, under the cover of walls and doors, Hannah was feeling a bit restless too.

Daniel mentioned his hired hands during supper. Hannah learned that Vernon Schwartz was his fourth cousin and had four kids, all with names that started with *S*. The other man working under Daniel's employ, Eli Plank, was apparently full of bad advice, which he liked to give out for free and Daniel insisted no one should take. It would be a nice change of atmosphere, getting to know the people around her. She had lived in the same house for nearly seven years and hadn't even known the names of most of her neighbors.

At the sound of a buggy outside, Hannah's heart jumped into her throat. Her daughters too, came to alert. "It's just a buggy. Nothing to worry about," Hannah assured them as much as herself.

"*Aenti* Edith said she isn't coming today. She has chores to do. Who could it be?" M.J. asked. Since when had her youngest resorted to calling Edith her aunt? They clustered near the sitting room window and peered out. Two women climbed down from the buggy in matching blue dresses and white aprons. One was tall and shapely and younger than Hannah, the other short and maybe ten years her senior. They collected plates and a cake carrier from the buggy floor, then headed toward the house. Hannah straightened to the fact that she was about to face her first visitors.

"It looks like we're not going to the mill for lunch today," she said, a bit disappointed. She hated that Daniel would be without his lunch, but she couldn't send the girls to deliver it by themselves, could she?

"Girls, remember, don't speak too much. Just smile, and be friendly." Hannah shot Catherine an extra look before nervously tidying her dress, apron and *kapp*. She couldn't remember the last time she'd cared so much about her looks, or how she'd fit in. She walked toward the front door, took a deep breath and opened it with a smile.

"Hello," Hannah said, stepping out, her daughters finding a place at her side. Their little hands primly gathered in front. To outsiders, they were adorable. To Hannah, they were really good at pretending.

"I'm Millie Troyer, your nearest neighbor, and this is Margaret Sayer. We've come to welcome you and your family to our community." Millie smiled, with a glint of sparkle in green eyes that contrasted boldly with her fair complexion.

"Please, come in." Hannah welcomed them inside. Thankfully, the kitchen was freshly cleaned, and the floors swept.

"I brought *kichlin*." Millie offered each girl a cookie from the plate in her hand before turning to Hannah. It tasted like bliss, with the warm chewy texture of cinnamon and molasses. Their local bakery back home had never made such delicious cookies like this.

"We feel terrible we only learned of your arrival today. Edith Schwartz isn't usually so secretive about newcomers, but Hazel Miller heard you moved in and married our sweet Daniel and told Eliza Lapp. She's a poor widow who lives just four or five farms from yours." Millie pointed south, juggled the plate still in her other hand. "Eliza isn't one for company, but Emma Byler, that's Hank Byler's *fraa*, she went to check in on her as she tends to do, and when Emma came by the orchard for a few melons from our garden, she told me all about it. I can't believe a week of days has come and gone and we didn't even know our Daniel found a *fraa* and brought her home to Miller's Creek," Millie said without taking a single breath.

Before replying, Hannah inhaled deeply, then said, "I'm sure Daniel was just giving us time to get settled." While Millie placed another cookie in her daughters' hands, Margaret strolled leisurely around the large kitchen. She ran a finger along the old hutch in the corner, her face pinched in disapproval. A bead of perspiration made a slow journey down between Hannah's shoulder blades. She mentally noted to add extra dusting to her list of duties. These women must think Daniel chose a lazy bride.

"Most marriages are performed with the community as witness," Margaret said, sounding doubtful.

"It was a simple, private ceremony," Hannah replied, earning her two quizzical looks from her visitors. She knew she should say as little as possible, knowing so little about Amish traditions still. Mentally, she ran through the facts she and Daniel had agreed upon, in case questions like this occurred.

"This pie looks *wunderbaar*," Hannah complimented Margaret, admiring the beautiful woman with ivory skin and pretty blond hair.

"Daniel is fond of my apple pie," Margaret said sharply. "I usually bring one by once a week, but was visiting family recently." Hannah almost gasped in surprise. Just as quick as Millie Troyer had made Hannah feel welcome with cookies and smiles, Margaret Sayer took it all back. It appeared that Margaret had only come to meet the woman who married Daniel, and found her unworthy. Feeling immediately insecure, Hannah put her partially eaten cookie down on the counter.

"I'm sure Hannah here knows Daniel's likes and dislikes well enough," Millie quickly chimed in. "What man doesn't live for a full belly and a clean house," she laughed. Hannah agreed, despite knowing those things didn't satisfy some men. Millie seemed kind enough, but the tension in the room was so thick you could cut it with a knife. As the girls took their cookies to the porch, Hannah put the kettle on for coffee. She'd finally figured out how to make a decent cup of coffee without the luxury of simply pushing a button.

"How did you and Daniel meet?" Margaret asked. Hannah turned from the stove, realizing that she was stubbornly sitting at the head of the kitchen table, in Daniel's chair, legs crossed with the upper one angrily swinging. "I speak to him nearly each week and he has never mentioned you to me before."

Everything suddenly became crystal clear. And Hannah felt a pang of guilt. Had she come between two sweethearts? This woman clearly had an interest in Daniel. She studied her cautiously. She was very pretty, frown and all. Had they been courting when Hannah and her girls were dropped on his doorstep? She and Daniel hadn't shared such information. Why hadn't Edith mentioned this to her before?

But one thing she knew for sure and certain—she had to stand firm, keep up the facade, for her children's sake. "He failed to mention your weekly conversations to me, as well," Hannah countered. "Daniel knew my late husband. After we lost him, I ran into Daniel and we... Well, how would one describe it?" She forced a bashful smile. "We connected rather well." It was only a small lie. Daniel knew nothing about Micah, except he'd put his family in danger, but they had come to grips with their roles. Hannah respected how he fulfilled his by playing dad to three little girls he had no connection to.

The screen door slammed and M.J. bounced in. Margaret didn't even flinch nor break eye contact with Hannah as her daughter toddled over to her.

"Oh, would you like another *kichli, liebling*?" Millie asked, handing her daughter another. "You are so sweet," Millie fussed.

"Danki." M.J. smiled. "I have a pet cow named Daisy." *Where did she learn that word?* Hannah wondered.

"Mudder, Rosemary needs you," Catherine said as she ran into the room. It was one thing for M.J. to try on the Amish words, but Catherine had been dead set against even wearing her prayer covering, though she was wearing it right now.

"Please excuse me for a moment." Hannah stepped

out of the kitchen quickly and found her daughters all huddled in the sitting room. "What's wrong?"

"Nothing, we just thought you needed rescuing," Catherine said. "That one lady asks too many questions. She doesn't seem to like you, and you do still call us the wrong names sometimes." Hannah pulled her into a hug and smiled.

"You are a wonderful daughter." Hannah kissed her cheek. "Or should I say, *wunderbaar*? But we have to deal with this. I can't hide in here until they leave."

"We could try," Catherine said, quirking a grin. Oh, how Hannah had missed that grin. Suddenly, the front door opened again. Hannah hoped that more company hadn't decided to show up. She and her daughters stepped back into the kitchen just as Daniel rushed into the room, sweat pouring from his face. He looked as if he had run all the way from the mill. Hannah wasn't quite sure why he'd done so, but the soured expression on Margaret seemed to be part of it.

"*Daed*, we have visitors. Millie brought pie." M.J. beamed and started rocking heel to toe adorably. Hannah had managed to contain her shock from their visitors but not from Daniel, who was equally surprised at her youngest's growing vocabulary.

"Millie brought *kichlin* for the *kinner*. I brought the apple pie," Margaret corrected. "Your favorite. Should you not be at the mill at this hour?" Margaret tilted her head and smiled coyly. Hannah knew it wasn't right, feeling as if this stranger was making no effort to hide her thoughts, but she didn't like thinking this woman— who didn't know they weren't really married—was flirting with her husband.

"Both will be appreciated by all of us, *jah*?" Daniel slowed his breathing as Hannah crossed the room and fetched a glass from the cabinet so she could give him some water.

"*Mudder* makes pies too," Catherine added. "She makes the best pies." Daniel flinched, and she could tell he was already figuring out that things weren't going so well.

"I work next door, so it's easy enough to sneak in and see my family during the day," Daniel said. It wasn't a total lie, he could if he wanted to see in on them during the day. She filled a glass with water and handed it to him. As he drank, they both leaned against the counter, shoulder to shoulder. They were in this together.

"Sometimes *Mudder* takes lunch to him so they can have more time together," Catherine added. Hannah was shocked that Catherine came to his defense. Daniel drained his glass and she refilled it a second time. "We even packed a basket for him today." Catherine pointed out, grinning. Her daughter might look like her, but this one had Micah written all over her. The little trickster!

"Oh, we must have come at a bad time," Millie began before Margaret quickly added, "Will your Catherine be joining school soon? Lydia is a *wunderbaar* teacher and has a talent for…outspoken *kinner*." Margaret's gaze landed on Catherine briefly before returning to Daniel.

Hannah stiffened. No one was going to talk about her children like that. But before she could say anything, Daniel spoke. "We just married, and the *kinner* are adjusting to a new community and a new house. I'm sure you can understand how we are all trying to enjoy this special time together." Hannah was relieved, hearing all the reassurance in his voice. Millie and Margaret both had to believe this was a true marriage or Margaret would spread unwanted gossip. Margaret's frown began to deepen.

"*Jah*, of course. New couples need time to themselves," Millie agreed, looking to Margaret as if reminding her of her place. "I would love for your *dochdern* to come visit and perhaps have a sleepover with my three girls." All three girls' faces lit up. Was the idea of making friends here the reason for their excitement? "My Ivy is just about your Catherine's age. Though the other two are a wee bit older and they love *kinner*. Anytime you two want a moment to yourselves, let me know, *jah*?" Millie darted a knowing smile between Hannah and Daniel. Hannah felt her face turn hot. But she recovered quickly.

"Oh, that would be so appreciated, Millie. I still have so much to tend to around the house, but if that offer still stands in a couple of weeks, Daniel and I will definitely bring the girls over to visit. He's been so hard at work at the mill—" she touched his arm affectionately "—we haven't had much time together. I haven't even seen most the area and think a tour would be so lovely." When Hannah smiled up at Daniel a second time, he met her gaze with a smoldering look that steeled her. She had only meant to sound convincing, to pretend to be the happy newlyweds. The way those eyes were looking down on her, she was convinced that he was much better at pretending than she was.

"We should go and leave you all to your lunch."

"*Danki*, Millie, Margaret." Daniel nodded curtly. As Millie said farewell to the girls, Hannah didn't miss the long look Margaret shot Daniel.

Feeling very much like a weed sprouting up between

two perfectly constructed stepping stones, Hannah stepped away from Daniel.

"Let me walk you both out," she offered kindly. She guided both women out and thanked them again for the treats and the warm welcome. Following proper etiquette ingrained in her from a young age, Hannah invited them to visit again, though she wasn't sure Margaret would take her up on that offer.

It was the right thing to do, being kind to Daniel's neighbors. She waved goodbye and took a long breath before entering the kitchen again.

Daniel stood at the counter helping Catherine fill the lunch basket. She didn't move, just watched as the two worked silently together, each in their own thoughts. At the table, her youngest two children nibbled on cookies. It was a simple scene, yet, one she had never been privileged to witness before now. She probably shouldn't be thinking how sweet they all looked.

Like a regular family.

She couldn't ignore how Daniel rushed home to see them. He was a natural protector, a man who was meant to be head of a household. From the moment they met, he kept surprising her. Every encounter, every small talk shared between them, was having her craving the next one.

"Mommy, I pretended real good, didn't I?" M.J. called out and all eyes turned to her.

"Yes, you did, dear." Marshaling the thoughts swirling in her head, Hannah moved farther into the room.

"It seems I have a house filled with *schmaert maedels*." Daniel tossed her a wry grin.

"What's a *maedel*?"

"A young lady," Daniel answered, tapping her nose. It had become his show of affection to her little one.

"Are you a *maedel* too?" Hannah chuckled at her daughter's cookie-coated fingers and parade of questions. It had been a lot of years since she felt young.

"*Nee*, she is a *fraa*, a married woman," Daniel explained. While M.J. practiced the new word, Daniel leaned back on the counter, folded his arms and simply stared at Hannah. It was a bit intimidating and made her begin to feel terribly self-conscious. Was he angry with her acts of affection moments ago? Did he sense the tension between her and the woman he could have married and lived a perfectly normal life with?

In his unflinching stare, Hannah smoothed her palms down her dress and made a quick motion to assure her *kapp* was straight. "She is also a young *mudder.*" His eyes perused her in full. Surely he was regretting this arrangement by now. The woman who left here just seconds ago was perfect.

"And possibly a great many other things I haven't discovered yet." Satisfied with his answers, M.J. resumed eating. Hannah on the other hand was shocked to the core. Less by his words than the intense look on Daniel's face. The churning in her belly stopped and was replaced with the soft flutters of attraction, affection and newness. She quickly placed a hand over her middle as if that alone would hide how he affected her.

It was then, in that fraction of a second, her words came back and strangled her. In answering Millie, Hannah had alluded to spending time with Daniel alone, seeing the area. Was he going to see she made good on those words? The very thought of long buggy rides across the valley or late evening strolls to the creek had her blood warming rapidly.

This time when their eyes collided, Daniel did smile and it didn't stop with his lips. It reached those hazel eyes until they smiled too. "It seems you can handle yourself just fine without me," he chuckled and gathered the basket on the counter. "I should get back to the mill before Eli puts up a fuss." He turned to the girls. "Don't be naming any more animals while I'm gone," he said playfully. Brushing past Hannah, he paused. "See you at supper, *fraa*." When the door shut, Hannah still hadn't moved.

Chapter Eight

Wednesday evening, Daniel walked home from the mill, clearing his head from the day's work and all the thoughts swirling in his head, using the time for prayer. It had always helped him before, when life got out of control. Now was one of those times. He was a husband and father in pretense only, but knowing it was all temporary, he had no idea how to take the helm. He wanted very much to love the girls freely. Provide them with stability, roots and a faith so strong they found healing just as he had. In short, they needed a father.

Then there was Hannah. When she looked at him and smiled yesterday, he couldn't help that his heart hammered, in fact he'd been defenseless against it. Her delicate beauty pulled him in. The way her eyes smiled at her daughters even when her mouth didn't move. It didn't go unnoticed how fast she had taken to his life, his world. The woman was determined to master anything and everything put in front of her. It caught him off guard, these feelings. He was a lonely man. And this was Michael's wife, an *Englisher* and a city dweller. But when he looked at her, he didn't see who she was before. Daniel saw Hannah, the Plain-dressed and protective mother with honey blond hair and eyes that made a man question everything. He'd never expected to be drawn to her when he agreed to this, but her air of fragility raised his protectiveness, and her eyes awakened his heart.

"*Gott*, don't let me get used to this. If You are going to take them away, make it swift," he prayed heavenward. He was not near as strong as he thought he was.

"Now you stop being nasty." Daniel heard the little voice as he closed the pasture gate and reached the yard.

M.J. stood in her new green dress, barefoot, pointing a crooked stick at his cantankerous rooster. "Trying to make friends with chickens now?" he teased. She turned toward him and beamed a little sunshine his way. It had been a long day, with orders piling up faster than he could cut them, and Bates had called to inform him of the current status of Corsetti, which was still undetermined. Coming home to her smiling face was just what he needed.

"*Hinkel. Aenti* Edith says it's not a chicken, but a *hinkel*." She shrugged adorably. "This one tries to bite Mommy every time she wants to get the eggs. I'm going to train him." Daniel wondered when she had started referring to Edith that way, then shook off the thought. Martha Jane was a wonder, fearless and social, and hoping to train a chicken to obey commands. Did his brother ever know how blessed he was?

"Even little Amish girls call them chickens, and for your information, that big fellow is a rooster. If he thinks you're afraid of him, he will take advantage."

She scrunched her little face. "*Nee*, I'm not afraid." She demonstrated by pushing her shoulders back and walking right up to the red rooster with colorful tail plumage. "Go back to bed until you can be nice to *Mudder*," she ordered, shaking her measly stick at him. Daniel stepped closer to intervene in case the old rooster had had enough, but suddenly found himself in awe when the rooster turned and stalked straight into the henhouse.

"How did you do that?"

"I dunno." She shrugged. "Maybe he is afraid of me." Daniel laughed so hard he thought he might start crying. "I made you happy," she added. "I like it!"

"*Jah*, you made me happy, and I like it too." If only all of life's troubles could be so easily cured with M.J.'s smiles and crooked sticks. "How was everyone today?"

"Catherine said I'm not allowed to call you *Daed*, since we already had one." She tapped her finger to her chin as if she were thinking. "*Mudder* was invited to a sewing party or sister party. I dunno what that is. She doesn't have sisters she said and looked sad. I don't think she wants to go. And Roslyn hasn't cried all day." Daniel appreciated the full report of the house.

"Sister's Day. That's sort of like sewing bees and frolics where the women of the community get together and quilt, or can food, or bake lots of sweets. It's a way of helping each other and taking care of everyone's needs."

"*Daed*, is there milking frolics too?" M.J. asked. The girl was taken with cows, that was for sure and certain.

"*Nee*, no milking frolics, I'm afraid. And you don't have to call me *Daed*. You can just call me Daniel."

"*Aenti* Edith taught me. It's how you say *daddy* in Amish. I am an Amish girl now, you know." Her face scrunched adorably. Powerless against her charm, Daniel lifted her off the ground and gave her a tickle.

"You laugh like one too," he jested as he carried her into the house.

Hannah had made a spicy rice dish with sausage for dinner. Daniel had never heard of it, but found it to his liking. The spices warmed his bones against the early October chill and cleared the sinuses. He was on his second helping when Hannah asked, "So Millie and Margaret mentioned sending the girls to school."

"I'm not going to an Amish school, Mom," Catherine said. "They probably don't even use real books."

"They do use real books, Catherine. And most Amish children are needed at home, so they have to learn everything *Englisch* kids do, but faster."

"Faster? What does that mean?" Catherine asked.

Daniel froze mid-bite at her sudden attention. He detected eagerness in the face of a challenge in this one and mentally stored the information away. He had noted little things about each of them. They all had their own different personalities. Rosemary trembled more at night than during the day, but she had jumped in to help her mother with household duties. M.J. liked reminding the world to smile, and making friends, even if they were angry roosters. She was eager to fit in, much like her mother, Daniel quietly assessed. Hannah wanted to fit in, and make everyone happy. Daniel could see that all the changes to her life were taking their toll on her. There was a weariness in her eyes. Common house noises made her stiffen, and he had a feeling she wasn't sleeping at night. He wished he knew how to ease her worries. But like with Catherine, he might have just found a way in.

"*Jah*, Amish children only go to school until eighth grade. They pass the same tests to do so as seniors do in *Englisch* high schools." Catherine crossed her arms over her chest, indicating she didn't believe him. "I think school is a *gut* idea. You all could make friends your own age, and I bet you'd learn faster than the other kids your age. It would be *gut* not to get behind in your lessons too." Daniel forked another bite of rice into his mouth and watched as Catherine's mind processed everything he'd said.

By the end of the meal, Daniel was certain Catherine would understand the importance of going to the local school. Standing, she collected her plate and turned to her mother. "Please don't make me go to an Amish school."

If he was going to get this one to comply to what was normal in his world, he would have to find another way to do it.

Like most evenings, Hannah followed Daniel to the porch after supper was cleared from the table. It was the only time they could speak without little ears about. "I can't force her to go to school here if she doesn't want to, Daniel. That wasn't part of the deal."

"It will be *gut* for her. I'll drive her myself and pick her up. It's normal, and normal is *gut, jah*?"

"She'll be angry we're making her go, and she'll be impossible to live with." Hannah didn't need the aggravation.

"Then blame me. Tell her I insist that she goes," he said gruffly. Hannah could tell he was still put off with her since Millie and Margaret had visited. Did he wish Margaret were here with him talking about sending children to school instead of her?

"I'm sorry I let my mouth run off like it did when Millie and Margaret visited that day. I didn't mean to come between you and Margaret. I was only trying to make this look real."

"I'm sorry too." She looked in his eyes, trying to read his thoughts, but to no avail.

"You didn't have to rush over here, you know. I can handle a few visitors from the community, including your girlfriend."

"*Nee*, I rushed over because you shouldn't be alone. I promised to help you and that includes dealing with people you don't know." And the price he was paying was too much. Her and the girls being here had cost him the chance for a real family of his own. For a long moment, she saw him for the decent man he was. He was a rare and wonderful human being. How many men would have gone to the same lengths he had for mere strangers? "And she is *not* my girlfriend."

Hannah stiffened. "When a woman bakes you pies weekly, she wants to be." Did he think her blind?

Daniel took a step closer. Close enough she could smell the scent of sawdust and sweat that penetrated his clothing.

"Married men don't have girlfriends," he said in a low tone.

"Some do." She quickly averted her gaze, regretting the slip of the tongue immediately. "She is very pretty and clearly cares for you."

"Does that bother you?" he queried.

She looked up at him; those hazel eyes searching

her for an answer were making her breathless. He was forcing her entire world to shift. "Yes, it bothers me. You've wasted your chance at a real wife by helping us. I'm not heartless, Daniel. We've disrupted your life, maybe even ruined it. Edith told me the truth, that we likely can't get an annulment when this is over. That we will have to stay married. We owe you so much for letting us be here…"

"My help is freely given. Maybe my life needed disrupting, and I have a real wife, however short-lived. I had a choice. We all have a choice. Nothing is ruined, Hannah." She couldn't believe that. She had taken advantage, spoiled his future, and he was making it sound as if she had not burdened him in any way.

"What about when we leave? This isn't our home. We will leave, eventually, Daniel. What about your future? My decision to agree to come here has taken that from you." She felt the first sting of tears threaten.

"Our future is in *Gott*'s hands. You are not that powerful, *liewe*." He grinned down at her. "And this is our home."

"You're not angry with me, are you?" She looked up, confused. Micah would have stirred up such a fuss at her boldness in front of others.

"*Nee*, I could never be angry with you. I'm committed to this. I care for your *dochdern*, I can't lie about that." Then she saw it. For just a second, she saw him, truly saw him. She had been missing all the signs right in front of her. Daniel was not the kind of man who lied to get what he wanted. But what was it he wanted? She took a step back, and reined in her common sense.

He cared for her girls, possibly loved them. He wanted what Micah never did. Daniel wanted children.

Hannah suspected he would sacrifice more for her daughters' sakes if asked. The quicker she understood that the better.

Her heart was in danger and she knew it. A woman would be a fool not to see what stood in front of her. Daniel Raber was a man to measure all men by.

"Micah didn't do that." The words slipped before she could stop them.

"What do you mean?" he asked.

"He never cared about something besides his job. Here you are, a stranger, sacrificing your entire future for us. I would understand if you want us to leave, to go someplace else." Daniel shook his head as if leaving wasn't an option.

"No place will be safer for you, for them, than here with me." Why was it so hard to breathe hearing him say that, to have him so close? They stood and stared at one another in a silence thick with choices, possibilities and regrets. She worried if they stood there much longer, she would make a fool of herself with him. Reveal her feelings. He was struggling too, some inner battle she wasn't privy to. As if only now noticing how close he was hovering over her, Daniel took two steps back.

"Catherine should start attending school next week. And it would be *gut* to have Rosemary helping with the animals. She's made for it. And…" He paused, grinned at the thought. "Let's have M.J. gather the eggs from now on."

Hannah was surprised by his demands that weren't actually very demanding. "But that rooster…" Daniel tossed her a smirk as he made his way down the porch steps, and then turned to face her again.

"She can handle him, trust me. That one is the least

of your concerns. I have a couple big orders this week, but after I think it's a *gut* time you learned to drive a buggy."

"I can't…" she started to protest.

"You can. You will take that to task too," Daniel said as he walked away from her.

Hannah stood on the porch and watched him go check on the animals, making his nightly rounds and see that all was as it should be before getting to bed. Daniel always had the same routine. A woman could set her watch by what time he woke each morning, milked the cow, went to work at the mill, returned home and walked over his farm to see no killers lurked about. Did he ever do anything spontaneous? She hoped not. Very few things in her life had ever been predictable, and Hannah found she suddenly liked predictable.

And hazel eyes.

Chapter Nine

Hannah triple-checked each daughter to make sure they were ready. Their *kapps* were stiff and white, their dresses ironed and even their new shoes shined, though Edith didn't press on doing so. If anyone in Miller's Creek mistook them for *Englisch* today, it would be for whatever poured out of one of her daughters' mouths, not for how they looked.

"Now, remember. Talk as little as possible, and don't use the Amish words Edith has been teaching you unless you feel comfortable with them." Hannah had been reluctant to try them herself, but M.J. thought each new word Edith taught her was more fascinating than the next. "Okay, Rosemary?" Hannah was only rewarded with a headshake. What Hannah wouldn't give to hear Rosemary mutter the simplest sound. Her silence was said to be temporary, but living on the road, hiding from a killer, was supposed to be temporary too, and here it was nearly three weeks later and temporary was still their lives. Hannah had decided today, as they planned on joining the community for church services, that temporary could deal with itself.

"What if someone doesn't think I'm an Amish girl?" M.J. asked.

"Just say we are from Indiana and that's how we talk." *Simple as that*, Hannah thought.

"Is that a lie? *Daed* says not to lie." M.J.'s face scrunched.

"He is not our dad," Catherine snapped. "Mom, make her stop calling him that." Hannah exhaled.

"M.J., you don't have to call Daniel Dad." Hannah reminded her a second time.

"But *Aenti* Edith says you are married so he is my *daed*. Mine is gone. Don't you want me to have one?" Hannah was speechless. How did one tell a five-year-old it was all pretend? Hannah and Catherine locked eyes. Even she had no quick reply right now.

"What I do want is for us to get going. We don't want to be late for church. We can talk about this later," Hannah stated as she ushered them out of the shared bedroom. It would be the first time any of them rode in a buggy, the first time going to an Amish church and the first time they would have to present themselves as a family in public. That was enough firsts to deal with for one day. Her nerves frayed, her stomach in knots, and even though the house held a slight chill this October morning, Hannah found herself perspiring.

Outside, Daniel lifted each girl into the buggy and instructed them to sit in the back, M.J. in the center, her sisters on each side, then held out a hand to Hannah.

"You don't need to help me, Daniel. I can do it," she insisted, putting her foot to the high step.

"I have no doubt, but humor me." Daniel grinned, taking her hand in his. As much as she hated to admit it, he did in fact make the climb easier. It was his warm, calloused hands that was hard to ignore. There was no way Daniel could be allowed to spark anything in her. Bryan would find Corsetti and then they'd soon return to the real world. *It's all just pretend*, she reminded herself.

At the sound of Daniel clicking his tongue, the horse jerked forward and the buggy began to move. Hannah looked over her shoulder to see that her girls weren't frightened in the least. Surprisingly even Catherine looked entertained. She had to admit, she too felt the air of excitement as the horse picked up speed.

"Just enjoy the ride," Daniel whispered to her. "It is a slower pace than you are used to traveling, for sure and certain." He smirked. "But slowing down has its own rewards."

As soon as they pulled onto the blacktop of the road, Hannah took in the passing scenery as she felt the slight jerks and pulls of the buggy. Watching Colt stretch and move was making her nauseous. She pulled her eyes away, looked at the driver again. Daniel was trusting their lives to the hooves of an animal. She forced herself to focus on the scenery again and not the scenarios playing in her mind.

Leaves had lost their lush emeralds and had traded them for bold reds, bright oranges, and a yellow that Hannah could only describe as mellow and earthy. Barns towered over homes, and homes were few and far between. Land rolled gently, pastures fenced in a backdrop of forest. How had she lived so long and not seen such beauty in person?

Hannah took special care to note all the mums and sunflowers lining walkways and lingering in gardens that looked barren elsewise. She had picked vegetables in Daniel's garden, learned how to can tomatoes thanks to Edith, but wondered what it would feel like to touch virgin soil, plant a seed, watch it grow. In his world, such a thing wasn't just a metaphor. All her life, she'd rushed from one thing to the next. What would it be like to slow down, enjoy the fruits of your labors? When she realized Daniel had been watching her, Hannah jerked back to reality.

"You look nice," he said, then faced the road again. "Are you nervous?"

Hannah glanced down at the new dress Edith had sewn for her. The rose-colored hue complemented her hair and skin rather nicely. Maybe she needed to learn how to sew. It wasn't right that Edith was teaching her so many things about life on an Amish farm, and she was making her and her daughters clothes too.

"A little," she admitted. "How far is the church?" She brushed her hands over her lap.

"We don't have a church building like the *Englisch* do. I thought Edith would have explained it to you." Giggles sounded behind them, and Daniel turned to cast a smile at her daughters in the back seat. They were enjoying the ride, and it couldn't be ignored how they were thriving here. It was all Daniel's doing. Daniel made a good father. His patience, the way he watched them when he thought no one was looking, and how he knew how to approach each one differently. She glanced over to him as he controlled the reins. Though he had suddenly stopped shaving, he looked fresh, crisp in his newly pressed shirt and jacket.

"We have services every other Sunday. Each family takes turns holding the service and the fellowship meal that follows in their home, or barn, whichever has the most room. Today, we are going to Sayer's farm. Bennie Sayer and his wife usually have services inside their home, and when weather is nice like today, the meal is eaten outside."

Hannah tensed immediately. "I didn't make anything. Why didn't you tell me there was a fellowship meal? Daniel, how can I show up empty-handed?" She was furious no one mentioned such an important detail until now. Even worse, he was smiling about it.

"You have just moved into a new home, with three children and a new husband. But if it makes you feel better, Edith made two peanut butter pies and a plate of cookies this morning while you were all sleeping late, again." He chuckled. "They are in the back of the buggy."

"You find this funny, don't you?" Hannah couldn't help but find herself drawn to him and his genial mood. Was it normal to find him so appealing when he was nothing like the man she had married? Then again, maybe that was what attracted her even more. Daniel was nothing like Micah at all.

"I do," he replied playfully. The beginnings of his beard gave him a more rugged look that Hannah found quite appealing. "But to keep you from being angry with me all day, I will tell you also that most of the service isn't in English. The service will last about three hours. Men sit on one side of the room, and women on the other."

"Anything else I should know?" How was Hannah supposed to convince three children to sit still for that long?

"Along with the other women, you will help serve the meal. Men eat first, then women and children."

He turned the buggy down a long gravel road and she watched the tension in his jaw work.

Was he holding something back? "What else are you not telling me?"

"Nothing. The community is filled with wonderful people and you might just enjoy yourself." Hannah shot him a disapproving frown though she secretly had to admit she was looking forward to seeing Millie again. "While you're here, you might as well enjoy it," he added.

When they pulled up to a smaller barn filled with tables, Daniel helped each of them down and placed a dessert in the children's hands. He said something in Amish to a younger man who led the horse and buggy around back. Hannah felt her hands start to tremble as she took in the scene. The lawn was crowded with people, many of them going in and out of the house and barn. A horse nickered nearby and she jerked, a faint sound escaping her throat. On impulse, Daniel reached for her hand.

"I will be with you, for now," Daniel said as he began leading her forward.

Hannah thought she might just be sick. There was over a hundred people here, and so far no Edith to guide her. Daniel had been kind to take her hand. In fact, she was surprisingly calm knowing he was taking control. For once, she didn't mind someone else was leading.

Daniel was right about one thing: sitting three hours on a backless wooden bench, listening to words in a language you didn't understand was exhausting. Hannah was proud of the girls for sitting still through it all. Even M.J. managed not to squirm or ask for the bathroom. It was proof they were all trying. Rosemary was skittish, but as soon as the women gathered in the kitchen to help put out food and drinks, her daughter was eager to be helpful.

"Does she not speak?" Hannah heard one woman whisper to another as Edith instructed Hannah to carry pies to the table just under the porch canopy. Another woman responded in a different language, and Hannah had no clue what she was saying. She promised herself she would try to learn more of the German dialect Edith called *Deitch*, though she made mention that here in the northern tip of the state, their language was very different from communities farther north. No matter what language, or version thereof, Hannah hated not knowing if she and her children were being gossiped about right in front of her.

"*Nee*, she is just very shy, but her sister makes up for her silence." Edith called out to M.J. and Hannah watched her daughter skip over, and start a full conversation about Daisy the cow and Marigold, the newest name she had concocted for one of Daniel's pesky goats, to the group of women who had been placing covered food dishes on an adjacent table.

Edith caught her attention then. "Hannah, this is Hazel Miller, she lives just a few miles from you." Hannah set down an apple pie on the table and brushed her palms on her apron before turning her attention to Hazel. She was a bit taller than Hannah. Fanned out wrinkles around her eyes suggested she might be in her fifties, but her skin glowed as fresh as a teenager's, unblemished and perfect.

"We heard our Daniel up and married an old sweetheart and thought we were being fed untruths. But I can see you are very much real, and such a *schee fraa* you are. I met your *kinner*. They are sweet." Hazel put her hands on her full hips and smiled welcomingly. Hannah quickly spied each daughter to note her whereabouts before answering.

"*Danki*. They can be sweet…in public," Hannah replied. The comment earned her a few innocent chuckles. She needed to talk with Daniel and decide how to handle these kinds of questions.

"Well, we were blessed when Daniel returned to us, and now even more blessed to have you and your *kinner* in our community too. I run the bakery in town. You should come by for *kaffi* and a scone someday," Hazel offered kindly.

"How kind of you," Hannah replied, wishing she could. No doubt, law enforcement was closing in on Corsetti, and time for drinking coffee and eating scones with Hazel was growing slim. It was too bad though, because Hazel reminded her of her foster mother, Anna, so much. Sitting for an hour with her would be a welcome respite to this unusual life she suddenly found herself living.

"*Wie geht's*, I'm Sara Plank. My Eli works for your Daniel." Sara was tall, thin and had the most beautiful green eyes Hannah had ever seen. She looked nothing like Hannah would have she imagined when Daniel spoke of his boisterous foreman.

"Nice to meet you." Hannah hoped her lack of Amish wasn't noticeable. She knew so few words but wasn't that confident in using them.

"That littlest one over there—" Sara pointed to three boys chasing grasshoppers in the nearby brittle grass, "—is Jesse. He is about the age of your Catherine, *jah*? The other two are his best friends." Sara chuck-led in a motherly tone. "Can't keep them apart." Han-nah watched the boys cluster together, comparing their catches, and laughed.

"So where did you say you were from, Hannah?" Margaret suddenly appeared in the growing cluster of women. Hannah was the new mysterious bride in their midst. She felt her stomach start to roll, never liking to be the center of attention. If the women weren't al-ready suspicious of her being here, Margaret would raise enough questions to warrant them to be. She knew jealousy was sin, but seeing Margaret dressed in a peri-winkle blue that accentuated all her finer qualities made Hannah feel like a wren among cardinals.

Across the yard, where a large huddle of men were standing in the open barn doorway, Hannah locked eyes with Daniel. He had been watching her get acquainted. She didn't need rescuing. Surely, she could handle a few Amish women after handling some of the nitpicky cli-ents she had endured in the past. So why did she feel so small, unworthy of their friendship? Then he smiled. It was just what she needed to gain her footing.

"We lived in Indiana. I believe I mentioned that when you brought over Daniel's favorite pie to the house the other day." Margaret's eyes narrowed. Even here, women had boundaries and Hannah was marking hers. Daniel said Margaret meant nothing to him, and she hoped that was the truth, because the last thing that she needed was a jaded sweetheart asking too many ques-tions and stirring up trouble, trouble that could cost her children their lives. "It was very…*gut*," Hannah added.

"But Daniel lived in Chicago before coming home. How did you two meet?" Margaret continued to prod.

Hannah struggled for an answer. Had Daniel lived long outside the Amish?

"Now, Margaret, let's not overwhelm her with such personal questions," Millie intruded. Hannah knew she liked Millie Troyer. "Hannah, you make sure to try the triple-berry pie." Millie pointed to the table of desserts. "Frances Byler makes it and it's the finest in the county." Millie looked beautiful in her teal dress.

"I was just curious about the kind of community she came from. If they are so different than our own, that's all," Margaret defended, looking as innocent as a tulip blossom. Hannah saw past the fresh ivory skin and rosy lips. Margaret was a pit bull, refusing to let go.

"I haven't been here long enough to answer that, but I can't imagine them being too different. Bishop Schwartz was very welcoming, and Edith…" Hannah smiled her way "…she's been so kind helping me and my daughters get the house in order." Hannah took a careful breath.

"It's our way to help one another, ain't so? We're so thrilled to have you here with us," Millie said warmly, shooting Margaret a warning glare.

"Well, I'm glad you and Daniel reconnected. You make a fine match," Hazel added.

"Hazel here is known for her matchmaking in our community," Edith informed, looping a hand around Hazel's arm in sisterly fashion.

"Seventeen couples and counting," Hazel replied proudly. "I did worry Daniel would never settle down. Didn't know his heart had been taken by an Amish *maedel* even when he lived among the *Englisch*. I'm just glad he came back to us, and suspect you had some influence in that." Hazel winked. "We all have much to thank you for." Hannah was speechless. These women thought she was the reason Daniel was back with the Amish. It sounded like his time in the English world was longer than a few short *rumspringa* years.

"I hate to lose one of our own to the *Englisch* world. I still can't get over why Dan Raber ran off like he did, taking our sweet Martha Jane and the *buwe* with her." Hannah cocked a brow but didn't dare pry Sara for details. That would make her look like she didn't know her own husband, exposing her for the liar she was.

It would explain why Daniel's accent wasn't as thick as everyone else's. Had that been why Bryan insisted she stay here? Did Daniel have a long enough history in her world that made him more inclined to help her family fit in to this one?

"Oh, now Michael, he was a handful, always running off and playing pranks on others," Hazel said.

"And stealing every *kichli* he could get his hands on," Millie added, earning her numerous head nods.

"Not Daniel. He was nothing like his *bruder*," Hazel added. *Brother?* Hannah stopped for a second, then busied herself cutting pies as she listened to the ladies talk about Daniel and his family.

"Oh, Margaret, please go fetch the dessert plates. We can't make Hannah do all the work," Hazel ordered, and Hannah almost chuckled aloud when Margaret's frown deepened.

"Don't mind her, Hannah. Margaret is just upset you snagged him first," Millie said, patting her arm. "Now, how are you adjusting, dear?"

Hannah wished she could tell them the truth: *Oh, I'm a fake widow named Magnolia who is ruining a man's one chance at love and family to keep my children safe from a killer. And oh, by the way, my real husband was a stranger to me too, secretly stealing money from mobsters and pretending to uphold the law.* Hannah hated lies, and she was lying to these wonderful women who had shown her nothing but kindness, and who made her feel as if she were one of them. She hoped God would forgive her.

"The girls are adjusting well. Rosemary is still a little shaken from all the changes but as you can see..." All eyes followed her gaze to M.J., now in Daniel's arms, telling a group of bearded men some tale that was earning their full attention. "That one has never met a stranger."

"He looks like a natural. I think our Daniel has finally found his place," Hazel said behind her. "You have given him what he needed most." Hannah scrutinized Daniel's well-proportioned frame and wavy dark hair peeking from beneath his straw hat. The way he held M.J., he looked like a father, smiling proudly as she entertained Daniel's friends. Hannah had to admit, regardless of how hard it was, anyone who didn't know them would think the two belonged together. M.J. would be heartbroken when they had to leave eventually. Daniel hung the stars in her eyes.

"You are young yet, maybe there will be *sohns* for him also," Sara chimed in. Hannah quickly hid her shock in a series of coughs.

"*Ach*, let's not put her on the spot now." Edith tapped Hannah's back but her wide smile said she liked Sara's way of thinking.

"Oh, and remember, I have an orchard. How about I bring over apples next week and we can start on pies and maybe teach the *kinner* to can pie filling and sauce for winter? Then you can tell me all about how Daniel asked you to marry him. I have always loved to hear such stories," Millie said, clutching her chest.

Hannah nodded. A day with Millie would be delightful, but chatting about romantic moments that didn't exist, not so much. The women were too kind, complimenting her and thinking her better than she was. How would they feel about her after…she left him? How would Daniel be looked at when his wife and children disappeared?

Hannah took a long, slow breath, calming her turbulent insides. She was making friends and falling in love with a world made of second hand comforts, but it was all a lie. They weren't the perfect family. Daniel wasn't her husband. He didn't love them.

He couldn't love her.

Chapter Ten

"So, you managed to get a *fraa* and *kinner* in one day without your community even knowing?" Daniel stiffened as Bennie Sayer strolled up beside them. He sat M.J. down, and instructed her to go find her mother. As soon as her little chubby legs disappeared around the corner, he addressed Bennie.

"You know full well I have never done anything halfway," Daniel chuckled lightheartedly. "How is your *mudder*? I heard she has been feeling poorly and didn't see her in attendance today." Daniel knew Margaret's father had only stomped over to find out why he had married a stranger and not his persistent daughter. A distraction was in order.

"Her heart condition has been giving her bouts of troubles lately," Bennie said, as he stood in front of him, feet set apart, gray eyes narrowing toward Daniel.

"We will continue to keep her in our prayers," Joshua said, untwisting a butterscotch candy wrapper and popping the candy into his mouth.

"Margaret has been most helpful. She cooks and cleans for her, and never complains. She's a *maedel* who knows what is important, *jah?*" Bennie's gaze remained on Daniel.

Daniel remained silent, and by the grace of *Gott*'s good timing, a voice called out, signaling the start of the fellowship meal so he didn't have to respond.

Daniel sat between Eli Plank and Vernon Schwartz at one of the long tables. In the distance, he saw M.J. playing with other children. Daniel watched closely when Aiden Shetler joined in. Ben and Barb's son was always finding himself in the middle of trouble and his M.J. needed no encouragement.

Rosemary, wearing the same blue hue as Millie, stood close by their neighbor at the desserts table as Hannah served ice water to men who were already seated. There was no sign of Catherine, but just as Daniel was about to excuse himself to seek her out, she appeared with Edith herding her toward the house. Whatever disturbance she had tried to muster, Edith was dealing with it so Hannah didn't have to. The woman had her hands full enough. Losing her husband and living in a strange place, all while learning a whole new way of life with three children. It was admirable how easy she had adapted. He had never met a woman who carried such a load and yet, as he watched her smile, working down the table, she made everything look easy. As if she belonged. He wished he weren't so attracted to her, but what man with two good eyes wouldn't be? She was small and dainty, could wrangle five-year-olds and pestering goats, and he noticed yesterday just how fast she could outrun an angry rooster too. She had known suffering in her life, and yet never complained. She didn't tire easily, and was a natural-born giver. The qualities he had always sought out in a possible wife.

"Water?" Hannah appeared at his side. She didn't look at him. Instead, she nervously looked to see how many eyes were watching them. He owed her for the remark to Millie, about letting the girls have a sleepover so they could spend time alone. Even though they both were pretending, Daniel couldn't resist making her blush for making him wonder what spending time alone with her would be like. He reached up as she poured his glass and touched her upper arm affectionately and smiled, just as any appreciative husband would have. It all backfired when she met his gaze. Daniel was dumbstruck. How could such a look of surprise, of vulnerable innocence, affect him so strongly? Hannah jerked, leaving a small splash of water on his arm, and hurried away. His instincts were fairly sound. She'd felt that too.

"You got stars in your eyes." Eli nudged him.

"*Jah*, I guess I do."

October was upon them. Days were warm. Nights ran chilly. Hannah let the cool breeze wash over her as they aimed their buggy toward home.

"That was interesting," Hannah said as the girls drifted to sleep behind them on the buggy ride home. Their bellies were full and they were worn out from playing.

"Was the service difficult to follow?"

"My High German is as good as my Pennsylvania Dutch," she teased him.

"*Ach*, well, when you learn one, you will learn the other." He'd said *when*. Had he meant to? Daniel was very careful with his words.

"You never told me you were raised in Chicago. Is that why Bryan thought this was such a good idea, because you once lived outside the Amish faith?" Daniel stiffened.

"Perhaps," Daniel replied. He wasn't going to make this easy on her, but Hannah knew how to be persistent.

"So what made you want to return and join the church?"

"I was born in the community, Hannah. But my father was unhappy here, and moved us away when I was young. I'm surprised anyone mentioned it. Feels like a very long time ago." He gave the horse a tap, and Colt responded, picking up the pace.

Hannah could sense that he didn't want to talk about his family or his time living in Chicago. "It's just that… you know a lot about me, that I grew up in foster homes, lost a husband and now I'm hiding out in the middle of nowhere with you. But I had to find out from strangers who you are." What was he afraid she would find out? "They believe I am an old girlfriend you just happened to run into. They think we have a history together."

"Edith must have spread that information."

"Well, spill it, mister. I can't act like your wife if every bit of news about you is a surprise to me."

"I lived in Chicago a long time ago, *jah*, but now I'm back here where I belong. There is nothing secretive about it," Daniel said prickly.

When he brought the buggy to a stop in the drive, Hannah stepped down with ease. Nudging Catherine awake, she helped her eldest from the buggy before fetching M.J. and cradling her sleepy daughter against her Without a word, Daniel lifted Rosemary to his shoulder as he and Hannah glared at one another.

"I'm going to my room," Catherine muttered as Hannah and Daniel moved through the foyer and headed toward the sitting room. They placed the two sleepy girls on opposite ends of the couch.

"She has a room?"

"Did you not say she could have one?"

"I thought they were still sleeping with you. I'm glad one of you is comfortable enough here," he whispered in a snarky tone before heading out the door. Hannah followed. No way was he going to act mad at her when she was the one who was angry.

"I'm not the only one who isn't comfortable. Who's Michael?" Hannah demanded.

Daniel stopped in his tracks. "We aren't talking about this now, Hannah. I agreed to offer you and your *dochdern* a safe place, food and shelter. But my life before you is none of your business." Daniel stormed off to the barn, leaving her with more questions than answers.

Hannah's life had taken some sharp detours at times, but right now it was Daniel Raber's side roads she was concerned about. How could she trust someone who couldn't be honest with her? Why was he being secretive with her all of a sudden?

Long after the skies grew dark and the children were tucked into their beds, Daniel still hadn't returned to the house. Hannah paced the kitchen floor like a nervous hen. Thunder boomed in the distance, jolting her already frayed nerves. Something scraped the sitting room windows; the barren rose bush she thought, but the eerie creaks and groans heightened her senses. It was an old house, she told herself, shifting and settling, searching for a comfy spot to wait out a storm. It had been a good many years since she felt alone, but tonight she felt more isolated than ever. She wanted Daniel to come inside, bring that sense of safety back into the house. She wanted answers to her many questions, but if he would just come in, she wouldn't address them tonight. She would just be thankful he returned and that would be that.

Her heart thudded to a stop when she heard the sound of boots on the porch outside. For a second, she played out the dreaded scenario. What if Corsetti had found them? What if he had found Daniel brooding in the barn, and now had come to kill her children? She backed against the counter, searched out anything she could use as a weapon when the door creaked open, then closed.

The lock clicked into place as it routinely did and her wild imagination vanished in an exhaled breath.

In the dark foyer, Daniel's tall silhouette stood. He removed his hat, hung it carefully on the third peg as always and removed his boots before stepping into the kitchen. When their eyes locked, Hannah could see the color drain from his face.

"You should be resting," he said in a deep tone as he moved to the sink and washed his hands. "Staying up every night, waiting for something bad to happen isn't healthy."

"I don't like this arrangement any more than you, but you did agree to it," she blurted out.

"*Jah*, I agreed to help you, but there are some things I can't share with you, Hannah. Not right now," he said firmly. Was there any man more confusing than Daniel Raber? She thought not.

"How can I trust a man I don't know with my children? M.J. is growing attached to you. Before church today, you promised them an adventure in order to get them to behave. You bribed them."

"It worked, didn't it?"

"And you let her name the cow and a goat. Can't you see how this is a problem? We don't know you." She backed up into the hutch. Dishes rattled but none fell.

"Do you want me to stop being kind to your children? Do you want me to stay distant, only protecting them from afar?" He pinned her with a look that could scare scales off fish.

"This was a mistake. This was all a big mistake. What have I done? Why did Micah do this to us? None of this should be happening." She dropped into a chair and began to sob. Daniel slowly crossed the floor and pulled out the seat beside her.

"You miss him. I'm sorry you have to go through this." Hannah's head snapped up. And she looked at him.

"One minute, life was good. My girls were happy and I had a job that wasn't too bad. Then I blinked and a cop was whisking me away, my children were inconsolable and Micah was dead. I blinked and here we are, wearing *kapps* and baking applesauce. I have no idea what I'm doing." Daniel leaned forward and took both her shaking hands.

"Neither do I, but if anyone can do this, it is you." Hannah looked at him as if he were speaking a different language. "We will both just practice not blinking so much," he said, letting go of her hands.

He was silent for a long moment, then said softly, "They were killed." Hannah looked at the man she thought could handle anything, his shoulders slumped, his head low.

"I'm sorry."

His heart couldn't take seeing Hannah in tears. She missed her husband, the life they shared, and here he was making things harder for her. It would be painful, the past usually was, but he had to give her something.

"My parents, they owned a store and it was robbed. The man only got two-hundred-and-nine dollars and killed them because he could."

"I… I shouldn't have…"

"No, you were right," Daniel admitted. He wanted to tell her the truth, but now was not the time. Marshal Bates was right about that. It was clear Hannah had suffered a lot in such a short time. Adding more salt to her wounds would be the wrong move. "We will pray, get some rest and face the next day. Then we will do that the next day and the next, for as long as it takes. Then you can go back to your real life." Did she still want that? *Stupid.* Of course, she wanted the life she was accustomed to. Freedoms his world didn't allow for.

"Real life. I don't think I even know what's real anymore," she scoffed. He lifted a hand, thumbed away a lonely tear sliding down her cheek.

"I don't have all the answers, but just remember you aren't alone." And she and the children never would be again, he promised himself. "I know it's not the same. I am not your husband in your heart. I know this has been difficult and you miss him."

She looked up under long, damp lashes. "I don't miss him," she confessed, more tears deciding to run south. "You probably think me a horrible person for saying that. But he became someone I didn't know anymore."

"I'm sure he loved you, despite the mess he got himself into." Daniel believed that. Michael would have never married her if he didn't love her. Hannah was so easy to love.

"In the beginning, he loved me, but then he just…"

stopped. I don't know why, not really." She shook her head. "I'm not sure I can forgive him for this." He studied her for a moment.

"I have much to forgive, myself. You are not alone with that struggle either. Some people can break your heart, but we still love them as *Gott* loves us." Daniel felt that familiar warmth in his veins he got every time he thought about his father. If he hadn't taken them all away from the community, forced them to live in such a dark and dangerous world, *Mudder* and Michael might still be alive. Hannah wasn't the only one who needed to practice forgiveness.

She got to her feet. "Good night, Daniel." She was gone before he could find a reason to stop her.

Hannah lay on the bed, as Rosemary and M.J. cuddled beside her. She touched her cheek where moments ago Daniel had brushed away her tears. If only he could fix everything. She had no place in this world. But what really awaited her upon returning to Indiana? Magnolia Reynolds could not just return to her real estate job or her life before. Her house was likely already being foreclosed upon, her things no longer her own. What did she have to return to? That was the big question.

When the sound of thunder roared to the west, Hannah shuddered. Was she always going to be this afraid, waiting for something bad to happen, as Daniel had said? *It's just thunder.* She snuffed out the bedside lantern, drew up the quilt, placed an arm over Rosemary next to her. The last thing Hannah recalled was a pair of hazel eyes, warm calloused fingers, and the scent of rain and earth on a man who made her wish her life had started out very different than the hand dealt her.

was for sure. Marshal Bates needed to know what he'd found, and Daniel needed to spend more time at home. He would change up his nightly routine too. Just in case this wasn't the first time someone had watched them.

The mysterious tire marks worried him all day. *Jah*, there were a dozen reasons for them, but there was one that was in the forefront of Daniel's thoughts as he walked home. Bates already had two men searching the area for clues, and even suggested leaving an officer to watch over the house. But that would draw attention, stirring up questions neither he nor Hannah were prepared to answer in their tight-knit community. But Daniel soon came to the realization that he couldn't refuse, not with his family's lives in danger. "*Gott*, watch over Hannah and the girls. Please hold them tight to You and give me whatever tools I need to protect them."

He stepped into the house; the strong aromas of cinnamon and cloves hung heavy in the air. Laughter spilled throughout the rooms. He tried to ignore the merriment, but found himself too weak to resist. Even after loss, there was laughter in his home. Was this not how things should be? His *onkel* spoke often on it. When a life was no more, we were to see that life as completed. It was hard to imagine his *mudder*—who should have had many years of life ahead of her, lots of grandchildren to coddle—a completed life. His father's decisions had taken that from her, had he not? And Michael. He too had made decisions that impacted others. How did *Gott* expect him just to look past those bad choices when they had followed him here, affected those he cared for? How was he supposed to simply forgive?

Removing his straw hat, he stepped farther into the house full of females. "Looks like you all are having too much fun in here," he said. Four beaming smiles greeted him. Even Catherine, who rarely smiled genuinely, did. M.J. ran to him and Daniel lifted her into his arms. He put on a happy face, for their sakes, but knowing that someone could, at any minute, take one of them from him, had his gut churning.

"Millie and *Mudder* are making pies and applesauce from all the apples. I got to smash the dough," M.J. said, slamming a tiny fist into her palm.

"Your Hannah here is going to teach me how to make fried apple pies like her grandmother," Millie added. Daniel lifted a corner of his lips, glad she was more settled today than she had been last night. He hated that he would have to tell her after supper about what he'd found today. But he had to tell her. Keeping his true identity from her was one thing, but keeping a possible threat nearby a secret was entirely something else.

"Rosemary's crust is the best. Millie said so," M.J. said comically.

Daniel glanced around the kitchen, but didn't see Rosemary. He placed M.J. back on her bare feet.

"Where is Rosemary?" Daniel asked Hannah. Her smile faded into a solemn expression.

"She's behind the house. I think she needed a minute to herself."

"I'll go check on her." He kept his voice calm but his breathing was rapid. Knowing someone had been lurking about the farm and mill meant they needed to be always vigilant.

When he rounded the house, Daniel's heart skipped a beat to see there was no sign of Rosemary. Scouring the yard, he quickly found her on the rise, near his two beehives. He let out an exasperated breath and slowly took his time approaching.

Rosemary wasn't afraid of horses, and since she was standing not ten feet from his hives, it seemed she wasn't afraid of bees either. She was entranced, watching them. Could this be what she needed? Nature nurturing her soul? He had sensed it each time they took a long stroll, *adventures* M.J. called them. Rosemary was always more relaxed outdoors.

When Daniel drew close, she sensed him and startled. "I'm sorry." She had been crying, alone, here on the hillside. It cut him, seeing this beautiful child heartbroken. She turned, ignoring him but not running away either. Daniel seized the opportunity to connect with her. "I lost my father too." Still, she stood stiffly, watching the bees jump from withering wildflower to milkweed. "I lost my home once also. I'm sorry you all had to leave so much behind."

Rosemary looked down at her hands, a blade of Timothy grass rolling between two fingers. He wanted to scoop her up, hold her and surround her with walls so strong, nothing dark could leak in. The surge of protectiveness grew stronger with her. She had witnessed a horrible thing, lost the one person meant to protect her and was a target. How could he even begin to help Rosemary when he couldn't fathom the battle being fought within her?

Rosemary turned shyly and slowly looked up to him. Those big brown eyes, glistening, were Michael's eyes staring back at him. "How can Mommy laugh?" she murmured, then burst into another run of tears.

A bullet couldn't have this much power, he reckoned. Daniel's chest exploded, sending a huff of air out of his lungs. *She spoke.* He tried to rein in his emotions, but succumbed to them. He wrapped both his arms around her, and surprisingly, Rosemary buried herself deeper in his embrace.

He hadn't really cried since the day he'd buried his parents, but Rosemary's pain, her shattered little heart, broke him. He lifted her up and felt his heart jolt when her arms clung to his neck.

"I know, my *lieb*, I know," he crooned as he felt her arms squeeze tighter.

They remained there, holding one another in quiet tears. When he sat her back down on her feet, they both sat in the tall grass, watching the bees dance. "One day you will laugh again too."

"Does she not care?" To hear her tiny voice, so strong and yet so fragile, awoke something in him he never knew he possessed.

"It doesn't mean she doesn't care. She has been through a lot too, and worries for you and your sisters. It's good your *mudder* is able to laugh. She needed to feel good and Millie helped her. Don't hold it against her. *Gott* is working on all of you, trying to help you heal." Rosemary nodded. She understood more than a six-year-old girl should.

"How about I tell you about those hives? I could teach you about bees. I have books too." She wiped her face with her sleeve and looked up at him with curiosity in her eyes. He smiled tenderly at her. His heart was big enough for all of them. He loved her and felt she loved him too. "Maybe come spring, you can have her bring you back to the farm and we can harvest the honey together." He could only hope Hannah would, because he was too deep in love to never see them again.

Rosemary nodded. They reached a milestone today, and did it together.

Yes, today was a good day.

Hannah stepped out onto the porch as late October presented a spectacular view. Tall evergreens held fast to their bold emerald, while rustic gold, orange and reds competed wildly with a stunning sunset. It was breathtaking.

Everything about Daniel's world held the very essence of peace and an unchained freedom despite doing everything without conveniences. She laughed. It was funny, considering being Amish meant strict rules and yet freedom carried on the cool autumn breezes, through the shedding trees and over the lush lawn where her daughters ran barefoot and pushed one another on the rope swing Daniel had surprised them with that very first day. It was a balm of awakening, this moment right here. In all her life, she had never felt such calm, so near to God, whom she prayed to vigorously yet it seemed He seldom heard her.

She glanced down at her simple cornflower-blue dress, her white apron front, and realized the decision to come here was the best thing that had ever happened to her. She looked nothing like Magnolia Reynolds anymore, felt nothing like her either, and that meant everything.

Millie and Edith weren't like the women she knew back in Indiana. She had never had too many close friends, moving around far too much to make lasting connections. Yet, Hannah knew when she left this place, she would miss them both terribly.

She suspected Millie knew some, if not all, of her plight, but she also sensed Millie was not the kind of woman who would dig for details. Millie was also a widow who understood about bouts of loneliness, and though her late husband, Ben, had been an upstanding father and husband, they were both raising daughters alone. They shared a connection.

Whatever had transpired between Daniel and Rosemary yesterday, she was glad to see Rosemary more relaxed and excited at the prospect of learning about bees. Hannah would never tell a soul, but she had cried softly in her pillow that night when Daniel told her of his intentions to teach her daughter how to care for bees. It was a simple thing, and yet, it was so very much. He was the kind of man they deserved, rather than the father given to them and then stolen away. Would God find her terrible for such thoughts? She chided herself for such thinking. She knew Micah loved them, even if he never wanted children.

Stepping back inside to check on dinner, she pulled out the large roast from the oven and checked the meat for doneness. Spooning out most of the juices in a separate pan, Hannah added a healthy spoonful of flour, and began whisking the mixture over the back burner. She liked a thick gravy, and hoped Daniel did too. He never complained about her cooking. He never left the table without offering a thank-you either. She found herself looking forward to their chats on the porch, watching the day fade away as he updated her on what news the marshals had or how many saw blades he had gone through filling his latest lumber orders. All the while her daughters would be giggling inside, playing new games and finding joy without cable TV to appease them. How different their lives could have been if she weren't so anxious to please, so quick to fall in love. And if she were being honest, too gullible to know what was going on right underneath her nose for years.

Maybe she still was gullible, because it was growing more and more difficult to deny what those long looks Daniel sometimes tossed her way did to her.

Around three that afternoon, Daniel took a quick buggy ride into town to meet with the local sheriff and pick up a few things Hannah had scribbled down for him at the store. He was glad the sheriff was taking the threat seriously and agreed to keep Hannah and the children's identities secret. At least there would be others looking out for them. Eli and Vernon could handle things well enough at the mill. Daniel needed to be closer to home until this was over. And if the marshal's gut instincts were right, it would all be over soon. Daniel wasn't sure how he felt about that.

Now instead of working, he was buying protective bee gear for a little girl so she had something to look forward to. He should be home, watching over the farm, making arrangements for the mill, not shopping. Then the thought hit him. It was time Hannah learned how to handle a horse and buggy.

Thirty minutes later, he entered the house with two paper bags in his arms. He had every intention of informing Hannah that she would be doing her own shopping from now on. When he reached the kitchen doorway, he paused and his earlier frustrations vanished. She looked so pretty in her new blue dress, her cheeks flushed from canning what looked to be apples, and that one curly tendril escaped and clinging to her delicate neck. She was humming too, a clear indication she was in a good mood.

"New dress?" he asked. Hannah startled, bringing one hand to her chest.

"You're home early," she exclaimed, as she turned back to the stove. "And yes, Edith is spoiling me. I think I want to learn to sew them myself. It isn't right she has to go to all this trouble. I am sure I can get the hang of it."

Daniel didn't doubt that one bit. "I'm sure she will be more than happy to teach you." A hint of something resembling hope rushed through him. Hannah, learning more about their life, and his life. Would she ever consider staying? It was a fanciful thought, one he knew better than to entertain. He was Amish, and she was *Englisch*. She was Michael's wife and he was simply the man who promised to look after her.

And what could he possibly offer her? Daniel had seen it for himself, the fancy clothes and expensive cars. Michael had taken her from being an orphan to living in a big house with everything her heart desired. Daniel could never give her more than this old house and a sawmiller's promise. He never could measure up to his brother, and after seeing his beautiful wife and falling for those sweet children, he knew he never would. They deserved everything this world had to offer them.

He reached up to touch the scar on his neck, now hidden under new growth. Here he was playing a part for his brother again, only this time a real heart was at stake.

"I think it's time you learn to drive a buggy," he announced.

"But... I can't do that," Hannah said a bit too quickly. Daniel dropped both grocery bags on the table and fished out the bee gear he had purchased for Rosemary.

"You can. I think shopping is better suited for you than me," Daniel added in a sharp tone.

"Because I'm a woman?" Her chin lifted.

"You're better at it than I am." He smirked. "City girls are experts, if memory serves me well."

"Not all city girls. I hate shopping and I know nothing about horses. Don't presume you know me, Daniel Raber. Besides, Edith says I can hire a driver if I really need to go anywhere." Even angry she was adorable. Daniel tried ignoring how much so.

"Drivers cost money."

"And what of the dangers? You can't expect me to go shopping with a maniac out there. And I have my own money, so don't bother using that as an excuse."

"Marshal Bates has men all over this town. They would be staked out in the front yard if they wouldn't draw so much attention. The sheriff plans on driving by the house a few times a day and checking to see if any new faces have come into town. If it was indeed Corsetti, they will find him."

"How can you be so sure?" Was she going to quarrel about trusting him, a stranger, again?

"I put my trust in *Gott*," he said, looking at her intensely.

"That's a foolish thing to do," Hannah murmured.

"I would love to argue this more with you, wife," he said, "but I have a date with a bee charmer this evening. Tomorrow, Edith will watch the children while I teach you how to handle a horse and buggy. Maybe you will learn a thing or two about trust then."

Daniel grinned and strolled out the door, leaving Hannah speechless.

Chapter Twelve

Hannah clasped the buggy reins in both hands and tried not to tremble. Her heart sped up, but she really wanted to do this. Not for Daniel, of course, but for herself. There was something satisfying in knowing how to handle oneself no matter what the circumstances. Fear always drove her, but Hannah learned long ago to power through those feelings.

"Now just pull back slowly if you feel she is getting ahead of you," Daniel coached from the seat next to her. November was almost upon them. A crisp breeze threatened, but she was sweating bullets thanks to her jangled nerves. Despite her fear of a half-ton animal, Hannah did what she always did: she continued on. She gave Maybelle a light tap of the reins and clicked her tongue as Daniel instructed. The horse moved gingerly, no jerk or eagerness in her aged flesh. That put her more at ease. She couldn't imagine handling Colt alone. The gelding was strong, eager and always ready to go. Maybelle was older and wiser, and Hannah sensed she knew exactly who the driver was.

"Veer right here. We should stick to the back roads."

Hannah did as he asked. "But this is pavement. Back roads aren't usually paved."

"It's on the way," Daniel said with a hint of humor in his tone. He was having way too much fun seeing her uncomfortable. "I told you there was nothing to it."

Hannah chuckled. "I bet if I let go of the reins, she would bring us back to the house easy enough."

"*Jah*, she would. Would you have preferred I hitched Colt up for you?" He lifted a brow.

"I think Maybelle will work fine for me for now." She could practice more, learn to harness the mare all by herself. Then she could do her own shopping and not depend on Edith and Daniel so much. He was right, but she didn't have to tell him that. Maybe if she got good enough, Hannah could take the girls and visit Edith. They hadn't seen inside her home yet, only the outside when they dropped the children off earlier. And Millie. Hannah had been yearning to see the orchard Millie spoke so much about. She had grown very close to both women and looked forward to spending more time cultivating those friendships as much as she could.

As tempting as it was to imagine her life here, Hannah knew she was no Margaret Sayer. She was the outsider. She wasn't born into communities full of unwavering faith. She was born into a world where nothing lasted and only the strong survived. Believing in God, praying for miracles, was one thing. Submitting wasn't even hard to fathom, but to become part of something, this lifestyle of faith and community, was a mirage. Nothing good ever lasted, she knew that all too well.

Besides, it wasn't like Daniel saw her as anything more than the mother of the three girls he had come to adore and protect. It was her children he cared for, and for that she was grateful.

A few minutes later, Hannah veered the buggy onto the gravel road Daniel pointed out. She had been right about backroads and felt her muscles tense as the buggy bounced over uneven ground. "So where does this trust part come in?"

"The horse must trust you and you must trust him, or else accidents happen," he said.

"So that's where I went wrong in life," she quipped. "I never had a horse." His laugh filled the evening air.

"But you have three wonderful girls."

"Three amazing, beautiful and perfect little girls," she corrected, meeting his smile with one of her own. Daniel was easygoing and seemed to already forget their previous quarrel. Micah would have never forgotten so easily.

"Do you ever feel guilty? For lying to all of your friends and family?"

"We have only withheld the truth to keep you—and them—safe, but *jah*, I do."

They rode in silence, up one road, down another. Hannah tried to focus on the evening, the scenery and Maybelle, but all she could focus on was the man next to her and how she disrupted his life.

An hour later, and one panicky instant with a speeding car, Daniel leaned back in the buggy seat and pretended to enjoy the ride back toward his *onkel*'s. Joshua had told Hannah the sign at the end of his and Edith's lane that read Poverty's Knob was there from the previous owners, and considering how empty his pockets stayed, he couldn't bear taking it down. Hannah had laughed about it before they left the girls to bake and play with Edith, but she wasn't laughing now as she sat stiffly beside him and in total control of the reins. Hannah, as he was beginning to see, learned at a masterful pace, but he sensed she didn't like control, or the responsibility that came with it. She didn't like lying either, which had earned her his utmost respect.

"So will I be driving Catherine to school in the morning?"

Hannah shot him a quick look. "I've spoken to her and she's finally agreed to go. I still think it isn't safe. What if those tire tracks were from someone spying on us?"

"No way of knowing for sure, but there are many looking into who made those tracks. School will be good for her and she will be surrounded by others all day." Hannah nodded her head. She understood his logic, but Daniel knew fear still rested in her mind.

"I like driving the buggy on the pavement better," she commented. He listened to the clip-clop of Maybelle's hooves striking in cadence. "The gravel is loose, and it feels like we may slide. I'm glad she handles so well." He watched her fingers tighten on the reins. She was letting the new sensation of control warm her. It made a lot of sense. So much of her life was out of her control, grabbing a piece of it wherever she could helped her gain something resembling strength. For it was strength he saw when he looked at her.

"Tell me more about the girls. How they were before you came here." She shot him a curious look, then focused back on the old gravel road ahead that he'd insisted on. It was easy for him to forget sometimes what connected them. Thankfully, she didn't press his motives and assumed he was simply making idle conversation.

"Well, after three false alarms, Catherine was born nineteen days late. Oh, and her first word was *no*," Hannah laughed.

"I suspected as much," Daniel said on a chuckle.

The cool breeze, mingled with the slow pace of Maybelle, had Hannah shivering and he quickly shucked his coat, wrapping it around her. *"Danki,"* she said, slipping her arms into the long sleeves. He knew Hannah was a small woman, but in his coat, she looked even smaller.

"Catherine was always independent and strong, even as a *boppli*." Daniel lifted a brow at her use of the Amish word for *baby*. Since her arrival, she had been reluctant to use his language. "She walked when she wanted, spoke full sentences when she was ready and even ate when she chose no matter the hour. Catherine lives life in her own timing, you could say. But—" she glanced his way "—whatever life throws at her, she will do well."

"And Martha Jane? What of her?"

"Besides *Mama*, her first words were *go-go*." Hannah broke into a warm smile. "And she was born early, of course."

Daniel laughed. "Of course, she had much to see in this world." Hannah chuckled with him. Did she know her eyes twinkled when she forgot why she was here?

"Exactly. She has always been on the go and never met a stranger she didn't want to be friends with."

"Or a rooster," Daniel added. It was nice, sharing this together. He wondered what she was like before too. Hannah had given him glimpses into her past, but nothing substantial. Talking about her children was a good distraction as she handled the horse and buggy. Her white-knuckle grip had already loosened again.

"Believe it or not, Rosemary was quite the adventurer. You should have seen her, Daniel." Her breath hitched and he nearly regretted broaching the topic. "She walked at seven months. When she was three, she rode her bike without training wheels. She used to chase bugs and catch bees with her fingers. She used to pick flowers." When she turned to face him again, the tears were falling down her cheeks, her grip of the reins going slack. "She used to sing all the time. She had the sweetest voice. And she had imaginary friends." The more she grieved for her daughter's lost innocence, the more her hands shook. Daniel took the reins from her and guided Maybelle into a hayfield to their right. He didn't dare tell her that Rosemary had spoken to him. Not now. Hannah had tried coaxing words out of her since they arrived and he could see how it broke her heart when nothing worked.

When she covered her face with her hands, Daniel pulled her to him, enveloping her with arms that would help carry this burden for her. "It will get better. It already has. Surely, you see that.

"*Gott* promises us that suffering doesn't last. We must see each new day for the blessing it truly is. Live in it with intent." The scent of her hair, the weight of her head against his chest felt right, and Daniel wanted to keep her there in his stronghold. "I'm sorry your husband is not here with you, helping you through this." Did she still mourn Michael? Did she wish he were here instead of him?

She looked up at him. "I failed him so badly. I tried so hard to make him happy but I failed. And the girls, they wanted to spend more time with him but there was always a case, a person in need, something more important than his own family. Is it wrong that I'm angry at him when it's me who failed him?" She sobbed harder. "I made his life miserable. I ruined everything."

"That can't be true, Hannah. He failed to follow the law, that's all. I'm sure he loved you and the girls more than you know. Some people just can't show love the same way as others do. None of this is your fault."

"Daniel, I couldn't convince him to go to church. I couldn't find a way to show him how important he was to his children. He wasn't happy. He didn't want us. What's worse, he died unhappy."

"*Nee*, I don't think that's true. You're just upset. Your husband had you, and three wonderful children." Daniel pulled away from her. How could she think herself not enough for any man? How could his brother not see the pearl he had been given?

"He left this world with no faith, no love and no idea how badly those little girls loved him. Because he didn't love me anymore, they suffered. Because I wasn't enough for him, my children thought their father didn't even like them. What kind of woman is given the perfect life and messes it up this badly?"

In her sudden breakdown, Hannah had told him everything he needed, but wished he didn't know. Daniel's jaw tightened. Michael had become no different than their father. He'd never been satisfied. Their own mother cried tears of guilty burdens, just like he imagined Hannah had. She'd tried to help *Daed* keep his faith, follow the straight and narrow. Instead, he abandoned everything they knew to be right, for *Englisch* things. His heart cracked anew. Michael too was a lost soul, and the pain etched in Hannah's eyes confirmed it.

"We are only responsible for our own actions. You can't blame yourself for another's sins." He squeezed her hand.

"He took all of it for granted. He stole and lied and put his children in danger. He was so kind, in the beginning. But you're right." She straightened and wiped her face. "He took it all for granted, didn't he?" Daniel nodded, sensing she needed his assurances, though learning about Michael this way hurt something awful. "Bryan said he had been stealing from these mob people for a long time. Why do people do that? Why does love just stop?" She thought he had the answers, desperately wanted him to have them. If she knew the truth, it might give her some closure, but Daniel couldn't tell her about Michael, what had shaped him into the man he became, no matter how much he wanted to right now.

"I don't know." Though part of him did. Putting oneself before others always invited sin.

"He wasn't the kind of person you would have liked. I was married to a man I didn't even know." She laughed. "Talk about repeating your mistakes."

Daniel didn't laugh. Hannah was the smartest person he knew. He didn't believe she made many mistakes and didn't want to be considered one. He couldn't stand seeing her like this. "I'm sorry he hurt you, but I feel he loved you, just maybe not the way he should have." Michael had chosen his lot in life, just as his *daed* had, but he would have never married Hannah if he hadn't loved her. That much he was sure of. How long would Daniel carry around this hardness in his heart for them?

Their mistakes weren't his to carry. Was that not what he had just tried to convince Hannah of?

It was time to put the past aside, stop dwelling in the shadows as Hannah was clearly doing herself. They needed to forgive. Forgive those who took advantage, who didn't care enough, who took the wrong paths. There was no way either of them could move forward without it.

Hannah had already endured abandonment from early on, and when she looked up at him, he saw the pain of it again in her teary blue eyes. Daniel felt his heart thunder, felt the ache of holding back when all he wanted to do was surround her in a love so great doubt had no place there.

It was time to separate the past from the present. "I know this isn't easy on you, handling all this alone, but…"

"But I am not alone, am I?" she said sharply, and he sensed his world was shifting again.

"*Nee*. We are never alone, Hannah. *Gott* is always there. He will wipe away your tears."

"I know that. I think I've always known that." She sniffed back another run of tears. "And so are you, Daniel Raber," she said. "You don't see it. What a treasure a few minutes of your attention does for them. My children feel safe with you. They trust you. I think they love you."

"They are easy to love," Daniel admitted out loud and felt there was more that needed to be said, but didn't dare cross that line.

"Why haven't you ever married?" she asked him. "You would make a wonderful father."

Because I was waiting for the right one, he wanted to say.

Instead, he teased her. "I am married, am I not?" He shrugged. "I never took the time for it. I dated a bit when I was younger."

"Did you have a girlfriend when you lived in Chicago?" Daniel was surprised by the question and felt his cheeks grow warm. "You probably dated dozens of girls. I bet Margaret isn't the only one in Miller's Creek who delivered a dish or two at your door."

"Do you really want to know this stuff?" he asked her. Hannah wiped the remaining tears from her face and nodded. "Okay. I dated a couple women, but none really suited me. They were more interested in material things than I was. Their faith wasn't sound and that meant the most to me. One cannot build a home on a weak foundation." He looked out over the field as the light chased shadows. "Not many in your world can accept mine. I never made it a secret that I had hopes of returning to my Amish roots. I was always honest about that."

"I could imagine how that went over," Hannah laughed. "I can't lie, when they told me I was coming here, what was expected of us, if I hadn't been so numb from all that had just happened, I would have probably run too."

"But you didn't." He stared at her intently, searching for what his heart was aching for but feared being denied.

"No, I didn't," she said softly. With that, his heart stirred.

"And now?" A flicker of surprise raced over her features. Did she like being an Amish bride? Would leaving be something she would regret? His heart yearned to know the answers.

"I think what you and Edith and Millie have is something special. I have never known community like you have. Millie and Edith are…friends. Not the kind you work with or who happen to be married to your spouse's friends, but real friends."

"So I'm not your friend." He tried looking offended.

"*Nee*, you're my husband, remember," she teased. "I've never canned applesauce before or made homemade cheese, but I like it." She sounded like M.J. and Daniel couldn't smother his reaction. "Don't laugh."

"I'm not laughing at you. I'm glad to hear we have made such an impression." In this light, the shimmering in her eyes pulled him in.

"You have, Daniel," she said in a softer, more serious tone. "Made an impression, I mean. My children feel loved here. That is a special thing, even if it's short-lived."

"It is." He shifted, angling his body to face her. For a brief moment, he forgot she was Michael's. Forgot the promise he had made that first morning. He wanted to show her just how much she deserved. "We all need and deserve love And love isn't short-lived or temporary, Hannah. Real love, it's everlasting." He never planned to have these feeling for…his wife, and now he wanted more. The urge to kiss her, draw her closer, had never been harder to resist. All he had to do was lean down. If he were just given the chance. Not as Michael's brother or the stranger that took her in, but the man he knew himself to be.

"The kind of love that never stops," Hannah whispered, her cool blue eyes looking up under long lashes still damp from crying. He lifted a hand and slowly cradled her cheek. The cool of her flesh collided with the warmth of his hand and he felt her give slowly.

A truck honked as it drove by, a customer whom Daniel recognized driving it, jolting them both back to the present. "I'm sorry," he quickly apologized, withdrawing his hand. "We should get back." How could he have almost kissed her?

Chapter Thirteen

Hannah was beside herself. Catherine hated school and there was no reassuring her. Being shifted from home to home, Hannah remembered what it was like starting a new school, how cruel some kids could be. And just four days in, Catherine had become the center of Jesse Plank and his teasing friends' world. No one liked being called names, or picked on. After supper, Hannah slipped outside to join Daniel for their regular nightly talk. The man seemed to have an answer for everything. Had he gone through some of the same things when he lived outside of the Amish community?

"It's getting colder." Hannah shivered as November winds blew over them. "I should probably learn to knit or something. The girls will need scarves." The swing Daniel and Joshua had hung in the oak tree swayed in the breeze.

"I should start hauling over more wood. Winter will be here before we know it," Daniel added, leaning on his post while Hannah leaned on hers. This had become their habit, a routine that they each looked forward to but never spoke about.

She stared out over the scenery. The land was slowly losing its autumn plumage, preparing itself for its winter slumber. She tried to imagine what it would look like covered in snow. Would the girls get to go sleighing on the neighboring hillsides and make snowmen? She shoved back the thought, and tried to focus on the reality. This was Daniel's home, not hers, and if things were on track as Daniel thought, then soon all of this would be over. No sense getting more comfortable than they already were. But he'd almost kissed her. Could she have simply imagined that too?

"I'd like to take Catherine to work with me tomorrow," Daniel said, bringing her back to the present. He cared for her children. Children were easy to love, he had said. Like puppies, all cute and sweet and clumsily adorable. At least her girls had this love now, when they needed it most. She thanked God each night for that. Though she hoped He would provide answers, the right words for her, when the time came to depart.

"Why?"

"Eli needs to know this teasing his *sohn* is tossing out has consequences. I won't have Catherine treated unkindly." Daniel's frown indicated he too was angry Catherine was having a hard time fitting in.

"You could just talk to Eli. I'm sure if he knows Jesse is calling her names, he will see it stops." Or Hannah could talk with Jesse's mother, Sara, herself. No mother would stand by her child being cruel to others.

"I could, but this way is better." Daniel shifted, his back now resting on the post. He looked as handsome as that first morning in his pale green shirt and suspenders and carrying a breakfast tray. "We cannot always stop others from acting a certain way, but we can decide how we handle it."

"And by handling it, you mean skipping school instead of turning the other cheek?" Her words earned her a narrowed look.

"Catherine has been through plenty and even little girls need a break." Hannah warmed to his absolute observations of her children. He continued, "I can let her answer the phone in the office. Maybe take her to lunch in town, just the two of us."

"Just the two of you?" Hannah asked, slightly befuddled.

"*Jah*, a day with my pretend daughter," he said, sliding his thumbs into his suspenders. "I hear it's a thing." He shrugged.

Hannah managed not to liquefy into a pool of mush right there. "I think that would be lovely," she choked out. Her daughter would have one of those luncheons she always dreamed of, the kind where you were made the center of your father's world. Did he know what he was promising? "That's very sweet of you, Daniel."

"I can be sweet," he teased, puffing out his chest playfully.

"And humble, I see," she mocked. If only all men were measured by this one, then marriages would be happy-ever-after and all children would feel they mattered. She suspected when Daniel Raber loved, it was a gift worth cherishing.

They grew silent. Above them, stars blinked to life. "So many stars," she muttered, in awe with the display above her. One of the few fond memories she still held dear was Anna telling her stories under the stars. She hadn't done that with the girls before. She would, before the air grew much colder. They were supposed to go camping that very weekend their world unraveled.

There were so many things Hannah had been denied in her childhood, but her daughters deserved all the wonderful moments and lessons of simplicity that might mold them into better people. And Daniel. They deserved being cared for by a man like Daniel Raber. She didn't need to hear the words to know he loved her children. It showed in the gleam in his eyes, the laughter in his voice, and in the way he attentively treated each of them.

Daniel sat on the top step, legs outstretched, and leaning back on his elbows. He was in no rush to end the evening and neither was she. Patting the wooden plank beside him, he urged for her to sit too.

Hannah lowered down beside him. He smelled of sawdust and sweat. Was she falling under the same infatuation as her daughters? Pondering what she was falling into, Hannah settled back and faced the glittering of night.

"He counts the number of the stars and calls them by their name," Daniel said.

She glanced over and noted he was still looking up. "That's a psalm," she said. "Though don't ask me which one," Hannah half laughed. Daniel looked over, and rested his hazel eyes on her. As long as she lived, Hannah would never find eyes so honest, so engaging.

"I'm not sure which one it is either." Daniel's lips quirked into a grin.

Hannah rubbed her arms up and down, took in a deep breath of cold night air. "I have never breathed so easily."

"It's slower, harder, a more restricted life here, but

yes—" he pulled his gaze from her and looked out again "—it's easy to breathe in."

"The pace gives you time to think, enjoy your hard work, and having no phone helps." She thought she would have missed having her cell phone by now. Oddly, Hannah hadn't missed it at all. Who else did she need to talk to? Everyone she knew or cared about was right here.

"You miss it? Living in Indiana, living the *Englisch* life?" He studied her again.

"I miss what could have been, but no, I don't think I do. I like having time to do things right. Not being rushed. I missed spending time with the girls when Micah insisted I went back to work. How about you? Do you miss Chicago?"

"I missed being here when I was in Chicago. *Nee*, I'm right where I am meant to be." His heart had been set long ago and she could see that in his reply.

"I've never been confident like that. God sort of tossed me around and I made the best of wherever I landed."

"*Gott* always has a plan, even if we don't see it."

"Yes, He does. I'm learning that better now. Edith speaks so much of me being here for a reason. Like it was meant to happen," she half laughed. "It has helped the girls deal with everything. They are adjusting well. We have enjoyed our time here with you, Daniel. I want you to know that. It means a lot to all of us."

"I like having you all here too," he said in that deep voice that often made her shudder. "I made you a promise. To offer you shelter and safety, until it's safe for you all to leave, but I will miss you all terribly."

Hannah took a shaky breath. Her daughters were

easy to love, but a part of her wanted to know how he felt about her. Would he miss her? "I've been meaning to tell you, the beard looks good on you. Edith told me why you are growing it."

His cheeks glowed pink. "*Jah*, it's one of the rules of the Order. Married men don't shave."

"And you are a married man now," she said, grinning.

"You still haven't brought me lunch yet," he said, leaning closer to her.

"You still want me to bring you lunch?" His voice had her floating, her breath quickening.

"Catherine did tell Millie and Margaret that you do bring lunch to see me some days." He lifted a brow, taking one corner of his smile with it.

"But that was just…"

He chuckled deep, and low, and very unsettling. "A lie. So, let's fix that."

"I still don't think it's a good idea, Daniel."

"You did run off my only prospect for a girlfriend, did you not?" he teased. She wasn't so off-kilter. Hannah had forgotten how men and women interacted, and it was clear Daniel was flirting.

"I guess I did." She smiled cunningly. "I'm sure the girls would like that very much."

"And you? Would you like that?" Was he just curious, or did he really want to know? Did she dare let her heart fall for another man, knowing he too would one day grow tired of her?

Looking at him, she moved her fingers toward the scar slowly being camouflaged in his newly grown facial hair. "Where did this come from?" She didn't touch him, but felt the warmth of him being so close.

"My *bruder*," he said flatly, and she withdrew her

hand immediately. Hannah watched him tense. Daniel had refused to talk about Michael before. Keeping silent, she waited. She wouldn't push. After a time, Daniel began to relax. Leaning forward, elbows on knees, she could see him battling with sharing this part of himself.

"I looked up to him, when I was young. He was just a year older than me." He threaded his fingers together, before continuing. "When we were *kinner*, he was always doing stupid things. Getting stuck in trees, painting the old deacon's dog and other things I would rather not say." His voice grew more gravelly but she could tell he had enjoyed that time in his life. She'd never had siblings of her own. Daniel had lost his parents but she was beginning to realize that he had lost his brother too. That had to be why it was so hard to speak of him. A year apart, they were most likely very close.

"Painting a dog?" Micah had once painted a dog, he had told her. Something about a grumpy old man telling his parents he caught him smoking cigarettes with friends.

"Jah," Daniel chuckled. *"Mudder* was madder than a wet cat over that one." Hannah could imagine.

"As a boy I thought he was the bravest person in the world. He was fearless. Nothing scared him. I got to tag along on what is it M.J. calls them, 'ventures?" They both laughed. "Michael was a lot like our *daed*. He never wanted this life and when *Daed* moved us to the city, things just changed. When he was around eleven or so, he wanted to be Indiana Jones, got a toy whip and that hat, you know the one, for his birthday." Hannah nodded but remained quiet as he worked through this telling of his brother.

Daniel pointed to the scar on his neck. "This was

from him practicing knocking a can off my shoulder."
Daniel cocked his head. "Michael had a way of leaving scars behind him."

When his knowing eyes held her, recognition slowly registered and Hannah bristled. *Indiana Jones. Painting dogs.* Could it be possible? That grin... She would have never guessed it. The story wasn't just Daniel's, it was Micah's too. What a fool she was not to have seen it sooner. Even the way his lips tightened when holding back, just like Rosemary's did. She shivered, but not from the cold. Was this really happening? She staggered to her feet.

"Are you okay?" Daniel reached to steady her but she jerked away from him quickly.

"Oh...yes. I'm sorry. I should go check on the girls. Good night, Daniel." Hannah rushed into the house feeling more betrayed than ever. She had fallen for another man who was a liar too.

Chapter Fourteen

Daniel did as he said he would and dragged an angry nine-year-old to the mill with him. Catherine looked no happier to be at work with him than going to school and dealing with Jesse Plank. That frown was in danger of becoming a permanent stain on her little face. When the teenaged years arrived, Hannah would be in trouble.

"I'm only nine," Catherine sassed, crossing both slender arms over her chest. "Isn't making me work like against the law or something?" Daniel rubbed a tense nerve at the back of his neck, and forced a smile. He could either pull his hair out or laugh dealing with Hannah's eldest. Then he remembered that little pocket of information he'd kept stashed away for just the right moment.

"Well, I'll tell you the truth. I brought you because I could really use your help. Are you any *gut* with numbers?" He knew she was. Hannah had mentioned how advanced Catherine was in math in her former school.

Her blue eyes, just like Hannah's, lit up, but she refused to answer him. Daniel continued. "And it so happens that Jesse Plank's dad works here. He talks all the time about how Jesse can muck twenty stalls in one afternoon."

"I can muck a stall. You made me, remember." She started tapping her foot against the wooden floor.

"*Jah*, and you do good work. Sometimes Eli brings Jesse here to work when school is out. That boy can count lumber footages faster than I can." He tested and she still remained stubbornly poised. "I guess boys just have better heads for such things. I thought maybe having an apprentice, someone to learn how to do the books and so forth, would be good for business. It was just a silly idea. I can run you back to school if you'd rather. I should have known this wasn't something you could do." Daniel opened the office door and waited for her to follow. After two long minutes, it worked like a charm. Challenging her, and using Jesse Plank to do it, was all the kindling he needed to strike that fire.

"No boy is smarter than me, especially Jesse Plank." She pulled off her jacket and tossed it over his office chair. "What does an apprentice do?"

Daniel had to do everything in his power not to smile.

By noon, Daniel stepped back into his mill office and found the floors swept, the windows scrubbed, two phone messages written surprisingly in neat handwriting on a notepad, and a stack of receipts and orders he had scattered about, organized. There was no way this child was only nine. Daniel was more than impressed. He was shocked by her hidden talents. Now if he could just knock down that last remaining wall. "I promised you lunch, and you have certainly earned it." Daniel motioned for her to follow him.

"Where are we going?" she asked as she followed him to the buggy and climbed in.

Daniel climbed up beside her and felt the warmth of accomplishment seeing her eager smile. "It's a surprise."

Just as they neared the diner in town, the skies opened up and it started to pour. Daniel quickly parked the buggy, tethered Colt and pulled Catherine into his arms. "Come on, munchkin. Can't have you getting your pretty *kapp* soaked." He covered her head with his straw hat, though it did little to ward off the downpour, and ran for the diner door, her giggles floating behind them.

Daniel guided her toward the center of the diner to an empty booth. "Let's sit over here."

"Why are we here?" She slid in the booth, her hair damp under her *kapp*.

"What can I get you two?" the waitress asked as she offered a handful of napkins to Catherine. "You are soaked, sweetie. How about some warm soup? Maybe a hot chocolate?" Catherine looked to Daniel, for permission perhaps.

"Order whatever you want," he encouraged.

"I would really like a hot dog and the hot chocolate too, thank you very much." Daniel was impressed with her manners.

"Same for me, with french fries please." The diner was well known for their homemade fries and, of course, pie. They ate in silence, sharing the fries, as they watched people stroll by the large diner window.

Daniel noted the green car sitting out front. The same one he recalled pulling in the same time he was running with Catherine in his arms toward the diner. The man behind the wheel wore dark glasses but the tint of the windows revealed little else. Daniel didn't know everyone in town, but he was certain this person didn't live in the area. No one got in or out of the car, and Daniel held his attention on it—and the shadowy driver—until it slowly backed out into the road and drove away. He would be sure to report what he saw to Bates soon.

When he turned to Catherine again, she dipped a fry into her ketchup and gave him a curious peek. "You're not, like, an undercover cop, are you?"

"No," he chuckled. "Just a Plain man who makes his living in lumber."

She studied him closer, chewed her mouthful. "So you are a real Amish person, helping us just because Bryan made you?"

"He didn't make me, I volunteered." Daniel claimed a fry, dipped it in her ketchup and ate it.

"So you're helping us because you want to?" She handed him a fry, a silent truce perhaps.

"I care very much about what happens to all of you." Catherine stared at him for another moment, processing his words. It was true she didn't rush her thoughts unless angry. Daniel gave her all the time she needed to consider her next question, because he knew she had more questions. He just hoped he had the right answers.

Breaking the silence between them, the waitress came over. "Can I get you two some dessert, maybe a coffee?" she asked.

"Ice cream and coffee would be nice, *danki*," Daniel replied. "Is that okay, *dochder*?" He smiled across the table. Catherine gave the waitress a nod but shot Daniel a narrowed look.

Then the waitress returned with their ice cream. "Here you go, you two. Rain looks to be letting up." She smiled at Catherine. "You might get home dryer than you were when you arrived." She patted Catherine's shoulder, gave Daniel a wry smile and walked away.

"Are you going to eat all of that?" he teased, reaching over with his spoon and stealing a bite of ice cream from her bowl.

"My dad was a detective," Catherine said, choosing her next bite carefully.

"He was very important, *jah*. You must miss him."

She shrugged. "He helped find people who got lost." She licked her spoon, stared out the window in a daze. "He was like a superhero."

"That he was," Daniel added.

"Real dads are busy. They work to pay for stuff and don't have time for ice cream and stuff." Her tone grew bitter. "You're not a real dad."

He let the insult roll off his sleeve. This was just a child trying to understand her place in the world. A child grieving for what she'd lost. "*Nee*, I am not. I like eating ice cream too well." Daniel snuck another bite from her bowl, half-teasing, but when she looked up to him again, he froze. She was serious. Had Michael never spent time with his children? Hannah had been angry when she said those things, but Daniel hadn't thought she meant Michael had never done *anything* with them. He thought Hannah only implied his busy life left him few moments to spare. A man's first duty was to his family. To teach his children they are valued, loved, and how to value and love others. He put the spoon down, and felt the first wave of nausea come about. Catherine's shoulders straightened; he could see that hard stubbornness making her all cold again.

"Catherine, I'm sorry about what has happened."

"It's not your fault," she muttered. "She doesn't think

we know, but I do. I know he wasn't a good guy. I heard Bryan and the tall guy say it. They say he took money and lied a lot."

"I'm sorry you heard that."

"I'm not telling my sisters." She pushed her spoon around the melting ice cream as if lost in the swirls and textures.

Daniel reached across the table, took hold of her tiny hand. "I know I'm not your *daed*. That this is all pretend until the man who hurt your father is found, but while we have this time together, I say, let's make the best of it."

"Like how?"

"We take the time to talk, maybe eat ice cream more often. If something bothers you, I want you to be able to talk to me, and your *mudder*. It bothers her when you're not happy and she doesn't know how to fix it." She pulled her hand free and toyed with her ice cream again.

"She always has to fix everything. When Dad wouldn't take Rosemary camping like he promised, she said she was going to take us. She always has to do what he forgets." She bit her bottom lip and looked up to him again. "I'll just talk to you so she doesn't have so much to worry about, since you're my pretend dad and all."

Progress, with a dash of guilt added. Would Hannah be upset at him for communicating with both Rosemary and Catherine? "She's your *mudder*. No one other than *Gott* will love you more than her."

"I know that." She took another bite of softened vanilla. "I'm nine, not stupid. She acts happy, but I know she's sad."

"My *mudder* did that. She was sad a lot, but we never knew."

"What was she sad about?" Catherine cocked her head and asked. They were connecting, bonding, and she was opening up to him. And Daniel found it wasn't that hard at all.

"My *daed*, well, he was a strange man."

"How?"

"Well, he thought living here, being Amish, was a terrible way to live."

"It's not so bad." She shrugged and took another spoonful of ice cream. Daniel grinned.

"He had strange thoughts, and tended to forget us sometimes too. He moved us away from the community to live among strangers." Kind of how he predicted Catherine felt right now. "My *mudder* helped us fit in, but *Daed* only cared about other things." Daniel had no intention of elaborating on the kinds of things that came first to his father.

"Our daddy did that too. He didn't like being home, or having kids," she said on a sigh. Her honesty cut him. "Especially M.J. He never talked to her." Was that why she craved friendships? Daniel shifted in the booth seat. "Sometimes he would look at Rosemary and make funny faces."

Because she looks like her grandmother, the mother he left behind weeping, Daniel thought. Would he ever be able to make up for the pain his brother inflicted?

"We may never understand everyone, but *Gott* promises we are never alone. Even when family fails us, we have community. Community is important to the Amish. You always have others to care for you, look out for you, as *Gott* intended."

"I like the name Catherine, you know, but don't tell."

She pinned him with a sharp look that Hannah often possessed.

"Catherine is a very strong name. It means pure. Catherines are understanding, and they take their time choosing their path. They do well at everything. They listen before speaking and are well loved within their family."

"I can do that." Her shoulders rose. "Listen and do well."

"I know you can. I could use some help at the mill on a regular basis." Her face lit up. "Don't get excited. We still must ask your *mudder*. You could help after school and maybe some Saturdays when I'm already working over there. Never without me."

"Really?"

"*Jah*. But you have to ignore Jesse Plank and finish all your chores. Plus, I expect you to help your *mudder*."

"I can help Mom, but can I hit Jesse Plank just once? Mom says girls don't hit, but boys shouldn't need to be hit."

Daniel chuckled. "Well, a good *maedel* would never do that." Then he leaned closer. "Even if it is well deserved. I have a feeling after today you won't have a problem with Jesse." Daniel had it on good authority Jesse was going to be punished for all his teasing.

"And after hot chocolate, he let me have two scoops of ice cream. I couldn't finish it and it melted but he never got mad," Catherine told Hannah as she tucked her into bed. She never thought she would see her child look happy again and it warmed her heart.

"Sounds like you had a really good day," Hannah said. Of course she did. Her own uncle loved her and spent the day with her. Hannah had been a fool, yet again, letting her heart be swept away by Daniel. She knew now Bryan bringing her here wasn't a coincidence. Daniel was Micah's brother. Another lie Micah had told her. He'd said his family was dead, that he was all alone in the world like her. That was how they had connected, why she'd kissed him that first time. It was the first lie of many and now Daniel too was a liar. Worse, Bryan had known it. She couldn't trust anyone.

"I saw a police car today and met the sheriff. Daniel says the sheriff here is checking up on us. That's nice," Catherine said, breaking Hannah out of her thoughts.

"It is. They drive by a lot, but I don't want you to bother your sisters about it. Rosemary might get scared if she knows."

Catherine nodded, understanding how her sister would be frightened by the extra security. "Are we safe here, Mom? Like, really safe, like Daniel says?"

"We are." Hannah wanted to believe it was true, but privately she wasn't so sure. First, there was the tire tracks at the mill a week ago, and now a strange man watching them eat ice cream.

"Did you know my name means I will do well when I grow up and my family loves me?"

Hannah smiled. "It is a strong name for a young lady."

"Daniel says I can work at the mill sometimes. Like on a Saturday when he has lots of paperwork, or when school is out. He thinks I'm smarter than Jesse Plank."

"Stay away from those boys who tease you." Hannah moved across the room to collect Catherine's clothes from the floor.

"He said I was freakishly tall and weird because I

didn't know we weren't supposed to dress up for Halloween," Catherine said.

"I'm sorry you didn't get to trick-or-treat this year." Hannah would never admit it, but she was glad to be rid of the ritual this year. She never was a fan of Halloween.

"It okay. I didn't want to anyhow. Daniel says Amish *maedels* don't do that and that hitting boys goes against God. But Jesse is going to be punished for being mean to me."

Hannah jerked in surprise. "Is he now?"

"Yep. Daniel won't let boys pick on me anymore, Mom," Catherine said as she yawned.

"Catherine, Daniel is very nice to do and say all of those things, but remember, darling, we won't be here forever." Hannah couldn't let this go on much longer. Now even her most stubborn child was growing attached to Daniel. To this life. Hannah finished hanging Catherine's dress on a peg on the wall and moved back to the bed. "When this is over, we'll find a nice house and start over." Hannah bent down and kissed Catherine's cheek.

"Dad never carried me out of the rain before. We never ate ice cream at a diner either. Was I so bad he didn't love me?"

"Oh, baby, no." Hannah gasped and enveloped her daughter in her arms. "Your father loved you very much. His job was just so important he could never be around as much as other dads."

"But why weren't we more important?" Catherine asked. Hannah knew the answer. She just wasn't sure how to tell her child. How did a mother teach honesty and integrity when she herself had lived a lie for ten years?

Chapter Fifteen

Daniel switched off the gas-powered mill when he saw the buggy approach. He hadn't talked to his *onkel* in a few days and right now he could use a bit of the bishop's wisdom.

"Had a free hour, thought to waste it on you." Joshua winked as he climbed down from the buggy. A light mist had encouraged fog to linger longer than usual. Daniel tethered the old mare to the mill office's porch post and led him inside.

"Looks different in here," his *onkel* observed. Daniel shuffled some papers into a neat stack and pushed them aside on the large desk.

"Catherine is a better organizer than I ever was." A nine-year-old had a better system of life than he did. When had his life become so disorganized? *When the bishop knocked on his door, that's when.*

"It wonders me how you all are." Joshua removed his black felt hat revealing a shiny bald spot on top of his head. "Edith wanted to give you all some space, but I think she is missing spending time with those *kinner* of yours."

"*Nee*, we are managing," Daniel said, unsure. "You needn't worry."

"You are my *schwesder*'s sohn. I will always worry." Joshua grinned. "Any word on this man the law is looking for?" Joshua reached into his pocket and pulled out a handful of mixed hard candies. He offered one to Daniel, who declined. For a man who constantly ate candy, those teeth sure looked healthy.

"They got a few leads. Some people spotted him in Indiana, but there's no word on if it's connected to whoever was sneaking around here."

Joshua raked his thin beard and remained silent.

"I haven't told Hannah all of that. I didn't want her to worry. The *kinner* are doing so well. I would hate to see Rosemary frightened again. The agents and sheriff all know."

"*Jah*, I've seen them driving about regularly. That's *gut*."

"Marshal Bates thinks he didn't even know Rosemary saw him. If she saw him."

His *onkel* shook his head. No one wanted to see children scared, put in harm's way. "Man is a fickle creature, tending to ignore what is placed in front of him, yet is relentless to have what isn't." He fixed Daniel with a chastised glare. "I will continue to pray for them, and you." Joshua went to the office window and watched the men run lumber through the edger. "Edith is quite taken with that little one."

"I'm quite taken with her myself." Daniel smiled, helpless against it.

"And her *mudder*." Joshua turned and pinned him with a probing look.

"She is Michael's wife, *Onkel*."

"*Nee*, she is Michael's widow. Hannah is your *fraa*. A second chance at a family *Gott* has blessed you with."

"This is all make believe, for safety's sake. Nothing more." His *onkel* wasn't buying it. Daniel tossed a wood-marking pencil aside. "She's been avoiding me for days," he added. What had changed from one day to the next, Daniel hadn't a clue.

"This situation won't always stand between you," Joshua said as he placed his hat back on his barren head. "She has taken to our ways well enough. Edith is going to teach her to sew dresses and coats tomorrow. She has a good start. Maybe she does not feel as you feel. Some come to us seeking a simpler path, one closer to *Gott*."

"She didn't come here willingly," Daniel reminded him. "We are partners, protecting the girls." Daniel lowered his head and angrily added, "Protecting this lie."

The bishop sighed heavily, then asked, "Is it really so hard for you, Daniel?" Daniel narrowed his brows in confusion. "Hard to admit you love your wife? That you're capable of loving? Most men would envy what you two have."

"No man would envy this, *Onkel*. She will leave someday. They all will." Taking his heart along with them.

"Not if you do things right. Haven't you ever considering courting her?"

"My bishop suggests I court my *fraa*?" Daniel laughed out loud at the very thought. "Now that's building the house before cutting the tree."

"I admit we put you in such a position. Your *mudder* loved you, loved you and Michael both. My dear *schwesder*, Martha, had such a kind heart. I see many of those qualities in Hannah." Daniel had too, which was why he was struggling so much. "She loved your *daed* even after he dragged her away from her family and her community. She loved your *bruder* even when he ran away. She wrote me, often. I know everything about him getting in trouble for drinking and stealing and even that time you got taken out of school for fighting."

"You knew about that?" Daniel blurted out. "Well, I didn't know any better then. And the guy would have beaten Michael." Daniel turned toward the window and shook his head. "He liked to start things and I always got stuck cleaning them up afterward."

"This isn't that, Daniel," Joshua assured.

"Feels like it most days." But on other days, it felt like Michael wasn't between them. That it was just him and Hannah and three little girls trying to live a life, one day at a time.

"If you love her, don't compare yourself. I know her life with Michael was not easy. She talks to Edith. I believe he wanted to leave her before he passed." Daniel's fist tightened. Hannah blamed herself, believed she had not been a good enough wife, and here his brother had been considering abandoning her, his children. His veins ran hot in the knowing.

"Michael was never content for long. He never put *Gott* and family before his own selfish wants. If Hannah knew this truth, that you are Michael's *bruder*, she would never think you the lesser man."

"No, she would think me a liar, keeping secrets from her, just as Michael did. She will never understand the full of it. She has been through so much." Daniel stopped. His *onkel* didn't need to hear what he was thinking.

"Then show her how not all men are alike, even those raised under the same roof."

And by showing her, his *onkel* was suggesting Daniel court her. It was ridiculous, a complete contradiction to the order of things, and yet, the very notion of courting Hannah struck a dusty chord in his chest.

A little after two that afternoon, Daniel veered his buggy into the school parking lot. He was early but Catherine burst out the schoolhouse doors and hopped up into the buggy before Daniel could blink. "How was school today?"

"I hate this place," she said angrily folding both arms over her chest.

"*Hate* is a strong word. My day was not so *gut* either." They were both in a foul mood, so instead of turning right toward home, he turned left. "I know what we both need." Twenty minutes later, Daniel watched as Catherine drank her milkshake noisily.

"We just drove a horse through McDonald's drive-through," she busted out laughing and Daniel laughed too.

"I once took Maybelle through a car wash. You should have seen people's faces then." She laughed again, and his heart did somersaults knowing he had a part in that. Without all the hardness, she was a delight. Daniel felt their friendship kindling and hoped she felt it too. No child should feel so alone, without a friend to turn to, without a *daed* to protect her.

"You ran out of there so fast today, I wondered if you didn't punch Jesse right before I showed up, and now I am an accomplice to your crime."

"He won't stop teasing me. I said you're welcome

wrong in Amish, and he said I talk funny, and my hair is too short because I can't keep it pinned up right. He said I must have had lice, because they shave your head when you have lice. I couldn't say it wasn't true without him knowing I'm a fake Amish girl."

"I remember my first week of school when we moved to Chicago. I had an older *bruder* so I thought I was safe from such things as teasing." An English school with hundreds of kids had been quite the experience after attending a small two-room Amish schoolhouse.

"I wish I had an older sister," Catherine said solemnly.

"It isn't all wonderful. He got me in more trouble than I could find alone. He would pick on other kids and start fights. Then I had to pretend to be the big *bruder*."

"Doesn't sound like a very nice brother," Catherine replied.

"He wasn't, but he was mine."

"You weren't mean like that, were you? Like your brother or Jesse?" Her big blue eyes looked up to him.

"*Nee.* One of us had to be responsible." He nudged her. "The eldest is supposed to look out for the youngest, but I loved him and didn't mind, much."

"So it is my job not to make things harder for Rosemary and M.J.?"

"Precisely. You are the eldest and must set a good example, and you are a very wise young *maedel*, Catherine Faith."

"I know." She grinned, cocked her head and smiled. "But Sunday for church, I am not letting him have any of *mudder*'s *kichlin*."

When they reached home, Daniel saw the dark vehicle at the end of his lane. He pulled on the reins, bringing Colt to a stop. The driver's side window rolled down and he recognized the man as one of the two agents who had been there the night Hannah and the girls arrived in his home.

"Hello."

"Mr. Raber," the agent greeted in a sturdy frown. "I'm agent Lawson. I'm here giving the locals a break. I'll be here until sunup, sir, until told otherwise." Lawson's arm rested on the window. His intense gaze told of a man who took his position seriously.

"Come to the house for supper. It's the least we can do for all your help."

"I might take you up on that." Lawson nearly cracked a grin. "There are only so many burgers and cups of stale coffee a man can tolerate."

The agent followed them to the house and Daniel welcomed him inside. "I brought company for supper, Hannah. Hope you don't mind," Daniel said as he entered a kitchen that smelled of tomato sauce and fresh garlic bread.

"Agent Lawson," Hannah said in a surprised voice as the tall man stepped into the room. "Is there any news?"

"No, ma'am. Just keeping watch over everything," Lawson said.

"Well, I'm glad you've come to join us. I hope you like baked spaghetti. The girls have been on me to make it. We have salad too, and an apple cobbler for dessert."

"It sounds wonderful, ma'am. Thank you for inviting me."

As Hannah and Catherine set the table, Daniel helped M.J. into the seat next to him. The agent sat in the empty chair at the far end of the table and once everyone had settled, Daniel lowered his head to commence the silent prayer. After a minute, Daniel cleared his throat, and all heads lifted. Hannah quickly began filling plates for everyone. "So, Mr. Lawson, where are you from, exactly?"

"A native Hoosier," he replied, offering up his plate. For the next half hour, the two of them talked like old friends. They spoke of restaurants they frequented, scenic towns they knew. Daniel began to feel the slow sting of jealousy creep into his gut. Especially since Hannah hadn't once looked his way throughout the meal. He helped M.J. cut her spaghetti into smaller pieces and tried to ignore his unease. Hannah didn't even offer him dessert. Daniel had to spoon out his own serving. Was she punishing him or simply keeping her distance?

After a meal that lasted longer than he wanted, Daniel escorted the agent to the door. He would sleep better tonight knowing someone else was looking out for the family, but he felt like the *Englischer* had worn out his welcome.

"Thanks again for the meal. Magnolia said she would run out breakfast come daybreak, but I don't see the sense in her going to all the trouble."

"I'll let *Hannah* know. *Gut nacht.*" Daniel closed the door and stomped back into the kitchen.

"If you plan on feeding him come morning, it will be me who takes it to him," he said before crossing the room and stomping out the kitchen door to do his evening rounds.

Daniel flipped on the flashlight and made his way toward the barn. Since when had he become possessive and brooding? Hannah of course simply enjoyed talking about home with someone who understood. Daniel shared no history with her, personally. And then he had to go on and act like a jealous *dummkopp*.

At his entrance, the goats all came to life and started bawling. Daniel went to fetch them a scoop of feed to quiet their ruckus.

"I see all of you are enjoying the spoils of the *kinner*." He shined a light on each one and noted just how overly fat they were getting.

"So do you all think I'm an idiot too?" He scooped out another bit of grain and watched as they took right to it. "Well, we might not have history, or anything close to normal," he said tossing the feed scoop back into the grain bin. "But that doesn't mean we can't have a future."

Chapter Sixteen

"I like this daddy. He's funner. He tells stories and thinks my hair is pretty even when it won't stay in my *kapp*." M.J. giggled. "He says my *kapp* can't hold all my pretty in, but I should hide it or some smelly boy might pull my curls."

"Your *daed* is right. Boys can be smelly. Now finish playing with the coloring books I brought you and eat your cake while I show your *mudder* how to cut a dress." Edith stepped into the kitchen where Hannah had already spread out a light green material across the family table.

"This is a nice shade," Hannah complimented. "I have only quilted some, but can't say I know a thing about sewing clothes from scratch."

"It is not so hard," Edith ensured as she began spreading out pattern pieces and explaining them. "Do the *kinner* like the swing Daniel and Joshua hung for them?"

"Yes. They love it." Hannah mimicked tracing a sleeve from her side of the kitchen table. "They play on it nearly every day. I could have saved a lot of money over the years if I'd just hung a swing," Hannah noted.

"You need a sewing machine. I shall speak to Daniel of it."

"Oh, no, please don't. Daniel has done plenty already. I have some money left from Bryan," Hannah said, trying to hold back her anger. Last thing she wanted was something else to owe Daniel for.

"*Nee*, you are not doing the asking, I am," Edith quirked. "I heard Catherine missed school. I hope it was not because of her troubles with Jesse Plank?"

Hannah looked up from the table. "She came home crying the other day and told me that he'd said she had lice. And that was why her hair isn't long like the other girls." She went back to marking material. "Micah always insisted they kept their hair cut short, but I convinced him shoulder-length was best."

"I wonder if that *bu* has any sense at all. Takes after Eli, that one. That man speaks his thoughts aloud more than he ties his own shoes," Edith said, ill-tempered. "That poor *kind*. She has been handed a hard blow. Well, I shall continue to pray for her."

"Daniel took her to work with him recently, then out for ice cream." Hannah looked up from her work. Edith would see how this could be a problem. The woman was keen about others.

"Daniel is a smart man. He has the *kinner*'s best interests at heart. Even so, it is good to see him happy."

"Happy? How is it possible he's so happy? We have disrupted his life completely."

"It is as plain as day you being here has made him happy. Family brings joy, and you would do well to accept that. *Gott* does not mean for us to be alone," Edith said.

"But he will be alone, when we leave. I'm concerned the children are growing too attached to him. I hope they find this guy Corsetti soon. I hate to see my children hurt more than they already have." Hannah looked up and noted Edith's sorrowful expression. "Edith? What is it?"

Edith sniffled. "I'm sorry, my dear. It is just… I would hate to see you go. I have come to care a great deal about you and the *kinner*."

"But this isn't our home. We can't stay and pretend that it is…forever."

"A home is a place where we feel love. You have been given a second chance to feel love here. So has your *dochdern*. *Gott* does not make mistakes. Does it not feel like you are loved?"

"Feels like straddling a fence," Hannah said. "Like we are neither fully in this world or the English one." She went on. "Besides, Daniel feels obligated to help us. That's all." Hannah reached for a marking pencil. "We are like the guest that never leaves. We have been here almost six weeks."

Edith chuckled. "Time enough. Now you stop all that fretting about what could be and focus on today. You are his *fraa*. Those are his *kinner*. Has he not provided and cared for each of you?"

"Well, yes, but…" They were Micah's children, not Daniel's.

"Have you not in return tended to his home?"

"Mostly but…" But Daniel was only doing what any honorable man would do, tend to his brother's family. Though she had to admit, Micah would have never gone so far for another.

"It is perfectly normal to feel something for Daniel. You two have been good for each other." Edith tilted

her head. Hannah let out a sigh. Edith had a gift for seeing what was hid furthest in the heart, and bringing it
to the surface. Hannah cared for him and there was no
hiding it from his *aenti*.

"There are things you don't know. Things I just
discovered about him, and me. It wouldn't be right."
Hannah shook her head, wishing they could talk about
something else.

"So he told you about Michael, did he?" Edith
crossed both arms over her ample chest.

"You knew?" Hannah gasped. Had her closest con-
fidante lied to her, as well? Hannah took a step back.
Was no one on this earth trustworthy?

"Of course." Edith waved a hand. "You weren't ready
to know. You have endured so much. You lost a husband, your *kinner* were in danger, and you were pulled
out of your world and brought to a strange place. All
this happened so fast. It was no lie to give you time to
gain your footing." Hannah believed her. Edith would
never purposely hurt her.

"Daniel doesn't know that I know, but he only agreed
to this because of who we are. He thought it was his
duty, tending to us as he has. He is an honorable man."
The most honorable and amazing man she had ever
known. "He cares because we are the only family he
has left."

"Maybe at first," Edith quickly agreed. "Daniel has
always had to pick up after Michael. He wanted to help
you, but that doesn't mean he doesn't have feelings of
his own. The two are not so very different, *jah*?" They
were different, Hannah recognized.

"But we come from two totally different worlds."

"*Nee*, you have both known each side of a fence.

You are not so different." Edith pinned her with that knowing look. Was Edith right? Daniel had lived in her world and now she lived in his. "It only matters which place holds your heart." That was the problem, Hannah thought. She didn't know where she belonged. What she did know was that Micah was nothing like Daniel, and how she was feeling about him wasn't the same either. But he had withheld the truth from her.

"Your past hardships do not mean you don't deserve love from a good man." It was scary how Edith knew exactly what she was thinking. "*Gott* wants us to give love and receive it. You have that here, with Daniel. You got through all of that, to be here where *Gott* wants you. How do you know that He didn't mold you for this life?"

"I don't know what love is, really. I can't be trusted with such a thing," Hannah murmured as tears threatened.

"Oh, stuff and nonsense. You are a grown woman with three *kinner* whom you have proven you would do anything for. I have no doubts you know what love is. I see it when you look at them." Edith went to her.

"I was a fool, Edith. My choices have already affected my children's lives, forever."

"I see it there, between the lines. I see you holding on to a past that hurts. Worry doesn't fix a thing or complete a single chore. It just gives us wrinkles in all the wrong places. Do you still love Michael so much your heart has no room for another?"

"I was so young, so eager for love, a family. I thought he loved me, believed he did...at first. I thought he knew me. He told me that his life had been similar to mine. I thought we shared that connection, that he understood me. I let him have my heart without stopping to think if I wanted to give it away so easily." The tears were unleashed.

"Ach, mei lieb." Edith held her hand.

"He didn't want children and I..." she laughed through her sobs "...wanted them so desperately. When Catherine was born, he was angry, but he got over it. But when I got pregnant with Rosemary, he thought I was doing it to make his life harder."

"Some men feel pressures us women can never understand," Edith said. "Their father was like this. My poor Joshua spent many a day begging him to change his ways. Martha Jane had a hard life married to that one."

Martha Jane, M.J. Hannah felt the air slip out of her. Had her daughter been given the very name of her grandmother? Daniel and Micah were two very different people. How had God made two brothers, born of the same house, so different? Micah was full of sweet charms and selfish wants. Daniel rarely spoke and hadn't a selfish bone in his body.

"Dan took them away from us, to the *Englisch* world, because he couldn't submit to *Gott*. He liked to drink and smoke, and I think Joshua feared he had a gambling habit, as well. It broke poor Martha's heart. You should know those *kinner* have the look of her. I saw it plain as day the first time I laid eyes on them." Was that what had drawn Daniel in so deeply with her daughters? "Martha was a gentle heart. Very giving. She would have loved meeting her *grosskinner*. Did Michael ever speak of her?"

"Never. He told me he had no family." Hannah lowered her head. "He lied, about everything. The girls, they needed him. They needed him to make them feel safe, loved. Make them feel like they mattered." She turned to Edith again. "He never bought them ice cream or let them have pets or read them stories at night. He never loved us."

"Not like Daniel."

"Daniel gave Rosemary the bees and M.J. the sun. He made Catherine smile, and reads books with her. They love him. They beg for his attention and…"

"He gives it. Because that is what fathers do." Edith touched her shoulder. "My heart hurts to know you lived a life such as this, but that does not mean you should accept that as the way life should be for your *kinner*. *Gott* loves you and you have a home here if you want it."

"I don't matter. It's the girls who do. Plus, I'm not even Amish. Even if that was a possibility, I can't."

"There are steps to be taken, *jah*. It wonders me if you want to know what those are." Edith smiled cunningly. Hannah wasn't sure what she wanted, but she knew being a burden on another man wasn't it. The front door slammed shut and Hannah jerked away, rushing to wipe the tears from her face.

"Why do I feel my ears burning?" Daniel teased as he walked into the room. Hannah turned her back to him and busied herself placing the cut-out pattern over the material. She couldn't let him see her crying, or asking questions. Catherine moved toward her.

"How was school today?"

"It was not good," Catherine said. Then she looked to Daniel and smiled. "But it got better. We had shakes and Daniel says I get my own pay for working at the mill."

"He did, did he?" Edith arched a brow. Hannah turned slightly and smiled at her daughter.

"Daniel, your *fraa* needs a sewing machine," Edith blurted out to Hannah's embarrassment.

"Then she shall have one. It would be good for the girls too. If you have plans on using it," he tested, looking to Hannah. She watched his smile fade when he caught sight of her teary eyes.

"I really don't think we will need one. It would be a waste of money considering we won't be here long enough to enjoy it." With that Hannah hurried from the room, putting as much distance between her and Daniel as possible. Pretending to love a man was just as hard as truly loving him.

The air grew chilly, and there was a hint of snow threatening. Daniel stoked the fire in the fireplace, and could tell from the sounds of things that Hannah was having trouble getting the girls to bed tonight. Putting the poker down, he climbed the stairs and went to tuck Rosemary in while Hannah wrangled M.J. into bed. They would have to be more careful how many sweets that one devoured after supper.

"Danki," Rosemary whispered as Daniel pulled an extra quilt from the chest at the end of her bed.

"I'm proud of you for sleeping in your own room." He unfolded the quilt.

"I can't be a baby forever. And I know there is a police car driving by the house a lot. So I'm not afraid."

"Have you said your prayers?"

"Yes. I like it here. I like Colt and milking Daisy. Did M.J. tell you she wants a cat?" Rosemary smiled.

"Jah, she did." Daniel smiled in return, then sat on the edge of her bed. "And that she named all the goats after princesses."

She was doing so well adjusting to life here. Far from the mute, frightened little girl he met on that dark September night several weeks ago.

"I think she would want a dog, an elephant and maybe a monkey if I allowed it." He leaned down, kissed her forehead and got to his feet again. "Need me to leave the lamp on longer?"

"I can see with the big moon outside. Daniel…" she paused "…I know *Aenti* Edith says we should call you *Daed* when we have visitors."

"*Jah.*" He held his breath.

"Can I call you *Daed* here too?"

"*Jah*, Rosemary. I would like that very much. *Gut nacht, liebling.*" Daniel fought back his emotions. Little girls needed to feel that the men in their life were strong, but right now he felt like a melted puddle of goo. He slipped into the hall, pulled Rosemary's door near shut, and there stood Hannah, her eyes brimming with tears.

Suddenly, she turned on a heel and ran down the stairs. He chided himself for not telling her about Rosemary speaking before making his own way downstairs to deal with the situation.

She stood in the family room, staring at the fire, red and orange dancing with each other. "How long… how long has she been talking to you?" Her voice was full of pain.

"Not long."

She spun angrily. "How…? Why…?" If one ever doubted she could be fury and backbone, all they had to do was see Hannah right now. At that moment, nothing soft or vulnerable existed. He had done that to her.

"I'm sorry, Hannah. I should have told you the first time it happened. I have no excuse. She is only now comfortable with it. I had hoped she would have opened up to everyone sooner, on her own, but…"

"But she trusts you."

"It was an accident, I think. She was upset one day and just blurted out a few words." He edged cautiously closer. "She worries about you, about more than little girls should. I'm sorry." Daniel would do anything to show just how sorry he was.

"I'm being selfish." She straightened her shoulders and lifted her chin.

"*Nee*, you are her mother. It is me who was selfish. I had no right. Rosemary is your daughter and…"

"And she is your niece." Daniel jerked to attention. How did she know? His heart dropped like a heavy stone into the bottom of his gut.

"I'm right, aren't I? Micah is…was… Michael and you are…his brother?" Daniel clenched his jaw but said nothing. "You kept secrets and lied to me." Hannah brushed the tears from her face and stormed past him.

Daniel reached out, took her arm to stop her. No more lies, no more pretending. "How did you know?"

Like that evening on the porch, she reached out to touch the scar no longer visible on his neck. "This. Micah told me that story. He loved Indiana Jones. And that dog. He painted that dog because your deacon reported him for smoking." His gaze landed on her eyes, the pain he'd added there. "He said his family was dead. It was just one of his many lies. He said you all abandoned him and then died. How could you not tell me?"

"Bates said it was safer not to. I wanted to, Hannah. I only found out about Michael, about his family, hours before you showed up at my door. You weren't the only one hurt and having to make decisions quickly."

"You knew this and still, you almost kissed me." The pain on her face was unbearable.

"I hope you can forgive me for that too. It won't happen again." How many mistakes was he going to keep making?

"You took us in because he was your brother. You felt obligated in taking care of his burdens. You are both made from the same cloth and it's woven together with nothing but lies." She jerked away from him but Daniel held firm.

He was selfish, like Michael, because he wanted something he could never possibly have. He wanted her. Daniel loosened his hold on her arm, but didn't let go completely. "I did what I thought was best…for you and your girls. My obligations have changed. I have my own reasons now." *Stupid Daniel.*

"And they are?" She stiffened.

"Those *kinner* up there sleeping." He pointed toward the stairs.

"I hate that they love you, even Catherine, though she would never admit it."

Her tone grew softer, less cutting. But did she love him? That's what Daniel wanted to know. Could she ever move past the mistakes of his family, see him as someone worthy of her? Could she forgive that he'd kept so many things from her?

They were close, a breath away. His other hand brushed a tendril of hair behind her ear. "I love them too," he admitted, his heart pounding in his chest. He needed to close the chasm between them. He'd worked so hard building that bridge and felt as if he was losing that now. Daniel couldn't let that happen.

So before she could utter another harsh word, he

kissed her. And to his surprise, she kissed him back. Hannah melted into him and everything that stood between them vanished. He was the first to pull away and missed her immediately.

"I'm sorry." She looked breathless, stunned. Both good signs that he hadn't burned that bridge. Relief washed over him.

"Me too." Even in firelight the blush on her cheeks was apparent.

"I should…"

"Get some rest," he quickly said, noting her dazed state. He watched her retreat back upstairs wishing he'd said something more. What he wanted was to kiss her again, but Daniel had surprised her plenty for one evening. And a kiss like that left a person a lot to think about. She needed time to think after his boldness. They both did.

Picking up the poker, he gave the fire a little stir and added another large log to keep for the night. Hannah had fit into his life and without knowing it, gave him a glimpse of what family truly meant. She thought him the expert, but it was her, in all her selfless love and fierce determination. No matter her plight, Hannah never quit. Daniel only hoped he could convince her not to start now.

Chapter Seventeen

Hannah managed to keep to herself the next few days and Daniel didn't show any signs of caring she did. Neither knew how to handle that unexpected kiss. Nor how to deal with such strong feelings that followed. At least Rosemary was speaking to her now. It was the highlight of Hannah's night, tucking her into bed, saying prayers together. Her daughter was healing, and surprisingly Hannah was too.

Until that kiss. She knew he regretted it, letting the moment seize his common sense, but it was making things difficult for her. She couldn't stop thinking about him.

She finished washing up and pinned on a clean dress and apron before going downstairs. She'd promised the girls they could play on the porch. As she began working out the tangles in her wet hair, Hannah stared out the kitchen window. The cool breeze of the season twirled up anything outside not rooted in the earth, but she felt nothing but warmth in this house and life that Daniel had made for himself—and for them.

"Mommy!" M.J. came bursting into the kitchen, her

kapp lopsided, her new coat unlatched. "Princess Fiona is dying!"

"Martha Jane, I told you not to go outside or to the barn without me or Daniel with you." She would have to nail M.J.'s dress to the floor to keep her close.

"We were on the porch. You said the porch was fine." Knowing Agent Lawson and the county sheriff were just down the lane, keeping watch, Hannah thought the porch was perfectly safe. "She's under the tree swing, dying. Mommy help her. Don't let Princess Fiona die." Her daughter produced real tears, something she rarely succumbed too. Hannah tossed her brush onto the counter and rushed outside to see what the fuss was all about.

Just as her daughter said, under the large oak in the front yard, lay Princess Fiona. The black nanny goat was lying on her side, her stomach twice its normal size. Hannah knelt beside her. "What have you got into?" A thousand scenarios ran through her mind. Poisonous plants she didn't know of, or maybe she had gotten into the feed and overeaten. Wasn't that what Daniel called founder? It wasn't until the nanny began to push that it became crystal clear what was happening.

"Catherine," she yelled toward the porch where Rosemary and Catherine stood. "Fetch a bucket of fresh water by the pump." Catherine bolted around the house without hesitating. "Rosemary, get a couple towels from the line." Like her eldest daughter, Rosemary didn't pause.

"Is she gonna die, Mommy?" M.J. whimpered.

"No, sweetie." Hannah smiled up to her daughter. "She is going to be a mommy."

M.J.'s eyes lit up. "A mommy? For real?" Hannah was just as surprised. Daniel fussed the girls were overfeeding the goats and making them into spoiled pets. He would be in for quite a shock when he returned home today.

"Now rub her head and talk to her like you do any other day. It will help keep her calm." Hannah wished Daniel were here, but after bringing Catherine home from school, he had a couple more hours before he left the mill for the day. It was cold and windy, the ground still slightly damp from misting most of the day, but Hannah knew it was too late to persuade the cantankerous animal to move into the barn. "Well, Princess Fiona, let's have a baby." Hannah tucked her damp hair behind her ears and rolled up her sleeves.

At first, Daniel suspected Hannah had killed the old pesky goat, but when Rosemary stood cradling something with four dangling legs, he knew. *Just what I needed, more pets for M.J. to give silly names to.* He looked heavenward before letting out a hearty laugh.

When he neared them, all four females beamed, but it was a set of blue eyes sparkling with sweet wonder that held him transfixed. Hannah carried a second black kid wrapped in a towel toward him in a proud stride.

"A boy. Well, two boys actually. Now we know why she was so moody." She laughed, her eyes sparking with life and enthusiasm he had never seen before. Her hair was partly damp, the wind playing with the strands. And he knew right then in that moment—Magnolia Reynolds was a woman born to a world that tried molding her to its own selfish way. She all but said so. But Hannah Raber was happy and he knew it took so little to give that to her. How had such a big world failed her he hadn't a clue, but he had every intention of giving her all that he had.

"Well—" he reached out and patted the kid's head, still warm and damp to the touch "—me and Colt *were* feeling outnumbered. We needed a few more males around here." A gust of wind sent his hat tumbling away. Catherine hurried to fetch it.

"You three want to help move them to the barn before milking?" he asked, still focused on Hannah, the way her hair danced about her beautiful features.

"Milking is done." She titled her head and floated him a proud smile. That same smile she'd given him when Millie and Margaret had arrived unannounced at his door. She wasn't angry anymore.

"Well then, *fraa*, thank you." He winked at her before heading toward the barn. Life was shifting and Daniel was glad it was.

Chapter Eighteen

There was something about a Thursday that always made Daniel uneasy. He'd left Kentucky for the *Englisch* world on a Thursday. And had returned to it on a Thursday. He'd become a husband and father on a Thursday too, and this cold November morning the wind woke him, warning him another shift was coming.

He slipped downstairs to make *kaffi* and add fresh wood on the fire so the children woke to warm floors. The house was quiet. He thought he would miss that, but was growing accustomed to the sounds of feet running across the upper hall, giggles that made concentration impossible and the sweet strawberry scent of Hannah's shampoo wafting from room to room.

He discovered Hannah was already up, moving about, lamplight illuminating her small curvy frame as she reached into the fridge and pulled out bacon and eggs and milk. She stilled, sensing him near, and when she turned to smile his way, Daniel wanted to kiss her just like he had before. He loved her, and he couldn't deny it anymore.

"Gut morgen."

"Gut morgen." Her soft voice made him smile inside. He thought about just how much he wanted to wake up to mornings just like this one. Every morning. "Coffee?"

"Jah, danki." Daniel lifted both suspenders over his shoulders as he watched her retrieve a cup from the cabinet nearby and begin filling it. He took a seat at the table, careful not to let it scrape the floor, waking the children. Getting up early had been instilled in him since childhood, but the girls didn't need to get used to it. They would soon leave, back to a life where 7:00 a.m., and not 4:30 a.m., was normal. "I'll see to the morning milking today. It's getting colder out."

"I don't mind. I think I'm finally getting the hang of it." She turned his direction. "As long as M.J. is there to talk Daisy through my tortures," Hannah laughed softly. She carried him over a cup, then turned back to start breakfast when he said nothing more. They were both stalling. Neither willing to discuss what was going on between them. He watched as she placed bacon in the cast-iron skillet, turned on the heat of the gas stove. He wanted to ask her to stay, but feared her answer. The thought of her leaving, the children leaving, was tearing him apart. He was committed to this life, this marriage. If she would only acknowledge that kiss, say something to give him a reason to hope, he could tell her. One thing Hannah had few of was choices. He wanted this choice to be hers.

The silence lingered longer than he could stand. Daniel drank down his coffee and silently sat his cup aside. As much as he loved the idea of simply sitting there, watching her as she began mixing ingredients for biscuits, he knew that was only going to torture him further. He carefully rose, retrieved his coat and hat from the third peg by the door, and slipped out in the cold dark morning.

Maybe that kiss didn't mean to her what it had to him after all.

Daniel's bones ached like a January night as he sawed log after log. Why hadn't he told her how he felt this morning? Because she was clearly leaving, that's why. She'd never asked for this life, the Plain life. How could he ask her to give up her world and become Amish?

The sheriff's car pulled up to the mill office. Daniel let Eli take over things and went to greet him. "Afternoon, Sheriff Corbin," Daniel said, drawing close. The sheriff had come to town from somewhere farther south a few years ago. Not quite forty, and an inch taller than Daniel, he looked more like a man who worked the fields than one who rode around in a patrol car all day. The sheriff was friendly, only serious when the need called for it, and was capable of maintaining a peaceful community that was half Amish, half English.

"Your marshal friend called the station this morning." Corbin removed his hat, running a wide palm over his short-cropped head. Daniel ushered him inside the office for privacy. Eli and Vernon would only assume he came to discuss the tire tracks from days ago.

"This Nicholas Corsetti fella is here, in town," Corbin told him.

"I should get back to the house then. The bishop's wife is there with Hannah and the two little ones. How do they know for sure?" Daniel felt his heart begin to race.

"Hotel manager over in Mason reported an out-oftowner taking up a room for about nine days there. Their sheriff's department didn't care much, but when the man called again yesterday, he claimed Room Service had complained about the man. Said he had a gun on him. They called it in, along with the description of the car, plates and the man's description. He checked out, but when they ran the information—" Corbin shook his head "—the car was registered to a man from Ohio. That man was found dead two weeks ago. It seems everything leads to this Corsetti fella."

"Bates had one man already here. Agent Lawson. Besides you, he drives by every so often, came to the house a couple evenings for a meal."

"Yeah, I met him. He sleeps over at the bed-and-breakfast."

"I should go fetch Catherine from school." Daniel moved toward the door. "Can you go to the house until I get there?"

"Sure, you want me to get the girl so you can get home?"

"*Nee*, that will only scare Catherine, and a sheriff's car pulling up to the Amish school might start a panic and stir up questions."

"I've got two deputies now. Once you get back, I'll see Brown sits on the porch round the clock."

"I'm sure Bates will see there are a few agents nearby too. *Danki*, Sheriff." Daniel reached for his hand.

"None required. You're one of ours, now they are too. No one is getting to them while I'm sheriff here."

Daniel prayed he was right.

Daniel pulled into the small gravel parking lot of the Amish school, a large gray building he had helped build himself. The school had indoor plumbing, three classrooms and a small dining area. The last time Daniel had been inside was last year's Christmas recital. He tethered the horse to one of the six posts and climbed down. Daniel waved at Silas Graber's new bride. She was often carting Silas's two boys to school, but Daniel suspected young Aiden was getting big enough to take on the responsibility soon. It was clear love had been kind to them all and her rounded frame said the former widower was better at crossing rivers and building bridges than Daniel was.

He stepped into the front door. "Daniel?" He looked over to Lydia Ann Byler, Catherine's teacher, a stack of papers in her hands, dodging out of a room to the left.

"Why are you here?" Her head tilted in confusion.

"To pick up *mei dochder*." Daniel met her with equal perplexity.

"But Catherine never attended today," Lydia said, her eyes growing wider as the words left her.

"I dropped her off, right here," Daniel said, his voice doing nothing to conceal his growing panic.

"Oh, my." Lydia's hands flew to her mouth. "Daniel, she hasn't been here all day. I thought you kept her home again. Oh, Daniel…" But he heard no more as he raced his buggy to the nearest phone a half mile away. Daniel called 911, then Bates.

News traveled fast in Amish communities. Before Hannah had a chance to grasp what the sheriff was saying, the sound of several buggies clattered up the lane. "I will never stop being amazed at how fast the Amish grapevine works," Sheriff Corbin said, shaking his head as he opened the front door. Hannah stepped out onto the porch, her vision blurring. A warm hand touched her shoulder, moved slowly down her back. Was Daniel fearful she would collapse as half of Miller's Creek began filling up the driveway?

"Is this because of my daughter missing?"

"Jah," Daniel said softly behind her. "They will all come to help and won't leave until we find her." She turned to face him.

"They will know, Daniel. They might already know," she said. He reached for her hand, a warm reminder that she wasn't alone.

"Only that our daughter is missing. And that we need their help." When he looked down on her with those serious hazel eyes, a slight wrinkle between them, Hannah knew Catherine's chances were better. Daniel was holding back anger, fury and fear, but that raw determination was right there in those eyes. Amish or not, she had no doubt he would do whatever it took to find Catherine and bring her home safely.

"We lied to them," she said softly. "Why would they want to help me find her?"

"They know why. Even *Gott* knows why. These people love her—and you. We won't stop until she's home."

Warmth filled her. His words stronger than the November chill. "You *will* find her, won't you?"

"Daniel." The sheriff broke between them. "That agent has a man missing but the vehicle has just been spotted not far from here." Corbin bounded off the steps, motioned to a deputy nearby and started giving orders.

"Joshua will see to getting everyone organized. I'm going with him. I will bring her home." Daniel kissed her before running after the sheriff.

"Oh, Hannah, we just heard someone has taken Catherine. I called as many as I could." Millie bound up the steps first, all three of her redheaded girls jumping out of the buggy and running behind her. Millie pulled Hannah into her arms, tears pouring from her face. Hannah looked over Millie's shoulder as Daniel climbed into the sheriff's car. Their eyes held until the car turned away and raced past buggies still arriving. She needed to trust now more than ever.

"You came," she cried into Millie's shoulder.

"We all came. It's what friends do," Millie replied.

Chapter Nineteen

"The agent said they had him cornered just down the road from your mill," the sheriff said over the sirens blaring. "He's on foot now, and she wasn't in the vehicle." Daniel's heart hammered in his chest. Had he already hurt her?

The car pulled into the mill lot where two large black vehicles and a deputy's car were already parked. Five men stood, guns drawn. Another man stepped out of the office, indicating Catherine wasn't inside. Daniel jumped out of the sheriff's car.

"Stay in the car, Daniel, and let us do our job."

"We think she is on foot and he's chasing after her," Lawson said, a smear of blood on his forehead. "Tracks go this way."

"Browning, you stay here with Daniel, call in Search and Rescue and have them standing by. I can't have them entering the woods with an armed man and we don't have enough deputies to escort them right now." The sheriff looked to Daniel. "We have to have him in custody before letting them search, sorry." Daniel appreciated the information but he wasn't happy about it.

Catherine was out there, somewhere, waiting for him to come get her.

"She knows the woods here. She might be heading home," Daniel put in. Catherine was smart, he reminded himself. She paid attention to details and Daniel had taken them all through the small wooded area on walks twice now. Besides the mill, she would want to go home, where it's safe, where she would think he was. He believed that in his heart.

Bates ordered a female agent back to the house, just in case. Daniel fought between staying put and rushing home. The agent was in a vehicle and pulling away before he could choose, making the decision for him.

Daniel watched the men all spread out and move into the forest. Browning, the sheriff's deputy remaining behind, turned to him. "They said she jumped from the vehicle and fled into the woods. Don't worry, Mr. Raber, you got a smart, tough girl. They'll find her." His assurances didn't help matters. Daniel knew she wouldn't give up without a fight. Some parts of Michael he was blessed to know she possessed, but there was a fifty-fifty chance this hired gun man would find her first.

"*Gott*, let them find her. Let her find her way home. Let this man be stopped, here and now."

The agent motioned for Daniel to get down and Daniel quickly hid behind the sheriff's car. Movement stirred between lumber stacks. The deputy squatted down in front of him. "Fastest answered prayer I've ever been privileged to witness. Stay here."

"Wait." Daniel reached out to stop him. "Look." Just under the eave of his mill shed, a faint flash of blue caught his eye. "She's hiding above the mill, in the rafters." Daniel's breath exhaled in relief. Now all he had to do was get to her before the gunman did.

"He's looking for her. I'll go around, try to flank him. You know how to use a gun?" The agent started to pull a second weapon from under his coat. Daniel looked around quickly. He spied a nice-sized stacking timber close by.

"*Nee*, I don't need one," Daniel replied. He hoped he would never have to be put in the position to take a life, but fear for Catherine, coupled with knowing if this man got away he would forever threaten his family, he wasn't sure what he would do if the moment presented itself. He had taken his vows to *Gott*, believed them, but in that moment, Daniel knew he would defend life if he was forced to.

The deputy slithered along the car, looked out and ran toward the office. Daniel watched as a few seconds later he made a run for a pile of logs to shield behind. He was edging closer to the killer while Catherine clung to the rafters, hoping not to be seen.

Daniel peeked over the car's hood, the killer, a small light-haired man in jeans, worked his way around another stack of lumber. He was getting closer to the mill, closer to Catherine. Daniel slid the short four-by-four used for stacking lumber off the ground from his right and gripped it tightly. "Please don't put me in this position, but forgive me if I do what I must to save her," he whispered before making a run toward the lumber piles.

"Come out, little one," the killer called out. "Just want to know what your sister knows. Give yourself up and I promise I won't hurt her. Be a good big sister now, come out here."

Daniel steeled his breathing, though his veins

pumped rapidly. The deputy had worked his way toward the lumber stacks. Daniel positioned himself opposite the killer. He could no longer see Browning, knowing he was closing in on the murderer, but Daniel couldn't see the killer either, just hear his steps carelessly stomping closer.

"If I take you in, they won't want her. You would be saving your sister."

Heart pounding in his chest, Daniel lifted the stacking timber, tightened his grip. Catherine would indeed give herself up for Rosemary. He knew she would. He couldn't give her time to do that.

"I see you," the monster's voice echoed out. "Nice hiding spot, Jasmine. Your daddy would be proud."

Catherine's voice made a faint cry as the deputy burst out of hiding. "Hold it! You're under arrest!" A shot rang out and Daniel let instincts take over good sense, stepping into the aisle. The killer's back was to him, not two feet away. His gun raised, but no dead deputy lay on the ground ahead. Daniel breathed a quick relief that Browning's agility had saved his life.

"Her name is Catherine," Daniel said. Nick Corsetti turned and Daniel swung as hard as he could, making contact and knocking the man hard into the lumber. He fell down, but before Daniel could react, the deputy was already on top of Corsetti, hitting his gun away.

"Nicolas Corsetti, you are under arrest for the murders of Micah Reynolds, Charles Brown and Nina Sanchez." The agent looked up to him. "Nice swing, Amish. Go get your daughter." Daniel didn't have to be told twice. Dropping the wooden weapon, he sprinted to Catherine.

"Come on down, Catherine." Daniel reached up into

the rafters as Catherine eased down into his arms. He didn't give her a chance to speak before he enveloped her in the safety of his arms.

"I'm sorry, *Daed*. I…"

"Shh. You are here, safe. That is all that matters." He held her for nearly two more minutes before sitting her down and checking for wounds. "Did you hurt yourself getting away?"

Nodding that she was, Catherine looked up at him with those wide blue eyes full of fear and tears. "You came for me," she cried out and he swept her back into his arms again.

"I will always come for you," he promised. "Nobody hurts my *maedel*."

Twenty minutes later, EMS had seen to Catherine while Nick Corsetti was being hauled off in the back of an SUV.

"I would put ice on that knee, maybe take some Tylenol, but surprisingly she's got nothing but bumps and bruises," the female paramedic informed him. "You are one brave little girl." Catherine shrugged.

"I know you're mad," she said, looking to Daniel.

"I'm thankful you are okay."

"But you're mad too. I see it."

"*Nee*, but you scared us half to death, Catherine. Why did you run off from school and let yourself get put in this position?"

"Why do I have to go to school when we are leaving?" She brushed away a few tears and tried looking angry. "Mom said we couldn't stay. So why? Why should I put up with Jesse Plank and his friends or the baby goats? Why should I care if I learn how to sew or make apple pies and muck stalls?" She slapped a hand on her leg. "Why should I help at the mill, counting footages and adding numbers? Why should I like you even if you save me from bad guys if we are leaving?" Then she burst into another run of tears.

"I'll let you two have a moment," the paramedic said, leaving them inside the ambulance alone. Daniel pulled her onto his lap, fighting a rush of tears of his own. He held her a moment longer, felt his heart break in two, before forcing her to look at him.

"Do you want to stay here and muck stalls and play with baby goats instead of hanging out in malls and watching your favorite shows?" He wanted to give her a choice, something none of them had been given so far.

"*Jah*, I do." Her teary blue eyes begged him. "I don't want to go back. I want this to be our home. We like it here, except for Jesse Plank. Everyone loves us. He never loved us," she said on a fresh run of sobs. In the distance, Sheriff Corbin leaned on his car, talking on his phone. Daniel knew he was telling Hannah that Catherine had been found and was safe.

"Your *daed* loved you, Catherine. Michael, I mean, Micah, just loved differently. It doesn't seem fair at nine, but I promise you. He loved you and one day you will understand that he did."

"You don't do...different like he did," she said bluntly. The truth of her nine-year-old wisdom tore a path down the center of his heart. Daniel knew Michael had loved his children, just as their father had loved him and Michael. He also knew that sometimes words weren't always enough. It was action, assurances that children needed to feel that love. Doing the right thing, even when you didn't want to. That's what made a father a father.

"No, *liebling*, I don't. But that doesn't mean he didn't love you."

"Can you make her let us stay? If you're married, can't you make her? Dad made her do things his way. Can't you *make* her?" Her plea bore desperation.

"That's not how marriage is. I can't force her to do anything, but I could try to convince her you are happy here." Daniel smiled. He'd never imagined this was a life any of them truly wanted.

"How do you know so much?" She wiped her face.

"Not sure about much," he chuckled. "But I understand you. I was nine when we left here and moved to Chicago." He rubbed her back in slow circles as she listened. "I know what it's like not to fit in someplace."

"Did you hate the city too?"

"*Jah*, I hated it. So loud and busy. People weren't very kind. I lived in a small house with my parents and brother, crammed between two other small houses. My parents ran a small store. School in your world is even scarier than here," he noted.

"Where are they now? Your mom and dad and brother? Do I have grandparents? We never had grandparents before."

"They are all gone, but I know Edith would gladly be your *grossmammi*." He watched but her expression didn't waver. Catherine was absorbing it all. It was what she did, considering her words carefully. It was a trait he liked to think she'd gained from him.

"You lost your family?" she asked, shivering against the cold.

"I did." Daniel removed his coat and wrapped her in it.

"But we are your family now, aren't we?"

414 His Amish Wife's Hidden Past

"You are, and I thank *Gott* every day for bringing you all into my life. I love you, Catherine."

"I love you too, Daniel. I'm sorry I got in that man's car and you had to save me. He said he worked with Bryan and I thought he was here to take care of us. He didn't know Rosemary wasn't in school. If he was watching over us, he would know that, right?"

"Right." Daniel smiled. *As smart as her mother.* "Just never get into a car again." He pulled her close again, breathed in the soft scent of sawdust and little girl.

"I won't."

"Wait, how did you get out of his car?" Daniel asked. Surely she hadn't done as the deputy suggested.

"When he slowed down, I jumped," she said as if it meant nothing. Daniel wasn't sure his heart was up for the challenge of Catherine Raber in five years from now.

"How about we get back to the house, so your *mudder* can see you are all right. We will keep this conversation to ourselves for now, but I will talk to her."

"Promise?" she asked.

"Promise." And Daniel never broke a promise.

Chapter Twenty

Daniel leaned against the kitchen counter as Hannah cradled Catherine on her lap. He would never know the gift he had given her this day. She was blessed to have all her children here with her, safe. Bryan told her about the arrest and the fact she had no home to go back to. The bank had already foreclosed and sold it without her there to try to make amends for Micah's debts. She didn't care.

Everything she cared about sat in this very room. Her favorite room of all the rooms she had in a lifetime. This kitchen, though plain, brought her more joy than any other. This is where she came when she woke each morning, prepared meals she had always wanted to. The long table was where she learned to cut dress patterns, how to make the perfect crust and where her family gathered together each day. The fridge ran on propane, had no ice maker installed and yet held the fresh milk she had gathered from the cow her daughter loved like a best friend. Her favorite pan sat on the back of the stove, waiting for her to make use of it.

"We can see about setting you and the girls up someplace nice. I think it's best you don't return or use your old names in case Marotta finds a reason not to believe Nick's confession."

"But it's almost Thanksgiving," Catherine blurted out.

"*Aenti* Edith and Millie and everyone is coming," M.J. added. "We can't miss the big Thanksgiving with our new family, can we?" M.J. looked to Hannah and put on one of her signature pouts. Gott *bless these two,* Daniel nearly said aloud.

Hannah looked to Daniel. She was waiting for his re-action, not those of the faces around her. "I think miss-ing Thanksgiving would be terrible too. It's just a few days away, and I have been looking forward to your dressing and gravy," he reasoned, hoping to buy more time. In fact, the longer he thought about it, Thanksgiv-ing, which was a Thursday, would be the perfect time to tell her how he felt.

Her damp blue eyes widened in surprise. Daniel noted her fingers were slightly trembling, but before she could grab hold of her apron front to steady them, Rose-mary reached up, grasping hold of one of her hands.

"A few more days," the soft voice pleaded. How could the woman not know he wanted her to stay? Even her children knew. He wanted to tell her right then, but not with so many eyes upon them.

"Can we do that?" Hannah looked to Bryan.

"It's your call, Mags. Nobody can answer that but you. You are free to come and go as you please, just keep the identities for now. If you choose to want newer ones, all you have to do is ask." Bryan took a sip of the coffee she had prepared for them while deputies and agents nibbled on sandwiches the women had laid out.

"I think the children and I would like to stay for Thanksgiving if Daniel doesn't mind."

She was clutching to every last minute and it made his heart swell knowing so. "You know I don't. And we have much to be thankful for." His eyes twinkled as he looked over the girls' faces.

"And you promised to make the turkey," Edith put in. "I'm not making all the desserts and the turkey too."

"We do have a lot to be thankful for. We are blessed our Catherine is safe." Millie placed an arm around Hannah's shoulders. "We are blessed with friends and love big enough to fill this room. You can't leave all of that." She couldn't and didn't know how she was going to after Thanksgiving either.

Hannah straightened. It was settled then. Another couple days, she would relish in it. Then she would decide where to go. She looked across the room at the man who taught her not all men were the same. The man who saved her daughter, and her. Edith's words rang in her ears. Daniel would always consider their marriage legal, and now she would too.

"Yeah!" M.J. yelled and jumped into Daniel's arms. "We get to stay. I like it." Daniel chuckled at her signature adage. "I need to go tell Daisy we are staying for Thanksgiving. And I get to milk a goat. This is the best day ever." She squealed.

"Milk a goat," Daniel said, taken aback.

"You said you can milk goats if they become mommies. Well, Princess Fiona is a mommy and she's my size."

Daniel shook his head. "I guess I did."

"You should join us," Hannah spoke to Bryan. Bryan was a friend, more than that. He had brought her here, where she and her children could heal. In that healing,

Hannah had found herself, her true self, in the last place she would have ever looked. This Plain world, she was made for. It taught her the value of community, friends and faith. She thought she knew God before, but now she felt closer to Him. Whatever His will was for her, she would obey. She would adapt. But she would never forget Daniel, the man who held her heart.

"I have to escort Corsetti back. No rest or holidays for my kind," Bryan chuckled and gave Catherine a shoulder pat. "But you all take your time, enjoy your holiday and call me once you know what you want to do. And no more getting into cars with strangers, kiddo." Catherine gave him her promise. He gave Hannah a long hug as they said their goodbyes.

Daniel couldn't help but notice the sly grin on Catherine's lips. He had a promise to uphold, and he would. Just a couple more days, because no longer would Thursdays break him.

Daniel walked the marshal and his men to the door. "Take good care of them," Bates said over a shoulder.

"I intend to." Daniel watched the vehicles, one by one, disappear over the east rise. Catherine was safe. The children were safe. He blew out a breath.

It was late at night before the last buggy pulled out of the drive. Daniel lifted Rosemary from his lap, her sleepy head rolling into his chest. "I should put this one down."

"Thank you, Daniel," Hannah said, turning from the sink. "I know what you did. Thank you for saving her."

"She saved herself," he replied. "I just happened to be there to notice," he said modestly.

"Will you read to us tonight?" M.J. asked.

"I would love to."

Chapter Twenty-One

A house full of females. Daniel never imagined he would one day have a house full of females, or that he would be happy about it. His mother would be laughing right now, a big smile on her face. In his mind's eye, he could see her gray eyes gleaming with joy, knowing her home was filled with family, with abundant love.

Millie, Hannah and Millie's older two daughters were elbow-deep in the kitchen, finishing the last of the meal. The women had grown close and had more in common than being widows and mothers. Their bond was sisterly, and it warmed Daniel's heart that Hannah was receiving a forever love of a sister she had never had before.

His *onkel* Joshua took it upon himself to carve the turkey that looked just about perfect. Hannah's cooking skills never ceased to amaze him.

He slipped outside for some fresh air. Sitting in the swing on the porch, he watched the children chase the two little goats around the yard. Ivy, Millie's youngest daughter, seemed just as eager to play chase as his own girls, her vibrant red hair bouncing out of the confines of her *kapp*.

Daniel couldn't help but grin as Rosemary ran, legs digging forward at breakneck speed, outrunning her elder sister as well as a girl five years her senior. The girl had wings. He no longer worried about her finding her footing, glad she and Hannah had finally knocked down their walls together. When Rosemary reached the fence lines, sliding to a stop in the damp grass, she smiled at him as if accomplishing a great feat. He smiled back. This was just another step of her feeling more alive, the little girl who sang and charmed bees, and felt loved.

"Girl can sure run," Joshua said, stepping out onto the porch.

"You should see Hannah run from a rooster. They come by it naturally," Daniel chuckled.

Joshua nursed a glass of tea, Hannah's well-brewed blend, and sat down beside him. "So, all this nonsense is done."

"*Jah*. They said there would be a court date, but they have enough on him that they don't need Rosemary. I wasn't going to let her testify anyhow." Neither Rosemary nor Catherine would ever see a monster's face again if he had any say in the matter.

"It isn't our way, *jah*. It wonders me what tomorrow may bring," Joshua said lightly as he took a drink.

"Now, *Onkel*, you know that is for *Gott* alone to know." Daniel gave him a sideways smirk. Joshua was just prodding for information.

"*Ach*, boy, tell an old man. I like a happy story as much as the next one and Edith has been worried Hannah is going to up and take those *kinner* away. You know she thinks of them like her own."

"I'm working on that," Daniel replied. "I gave her flowers. Well, left them in her room for when she woke."

"In November?"

"We have a florist in town," Daniel laughed.

"And?"

"House has been full of people since she woke. But I'm getting to it." He did note the flowers now sat in the center of the sitting room coffee table and her smile was much brighter today. For two days, they had barely spoken, neither of them knowing how to take the next step. Having three children underfoot and constant visitors about didn't help much either.

Hannah stepped outside and called everyone inside. She was wearing her chicory-blue dress, his favorite. He hoped it wasn't by accident.

After grace was said, and the meal was devoured, Hannah and the women begin clearing the table. Catherine gave him a sharp glare. Daniel leaned toward her. "I don't break promises, but you need some patience."

"I need you to make this a better day than it has been already. You promised last night you would talk to her today," Catherine urged. "Do you want us to leave?" Daniel stood, gave her a wink and made his way over to Hannah.

M.J. tugged at her apron and Hannah bent down to her. "What is it?" Her little girl bit her lip, looking almost worried.

"Is the bad man gone now?"

Hannah knelt and hugged her. "Oh, yes. He is gone. Everything is all right now. We are all safe."

"So we don't have to play pretend anymore," M.J.

whispered loudly. Hannah jerked to attention, her eyes catching Millie's right away. Millie smiled, waved off the worry. No one would speak it out loud, but Hannah's coming here was no longer a secret. Daniel liked that, feeling no pressure to uphold so much.

"No, M.J.," Daniel spoke up. "No more pretending. Now help the ladies clean up and don't eat all that pie before we get back."

"Where are you going?"

"I'm going courting," Daniel said and watched Hannah's eyes widen. Giggles from the table made her cheeks rosier than the already hot kitchen had. "Come, Mrs. Raber." Daniel held out a hand and she shyly slipped her fingers into it.

"Where are we going?" she asked as he reached for her coat and shawl, helped her slip into them.

"Anywhere we want." He smiled down to her, relishing the soft features of her face, the look of affection in her eyes, and the excitement of anticipation.

The air was cold enough Hannah could see her own breath, but inside her heart was pounding enough that she figured if frostbite was a potential threat, she wouldn't notice. Sitting beside the man she loved, heading to an unknown destination without the need to glance over their shoulders.

"I had a talk with the girls. They don't want to leave." Daniel veered Colt onto the main road and toward Millie's orchard.

"I know. They love it here."

"I'm sure Bates can help you start from anywhere, give you back some familiarities you have been without these few months."

"He could." But she didn't want that. How could she tell him what she truly wanted? Men like him required a strong, confident woman, and Hannah was neither.

"I have grown to love your *dochdern*." So he wasn't asking her to stay. Her heart plummeted. Daniel feared losing her daughters. Hannah felt the first tears touch her cold cheek as he veered off the gravel road and pulled into the orchard grass. The trees were dormant, barren, like her life right now felt. Cold and miserable and fruitless.

"I know you care about them. You are welcome to come see them anytime, but I can't stay and keep doing this, this pretend marriage." Daniel turned to face her. His hand reached up, brushed the tears from her cheek. "I already lived that, and I can't do it again. I just want to live a simple, quiet life with my children."

"If you want to go, I won't stop you, but…" His voice lowered, his warm fingers pressed closer against her flesh. "I want more."

"You want me to stay for them, for you to not lose them?"

"I want you to stay because I love you, Hannah. Stay because I can't imagine a life without you in it."

"Daniel, I know what the children mean to you…"

"No, Hannah," he stopped her. "I have struggled with this a while. What I feel for you. I tried not to. You were Michael's wife. How could I fall in love with you? How could I give you the life you were accustomed to? But I have to be honest, even that first night I saw you, I knew." He leaned in closer. "The girls were easy to love, you, my dear wife, were impossible not to."

"Do you really mean that, Daniel? You aren't just saying you are willing to keep me because of them?"

He leaned down and kissed her, soft and tenderly. "I love you because you are everything I searched for in a woman all my life but never found." His lips brushed hers once more. "I love you because you value everything that matters—God, family and community." He kissed her cheek. "I love you because I can't stand not to be near you. I can't imagine you not beside me when I wake, when I fall asleep. I can't not love you, Hannah Raber."

"I love you too, Daniel, but you have to be sure. I can't spend the rest of my life feeling like a bad choice or someone you will tire of. I can't stay just so in ten years you will be bored with me."

"How could I when I can't even get enough of you." His smile became another kiss, hopeful and sweet, an unspoken promise to years of happiness to come.

He pulled away slowly. "We can build a life here. Together." That's all she ever wanted.

"And add to it." She looked up with hopeful eyes and his heart wasn't sure it could take much more. "I love children," she admitted.

"I would love to have more children with you, Hannah Raber."

"*Ich liebe dich*, Daniel Raber."

"I love you too, Hannah Raber."

Throwing caution to the wind, Hannah rushed forward and kissed him again. Whatever came, he would always hold her up and she him.

* * * * *